III
A STAB OF HOT PAIN FLOODED THROUGH HER

She collapsed to one side, and if the partition hadn't propped her up she would have fallen.

Something in her drink. But she'd watched the barman pour it herself . . .

As if through layers of cotton wool, she heard footsteps coming down into the toilet. At the same time, the lock on the adjacent cubicle was released and someone emerged from it. The door facing her swung open revealing two men. One of them she recognized as the barman; the other, much younger, was a stranger to her.

The barman moved forward, but a voice commanded, "No, Pat," and he stepped to one side, disclosing yet a third man. Roz's last coherent thought was that she knew him. Who? Where could she have—

Then she knew. She opened her mouth to scream but her tongue filled her mouth and all that came out was a long hiss of dread.

"Good evening, Miss For̶b̶———̶ the Krait.

Also by John Trenhaile

KRYSALIS

Published by
HarperPaperbacks

ACTS OF BETRAYAL

JOHN TRENHAILE

HarperPaperbacks
A Division of HarperCollinsPublishers

HarperPaperbacks *A Division of* HarperCollins*Publishers*
10 East 53rd Street, New York, N.Y. 10022

Copyright © 1991 by Dongfeng Enterprises Ltd.
All rights reserved. No part of this book may be used or reproduced in any manner whatsoever without written permission of the publisher, except in the case of brief quotations embodied in critical articles and reviews. For information address HarperCollins*Publishers,*
10 East 53rd Street, New York, N.Y. 10022.

Hardcover editions of this book were published in 1990 in Great Britain by William Collins Ltd. and in 1991 in the U.S. by HarperCollins*Publishers.*

Cover illustration by Kirk Reinert

First HarperPaperbacks printing: November 1992

Printed in the United States of America

HarperPaperbacks and colophon are trademarks of HarperCollins*Publishers*

❖ 10 9 8 7 6 5 4 3 2 1

For Matthew, my son, with love

The fruit of my experience has this bitter after-taste: that I do not now believe that any one of the hundreds of executions I carried out has in any way acted as a deterrent against future murder.

Capital punishment, in my view, achieved nothing except revenge.

—Albert Pierrepoint
Executioner Pierrepoint: An Autobiography

AUTHOR'S NOTE

I want to express gratitude to all those people at the *Times* who so kindly went out of their way to educate me in the ways of a great national newspaper, with particular thanks to Tony Norbury.

The present editor and deputy editor of that newspaper bear no resemblance to their fictional counterparts in this novel, as anyone who knows them can testify. That aside, I hope readers will take my decision to portray the *Times* without any attempt at disguise as the tribute I intend.

PART ONE
COMMITTAL

CHAPTER

1

LONDON. JULY

Afterward, of course, everybody was quick to clamber on the bandwagon, demanding to know: "At what point could this ridiculous treason trial have been stopped, and why wasn't it?" But that was afterward; and few words were ever wasted on the question of when or how the thing *began*. It started on a wet and blustery Thursday morning, in a large room on the ground floor at the back of Number 10 Downing Street, overlooking the gardens; everybody knew that for a fact.

As the cabinet secretary stepped over the threshold he saw that this was to be a two-blue occasion and he shuddered slightly, but when he murmured "Good morning, Prime Minister," his voice was its usual firm self.

"Good morning, Robin."

The prime minister was wearing a dark blue suit; on the blotter in front of her lay a single sheet of the lined blue paper they used in the Political Office next door. The cabinet secretary disliked this blue paper intensely, because it was used to convey unsieved information to and from the PM. When coupled with her present fetching, if severe, dark blue ensemble, an *electoral* ensemble as he mentally described it, that signaled danger.

"Wretched weather," the prime minister commented.

The cabinet secretary glanced out of the nearest window, slashed by ugly streaks of rain. "Quite."

"Not polo weather at all."

So that was it. She was going to take a personal interest in the Thornton case.

Now voices could be heard in the corridor, "the male voice choir," as they were known in Whitehall, because all the members of the cabinet were men and they sang the same tune to the beat of one conductor. The double doors opened; "Are we early?" inquired a jocular voice.

"Not at all."

"Morning, Margaret . . . " "Morning, Prime Minister . . . "

The cabinet secretary examined his fingernails. He wondered who would notice the combination of Oxford and Cambridge blues—electric clothes, summer-sky paper—and concluded that none of them would. They were taking longer than usual to settle, which was unwise of them today . . .

The prime minister rapped on the table. Conversation died quickly, but long before the last word had been spoken she was off and running.

"All right, I'm changing the agenda, minutes later, now, the Thornton case. David, I understand he's been remanded on a charge of attempted murder."

"Yes."

"Why?"

The monosyllable was delivered in that famous low tone reminiscent of a church organ. It caught the home secretary on the hop, just as he finished blowing his nose and was about to put his handkerchief back in his pocket.

"Well, I don't know about anyone else, but it seemed the right charge to me . . . " The home secretary glanced to either side of him, anxious to garner some support before he stepped into the minefield that by now even the slowest ministers saw in front of them. "Perhaps Patrick could . . . "

The cabinet secretary wrote "A-G," short for attorney-general, and waited.

"Well what about it, Patrick?"

"He tried to kill the Queen, Prime Minister. What were we supposed to charge him with—indecent assault?"

The prime minister's voice scythed across the beginnings of nervous laughter. "High treason?"

In the silence that followed, the cabinet secretary counted up to seven.

"I'm afraid you've . . . lost me there, Prime Minister. High . . . ?"

"I'll read you something . . . "

The prime minister rustled that tiresome sheet of blue paper. She held her right hand to her forehead and rested her left forearm on the blotter, a characteristic posture that somehow conveyed passion mixed with ice-still intensity.

"Treason is committed when a man, and I quote, 'doth compass or imagine the death of our lord the King, or of our lady his Queen or of their eldest son and heir.' Those words come from the Statute of Treasons, 1351. So it was law even when *I* was studying for the bar."

This time there was no laughter. "If what that man Thornton did wasn't treason," she said trenchantly, "I don't know what is. Yes, Patrick?"

She's like a judge, thought the cabinet secretary, already presiding over Thornton's trial, black cap to hand.

"Excuse me, Prime Minister, but there's something to be considered quite carefully, I'd have thought." The attorney-general sounded agitated. "The penalty for high treason—"

"Is death." Her voice manifested neither satisfaction nor distaste. She went back to the sheet of paper in front of her, obviously quoting from it. "Penalty: death; see Treason Acts of 1790, 1814, and section 6 of the Treason Act, 1817."

"Precisely. It would look pretty footling to try a man for treason, one of the few remaining capital crimes, the *only* one, I think, with all the to-do in the press and so on, and then reprieve him. Why bother?" The attorney-general sat back, hands spread wide in an appeal to sweet reason.

"Reprieves are David's department, not yours."

And then, yes, they did get it. The beauty of it or the horror, depending on the individual's point of view. The bare, or barefaced, simplicity. The suicidal boldness.

"Let me get this straight . . . " (chancellor, minuted the cabinet secretary, in his neat italic hand). " . . . You would like to see him tried for treason, this Thornton character, because then, assuming he was convicted, and assuming David here decided that the law must take its course, Thornton would become the first man to hang in England for a quarter of a century . . . Margaret, is that really wise. I mean . . . "

"Yes, John? What *do* you mean?"

"Well, there's the European Convention on Human Rights, for a start!"

The prime minister did not even bother to glance at the sheet of blue paper. "We haven't signed the Sixth Protocol, which I take it is what you're referring to."

"But we will. I mean, one day . . . "

"Europe *this*, Europe *that!* I am fed up with being

told at every turn what Europe will and won't allow a democratically elected government to do. *One*, we haven't adopted the Sixth Protocol outlawing capital punishment in peacetime, *two*, we won't, *three*, even if we did, there's provision for exceptional circumstances and if these circumstances aren't exceptional then the English language has lost its meaning."

When the silence had gone on long enough, the prime minister embarked on a further discourse. "You've read the polls, you know what they say. We've lost touch. And there are the running-sore areas, of which Law and Order is far and away the most important. You know what I think about that: the rot set in in 1965, when first they suspended the death penalty."

The cabinet secretary relished that "they." Whenever she said "we," it smacked of interminable continuity, the mythic power behind dynastic rule. But "they" was a reminder that the devil Labor went about as a roaring lion, ready to devour.

"Even that huge, wet, anti-hanging majority could hardly complain if Thornton were hanged for treason." She emphasized her next words by bringing her fist down on the table top. "Because *that's* the *law* of the *land*."

She made it sound like the Holy Trinity instead.

"What about Amnesty International?" asked a worried voice.

The prime minister tossed her head. "Who runs this country: Parliament, or Amnesty?"

"But it could be seriously counterproductive, I'd have thought." Now it was the home secretary's turn to lean forward, thus betraying his anxiety. "The Queen escaped unharmed. Thornton wasn't even pointing the gun at her."

"Or the Queen Mother," someone else put in.

"Quite. Thornton merely carried the gun into Windsor Great Park; how can we hang someone for that?"

But the sheet of blue paper was equal to the occasion. "Craig and Bentley," the prime minister snapped.

"Exactly," said the attorney-general. "What a mess that was! It's because young Bentley was hanged—"

"Or was it Craig?" the home secretary asked, frowning.

"Oh, what does it *matter*?" the attorney-general cried. "The point I'm making is that because the innocent one was hanged, the one who didn't have the gun, that's why Parliament abolished the death penalty in the first place."

"Bentley didn't try to kill the Queen," the prime minister interjected. "His crime lacked any emotional impact, so there isn't a parallel."

"No emo . . . He was party to a *murder*, Margaret! Are you—"

"Thornton could be our platform for reinstating the death penalty."

This time the cabinet secretary got up to a count of ten before anyone spoke.

"You want to reinstate it?" The chancellor's voice was hushed. "By the *back* door?"

"Certainly not. If Thornton's guilty, and he's hanged, I'd expect it to be regarded as the best thing we've done in years. By that time, we could be in the early run-up to an election which the pollsters predict we're in danger of losing, but which I know we'll win. See what happens to the anti-hanging brigade then! A lot of them will be out of a seat; others will have their majorities slashed. And we'll be in on a proper mandate to bring back hanging, *because* we weren't afraid to hang when the times called for it."

"But, Margaret—"

"*No.* I'm not interested in buts, not at this stage. It's not for me to tell the Law Officers of the Crown how to do their jobs. All I'm suggesting is that they should at least consider charging him with treason and watching developments. That's all."

The youngest member of cabinet, a recent appointment and a longtime favorite of the prime minister, placed his elbows on the table, cupping his chin in his hands. "I 'ad that attorney-general in the back of my cab once," he said, to nobody in particular. "They should string 'im up, guv; that's the only language them politicians understand."

The newcomer's name was Brian Oakley; but because the cabinet secretary had an aversion to minuting "BO" he wrote "Oak" in the margin instead. The prime minister threw back her head and laughed out loud, delighted.

"It could work," Oakley added quietly. "My wife's already had some of that, at the school where she teaches. In slightly more dignified language, of course. The Queen Mum factor . . . "

"Thornton's been charged with attempted murder," the attorney-general said dismissively, intending to halt the discussion. "It's too late to backtrack."

"It is *not.*" The blue paper worked its by-now familiar magic. "You can . . . where is it . . . you can ask a judge to prefer an indictment for treason, even though he's already been charged with something else, under section two of the Administration of Justice (Miscellaneous Provisions) Act, 1933." Her smile was wintry. "You really should try reading some law, Patrick, it can be so fascinating."

The attorney-general looked her in the eye. "I thought you said you weren't telling the Law Officers what to do," he commented.

"I'm offering them advice, as is my duty. Nevertheless, I'd be interested to know cabinet's response overall. So let's count heads, shall we?"

While the vote was being taken, the cabinet secretary wrote his guesstimate in the margin. He was
not totally surprised when the prime minister
picked up two more votes than he'd allowed for.

After cabinet, she made a point of asking him for
a draft minute of the first item on the morning's
revised agenda to be prepared in a hurry. He found
her eating a sandwich in her first-floor study, a
sanctum recently softened by the addition of floral
curtains and a patterned sofa that accorded ill with
their surrounding Georgian severities.

He placed the draft minute in front of her. She
scanned it quickly, reaching for her pen, and crossed
out several names. "Keep it general, Robin. 'Certain
ministers were of the view,' that kind of thing.
Porridge—colorless, tasteless."

It was certainly that, he thought.

"It's going to be a tough enough ride without
implicating individuals."

"Certainly, Prime Minister."

He would have proffered an opinion about the
wisdom of embarking on this "tough ride" if she had
asked for one, but he knew she would not ask and
she did not. Instead she scored through several more
words with a snort of derision. "It was *Bentley* that
they hanged. Oh, for goodness' *sake* . . . "

CHAPTER

2

WAPPING. THE PRESENT

For the deputy editor of the *Times*, however, it began in quite a different way—began, in fact, as it was to end, with red roses wrapped in cellophane.

"I said delivered to Norwich," Roz Forbes said to the cringing florist at the other end of the line. "You've had my parents' address on file for eight and a half years."

A messenger flung open the door of her office, skimmed a sheaf of papers across her desk with the words "Morning conference" and was gone.

"What's more," Roz continued as if nothing had happened, "I said specifically I wanted them in bud." She picked up the bouquet, eyed it distastefully and dropped it onto the desk next to the agenda for the eleven o'clock editorial conference.

"Only today's the anniversary of my grandmother's death," she went on, "and my mother will be leaving the house for the garden of remembrance at noon, which doesn't leave you much time." Her voice was clipped, polite, and very firm. "If they've

11

not been delivered by then, please delete my name from your accounts file. Thank you."

She put down the phone across a cooperative mumble, thinking that if only she'd gone up to be with her parents, there wouldn't have been a problem. If! If! If!

Sam, her elder brother, was a GP, worked off his feet twenty-five hours a day but somehow never too pushed to find time for the annual visit to where gran's ashes were scattered. When their father, Donald, had been senior doctor in Sam's practice, he'd always found time, too. Only Roz couldn't ever seem to make it.

"Never mind, darling," her mother would undoubtedly say later. "I really don't know why we still bother. You're the one sensible one among us!" And then Roz would say, "Maybe next year." And then mother would—

Simultaneously the phone rang and the door opened again, this time to admit Joe Simmonds, the *Times*'s legal correspondent. Roz grabbed the telephone, glad to be cut off from a pointless train of thought.

"Come in, Joe," she mouthed to the newcomer. "No, sorry, Henry, just talking to . . . good. We'll need a bigger paper tonight; can you send up the book and then talk to the production editor . . . two pages, great, 'bye."

She put down the phone and treated Joe Simmonds to a wide smile. "Your piece on 'Krait' Brennan," she said. "Loved it."

"Any chance of above the fold?"

"You bet. And I need nine hundred words on the Thornton trial for the op-ed."

Joe sat down opposite her. "Aren't you going it a bit?" he asked.

Roz snorted. "This bloody trial sucks," she said. "And I'll tell you something: I'm going to make sure Frank doesn't hang. It's the only thing I give a damn about, *period*."

"I think England's already aware of your views on the subject."

"Invoking an antiquated piece of legal—"

He held up his hands in surrender and she grimaced, running her hands through her long black hair, acknowledging that she was in danger of going over the top. Then she saw Joe's smile and knew that her credibility remained intact, with him at least.

"Nine hundred words," she said. "Okay?"

She went over to her wall chart, where she ran a red check through "Gran's d./anniv." Next to the chart hung a cork board. On it was a blown-up black-and-white photograph of a man's head, half turned toward the camera, looking down and to the right. His features were fuzzy, but he had fair hair and he was smiling remotely, as if at some inner vision.

"It's an improvement," Joe said. "The mustache and so on."

Roz had inked in a Toulouse-Lautrec-style set of whiskers, rendering an already unfocused image even more obscure.

"I think so," she agreed.

"Brennan?"

"The latest one, yes. My God . . . " She flung out her arms, as if appealing to the man on the cork board. "He must be the most photographed terrorist in the history of the world, yet nobody ever recognizes him until it's too late."

"Where was that taken?"

"Oslo, last month."

"Oslo . . . ah, the car bombing."

"Right." Roz pointed to the photo. "A tourist took that; I ask you! Just as the bloody thing went off, some Yank with an Instamatic takes a street scene and Brennan's right there, in the frame, along with a Coca-Cola sign and two lovely nineteenth-century facades."

"But they never got him."

"Naah!" She straightened a few odds and ends on

her desk. "All right," she said. "I'm ready. How do I look?"

"Great."

"Once more, with feeling?"

"Great!"

She liked Joe, a genial man in his late forties whose skull, almost bald, shone deep tan under the lights. A sun worshiper? No, gardening freak, that's right! Roz had a retentive memory for whatever interested her, and at the top of that list by a long way came her fellow human beings.

She rooted around in her handbag in search of a mirror. Not bad: hair full of body with a will of its own; pale green eyes, a little bloodshot today (but who needed sleep when death would one day let you catch up?); nice skin for forty-three, thank you very much (pity about the neck), if a bit pale, but then holidays in the sun were like sleep, dispensable. She held the mirror farther away, widening her field of inspection. Black corduroy jacket over dark gray skirt, white blouse, gold brooch . . . yup. 'Twould do. She made a moue at herself, and Joe whistled.

"Oh, piss off," Roz said cheerfully, stuffing the mirror back in her bag. She picked up a thick dog-eared file. "Let's go and throw tomatoes at the Lord Chief Justice of England."

"Think what a headline *that* would make."

"Seriously," she said as they walked briskly along the corridor to the lifts, "I am *angry*!" And then, unconsciously echoing a member of cabinet seven months earlier, she went on: "A man's found carrying a loaded gun with his fingerprints all over it. That's the beginning and end of the case against him. He'd get five years maximum except for one thing: he was carrying the gun toward the Queen of England. And because of that, they can hang him."

"Yes."

"You say Yes, but I can't understand *why*!"

"The law of treason's very old. It dates back to a time of great unrest, great national danger. As long as it's on the statute book . . . " Joe shrugged, then allowed himself a sly smile. "You should have read my series of articles on it."

"I did. And the more I read, the angrier I got. Trouble is, most people are angry with *Thornton*."

"At least you admit it."

"'Hanging's too good for him.' You hear that everywhere, in the pub, the tube, the Beeb." She jabbed the "Down" button with her thumb and sighed. "Johnny was saying . . . "

Johnny Dawson was her "man"; her longtime journo's mind put it in quotes even to herself. Two busy people, one of them male, divorced, and panic-stricken: no recipe for a successful marriage there, better not to live together, keep it simple, keep it light, oh well. Johnny made political documentaries in places like Jakarta, Chile, and Calcutta; in fact, just lately, the one place he hardly ever seemed to go to study and capture local conditions was her bed. Johnny liked to drink in Shepherd's Bush; God knew why, when he could mix with real people, but there you are; he said that opinion makers were under stress and it slowed them down. Hard-line lefties wanted to bring back the rope for child molesting, whereas dyed-in-the-wool conservatives were saying that Herself had gone too far, at last. Oldtime friends fought at editorial conferences. In England nothing was getting done, nothing *would* get done until after this travesty of a trial was over. So Johnny had buggered off to Central America, where they thought as they shot: straight. Lucky him, Roz thought ruefully.

God, she missed him.

The lift came. "I've got to visit the library," she said to Joe, patting the file. "Drop off this Krait stuff. I wouldn't mind if they were going to hang

Brennan. Yes I would—why bring ourselves down to his level?"

Joe was silent. She knew he disagreed, but the last thing she wanted this morning was an argument. For the past few months she'd grabbed every opportunity she could to keep the paper on course for collision with grass roots opinion, in the name of civilized conduct and good governance. She was making enemies left, right, and what used to be called center, only there was no center anymore. Joe still liked her, in spite of everything. Keep it that way.

She returned Brennan's file to the library, repository of all that the *Times* had managed to discover over the years, pausing to check with the head of information retrieval that the Thornton defense team were continuing to have full access to the paper's database. Then she and Joe headed for the gatehouse, where a minicab was waiting for them.

"The Old Bailey," Joe told the driver. But it wasn't as simple as that, because they were forced to abandon the car at a police barricade halfway down Newgate Street. Ahead of them, on the other side of the crossroads, Roz could see demonstrators outside the Friends Provident Building, hordes of them, carrying banners. As they approached, the demonstrators' slogans merged out of the surrounding babble.

"What do we want?"

"Tories *out!*"

"Why do we want it?"

"Fascist *scum!*"

"When do we want it?"

"Now! Now! *Now!*"

Roz's quick eye estimated a hundred policemen, two lines of fifty. No riot shields, no guns. Yet.

They hurried on, turning left down the hill, past the original wing of the Old Bailey, all its doors barred and guarded, until they were outside the carbuncular new addition. And there they met the monkeys.

She loved that word. Tabloid photographers were monkeys, because they spent so much time up trees in search of naughty pictures. And their journalist colleagues, the gentlemen of the gutter press, were blunts, because at crucial moments, when the Duchess bared her all, or if a story broke while the pubs were open, their pencils always turned out to be blunt. She recognized only some of them. But to a man they knew her. The chorus of wolf whistles might have nettled another woman, less feisty than Roz. It set her blood racing.

"Give us a good 'un," somebody shouted; and— "Wow!" Roz said, "the *Mirror*'s hard up if they've sent you, Mickey. Everybody else on strike, or just sloshed as usual?"

"Get off! Should work for a quality paper, Rozzie. See what the real world's like." Mickey raised his camera. "Come on, page three's empty."

She brought her face close to his, forcing her lips, already naturally rounded, into a sexy pout. "Are you suggesting I should divest myself?" she asked him gravely; and a howl went up from his colleagues.

"Go on, dear . . . " "Dare you!" "Give us a low shot, then." And, right at the end, when the hulla-baloo had almost died down, a small voice saying to a colleague, "What does it mean, then, divest . . . ?"

"I can see it," she went on, gazing into the space above Mickey's head. "Gorgeous, pouting *Times* bird Roz toplessly titillating . . . and that's just tomorrow's editorial!"

Their laughter wafted her through the revolving doors with old friendships still in repair, and maybe a few new ones in the making, who knew?

Inside, a policewoman searched her bag and direct-ed her through an electronic security arch. As they went up the broad, shallow flight of steps to the courtrooms she caught a glimpse of a "blunt" she knew well, Ben Saunders being matey with a fat man in a blue suit whose tie was half undone—CID, she guessed. Typical Ben, never off the job. She caught his eye, waiting for his grin of acknowledgment before catching up with Joe in the court corridor.

The air smelled sweaty, electric. Too many people stood close together, their voices lowered against the possibility of being overheard. She could imagine some great convulsion of nature hovering in the wings, ready to sweep them up—the sultry, sulky lull before a storm—and felt relieved when Joe hustled them into the court.

Her restless, photographic eye could absorb only a few details during their shuffle along the front row of the narrow press box. Number Two court at the Old Bailey was a huge, high room fitted out in oak, even down to the Royal Arms carved above the bench. She had expected it to be larger, but still she knew she was somewhere imposing: one of those places history sought out in order to get itself made.

As she settled into her seat, she noted with pleasure that the Thornton supporters' club was there in force: her opposite number on the *Guardian*, wearing his grimmest frown, two or three liberal and some not so liberal but nevertheless fellow-traveling crusaders, one unexpected adherent from a tabloid. Roz had a smile for each of them. But they were too few for her liking.

She drew a deep breath and turned her attention to the case. Not much seemed to be happening; it was as if every sound in the vast old building had been sucked out of the atmosphere by extraordinary fans, leaving only purified silence. No, not quite . . . after a few seconds she became aware of a very clear, well-modulated, and beautiful voice, which seemed to hover somewhere above her from an unidentifiable source, as if God were addressing the faithful. Roz knew then that she had reached the absolute dead center of what would be her universe until this trial was over; and the knowledge unnerved her, because the voice, as well as being marvelous in its clarity, conveyed to all who heard it the reality of power.

It was the voice of the judge.

She knew from Joe's briefing notes that this was the lord chief justice of England. He sat well back in an ornate, oak-and-green-leather chair. His robes were bright red with ash-gray cuffs; across his torso, from right shoulder to left waist, stretched a broad scarf, and around his neck hung a long black strip of cloth confined by the scarf. A floppy red ribbon adorned each shoulder. His wig was neither white nor gray, but something in between; it looked soiled. Because Roz was sitting at a lower level than the judge she could not see the bench itself, but over the lip of it peeped the fingers of a pair of kid gloves. They looked grubby, too.

Roz felt the first twinge of disappointment. If they were going to kill an old friend of hers, she wanted nothing cheap.

The judge finished speaking. He had, she realized, been warning the jury to ignore whatever they might have read in the papers about the events with which the trial was concerned, an admonition hardly calculated to win the heart of the deputy editor of the *Times*. Now he sat back, resting his arms on those of the heavy oak chair, and said, "Very well," in the way a man speaks when he is bored.

Across the court from Roz, a barrister stood up, hitching his gown more snugly over his shoulders: the attorney-general of England, whose duty it was to prosecute for high crimes against the State. He placed his hands on either side of the lectern in front of him and began to speak.

"May it please your Lordship, members of the jury . . . "

Roz looked at Frank Thornton for the first time.

He sat in the glass-paneled dock on her left, flanked by two officers. He wore a gray suit over a white shirt and blue tie. His thinning hair had been brushed back tidily to reveal a high forehead. He was clean shaven.

Those were the good things. Other details troubled her.

He was forty-four years old and looked sixty. His face resembled that of a man who has only just started to recover from a wasting illness and is having one of his frequent bad days. His complexion put her in mind of bread dough that had been left to rise too long. He sat with rounded shoulders, as if this were not the first day of the trial but the last, and all that remained for him was to preserve some outward show of dignity while the judge passed sentence of death.

Because Roz had visited Frank several times, she knew what those lonely months spent on high-security remand must have done to him. But those visits had not prepared her for the sight of him somehow giving evidence against himself just by sitting there, hunched and looking like hell.

He turned slightly, and saw her. For a long moment his expression remained fixed. Then he smiled, and suddenly he became alive. Roz heaved a sigh of relief. For years she had monitored his career from afar, watching him scale the heights of wealth and success; here, at last and thank God, was the man she had watched.

She smiled back. She lifted her hand. She inflated him like a balloon and she knew that she must come to court often to pump more spirit into him, keep him there, floating safely above the wolves who everywhere prowled around. That way, perhaps, she who once had ruined him could now save him.

Without taking her eyes from Frank's face, she

went back to concentrating on the attorney-general's speech.

" . . . in other words, if you plot to kill the Queen, and then go on to do something practical about it, you're guilty of high treason. But note— you don't actually have to fire the gun, and you certainly don't have to kill anyone at all. It's enough if you go around armed for the purpose of killing the Queen. It's enough if you provided arms for that purpose. And it's also enough if you sit down to conspire with other people to work out how the Queen should be killed. We on the Crown side say that Mr. Thornton did all those things. And now I'll tell you how it came about."

Roz thought that if God were to grant her one wish she would use it to stop the attorney-general calling Frank "Mr." Being polite didn't do anything except make the prosecutor seem so damned *nice*.

"The facts, members of the jury, are simple enough. On 21st June last, there was a polo match at Windsor. The Queen and the Queen Mother were to be there. Many guests had been invited, among them Mr. Thornton who, as a friend of the American ambassador here in London, and senior vice president in charge of a large oil company's English operations, was very much the kind of person likely to receive an invitation. It is the Crown's case that the IRA, who were behind this grisly business from start to finish, would have known that. The police received a tip-off. Mr. Thornton arrived in a convoy led by the American ambassador's limousine. When Mr. Thornton's own car reached the first checkpoint outside Windsor Great Park, it was stopped by armed police officers, backed up by members of the Special Air Services Regiment. A thorough search was made. In a compartment on the righthand side of the car, a police officer found . . . this. Exhibit one, please."

A table occupied most of the well of the court. On

it sat a number of files kept together in large boxes
that had once contained copier paper, the contents
marked on the top in bold black marker ink. In addition there were heaps of buff, comb-bound albums
marked "Police Photographic Department," and various objects to which someone had attached labels. An
usher now picked up one of the latter and handed it to
the attorney-general.

"This, members of the jury, is a French
Manurhin MR-73 revolver. You will hear about its
capabilities from experts in due course, but for the
moment all I want to emphasize is the weapon's
power. It's not a toy, not what's sometimes called a
lady's gun. One bullet from this, properly aimed,
would kill."

Directly opposite Roz was Andrew Mottram, QC,
who led for the defense. He sat with his chin resting
in his left hand, which gave his face the scrunched-
up look of a lugubrious bloodhound. In his right he
held a thick bundle of highlighter pens held together by an elastic band. Suddenly he dropped them
over the front of his writing bench. It looked like an
accident. Roz had caught the quick flick of his
hand, and knew that it wasn't.

The usher moved toward the pens, obviously
intending to retrieve them, but Mottram waved her
aside. He rose and heaved his enormous weight
along the narrow row of seats, moving sideways like
a ponderous Tweedledum—Roz hastily revised it to
Tweedledee, there was nothing dumb about
Mottram—right shoulder up, left shoulder down,
right shoulder down, left shoulder up, until he came
to the steps. There, wrapping his gown around him
as if he feared it might collect dust, he eased his
way down to the well of the court, which by now
was as silent as a chapel of rest.

He bent over to pick up the bundle of pens and
straightened himself, wheezing slightly. As he did

so he spread his hands to the jury in a discreet but visible gesture, rolled his eyebrows to heaven, and shrugged. It was all over in a trice, but everyone saw. The whole performance spoke volumes. Got to lose weight, he was saying. Must cut down to twenty a day. God, what a farce it all is . . .

He hauled himself back into place, using the handrails to support his bulk. Roz could sense the laughter pent up all around her, but the silence remained unbroken.

Then the lord chief justice said: "Morning exercises over, Mr. Mottram?" and the court erupted.

Roz saw a friendly smile play about the chief's lips as he adjusted his wig, and with a tiny thrill she thought, "Check to the King!" Watch Mottram, she mentally enjoined the jury, and we'll all keep sane.

But for the moment the attorney-general still held sway.

"Now why, you may ask, members of the jury, should Mr. Thornton's car have contained this gun, this loaded gun? Let me say at once that Mr. Thornton, when challenged, denied all knowledge of the weapon. But there are three important matters to which I must draw your attention."

His delivery's slipping, Roz thought excitedly. He's lost that matey touch. Listen to the schoolmaster, my little darlings in the box above my head, and make up your minds to skip class . . .

"First. Mr. Thornton's fingerprints were on that gun, and no one else's were. Secondly, there is the tip-off I mentioned earlier. A member of the IRA, who had been sentenced to life imprisonment and was serving that sentence in Dartmoor prison, contacted the authorities and asked to make a statement. It was he who laid bare a conspiracy to murder the Queen and the Queen Mother on a certain day in the future, using a particular kind of gun, and it was he who implicated the defendant in that plot. He turned out to be right about the gun; the Crown of course say that he was right about Mr. Thornton's participation, too."

He leaned forward to rest an elbow on the lectern, using the same hand to emphasize his next point. "It scarcely needs me to tell you, members of the jury, that the evidence of a convicted terrorist will have to be weighed by you with care and great suspicion. You will see this man, Padraic Tumin, in the witness box, and you must judge for yourselves."

He stood upright again. "Thirdly," he said; and all the muscles in Roz's stomach clenched, for the prosecutor's smile told her that he had saved the best until last.

"Thirdly, you will hear from another witness, of a very different kind, that Mr. Thornton was indeed implicated in this conspiracy: Alistair Scrutton. Like Mr. Thornton, Mr. Scrutton is a barrister, and until recently he counted himself among the defendant's friends. I say 'until recently,' because of an unfortunate incident that occurred at the funeral of this witness's late wife, Louise, about which you will hear. Unlike the defendant, Mr. Scrutton did not leave the bar to pursue another career; he rose in his profession to become a distinguished Queen's Counsel. And it may well be, members of the jury, that you will find the evidence of Alistair Scrutton even more convincing than Tumin's."

He reached behind him. Senior Treasury Counsel placed a notebook in his hands. The attorney-general opened it, paused for a moment, then resumed, "That's the broad picture. Now I want to flesh it out a little. Let's start by going back in time to July 1967, when Mr. Thornton and Mr. Scrutton were called to the bar . . . "

CHAPTER
3

LONDON. THE MIDDLE TEMPLE.
JULY 1967

A hand descended on Frank's tense shoulder and he yelped.

"Sorry," Alistair Scrutton said. "Thoughtless of me. I was wondering if you had a spare wing collar. Mine seems to have gone walkies."

They were in the gents toilet of the Middle Temple library, which was where you had to change into your rig before being called to the bar. That evening, the streets of London still oozed heat, like a griddle that has been turned off but not had time to cool; although the Middle Temple men's room rather resembled an oven in good working order. It smelled of sweat, the acrid variety that goes with fear. Young men stood in front of tiny mirrors, jostling for a place while they fiddled with the paraphernalia of an ancient and arcane profession: clerical bands representing the tablets of the Law handed to Moses; stiff white collars with pointed tips, wholly resistant to any attempt at the insertion of a collar stud; wigs made from horsehair (taken only from the mane, never the tail) that scratched sensitive scalps.

"Wing collar, of course," Frank said, and rummaged in his brand-new blue barrister's bag. Coming upright again, he cast an envious glance at his friend and thought, How typical! I spent the entire afternoon checking my kit, making sure I had two of everything that might break or get dirty, before trekking in from Raynes Park; and here's Alistair, looking as though he's just come off some tennis court, whose parents, his "people" as he likes to call them, have doubtless run him down from Highgate in the Jag (unless he drove himself in the MGB they gave him to celebrate his acceptance by Trinity). I got here an hour early. He's arrived in the nick of time. My shirt's a wet rag, the bottom of my suit's shiny, my shoes date back to school; and he looks like an ad for Savile Row.

The room was emptying. Frank glanced nervously at his watch. The prospect of being late appalled him, yes, but foreknowledge of what would happen later terrified him even more. He was going to have to stand up and speak in public. It wouldn't be the first time, he'd been practicing for weeks, but . . . but, well, he'd rather be dead, that's all.

"There." Alistair pulled on his gown and swiveled gracefully. "How do I look? *Damn!* Dog hairs . . . "

He picked at his waistcoat. Freddie, Alistair's golden retriever, liked nothing better than to find one of his master's suits draped over a chair and roll in it. Frank, who had witnessed this many times and was fond of Freddie, smiled. But . . . how to answer Alistair's question? How *did* he look?

He was taller than Frank, largely because, unlike him, he didn't stoop, and even at twenty-two his body had the solid appearance that was to stay with him into middle age. Now it was mostly muscle and sportsman's flesh, but you could already guess where later some of it would degenerate into flab. Alistair's love of the outdoor life kept him moving lightly, as if some portion of his body consisted of helium. He had a strong, dimpled chin with a tendency to jut, like his ears. Large lips, bright red against his tan, tapered to either side to form a sensual mouth. And Frank was one of the few people who knew that his perfectly sculpted nose was in fact just that, repaired by plastic surgery after a riding accident when Alistair was fifteen.

"You look," he said, "as you always do. A golden-haired godlet."

Alistair roared. His laugh was, without doubt, his worst feature. He laughed artificially, in a series of halting coughs that bore no relation to his otherwise melodious baritone. "Who says?"

"Louise. She saw that photo of you and me in a punt on the Cherwell. It's late, hadn't we better—"

"They'll wait," Alistair said with clipped assurance. He swept back the long, blond hair that had prompted Louise, Frank's girlfriend, to make her comment, and lowered his wig onto his head, Charlemagne crowning himself. For a moment he surveyed his image in the mirror through wide eyes of nut-brown sherry hue, before turning away to place an arm around Frank's shoulders.

"We made it, didn't we?" he said quietly. "Let's go."

In the square outside the hall where they would be called to the bar their respective parents were waiting, but Frank did not see them. As they approached, he had eyes for only one face, which seemed to loom out of a background suddenly gone dark against his own, personal source of sunlight.

He felt his heart beat faster, and this time not with terror. Joy imbued every part of him, as if someone had injected it directly into the vein. He felt an absurd desire to do something wild, to skip up to Louise Shelley and waltz around the square with her until they dropped . . . but then he remembered where he was, and instead he assumed a slight sneer to mask his impulse, despising himself for being so conventional, so insecure.

Louise was less inhibited. When she caught sight of him her eyes slackened into a dreamy look and her lips opened, the lower one revealing a trace of moisture, until there was no hint of country girl innocence left.

Even allowing for Frank's understandable bias, she was beautiful. Photographs showed her as merely pretty, but when you met her in the flesh you saw the strength of character aflame in her eyes, and she became beautiful. She had very small teeth, one of the lower left ones not quite straight, defying years of metal braces. When his tongue explored her mouth, its tip came back again and again to that awkward, uneven tooth, playing with it, caressing the feature that had somehow come to represent the deep, dark mystery of Louise.

They'd known each other for just over a year, had been sleeping together whenever they could for the last six months, and his throat still constricted at the sight of her.

She stood a little to one side from the rest of the group, acknowledging that this night belonged to others. But her eyes never left his face and Frank knew it. He had to make a real effort to ignore Louise while he paid his social dues.

"Hello, Mr. Scrutton," he said. "Mrs. Scrutton . . . "

He imagined, wrongly, that the Scruttons despised him and his parents for being lower-middle-class. The cerebral part of him conceded that Alistair's "people" were interested in everybody and were prepared to get on with whoever didn't frighten the horses, because from where they were standing, on the exalted heights of social achievement, you had a very good view of what was important and what was trivial. But no one lived a purely cerebral life.

"I thought you boys had got lost." The words burst out of Mrs. Thornton, as if she'd been holding in the words all day.

"Oh, *mother* . . . hello." Frank nodded at Louise. "Darling," he muttered.

Louise smiled, keeping her lips closed and her thoughts to herself.

"Frank, wonderful to see you." Charles Scrutton's voice matched his huge height. "Congratulations!"

Frank's mother started to say something, but Charles Scrutton's boom could not easily be swamped. "I was just saying to Eileen here, how proud she must be."

Every visible part of Eileen Thornton turned pink. She stuttered and fell silent, leaving it to her husband to pick up the reins. "Yes," he said proudly. "Young Frank's done all right. His granddad was an ironmonger and I've been a solicitors' clerk all m'life. 'Course, they want to change that." He laughed, making Frank shuffle his feet; a four-ale bar laugh, how he'd always hated it. "Legal executives," Sid Thornton went on. "That's the name of the game now."

Eileen grabbed his wrist and pinched it. "Yes, all right," she said impatiently. Frank knew that's what she'd said because he'd had years in which to interpret her mutterings, but no one else could have understood. Until this moment he had avoided looking directly at either of his parents. Now he stared directly into his mother's eyes, letting her read his displeasure, and said, "We really ought to be making a move."

"Oh, yes." Alistair's mother, Belinda Scrutton,

intervened, her voice bright with sympathy for
Frank's embarrassment. She wore a dark blue dress
belted at the waist; her hat matched both dress and
tie tone for tone, tint for tint. Looking at her, Frank
knew that his own mother should have worn a hat
to this occasion.

They began to move in a group toward the
entrance to the hall, almost the last stragglers in the
crowd. Charles placed an arm around Sid
Thornton's shoulders—a family trait, the Scruttons
all were "touchers"—and Frank heard him say,
"Legal Executives now, is it? I never know why
they can't leave well enough alone. When I formed
my present outfit we had a perfectly presentable
bod doing the sums, but . . . "

Louise slipped a hand into his and he heard no
more. "Hi," she whispered. "Don't be nervous.
You're the brightest and the best, Kid."

She called him "Kid" in bed. He'd been a virgin
when he met her, whereas Louise, a nurse at the
hospital where he'd gone to have his hand seen to
after catching it in a door, already knew her anato-
my inside out. With her, he could be the Kid he'd
never been at home.

"Thanks," he managed to mumble.

Looking at her, he realized she knew how terrified he felt. After dinner, he had been selected to
speak in a "moot," a kind of legal debate. Even
though she couldn't be by his side then, she was
still the only person in the world who had the
power to help him.

"This must be Louise," murmured a voice at his
shoulder. "She of golden godlet fame. Introduce,
introduce."

"Oh . . . Louise Shelley, Alistair Scrutton. We
shared a set at Trinity."

Alistair's hand held hers longer than was necessary, or so it seemed to Frank. And—was it imagina-

tion?—she let him do it with something akin to pleasure. Jealousy sparked inside him, making him feel ugly. Don't ruin it, an inner voice warned urgently. It's nothing. *Keep hold.*

They entered the hall. Parents and other hangers-on were shepherded to the back; Alistair and Frank took their places forward. As they settled into their seats, Alistair said, "What a dark horse you are, Frank. She's terrific."

"Thanks."

"Pity she can't see the moot afterward. I'd feel distinctly inspired. Got your notes?"

Frank mastered the sick feeling that had lurched into his stomach at mention of the word "moot" and patted his jacket pocket.

"Great. Ah. We're off!"

His last words were prompted by a thunderous crash from the rear of the hall, which fell silent. The Middle Temple porter, wearing his fur-trimmed blue gown, stood on the threshold, framed by one of two doorways let into a mighty oak screen. Now he raised his staff a second time and brought its heel down hard on the floor, repeating the crash that had silenced the assembly a moment ago. He did it a third time. Only then did he begin to advance down the hall.

Behind him came thirty or forty men, for the most part in middle age, though some were a good deal older. The procession moved forward at a steady pace, eventually ascending the dais that stretched the whole width of the hall at its far end, beneath Van Dyck's portrait of Charles I astride a horse.

These were the benchers, senior barristers who governed the inn of court. Frank looked along the line of faces. Some were kind, some thoughtful, a few arrogant and cruel. How would his own face map itself, years from now?

The senior bencher, who was called the treasurer, walked toward a microphone that had been placed at the front of the dais by the porter, and the ceremony began. There were many students, but time flushed away faster than water through a sluice. It seemed like only seconds before the treasurer intoned: "Francis Graham Thornton."

Lingering fears of the moot vanished, to be replaced temporarily by something far worse. He stood up too quickly, managing to trip over Alistair's feet. A hand grasped his wrist, gave it a squeeze; then he was floating free. His shoes made a horrendous noise on the floor. The treasurer, standing behind the Ancients' Table, appeared to him as sharp as if viewed through a fish lens; everything else was blurred. Frank concentrated on putting one foot in front of another. His breathing became shallow, sweat broke out through every pore, his heart knocked around inside his breast like a steam engine struggling to start.

At last he stood before the Ancients' Table in his last seconds of life as nothing: a soggy, perspiration-stained chrysalis awaiting its moment of beauty.

The treasurer consulted his list. "Francis Graham Thornton, by the authority vested in me as treasurer of the Middle Temple, I do call you to the bar and publish you barrister."

He smiled, and extended his right hand. Frank reached across the table to shake it. Then someone was pushing a fountain pen in front of him and directing him to the register, while the name of the next student was called. Frank caught a glimpse of Alistair's signature farther up the page, bold and distinctive, before appending his own. He bit his lip in frustration. He had signed as if in the grip of a terminal palsy. The chunk of spider's web on the page bore no relation to his name. He tried to embellish it with a touch here, a stroke there, but all he succeeded in doing was make a small smudge. *Leave it!* shrieked a voice inside his head. *Don't make it worse than it is already . . .*

The next student was waiting to sign. He straightened up, wheeled around, and marched back to his place. As he sank down in his seat with a sigh of relief, Alistair murmured in his ear, "Welcome, my learned friend."

His name had been almost the last to be called. Before Frank's heartbeat had quite returned to normal, they were going out into the summer twilight, where his mother, to his great embarrassment, pecked him on the cheek. But mothers everywhere were doing the same thing to equally bashful young men, so that wasn't so bad. Louise followed suit, although she put her arms around him to do it and for some reason he didn't mind that at all, was proud of it in fact, and hoped that a lot of people would notice. "A kiss is just a kiss," said the old song; but it wasn't. Everything depended on who kissed whom. Judas Iscariot knew.

"We must be getting back," his mother said. "Father's got to go to work tomorrow. I hope the dinner and everything goes well. Try not to be too late." She hesitated. "I'm very proud of you, Frank. You're the only one in our family to have done anything."

"What time should I come back?" Louise asked, once his parents were safely away.

"Nine. Better say nine-thirty. You don't have to wait, you know. I could come straight to the flat."

"I know. But I want to stay."

They were staring into each other's eyes when Alistair, who had despatched his own folks, came up to them and said, "What about a night club afterward? Frank and I could use a drink or six after we've done our party piece."

Frank started to prepare a gracious refusal. To his

astonishment, however, Louise said, "Sounds fun."

He stared at her, as if half-afraid some elemental spirit had taken possession of her body and she stood in need of exorcism. "You're serious?"

She must have heard the anguish in his voice, but she said, "Why not? We ought to celebrate." She flashed a smile at Alistair, who was quick to return it, before turning back to Frank. "Don't be a spoilsport."

"Fine," he managed to say. "Fine with me."

Afterward, as they went into dinner, he reasoned with himself that she was, after all, right. This was a once-in-a-lifetime occasion, like losing your virginity. A nightclub, why not? Champagne. It would make Louise happy, which in turn would make him happy. Great.

They dined, as usual, in "messes" of four people.

"To you," Frank toasted Alistair; "to the next Lord Chief Justice of England, bar . . . what shall we say, five?"

"Three." Alistair did not rise to Frank's teasing tone. "They tend to serve for between ten and sixteen years; I checked. I'll be the next Chief but three."

"You really want that job, don't you?"

"Yes." Alistair picked up his glass, swilled the wine around, and drank. "I'd do anything to have it."

"Anything?"

Frank's smile was arch; but there was nothing to match it in Alistair's expression when he replied, "Anything at all."

His mouth set hard, the clefts on either side etched deeply. He'd never spoken of his ambition except in this way: as a reasonable assessment of what would come to pass.

Would Louise prefer a man with such prospects? Frank wondered. He sipped wine, resisting the impulse to swallow it back. He must keep a clear head. Alistair, he noticed, was drinking steadily, without apparent effect.

"By the way," Alistair said, "have you found a pupilage yet?"

Frank shook his head. "Still looking."

Alistair pointed with his glass. "See that bencher, sitting at the end? The fat cove? That's Dennis Lighterman. He's in my set. I'll ask him if he knows of a vacancy."

Frank smiled. Alistair had long ago secured a "pupilage," an arrangement whereby an experienced barrister took on a newly-called fledgling and bade him stick to his master like glue. Whatever papers the master read, the pupil read too. If the instructions were to write an opinion, the pupil wrote one first; if to draft a document, then the pupil tried his hand at drafting it. On the assumption that he did well, then, if he was lucky, the chambers where he worked would invite him to join them as a "tenant." Since no barrister could practice unless he was a tenant of established chambers, the importance of a good pupilage in the right place and at the right time was obvious.

Alistair's father had found his pupilage for him. England, Frank reminded himself without bitterness, was not yet quite a meritocracy. He did not resent Alistair's slightly patronizing tone as he made his offer to speak to Lighterman, for was not Alistair Frank's very own connection? His *only* one, in fact?

The treasurer said grace; port was served. Almost time for the moot to begin.

Three "judges," in real life a law lord, a queen's counsel, and the president of the Probate, Divorce & Admiralty Division moved to sit halfway down one side of the hall with their backs to the wall. A dining table was hauled in front of them to act as makeshift "bench." From another table set opposite them, Frank and Alistair must represent Oxford as advocates in the coming moot against Cambridge.

Frank took his place, drawing a sheaf of notes from his pocket. His stiff collar had rubbed his neck raw and by now sweat was chapping the skin, making every movement of his head a minor annoyance. He raised his eyes a fraction to find himself under scrutiny from the law lord. The latter eyed Frank through round, black-rimmed spectacles, his mouth downturned in a scimitar-shaped crescent, a punter in the paddock about to back his fancy; and Frank could see that the man didn't fancy *him*, whether over the sticks or along the flat.

He swallowed and began to reread his notes, until at last the master of moots came to his rescue by standing up and booming, "Ladies and gentlemen, your attention, *if* you please . . . "

The lazy hum of after-dinner conversation died away. By now, people had arranged themselves in a rough semicircle with the three judges sitting along its diameter.

"Tonight, we reach the finals of our annual mooting competition, which, some may say, appropriately enough is between our two most ancient universities."

There were a few "hear hear's," some good-natured booing. The law lord removed his spectacles and polished them with a silk handkerchief drawn from his sleeve. The scimitar-shaped cut of his lips had degenerated into a horseshoe.

"A few of our guests may not, to use the lingo, 'know the score,'" the master continued, "so here goes with a potted explanation, or, for former pupils of mine here present, a potty explanation, of what we're about."

Frank knew that he ought to feel grateful to this jocular man for lightening the atmosphere, but he wanted the moot to start. Then he'd be doing what he'd yearned to do ever since he was a teenager embarking on his first awkward love affair: with the Law. The Law had seduced him into working long hours in the library when others were enjoying themselves. Much as his fellows drifted from girl to girl or from pub to pub, so he pursued a different scent, taking up this or that case, only to find that it opened up another vista, a further line of inquiry, just one more strand in a web that was already hundreds of years old and could, with his modest help, last another thousand.

The pub-crawlers and the girl-chasers were absent tonight. They had fallen by the wayside. Not he. Not Francis Graham Thornton, barrister-at-law.

"A moot," the master continued, "is an argument on a point of law. The facts of the case are set out on a sheet of paper—I do hope you've all got copies—and at the bottom of the page it tells us what's happened up to now. In this case, the plaintiff won in front of the High Court judge, but the defendant appealed to the Court of Appeal, you'll all know that old music hall song, 'She was only a judge's daughter, but she didn't appeal to me,' I'll pause for groans."

The audience was happy to oblige.

"The defendant appealed, and won, but the plaintiff wasn't going to take that lying down, and so now we have to imagine ourselves in the House of Lords, that home of lost causes and long pauses, for the final lap. In the red corner—" He shot out an arm. "—Cambridge, for the appellants. In the blue corner, the dark blue corner I should say, Oxford, for the respondents. Each side has twenty minutes. Judgment will be delivered on the point of law, but, more importantly, a second judgment will be given with regard to the advocacy. Ladies and gentlemen, the case is: Miss Spinster against the Great Big Shipping Company."

Senior counsel for Cambridge, whose name was Anderson, rose. The process took forever. He was tall and had outsize feet; a curl of red hair escaped from beneath his wig, which matched his complexion for whiteness. Frank surreptitiously checked that none of his own hair was showing.

"May it please your Lordships," Anderson began, his voice sounding thinly unimpressive after the master's jovial boom. "This is a sad case. A very sad case . . ."

"Sad delivery," Alistair muttered, sounding pleased.

"Miss Spinster, the plaintiff, decided to take a cruise. She bought her ticket from the defendants. Unfortunately for her, a member of the crew became enamored of her. As she was going down the gangplank at Casablanca, her admirer, finally unable to restrain his passion, rushed forward to embrace her. The effect of this, however, was the opposite of what he intended. He clasped her in his arms. She staggered under his weight. They fell into the sea together. There, they landed upon a passing shark, which ate a portion of the plaintiff's right . . ." He paused, palpably reluctant to say the next word. "Buttock."

Laughter, which had been building up behind a dam of good-natured respect for the advocate, burst forth. Anderson flushed. He rocked backward and forward in his size twelve shoes, not knowing where to look.

Now the president of the PDA division took a hand. "Is the shark a party to this litigation?" he asked.

Anderson gawked at him, while the laughter ebbed and flowed around his hapless head. "I'm sorry, m-my L-Lord?"

"Must have been a shock, being landed on by Miss Spinster. I mean, there you are, minding your own business on the bottom of Casablanca harbor, sunny day no doubt, wondering what's for lunch—"

"Miss Spinster, by the sound of it," said the law lord.

"Quite. I wondered if the shark was suing anybody, that's all."

Pick it up and run with it, you fool! Frank wanted to shout. "Tell him Oxford represent the shark, 'as your Lordships will not be surprised to learn, ha-ha. Something fishy about Oxford's case, nudge-nudge.'"

What Anderson actually said was, "I don't think so."

The law lord tossed his glasses onto the table, evidently regretting his momentary lapse into good humor.

Anderson stammered on: "The trial judge found the following facts. First, Miss Spinster was a corker of the first water—"

There was another gale of laughter, but Anderson, would-be general turned lame foot-soldier, simply read on: "—and it was therefore foreseeable that a member of the ship's crew would fall in love with her. Secondly, it could not reasonably have been foreseen that there would be sharks in Casablanca harbor at that time of year. Thirdly . . . "

People began to look at their watches, examine the unique ceiling or chat among themselves. Frank suddenly realized that this opponent didn't think the moot was funny. He could not imagine what it must be like to live in Anderson's world.

The Cambridge leader finally sat down, having overstayed his welcome by several minutes. His junior spoke next, one of those confident but uninspired young men who form the working bar's backbone. The judges gave him an easy ride, examiners prepared to pass this candidate on the nod.

Then came Alistair's turn.

He swung his legs over the low bench and stood up on the far side of it—a tactic that neither of the Cambridge advocates had seen fit to adopt—thus freeing himself of the table's physical constriction. "Good old Alistair," Frank thought fondly. Chalk up one for Oxford.

If Alistair had notes, they weren't visible. He pursed his lips and raised his head, as if studying the concealed lighting above the judges. For a quarter of a minute he said absolutely nothing. Then he spoke.

"My lords."

He lowered his head and turned it slightly, now examining his opponents out of the corner of one eye.

"A lady of uncertain years decides to venture forth on holiday." Pause. "She goes alone."

There was some tittering. On the "bench," the queen's counsel sat back with a broad grin splitting his face.

"This lady of a certain age is, we may be sure . . . " Alistair took out a handkerchief, dabbed his forehead, and squinted at the roof. ". . . of irreproachable character and morals." He replaced the handkerchief. "And it would be *wholly wrong* for any of your lordships"—he pointed at them, his finger lingering briefly on each—"to *speculate* . . . as to her motives . . . intentions . . . " His shoulders rose in a shrug, he spread his hands: "desires . . . "

The spectators no longer dutifully pretended to look interested, they were with the speaker heart and soul.

"Nothing in the papers indicates what this woman of untold summers and seemingly nonexistent emotional ties thought she was doing adrift on the high seas with a boatload of lusty sailors, and I cannot emphasize too strongly"—again the admoni-

tory finger—"the *extreme* impropriety of your lordships forming an opinion one way or the other."
Pause. "Especially the other."

When the laughter had subsided the president of
the PDA division said, "You keep harping on about
her age, Mr. Scrutton. Do we know how old she
actually was?"

"My lord, when Miss Spinster gave evidence, she
was coyly reticent on the subject."

"You didn't press her?"

"I did, but it was a little difficult because her
hearing aid had a tendency to fail, and when under
stressful cross-examination her false teeth would
sometimes—"

He could not continue for several minutes. Frank
dutifully reminded himself that he was part of a
team and it really didn't matter who got the credit
as long as Oxford won. But the prospect of having to
stand up in a few hundred seconds' time and follow
this left him chilled.

Those seconds filtered down the drain as if the
sheer weight of them had cleared some blockage,
speeding the flow. In what seemed like no time at
all, Alistair had resumed his seat next to Frank,
having spoken no word of law, to savor the roar of
laughter that greeted his final witticism. The smile
he turned on Frank was unusual, for him. It seemed
to challenge: "Top that."

Senior counsel was known as "the leader." And
when one led, Frank thought bitterly as he swung
his legs over the bench, another must inevitably follow. Many are called, but *one* is chosen . . .

He was having to concentrate on too many problems. The physical need to stand up, turn, and
speak; determination to dredge up at least one good
joke; trying to decide which of the Cambridge
team's points he should answer (for Alistair had
dealt with none of them); these things fought inside

his head like an air traffic controller, flight engineer, and co-pilot competing for the attention of an airline captain as he brought his jet in to land. So it was perfectly understandable that Frank should catch his foot in the underside of the bench and fall flat on his face.

The physical pain was nothing compared to his humiliation. An "ooh" of pity floated through the hall. As he picked himself up his head spun and he knew that this was ruin, the end of everything. Far better just to throw down his notes and flee. Lower than this, you could not go. Less than this, you could not have.

The law lord said: "Are you all—"

But Frank, not really knowing what he was doing or why, interrupted him. Words came into his brain. Without troubling himself as to their meaning, he allowed them utterance.

"Your lordships have seen the fall," he said in a clear, crisp voice. "Now you're going to get the submission."

And in that moment, his career began.

For the first time that evening, there was applause mixed in with the laughter. The scalding rock of shame on which he'd been spreadeagled a moment before magically transformed itself into a warm bath of entirely proper self-esteem. He glanced down at Alistair to find him sitting with both elbows on the table, palms to his cheeks, staring straight ahead. Frank couldn't read his expression and suddenly didn't need to. He had a case to present.

Afterward, he could not remember what he had said, but he could without effort bring back the laughter that swirled around him like a breeze from some hitherto undreamed-of land. It bore dangerous, exciting scents: success, the faint but sickly odor of pride, more than a hint of confidence. So that when it was time for judgment, and he heard the law lord say, "We find it difficult to decide, but we feel that Oxford scraped through, particularly thanks to Mr. Thornton," he was ready enough to claim triumph, with all due modesty, as his due.

"That was okay, I think," he said to Alistair as they stood up. "Pity we lost on the law, but I suppose you can't have everything."

"Yes, you can." Alistair might have been angry, or pleased, or neither of those things. "It's just a question of finding the knack. That's what life's all about. The knack."

He walked away without excusing himself and a moment later Frank saw him in conversation with the law lord.

"Thornton, can I have a word?"

He turned and to his surprise saw the "fat cove" whom Alistair had pointed out earlier standing at his elbow.

"I'm Dennis Lighterman," he said. "Well done. You slaughtered them. Fixed up with a pupilage yet?"

"Not yet."

"What are you looking for?"

"Common law chambers. Some commercial, if possible."

Lighterman nodded. "I wasn't planning to take a pupil this year, because I thought I'd earned a break. Look, if you still haven't found anything in another week or so, come and talk to me and I'll give you a whirl for six months. All right?"

"Thank you," Frank managed to stutter. "Thank you, thank you, thank you."

He wanted to say more, but before he could gather himself together Lighterman had gone. Frank stood staring into space for a few moments before realizing that he must tell Alistair.

His friend was still in conversation with the law

lord, now joined by the Queen's Counsel. Frank approached timidly, not wanting to disturb them but desperate to grab his friend's attention. The law lord saw him and stopped in mid-sentence.

"Well done," he said tersely. He turned to the Queen's Counsel and said, "It doesn't matter what else you can do, as long as you can stop the old bugger up there"—he jerked his head to where he'd been presiding over the moot—"in his tracks."

Frank was too amazed to speak.

"All the best, Thornton," said the law lord. "Look forward to having you appear in front of me down the road."

He moved away, taking the Queen's Counsel with him. Frank looked at Alistair. "Lighterman's offered me six months."

Alistair's lips tightened. He inclined his head. "That's wonderful, Frank," he said quietly.

"Come on. Louise will be waiting."

They emerged into the evening dusk to find that the heat had scarcely abated. Frank looked skyward. The moon and stars were obscured. As he lowered his head, heavy spots of rain began to fall, just a few at first, and then, without warning, a torrential downpour engulfed them.

"Damn," he heard Alistair mutter. "Damn, damn, damn."

Frank looked eagerly to right and left. Under the tree by the fountain in the square he could just make out something white. "Louise," he shouted. And before she could answer he was running to take her in his arms.

They stood clasped together in the pouring rain for a moment; then he cupped her face with his hands and kissed her long and hard.

"We won," he said. "And I've got a pupilage."

She tried to speak, but he silenced her with a finger placed across her lips.

"Louise," he said quietly. "Please, will you marry me?"

She gasped, held him at arm's length. For a long time neither of them spoke. Then, just as he thought she wouldn't reply, he heard her whisper, "Yes. Oh, *yes!*"

He took her in his arms again and swung her around half a dozen times. When he finally put her down he was facing the hall. A dark figure stood in the pool of light at the top of the steps, staring at them; Frank saw that it was Alistair. Then his friend thrust his hands into his pockets and turned away with a frown. His shoulders were hunched. He kicked one foot against the wall.

Frank rested his forehead against Louise's shoulder. "Oh, *God!*" he murmured.

"Darling, what is it?"

"Nothing," he returned with a smile.

But it couldn't be swept aside as easily as that. Alistair was jealous.

CHAPTER

4

HEATHROW AIRPORT.
THE PRESENT

Martin Brennan came off Pan Am's overnight flight from Seattle in excellent form. On his way to immigration he maintained the same steady pace, neither fast nor slow, seemingly a man with nothing much on his mind and time to kill before his first appointment. Brennan knew that many people would look at him while he remained in this airport, knew that some of them were looking *for* him, afraid that it was not only time he had to kill.

Fear ground in his belly like shards of cracked glass, making him feel truly alive for the first time in weeks. Terror was about the only thing left to him now when he wanted confirmation that he was still a human being. He welcomed its insidious approach as other people might greet an ex-lover: someone who once had possessed the power to move but now could stir nothing but dulled affection, and perhaps a touch of curiosity. Fear was Brennan's old, old friend.

Beyond the corridor's glass wall, tarmac glistened

in a white, watery sun. Pools of water lay everywhere, showing up the unevenness of the surface.
Brennan smiled absentmindedly. Rain and green
fields, those were all of his important memories:
the ones that shaped a man. Emerald Ireland, with
its drab landscape. England. Thailand, the rice
standing tall before the monsoons came. Sometimes
in his life there was sun; he'd never lacked for rain.

On the other side of a partition he saw passengers
headed in the opposite direction, escaping from the
wet and cold of an English winter. A family of four
caught his eye, mother, father and two teenage children, brothers. Where might they be going?
Terminal Three, long-haul . . . The Caribbean, now
there would be a nice thing. He could imagine the
boys fighting the Alantic breakers, like Sean.

Brennan walked on, a muscle twitching in his
temple. Memories had a way of coming up behind
you quietly, like a *Garda* who knew his stuff, sock-
ing you to the boundaries of unconsciousness.

Don't duck it, *face it*!

Well, now . . .

Memory of a misty summer's day in County
Sligo. Of Sean, eldest of twelve children born to
farmers, peasants really, and Martin, the next in
years but still no more than a kid. A kid in love
with his eldest brother who also happened to be his
God.

Sean always took care of Martin, and took his
part, too, in the playground, when he was bullied; at
home, if Dad was angry. Sometimes there was a bit
of cake going, one slice for everyone, but Sean
would still share his slice with Martin, and as for
Martin himself, why! he would have foresworn cake
forever if he'd thought that by doing so he could
give his brother one second of happiness.

That day, Sean had roused him from sleep at dawn, coming to lie down next to him where he was curled up with only a sleeping bag between him and the floor in a room the eight boys shared, sleeping in bunk beds, on mattresses, on whatever could be scrounged that was halfway soft.

"Come," this God had said to Martin; and he had arisen joyfully, running with his brother through the greens and purples and blues of the far west to the beach where the waves rode in with majestic slowness, fatigued by their long haul across the ocean but too proud to show it. And suddenly, as if Sean had done his magic yet again, the clouds had parted, the drizzle had stopped, and there, on the border between sea mist and pale blue sky, a rainbow had sprouted, a wondrous bridge to carry them over the sea to the Western Isles . . .

"Come," God had said; and he'd stripped off all his clothes, not worried how they might dry themselves after, before running to where Sean was already at war with waves higher than his shoulders. As Martin watched, he'd flung himself forward and begun to pound his way through the surf in a challenge to the whole might of the sea, fearless, defiant, utterly unafraid.

Martin rushed to join him.

A wave stronger than the rest sucked him into its undertow, dragging him out. His cries were lost in the wind, but Sean heard. Without a second's pause, he hauled his body through the currents toward his brother as he sank for the third time. Martin felt ironclad arms around his chest and stopped struggling, for he knew that all would now be well.

Sean had pulled him back up the beach, where they lay together, side by side, panting, until Sean threw an arm over Martin's shoulder and gently butted the side of his head with his own.

"You need to toughen up," he said. "I'll look

after you, though. I'll take care of you, Martin, my
lovely Martin. We'll always be together." His
mouth darted forward to leave a quick kiss on his
brother's cheek. "You and me."

He was wrong. "Come," God said; but another
god on a different day, and so Sean had gone to his
maker . . .

One memory of Sean. One among many . . .

Brennan's hand ached. He was clutching the handle of his briefcase so tightly that the muscles had
locked; it required a conscious effort of will to
release them. The family of four on the other side of
the partition had disappeared, mother, father, two
sons gone to play in the Atlantic surf. He, too, must
go on.

The first thing he saw as he entered immigration
was his own face staring at him.

This poster wasn't the best he'd ever seen, not by
a long way, but you could say it was half-decent,
now. He glanced at it for a few seconds, timing the
look meticulously so that whoever was watching
him would perceive only a citizen concerned with a
matter of public importance. HAVE YOU SEEN THIS
MAN? implored the poster; then came the photo, the
one he'd gone to such trouble to set up in Oslo;
after that, his name, in even bolder typeface: **MAR-
TIN BRENNAN.** There was some more writing
underneath, which he couldn't read, and finally the
abjuration:

Do Not Approach Him. He Is Dangerous.

He looked up at the signs. He wasn't a UK
national and he didn't travel on an EEC passport, so
he must be "Other," he supposed. Since he went
through all of life feeling "other," he wasn't slight-
ed, not in the least.

The queue was a long one. Because he knew they

would be watching him by now, watching *all* the passengers, he kept his face impassive and pointing to the front. The only outlet for tension that he allowed himself was occasionally to rise up on his toes, then rock back on his heels, the innocent actions of a man still assuming command of his body after too long spent in a plane.

Oslo had been okay, he thought, keeping his eyes on the neck of the man in front of him. Blowing up the French military attaché, now who on earth would be wanting to do that, and such a nice fellow, too? He smiled. The stage Irishman in him always appeared at moments like this: another persona to counterbalance the wonderful fear. "Moi leet-le leprechaun," he called it. The leprechaun had been with him for a long time now. Since a certain night on the border . . .

Brennan raised his eyes to the ceiling, as if the newly installed array of aluminum pipes intrigued him. The hell with the border. *Oslo. Think about Oslo.*

A nice, quiet Scandinavian country. Wide open. "It couldn't happen here," ought to be stamped inside every Norwegian's birth certificate. A pointless act of terrorism, somewhere to the northeast of England, somewhere distant. And the photograph he was looking at now, enlarged from one of twenty or so snapped that day by an apparently ordinary tourist who happened to be standing in the right place when the plastic explosive went up. An ordinary, but now much richer American tourist . . .

The man in front of him handed his passport to the immigration officer. Brennan was next.

The eyes in the poster seemed to follow him. He stared back at it. The passenger ahead of him was bending to pick up his hand luggage. It was then that Brennan finally focused.

He often likened his work to that of an infantry-

man in time of war: days of mind-destructive boredom, spent sitting around just keeping your kit in
order, punctuated by a few seconds of the most
intensely demanding activity ever devised by man.
But for those seconds, you had to be one hundred
percent fit and your concentration had to be perfect,
because if it slipped for a moment, you were dead.

He concentrated his whole mind on the immigration officer and stepped forward. "Good morning."

The man shifted on his seat, as if his underpants
had become entangled in his balls, and nodded.
Brennan began the familiar count. Passport out of
pocket, one, two, three. On the desk, count of one.
Slide it across, count of two.

The officer opened the US passport and examined
the photograph. He raised his eyes, lowered them
again. Brennan saw his glance divert to the poster,
but not a muscle of his own face moved. He'd been
expecting that, and was ready for it. He was prepared also for the inner reaction which nearly (not
quite) tricked him into saying, "Terrible fellow,
that Krait; when do you think they'll catch him?"
because Siri Chaloem, his mentor, had long ago
taught him that they were on the watch for the
funny business, the seemingly casual remark that
served only to pinpoint a nervous traveler. The time
when prey could play games with its hunter
belonged to the Sixties, and history. So he held himself silently immobile, in the knowledge that the
face on the poster bore no relation to the suntanned,
silver-haired, and mustached individual patiently
seeking leave to enter England on this milk-white
sunny morning.

"What's the purpose of your visit, Mr. Lloyd?"

"I'm here to attend a conference."

"How long are you planning to stay?"

"I leave on Saturday week."

That should have been all, but it wasn't. The

Krait's latest atrocity had them rattled, or perhaps it was on account of the Thornton trial; for whatever reason, the officer said, "May I see your ticket, please?"

One, two, *three*.

"Surely." Brennan's American-accented voice betrayed no emotion, except perhaps a desire to oblige officialdom. He handed over the ticket. He was confirmed on a flight to Seattle on February 17, the day he'd mentioned.

The officer gave back the ticket and studied Brennan for a moment longer. Brennan smiled at him, conscious of nothing. Afterward, when it was over, his body would make him pay in a dozen different ways for these extra, drawn-out minutes, but right now he was who he said he was.

"Enjoy your stay," the officer said as he stamped the passport with permission for the Krait to enter England.

"Thank you. God bless."

The officer laughed.

Brennan's right leg was trembling. He saw the sign for the men's toilet and somehow resisted the desire to barge his way in. Once he admitted they'd got him rattled he was done for. *Later.* But as he walked down the ramp to the baggage reclaim area he knew he wasn't quite in training, not yet. He should have chosen a harder target than Oslo, somewhere that would have stretched him into shape.

He clenched his teeth. So far it had all been dry run. The worst still lay ahead.

"If you feel yourself slipping," a voice whispered in his ear, "never look down. Then all will be well." The unseen speaker laughed. "*Nai nam mi pla, nai na mi khao.* 'There are fish in the water, there's rice in the field.'"

"Thank you, Siri," he whispered.

He put his briefcase down next to the carousel and

began a careful examination of the bags passing by.

Brennan was an expert at the luggage game, had cut his teeth on it. Even now he sometimes kept up with developments in airport security by taking temporary work as a baggage handler, an exercise which usually paid dividends in the form of valuables stolen from unlocked cases. But he'd been out of this field for a long time, and as he watched the carousel he felt another prick of treacherous, welcome fear reach for his lower gut.

His flight had originated in San Francisco, Seattle being its only transit stop. In San Francisco, two passengers had checked in within a few minutes of each other. The first of them, Brennan, had one suitcase, a gray Revelation with combination locks. The second passenger had checked in an identical piece of luggage.

Twenty minutes later, a baggage handler had opened one of these gray Revelation suitcases *after* it had passed through the x-ray machine, and added a Beretta pistol to the contents before loading it onto the London-bound plane. This case was owned by the second passenger, a Mr. Johnson, traveling all the way to London. "Mr. Johnson," however, never passed through UK immigration; somewhere over the Atlantic the man who had checked in under that name became Mr. Challas traveling on a Greek passport. As soon as he arrived at Heathrow he went to the transit desk where he presented another ticket and flew out to Holland within the hour.

His case remained in London.

So now the Krait was looking for a gray Revelation with combination locks. Not an easy task; there were so many that looked much like his. Ah, yes—there it was, his own suitcase, not the one belonging to "Mr. Johnson." He let it pass by, glancing at his watch, then holding it to his ear to check that it was still working. A man could hardly be expected to worry about his timepiece and notice his bags at the same time, now could he . . . ?

Then, after what seemed like ages, another gray Revelation was coming his way. Like Brennan's own, the one he had just allowed to pass, it bore a blue and gold IAPA Bag-Guard tag. He heaved it off the carousel and made for the nearest customs officer.

This was where years of training counted: the place where the wheat got sorted from the chaff, the men from the boys, the Krait from all the rest.

As he weaved his way around the two overlapping screens, bag in one hand, briefcase in the other, he was smiling. He could afford to. If they found the gun in his luggage he would affect horror, produce his baggage check, and prove that he was not the owner of this case. While they initiated a search for the elusive Mr. Johnson/Challas, some airline official would be heaving his own suitcase off the carousel and putting it with all the other unclaimed stuff that accumulated in every airport throughout the world on every day of the year—just another gray Revelation suitcase, with combination locks and a Bag-Guard tag. And there they would eventually find it, the police and MI5 and Special Branch and Uncle Tom Cobbly and all. Then what else could they do except release him?

But he would prefer not to have to go through that rigmarole. His suntan was neither as deep nor as permanent as it looked, silver hair-dye would wash out sooner or later, his metabolism must one day return to normal after the calorie-rich banquets he'd been using to flesh out his figure over the past week. And there was another reason, even more important, why he did not want to be stopped, for that would abort the biggest, most difficult operation he'd ever contemplated.

In certain circumstances, he could become an

opinion maker, the most influential in England. It
would be possible for him to change the way the
British public viewed the IRA in general and himself in particular. Under certain conditions, he
might bring down a government, thereby altering
the course of history. And not the least remarkable
feature of this plan was that he could achieve it
without spilling one drop of innocent blood.

In certain circumstances. Under certain conditions.

So as he began the long, long walk between the
rows of waiting customs officers he uttered up a
prayer: "Not this time. Please, not now." He did not
know to whom he was praying. The Christian god,
perhaps. Buddha. Siri. Sean.

One of these deities must have felt cheated by
Brennan's decision to mail his prayer without an
address on the outside, for when he was halfway
down the row a customs officer to his left stepped
out and lifted an arm.

"Over here, please, sir . . . where are you coming
from?"

Odd question, Brennan thought absently as he
lifted his suitcase onto the metal bench. They said
that to you in the States, when they wanted to
probe inside your head. He was coming from
nowhere.

"Seattle."

"Business trip?"

"Of a kind." He smiled. "My business is not of
this world."

The customs man did not seem to find this reply
in any way strange. He was in his early twenties,
Brennan guessed; lean and keen with it. His eyes
had a fixed stare which he kept focused on the
Krait's own, as if challenging him to chicken first.
Now he launched into a rigmarole about the signifi-
cance of coming through the Green Channel, penal-

ties, had he read the list of allowances . . . ?

While he spoke, Brennan methodically unfastened his briefcase. He also spun the Revelation's combination locks, but did not open it.

Languidly he recognized that he ought to be experiencing the naked terror which was his gift to others. There should be sweat on his face, a stutter in his voice, an infinite number of messages transmitted in the body language officers like this one had been trained to detect. None of these things happened. Just as in a previous decade he had survived the vicious months of schooling at East Germany's Pankow and Camp Matanzas in Cuba, so earlier this morning he had endured the fear, the encounter with Sean. That was then; now was now. So although he looked into the officer's eyes, a trick of meditation enabled him to superimpose over them this landscape of flat snow, stretching to a horizon where all the blinding whiteness met pale blue sky. Brennan looked deep into himself, and saw a void. He saw his own soul.

"I have nothing to declare," he said, having listened carefully to the goods enumerated by the customs man.

The inspector laid one hand on the Revelation, then decided to start by searching the briefcase. "What's this, sir?" He held up a tattered, saffron-colored object.

"It's a fan." Brennan gently took it from him and opened it to reveal embroidery. "A Buddhist monk's fan. That's the number of the Buddhist era, there, that's 2510. And the Chinese is its emblem, the goat."

"But you're not a monk, are you, sir?"

"No. A friend gave it to me, in Thailand. I always carry it with me when I'm traveling. To keep cool."

The inspector turned to the suitcase. He opened a flap and began to pick over the clean shirts lying on top.

The gun would be immediately underneath them, Brennan guessed. He looked away, putting off the moment when he must register, with shock, that this was not his own suitcase after all.

The officer swung the flap shut. "That's all right, sir." Politeness had given way to boredom; the young man's eyes were already scanning the other passengers filtering past his station.

Brennan closed the suitcase.

Outside, barriers kept back the crowds of people who had come to meet arriving passengers; he had to walk down a long, ever-narrowing exit channel, keeping his eyes fixed straight ahead, not running, not staggering, because the relief was getting to him now and he knew it was premature, they always watched as you came out of customs, that's when they caught you, when you believed you were safe, just put one foot in front of the other, boyo, think of Siri's fan, it worked a treat, as usual; left, right, left . . .

The two men were in the exact spot he'd told them to wait, halfway between the end of the exit channel and the Meeting Point, to one side, in front of the money changers. He quickened his pace slightly.

Then he saw the pair of British army grunts in fatigues, brandishing automatic rifles. For a spectacularly mad moment the Krait's vision of whiteness and powder blue sky melded with the hot, airless reality around him, nausea surged, his stride almost faltered. The soldiers were talking to O'Halloran and Condon, the men who'd come to meet him.

He continued to go forward. He had nowhere else to go.

Condon, seeing him approach, stiffened. The taller of the two squaddies registered this reaction and turned, his face expressionless. As Brennan came up to the group, the tall soldier, who wore corporal's stripes, gestured at O'Halloran and

Condon. "I was just saying to your friends here . . . all in the army together today, eh?"

"That's right," said the Krait.

The soldiers laughed and moved away. When they were out of earshot Brennan murmured, "I think, my dear friends, that after such a long flight, after so many tribulations, we should say a short prayer of thanks for my safe arrival. Oh Lord, who has given your servants every blessing . . . "

The other two bowed their heads and clasped their hands in front of them. None of the passersby thought anything of it, for all three men wore familiar blue serge uniforms, caps, and maroon collar tabs.

Two silver badges on Brennan's epaulettes showed him to be a full colonel in the Salvation Army.

CHAPTER 5

LONDON. THE PRESENT

Fleet Street's Temple Tandoori restaurant was long, rather than wide; and the farther back you went the darker it became, so that Roz felt as if she were penetrating a cave. She found Ben Saunders already there, right at the far end, where virtually the only light was provided by one small candle in an orange glass globe.

As he pushed some newspapers to one side, making room for her, Roz saw with surprise that he had been engrossed in reading that morning's contributions from the Thornton supporters' club, the select handful of journalists who, whether with their proprietor's support or in the teeth of his opposition, were damning the treason trial for the cruel travesty it was.

"Seen the light at last?" she said archly.

"Cheaper than bog rolls, actually. There's something really wonderful about clipping the photo of a well-loved professional colleague and using it to—"

"I *see.*"

She and Ben were on opposite sides. Roz was

leading the crusade against what she perceived as a perversion of the course of justice, although because she read the letters page she knew that her readers were divided. Ben's tabloid, like nearly all the others, supported the decision to prosecute Thornton for treason; it was what its readership expected and the paper did not disappoint them. Why, then, had she agreed to have lunch with the archfiend himself? Because she needed his help.

He offered her the menu, but she waved it away. "I'll have a prawn biriani and a couple of those spicy poppadoms."

"Lager all right for you, or does the *Times* only drink dry white wine?"

"Have they got Evian?"

Ben rolled his eyes to heaven. "Lord love a . . . " He raised his voice. "Oi! Titch!" When the waiter turned in his direction he screwed up his mouth into a piratical scowl and winked. The boy lounged over with a grin. Ben placed their order, insisting that the drinks come quickly.

He raised his glass in a toast. "Jack Ketch."

"Not funny." She took a sip of Evian water and looked over her shoulder to where a glimmer of light showed by the window. "Why this place?"

"I used to know it when we were all still on the Street. Handy for El Vino's. And I don't want to be seen with the likes of you, thanks very much. Mine's a decent family newspaper. If my readers thought I'd been hobnobbing with the anti-hanging league, circ. would drop like a brick through soft shit."

Roz sighed. "Can we cut the act? We all know you're a seedy home editor on a seedier tabloid. We know that. You don't have to prove it."

"Ah, but maybe I like proving it. Maybe I need convincing that my cozy little world of vicars and choirboys isn't for the chop."

Ben's appearance corroborated that. He had thinning ginger hair worn too long for someone of his age, and although she couldn't see it in this light she knew that the shoulders of his cheap suit would be dusted with dandruff, as usual. A big beer-gut strained against his nylon shirt, which had lost not one button but two. His tie knot hung suspended somewhere around the level of his nipples. His jowls sagged heavily, like the chest to which those self-same nipples were attached, and the bags under his eyes told their own story. He could have smartened himself up, but he chose not to, because this was how he really felt about things. Roz had a sneaking respect for that.

"You're backing a loser, Roz. You and old Aunty *Times.*"

Titch brought the poppadoms. Roz broke off a chunk and munched on it moodily, staring at the tablecloth.

"How's Johnny?"

"Ask him," she all but snapped. "You've got a fax machine that speaks Swahili. Or is it Quechuan?" She felt her sudden stab of anger turn into something uglier. "God, you really know how to create an ambience, don't you?"

"Ambi-what?"

"Shove it."

"Look, it was you asked for this meeting."

"I know, and I'm sorry." For an instant she was tempted to fling her napkin onto the table and stand up in a grand, theatrical gesture. But before she could decide whether it would be worth it in terms of sacrificed self-respect, Ben said, "What do you really want, Rozzie?"

She peered at him across the table, while the question rattled around inside her brain. She'd known Ben Saunders for years, starting when they were both on the bottom rungs of different ladders.

She'd always wanted to do serious journalism, whereas he liked the warm world of beer-lubricated confidences, the sensation of being "in" with your own clique of semi-honest policemen, doors slammed in your face, money changing hands for that big front page exclusive. A puritanical voyeur was how Roz thought of him in her more savage moments.

"What do I want . . . ?" She laughed, not happily. "I want to be editor of the *Times*. I want to get married and live happily ever after. I want to save Frank Thornton's life."

Ben was examining her across the table, a hard look in his eyes. "Right," he said. "Fine. Let's take a look at that, shall we? One, editor. Unfortunately for you, Howard Boissart's got that job, and he's not likely to shift in a hurry. Two, marriage. Johnny's in wherever, and notwithstanding half a dozen eligibles queuing up for the privilege you seem to be stuck on him, so that goes onto the back burner too. Which leaves Thornton. You tell me you want to save him. You've been telling me that these last six months. So let's fix our eyes on that ball, mm?"

Roz flushed, then decided to let it go. "What have you got for me?"

He pulled a sheaf of notes from his pocket, just as Titch arrived with their food. "I've got to admit," he said, between the first few hunger-quelling mouthfuls, "that this isn't half one line of inquiry you started me on. Lots of lovely rotting meat . . . here, you wanna try this Rogan Ghosh?"

"No, thanks."

"Scrutton," he went on. "You could just be right about him. He's the key, if anyone is."

Roz put down her fork, placed her elbows on the table and clasped her hands in front of her mouth. "Keep it low," she murmured. "Please."

"Using my terraces voice, was I?"

"Yup. You still take Kevin to the game on Saturdays, or is he too old?"

"Nah. His mum doesn't like him going, but Kev tells her to shove it, now." For a while he chewed without speaking—it would be wrong to say "in silence"—and Roz half regretted the impulse that had made her ask after Ben's only son by his ex-wife. But when he spoke again, his tone was less strident, and this time she regretted only not having asked earlier.

"Scrutton, then," he said more quietly. "Alistair Scrutton QC, barrister to the high-and-mighty, tipped in some quarters to be the next QB High Court judge."

"QB . . . oh, Queen's Bench."

"Right. Though if Thornton's IRA friends had had their way, I guess Alistair would sit in the *King's* Bench division."

"Go on."

Ben leafed through his notes with a frown, as if not quite sure they were the ones he'd brought with him. At last he stuffed them back into his pocket and picked up his spoon and fork. Roz, unable to contain herself any longer, reached out to grip his right hand. "I'll have them heat it up for you again later," she grated. "Now *tell*!"

"Okay. Scrutton gambles. He likes the gee-gees, but he's a casino man as well."

Roz exclaimed impatiently. "So what?"

"He's a traveler, too. Costa Smeralda. Dordogne. Cruising the Caribbean. Enjoys his hols, does Alistair. Lots of dosh, Roz."

"Of course, he's a QC."

"Maybe. But when I see a big roller who likes to go international several times a year, I ask myself, now is that dirty money he's playing with?"

"*Dirty* money?"

"Gambling is a well-known way of laundering

illicit gains, as the qualities call 'em."

"You mean Scrutton's a crook and he needs to cover up? Oh, come on."

He stared at her and there was no humor in his eyes. "What would you say if I told you I believe it's true?" he said at last.

"I'd say the strain of living permanently on the threshold of alcoholism, coupled with the nastiness at your place of work, had finally combined to send you over the top, my love."

He shrugged and went on eating. Roz watched him for several minutes. She couldn't understand his lack of concern. Granted, for one ridiculous moment, that there was a half-grain of truth in what he'd just said; even allowing for the fact that his paper was backing the treason trial; shouldn't he have been the tiniest bit excited at having unearthed dirt on a prominent, public figure?

"What kind of crook is he then?" she asked.

"Not telling. Not yet."

Roz did her professional sums. "You haven't got a witness," she said dully. "Have you?"

He screwed his mouth up and shook his head. "Not a one, my darling-oh. Not a single, solitary one who wants to see his grieving widow shoot off to Monte with the old life insurance money."

"It's that bad?" Roz said; and the tremor in her own voice surprised her.

He finished his last spoonful of rice and pushed away his plate.

"I started just as you asked me to," he began. "Down at Pennington Street, you don't horde the kind of stuff we do; you wanted me to sort the dirty linen. So I went to our libel back files. That's where we keep the stuff we can't prove, yet, and which it would be deadly to take a punt on in the blind hope *that*. Wealthy magnates who'd sue if we told the public about their liking for masochistic tarts.

Archdeacons who fiddled the new church spire fund. That kind of thing."

"And Scrutton was there?"

Ben nodded. "A one-liner. Our Bangkok stringer, drinking in the wrong bar with strictly the wrong people. As publishable as last week's weather report."

"So what did you do?"

"I took a little holiday. Always wanted to see Hong Kong and places east."

"Ah, the stuff Frank dredged up when he was defending Scrutton's defamation action—"

"—after so sensibly accusing Alistair of murdering his own wife. Right. Your Frankie did a lot of good research about the Hong Kong connection; all I had to do was pick up where he left off."

"And?"

"And after a while, I said to myself, I said, 'Ben, my boy, you're being taken for a ride and it sure as hell ain't on any air-conditioned bus complete with tour guide.'"

"But *what* were these people telling you? Why do you have to be so damn mysterious?"

"Because until I've got someone willing to stand up in court and take the oath, the fewer people who know about this the better."

She wanted to protest, but hard-earned professional experience told her he was right about that. "There must be *something* you can prove?"

"Airline ticketing. Alistair does a lot of work on what they call the 'Bamboo Circuit': Hong Kong and Singapore. He goes out there two or three times every year. After each case, he routes himself home through Thailand, or Malaysia—there's good gambling there, too, up at the Genting Highlands. He likes Bangkok, and he often takes a side trip up north, to Chiang Mai or Chiang Rai. I can prove all that: copies of ticket stubs and so on. But I can prove exactly the same about half a dozen top commercial silks and it doesn't mean a thing."

She thought for a while. "It makes me so angry," she said slowly. "I know Frank's been framed. I know that he and Scrutton were enemies. And I *sense* that Scrutton's more than capable of being involved in this."

"But proving it . . . "

"Yes." She tossed her head. "One thing puzzles me. How come you've managed to collect a dossier on Scrutton and the police haven't?"

He pushed his chair back from the table and spread his hands wide. "First and foremost, we get to hear a lot of things the police don't, because our networks are different. And it cuts both ways: there's stuff lying in files in New Scotland Yard that I'd give next year's bonus to see and never will. Second, even if the police did get to hear anything about Alistair, which I doubt—remember, I was *fed* this info, Roz, I didn't discover it all by myself— they'd still need a witness before they could act. Which is where we came in, isn't it?"

"All right. Forget about friend Alistair. What have you got on Valance?"

"Ah. You know as much about him as I do, really. Former senior clerk in Scrutton's chambers, sent down in 1985 for sex with minors."

"I bet you didn't have to walk far to dredge up that!"

He grinned. "Didn't have to walk at all, I keep the best stuff in my desk drawer. Now Valance was an interesting character. He made Scrutton's career. One of his bright young men, was Alistair."

"And they were very close."

"So the rumor goes. When Valance got nicked for having his hands up the wrong knickers, Scrutton moved heaven and earth to get him the best defense brief going. A lot of people in his position would have been pretty quick through the back door, thank you, but not Alistair. Folk admired him for that."

"So what's Valance got to say for himself?"

"Nothing. He's disappeared. Reg Valance was released from the Scrubs last December, three days before Christmas. He was met at the gate and that was the last anyone saw of him. If he's earning, the Income Tax boys don't know about it. He's not claiming the dole, that's for sure."

Roz stared at him. "How can you know that?"

"My love . . . " Ben heaved a sigh. "You're asking that, proves you'll never be up to working for a *proper* newspaper."

"Sorry," she said meekly.

"You're just not *qualified*."

"Right," she agreed. "Court and social, that's me."

For the first time in a long while, Ben laughed; and Roz realized that this inquiry had got to him. Not too many things got to Ben.

"One more question," she said. "Are you scared?"

"Am I scared . . . ?" He'd been looking at a point over her right shoulder. Now his eyes slowly focused on hers. "Yes."

"You don't want to go on with this?"

"On the contrary, my sweet, I would not let go of this for all the kopecks in the Kremlin."

"But—"

"When you asked me to do this, why do you think I agreed?" He took out a pack of cigarettes and lit up. "I mean, it was hardly your usual request, now was it? Why should one journo ask a rival to find out things for her?"

"We don't have the same kind of database."

"Yes, that. And Howard was being tiresome, wasn't he?"

Roz looked away.

"Howard was being tiresome about you using the *Times* to oppose the government on a particularly sensitive and divisive issue. Howard kept looking over his shoulder at the place where Her Maj's sword was due to descend one day, if he played his cards right. So that's why you asked, why you *had* to ask. Now. Why did I accept?"

She laughed her famous laugh, causing other patrons of the restaurant to stare. "Because you're one regular guy!"

He wasn't playing. "Because we're friends. At first, that's what this was all about. Now's different."

His eyes held hers. She found something cold, unappealing in their narrowed confines.

"How much do you know, really *know*, about the scummy tabloid press that fouls up the mud beneath your Gucci *Times*-special-offer-of-the-month shoes, Rozzie?" He pounded the table with his fist, telling her his tension had reached danger level. "I mean, *know*!"

"Not much." She wanted him to go on talking. "Nothing, really."

"Right. Because you work for a paper where bums stay on seats for more than one month at a time. Where you don't have two conferences a day just to discuss circulation, *twice a fucking day!* Just to see how the bloody *Express* is doing, and the *Sun*, and bloody *Beano* next week, I shouldn't wonder."

He squeezed both hands into fists on the cloth in front of him, raised them, and brought them down, hard. His face was working to such a degree that for an instant Roz feared he might be about to have a seizure.

"I will tell you something, Roz," he said to the cloth between them. "One day, somewhere, a home ed is going to come back from his lunch at five o'clock and find on his desk a glossy, full-color longshot of a Royal giving another woman's husband a blow job. And he is going to fucking publish that. Not tomorrow. Not next week. Not even next year. But someday. Within my lifetime. Because if *he* doesn't, the opposition will, and then *he'll* be out of a job."

She knew he wasn't joking. She even thought he was right.

"Tabloids," he said, "are all about going that little bit too far and not getting burned. Each year, you push the frontier back, and push, and push . . . and it's like a game you play with the other lot. Poker. Bluff. 'We're going with this, because if we don't the *Sun* will; the *Mirror* won't dare run that one, so we can afford to spike it, too.' It's all about jobs, Roz. Keeping them because you got it right one more day." He expelled a long breath. "It's not like being a paper of record, lovely. It really ain't. More beer?—oh, sorry, I forgot, it's water, isn't it. I'm going to have another beer. Or two. Titch! Cummover'ere . . . "

When his refill was sitting in front of him, Ben said, "It is thought . . . in certain high quarters . . . that I'm not cutting the mustard like I used to."

"And are you?"

"No. But if I save Frank Thornton from the gallows, I'll own whole fields of mustard, Roz. *Counties* of it. And I'll employ people to cut it for me, now won't I?"

"A moment ago I thought you wanted to hang him high?"

"Ah!" He raised an admonishing forefinger and wagged it at her. "But not on a miscarriage of justice, dearie. Not on perjured evidence. And let's have it in the open: that's the deal. You make the running, but I run the scoop."

Roz had known him for many years. She was positive that underneath the grime and the grease there lurked a real person, someone with ideals, and a brain, and a heart that was capable of working when put to it.

"That's a lovely story you've just told me about yourself," she said. "Human. But I wouldn't use it, not if it was my night to put the paper to bed."

"And why?"

"Because you know this trial sucks, just as much as I do. You know it's political, and staged to win votes, and a bad sign of worse to come, and it makes you want to vomit."

He had picked up his cigarette pack and stood it on end. While she was talking he'd taken to sliding his fingers down it to the cloth, flipping it and repeating the action, over and over again. The silence between them was marred by a kind of gritty static, like a makeshift radio link in the front line of battle.

"I'll have a scotch," she said. "Since it's my expenses we're fiddling. A *small* one."

He used the opportunity to order yet another pint of lager. When the drinks came Roz lifted her glass. "Cheers," she said.

Ben managed a smile. "The Fourth, bloody, Broadwater Farm . . . Estate."

They drank.

"Look, Roz." He reached out to brush her hand, ever so lightly. "I know this trial has got to you. I know you think it's a terrible miscarriage of justice, and that. But the law's the law. *If* Thornton did what they say he did, then that was treason. You don't like it, maybe even *I* don't like it, but that's the law."

"I know. But—"

"Hear me out. Thornton's nothing to me. I can see both sides. Yes, he's got a good background, no, he's got no record, yes, he's an unlikely terrorist. But the prosecution have got a damn good case, haven't they? The gun. Fingerprints. And Scrutton."

He drank, saying nothing for a few moments, but continuing to watch her, as if not sure how far he could go. At last he said, "So let's get to the big one, Rozzie, my love. *The* question. What's suddenly prompted you to get your ladylike hands so very, very dirty?"

"A love of justice. My sense of outrage."

"Funny, I thought it was because you'd got yourself knocked up and Thornton's the father and you're worried about the old monthly allowance not coming through if he's topped."

"Oh, look—"

"No. You look. My job's on the line, you were right about that. I'm spending my own money, what there is left of it after Annie's dipped into my bank account, on following leads that get me nowhere. My life's been threatened, more than once—da-*da*!" He threw up his hands and opened his eyes wide in mock horror. "It's down to you, and I want to know what it's all about, Roz. I've got a right to know."

"I've told you—"

"Bullshit! It's personal, isn't it. You and Thornton. Eh?"

Roz swallowed the remains of her whisky. "I owe him," she said abruptly.

"A biggie?"

She nodded.

"Since when?"

"The ark."

"Smuggled his pet goldfish on board, did you?"

"Puppy, actually."

"I see."

Roz felt a sudden need to confide. She wanted to tell him. She'd wanted to tell somebody, anybody, for years now, but . . .

"Look," she said, taking one of his hands between her own. "I once did something that affected Thornton badly. I've always regretted it. While I was doing it, I regretted it."

"So this is redemption time?"

She closed her eyes and nodded. Half a confession, she discovered, was worse than none at all.

"What was this terrible thing you did?"

She eyed him coldly. "Off the record?"

"Oh, Jesus, Roz! We're *friends*!"

But she repeated "Off the record," and would not speak again until he had nodded assent.

"I . . . " Roz heaved a long sigh. "It was at the start of their careers. Thornton and Scrutton I'm talking about now."

Confession came hard to her, but in the end she told him the lot. Surprising how little time that took. While she spoke, Ben looked at her. The minute movements of his eyes brought to mind a computerized scanner, covering every atom of its subject, logging it all away for future reference.

"God," he said, when she had finished. "Who'd have thought it? Deputy editor of the *Times*, and all. Well, well."

"Do you see now why it matters so much?"

He neither nodded nor shook his head. He didn't say a word. He just sat there, staring at her, as if she was a stranger.

"Got to go," Roz said at last, standing up. "I'll take care of the bill on my way out. Want another lager?"

He said No.

"Find Valance for me, Ben. You're all we've got."

"All?" He raised an eyebrow.

"Lawyers have been working on this defense for months now. They've got nowhere. You're our last chance, our *only* chance."

She was on the point of moving away when he said, "I want you to think about something."

She glanced at her watch. "What?"

"If Thornton's been framed . . . *if* . . . who did it, and why?"

Roz reluctantly sat down again. "My guess is that when Scrutton sued him for slander he began to dig around and he came up with something."

"Thornton had become a pain in some important arse or other, so Scrutton's little friends wanted him wasted?"

"More or less."

He shook his head. "There's easier ways. I could get in a cab, now, and drive less than half an hour and find at least a couple of guys who'd sort out Thornton with a crowbar and a length of chain. Not a Rolls-Royce job, but at the end of it your Frankie would be very, very silent for a very, very long time. And we're talking a few hundred quid there, Roz. Any idea what this trial's costing the taxpayer?"

She said nothing.

"Roz, have you ever seriously faced the possibility that Frank Thornton might actually be guilty?"

Yes, she had faced that possibility. When Frank came to give evidence, he was going to be asked about the events of a particular, crucial evening, for which he claimed to have an alibi. Roz had questioned him about it many times. But he would not tell her where he had been that evening, nor would he explain why he would not tell her.

He might be guilty.

When Roz said nothing, Ben sat back. "Just a thought," he said. "Run it through the old computer, eh? I won't have that beer, but a Courvoisier would slip down nicely, if it's all the same to you . . . "

CHAPTER

6

LONDON. THE PRESENT

T he last time I lunched at the Bailey," Alistair Scrutton drawled, "it was with the Lord Mayor." He pushed the lunch tray aside, making no attempt to conceal his distaste. "Steak au poivre, as I recall."

His guard sat leaning forward to read the *Sun*. He was in his mid-twenties, Scrutton guessed, with a fat face and a grossly overweight body assembled like a series of different-sized tires piled one on top of the other. His only exercise was likely to be raising cans of ale on Saturday nights after watching one of those warlike matches to which his chosen newspaper devoted so many pages. "A game for hooligans, played by gentlemen." Or was that rugby? Scrutton couldn't remember, but it never seemed to matter when he trotted out the *bon mot* at dinner; if he muddled up the joke, none of the people with whom he socialized were likely to be in a position to correct him. He was fond of his own variation: "A game for murderers, played by terrorists," he'd told the lord mayor, not a dozen yards from where they were sitting now.

"Football?" inquired one of the aldermen. "Wimbledon," Scrutton had flashed back. Satisfying, that. Damned satisfying . . .

Today, however, the two men sat in a tiny, whitewashed room with one barred window set high in the wall. It smelled of the fat officer's sweat, although Scrutton scarcely noticed the stink any more. The authorities had been protecting him for months, first in his own home and now at the Bailey. He didn't care overmuch, because the presence of bodyguards made him feel precious.

Scrutton slept quite well, the drink saw to that, and he'd had all his suits taken in, so outwardly he didn't look much different. When he climbed those stairs into court, and raised the Bible in his right hand, no one would see other than a successful public man, suffering from slight but perfectly understandable strain. No one would know the truth.

As the word "truth" leapt into Scrutton's mind, his hands clenched. No one must know the truth. Ever.

"The lavatory," he said abruptly. "If you'd be so kind."

The officer looked up, letting coldness show. He didn't like his charge—not surprising, thought Scrutton, a social class thing, that—but, more interestingly, he loathed the trial. Earlier, Scrutton had made some attempt at chumminess; after all, they were going to be together for some time and he wanted friends, anyone would do, really . . . He'd murmured something unctuous about how fascinating it was to see another treason trial after so many years, and the officer had cut him short. Had actually interrupted him, Alistair one-of-Her-Majesty's-Counsel-learned-in-the-law Scrutton! "Bloody farce," he'd said. "If you ask me." (As if Scrutton would!) They'd scarcely spoken since.

The officer unlocked the door to the passage outside and gestured Scrutton through it. At the far end was a lift but apparently they weren't allowed to use it, so they climbed the steps, Scrutton hoping the officer wouldn't notice how he held onto one of the hand rails.

As they reached street level, shielded from what lay around the corner by the lift shaft, Scrutton heard a bell ring and suddenly the place was filled with noise: cars, many voices raised in raucous protest, a bullhorn.

"Roz Forbes," he heard a woman's voice say. "*Times*. I went round the front but they told me to use this entrance from now on, okay?"

The officer held Scrutton back until the door was closed again, and another set of footsteps had lost themselves in the upper regions. Only then did they traverse the entrance lobby, go through a porter's cubbyhole, and find the lavatory. While the officer waited outside, Scrutton emptied his bladder, then stood in front of a mirror to tidy his hair. Instinctively he reached out for a brush, before remembering that this was not the Athenaeum. He sighed. But his reflected image told him that he was holding up well. A bit tired, that's all.

Gazing at himself in the mirror, Scrutton noted how his lips had thinned over the years, making his normal expression a sour one. So many middle-aged lawyers had that impatient, hostile look. The "jealous mistress" did that to you. She sucked you dry, leaving you with the personality and external appearance of an old lemon. Years of battling with ignorant judges and somehow managing to stay polite. Patronizing small clients, fawning on important ones. Finding your solicitor had lost the papers the night before the trial. Working to midnight seven days a week. Tolerating incompetent juniors. Wresting a comprehensible proposition of law from a hundred and more old cases. Telling yourself constantly that you were right, and the other side, the judge, the House of Lords, all were wrong. Making yourself believe it.

Somewhere along the line the juice and the sweetness left you.

He absently picked a couple of sand-colored dog hairs from his lapel, and smiled. Good old Freddie! (Freddie being his retriever.) Soon be the weekend, then time for a tramp and a half . . .

Why had Roz Forbes come to the Old Bailey?

He'd sensed, in an obscure kind of way, that she was responsible for the *Times*'s half-baked attitude to this trial. You could always tell when she'd written the first leader. Then, a couple of days later, another hand would pen what almost amounted to a retraction. So different from the rest of the press, which had adopted and then stuck to its battle lines even before the committal proceedings.

Back in what he'd come to think of as his "cell," Scrutton picked up that day's *Times* and turned to its editorial page. The first leader was headlined: "A Not So Blind Lady?" He read on:

The statue of justice atop the Central Criminal Court has long provided our legal system with its most potent symbol. The scales she carries weigh facts and arguments; the sword in her other hand punishes those found wanting. These things, every schoolboy knows. What every schoolboy does not fully understand is why the lady is blindfolded. The answer traditionally given is that she must be impartial; you cannot favor what you do not see.

The real reason, however, is that she was born handicapped; and governments like her that way . . .

As Scrutton folded up the newspaper with a frown, something snagged his gaze, drawing it down to his jacket sleeve. More of Freddie's hairs. Funny how he'd always ended up calling the retrievers

Freddie. Must be a long line of them, now, stretching back into the past. Quite a dynasty.

That year after call to the bar, when Roz Forbes . . . Yes. He'd had a retriever in those days, too. The first ever Freddie.

CHAPTER
7

LONDON. SUMMER 1968

E re's a right bugger's muddle." Reg Valance sounded pleased. "Mr. Thornton's gone and got himself a tiddler, nice little plea at Uxbridge mags, and Mr. Lighterman's uncovered in the Court of Appeal."

Alistair Scrutton and Valance were the only two people present in the clerks' room. Scrutton therefore knew that Valance must be talking to him. A year ago, he would have assumed that the senior clerk was speaking Japanese and let it go at that. Now, however, he translated as effortlessly as any long-term resident. Frank, lucky chap, had actually been given a brief: go along to Uxbridge Magistrates' Court and there plead guilty on behalf of a client before making a speech in mitigation of sentence. Meanwhile, his pupil-master, Lighterman, was appearing in another court as assistant to a more senior lawyer, and had been relying on Frank to stand in for him there while he argued a different case in the Court of Appeal.

"Here we all are, nine-thirty and not a whore in the house painted," Valance said cheerily. "What's a boy to do?"

The rules of professional conduct were strict. A QC

appearing in court must have a junior barrister to help him. If Lighterman couldn't sit behind his leader, it was Valance's duty to rustle up someone to take his place. Scrutton felt his heart begin to beat faster.

"What's Mr. Thornton got?" he asked casually.

"D. and D."

Drunk and disorderly. Scrutton flushed. Why had Valance preferred Thornton over him for the job? Frank was always being given these miserable cases to do. There were twenty-seven barristers here and five pupils; it was a busy set, with plenty of work, but most of it was high-class commercial, and competition for the rare "tiddlers" was high. That was when pupils traditionally got their chance to show what they could do. Yet he'd been into court only twice, and on one of those occasions he hadn't even been called on to speak.

Perhaps Valance had been saving him for a special job. Perhaps this was the day . . .

"Is Mr. Lighterman being led in the CA?" he asked in what he hoped was a casual voice.

"Nah. Client's got no shekels, he says." Valance sniffed, a loud, richly catarrhal performance. "*Oi vay!* Know what I mean?"

Scrutton smiled, but said nothing.

"Would you be available today, Mr. Scrutton? By any chance? Not Ascot, nothing important on?"

"Ooh, I daresay I could phone the Palace and get myself excused."

"Why don't you do that, then, and after you're through go and sit behind Mr. Godber in Court Fifteen."

"Thanks."

"Think I'll ring up Mr. Godber's clerk, give 'im an 'eart attack."

Scrutton watched him dial. He loathed Valance with a passion, while recognizing that he did a weird job superbly.

For the most part, clerks were of lowly education and lowlier middle-class background. Despite their lack of formal qualifications, they wielded awesome power. It was the senior clerk's responsibility to allocate work from the vast pool of briefs that came in without a particular barrister's name on the front. When doing this, they were like punters backing their fancy. They'd give a promising pupil a run over the gallops. If the outing went well, that pupil might graduate to low jumps. Might: clerks answered to no one.

A pupil who disappointed on his first outing didn't run again.

As Scrutton watched Valance relish telling his opposite number in Mr. Godber's chambers that the QC's junior had gone missing, it occurred to him that God kept a drawer full of a particular physical type that he dipped into whenever there was call for another clerk. Small build. Lined face. Thin as a rake. Balding. Bulbous, veined nose, that came in varying shades of red and had often, at some indeterminate point in the past, been broken. Canny. Alert, as a rat is alert. Cheeky and subservient by turns. This drawer of God's was in the same chest where he kept bookies' runners, boxing promoters, and bouncers; sometimes he opened the wrong one by mistake, setting a fat man down in the Temple to sweat buckets, or misallocating a dyed-in-the-wool clerk to a used-car showroom. Scrutton's stockbroker, a youth of approximately his own age, might have narrowly missed being a barristers' clerk.

The one thing all the occupants of this particular chest of drawers had in common was common sense. They moved and they shook when they saw the main chance, which they did often.

"Right," Valance said, replacing the phone. "That's fixed, then. Now, Mr. Scrutton, you come over 'ere and listen to old Uncle Reg."

Scrutton approached Valance's cluttered desk.

"This case is a nasty can of rotten dog food. Court's sitting in camera, that's Latin. Know your Latin, do you?"

"Some."

"Three great Latin sayings my father taught me when he was senior clerk in these chambers. *Res judicata*, *res integra*, and raise your 'at when you talk to me."

Scrutton laughed dutifully, although he had heard Valance say this more times than he could count.

"'In camera' means in private. No public, no reporters. *Especially* no press, got it?"

"Got it."

"Industrial secrets. Plaintiff's a big chemical company, rolling in it."

Scrutton already knew that from conversations he'd had with Frank Thornton. He also remembered how the family trust established by his father owned shares in the plaintiff, although he saw no point in troubling Reg with that potentially awkard fact.

"Their top three directors walked off with the formu-*lie*, client list, you name it. Going to set up on their own. That's what Mr. Godber and Mr. Lighterman have been saying all week. Other side deny everything, of course. Now if one word of this leaks out, *one word*, mind, they'll be all hell to pay. So you be like old Bre'r Rabbit: sit tight an say nuffink."

"Right."

"Another bit of advice. Give Mr. Thornton's notebook the once-over, you'll find it in Mr. Lighterman's room. Lovely notetaker, Mr. Thornton. A real worker. Same as you. I never knew two pupils work the hours you two do."

"Thanks."

"No charge. If Mr. Thornton could just brighten himself up a bit, he'd turn into something. Tip him the wink, why don't you?"

"I'll do that." *Like hell*, Scrutton thought savagely.

"Come lunchtime, if you need anything, Uncle Reg'll be in his other office."

Scrutton walked out of the room with Valance's high-pitched laugh resonating in his head like the start of a migraine. The "other office" was the Lamb and Flag's saloon bar; Scrutton would no more have thought of seeking Valance there than he would have endured the public stands at Epsom.

But he didn't waste much thought on Valance. This opportunity was too important.

He and Frank had begun life in these chambers as six-months pupils. In March, their status had been renewed for a further six months. Soon their time would be up; come September, they would either be offered tenancies or have to find further pupilages elsewhere. Scrutton had done his sums. He knew that there would be a vacancy for *one* new tenant at the start of the new legal year.

Five pupils; one tenancy. Lester McDonald, the oldest pupil, had declared himself out of the running, since he wanted a job in industry and was serving time in chambers only as a means of completing his qualification. Of the others, one was only just starting his first six months and the other was totally useless. Which meant that the toss-up would be between him and Frank.

It went without saying that Frank had the better brain. Thanks to Valance, he also had the greater court experience. And he and Alistair were friends. So as Scrutton sat down at Frank's table he dreamily murmured Reg Valance's favorite plea: "What's a boy to do?"

And what's a girl to do? For the first time since leaving the clerk's room Scrutton found something to smile about. He'd been seeing Louise, Frank's fiancée, on the side. Frank had gone to Manchester with Lighterman on a case that involved three nights away from home. Scrutton telephoned Louise, pretending he wanted to talk to his friend, and affected surprise when she said he wasn't there. "Didn't he tell you he was going away?" she'd asked. And he'd replied, "Professionally, Frank is *ultra* correct." She'd laughed. Something at the back of that laugh made him bold. He had invited her to the theater the following night and not been overcome with surprise when she accepted. They'd met several times since then. On their second outing, she'd said: "I think it would be best if we didn't mention this to Frank . . . "

He found the notebook easily. It lay on top of the pile. Frank, as usual, had written his name in the center of the front cover, using large script, and surrounded it with a picturesque border. Scrutton found this extremely distasteful, a throwback to the doodling of one's schooldays. You had to write your name on the outside of a notebook, of course you did, because no one must *ever* be given an excuse to look inside at what was, after all, confidential matter. But the flamboyancy of Frank's script was strictly *infra dig.*

He opened the book. Page after page of legible script unfolded before Scrutton's eyes, contrasting rudely with the shopping-list scribble of his own notes. He scanned quickly through, in an attempt to pick up the essence of the case.

Suddenly a passage caught his eye and he stopped. He read the words several times before their full meaning sank in. Then he flagged the vital page with a sheet of foolscap.

Frank's notebook was blue. Scrutton hurried to the stationery store, where he collected a virgin notebook for his own use, deliberately choosing one with a pink cover, because there must be no room for confusion, not today. Then he raced across the Strand to the law courts where he donned his robes and sought out

Court Fifteen. There he walked up and down the corridor, drawing deeply on a cigarette, while he tried to work out how he might transform that single paragraph of notes into a fortune.

The plaintiff was a relative newcomer to the Stock Exchange list and its shares looked cheap. It was easy to believe that Frank's notebook was correct: the company had recently received a strong, reliable hint that a larger rival was preparing a hostile takeover bid. Names were named. Once that news became public, its share price would soar. But if at the same time word broke that it was locking horns in court with its former directors, who'd walked off with the equivalent of the family silver . . .

He had to do something. He couldn't just let the opportunity of a lifetime slip from between his fingers. But if he were found out . . .

Time was passing; before long Godber, the leader, must show up and then it would be too late. Scrutton stubbed out his cigarette half-smoked and scuttled down the corridor to where he knew there was a pay phone.

"Dad," he said when he heard the familiar voice at the other end. "Can't talk long, got a pen handy?"

Then he paused. He was under no illusions. If he went ahead with this, and was caught, that would be the end of his career. But if he allowed such a golden opportunity to pass him by, what kind of lawyer was he, anyway?

Big rewards, bigger risks.

"Listen, dad: something for the trustees, not, repeat *not* for you." He mentioned the plaintiff company's name. "Strongest possible buy imaginable, but be ready to jump off yesterday. You didn't get this from me, and make damn sure the trustees didn't get it from you."

Scrutton ran back to court, where Godber, the client's leading counsel, found time for one tense greeting before the case was called.

Scrutton put Frank's notebook on the seat beside him, under a pile of law reports, and while a barrister on the other side read out a lengthy document, he scrabbled through Lighterman's set of papers in search of the source for that one, vital paragraph in Frank's notebook. He found it in an affidavit sworn by the plaintiff's managing director. Slowly he began to piece the case together.

The clock set high on the oak-paneled wall seemed to be stuck in some warped corner of eternity. When at last the judge rose it said three minutes to one. Scrutton picked up both notebooks, his own and Frank's, before crawling out of court, drenched in sweat. He went to sit on one of the benches opposite the double doors bearing their ominous warning "Court in Camera: No Entry," while solicitors, barristers, and clients filtered out of court and formed groups, heads nodding anxiously together.

He must phone his father and cancel the earlier call. It was too dangerous. If he were caught . . .

"Hello."

He looked around. Sitting on the same bench, to his right, was the prettiest woman he'd ever seen. Woman was wrong, though; she looked young enough to be anyone's sweetheart. Such lovely straight black hair, cut short but obviously luxuriant to the touch— already he found himself wanting to touch it—and those pale green eyes, so searching and true . . . She sat leaning forward, a reporter's shorthand book resting on her crossed legs, tapping her teeth with a ballpoint pen. Seeing him look at her, she smiled. What a gorgeous smile, he thought, full of honest charm, but come-hither dimples, too; and that shade of lipstick suits her perfectly. Bet she's fun in bed . . .

"Anything for me?" she asked, a touch forlornly he thought.

"You're press?"

"Yes."

"Sorry."

She sighed. "Oh, well. Guess that's it for today, then."

She stared down at her lap, but he could see the look of disappointment on her face and it was enough to drive out all thoughts of the case, the takeover, phoning his father.

"What's your name?" he asked gently.

"Forbes. Roz Forbes."

She opened her mouth to speak again, but then a loud voice called: "Scrutton . . . anyone seen Alistair Scrutton?"

Godber stood halfway down the corridor, scanning the passersby. Scrutton rose in confusion and ran toward the QC, face flushing up to the rim of his wig.

"Sorry," he blurted out, "I—"

"I want a word." Godber took him by the arm and led him down a side corridor. The QC's face looked somber. He leaned against the wall and removed his wig, using the back of the same hand to wipe his brow. "Listen, Scrutton, the judge saw a new face in court today—yours—and sent his clerk out with a message when he rose. He wants me to remind you about the injunction he made at the start of the hearing."

Scrutton's heart catapulted up to his throat. What was all this about an injunction? If anyone disobeyed an injunction, he went to prison. Frank's notes hadn't said anything about it . . . *damn*, might have been in the first couple of pages, he'd skipped them . . .

"What injunction?" he stuttered.

"The judge made an order on day one, prohibiting anyone connected with this, this . . . " Godber looked exhausted; he seemed to find it hard to put two words together. "This *thing*, from disclosing any information about it to anyone. Primarily that was directed against the defendants, who are grade-one shits. But it affects you just as it affects me. And I'm sure I don't have to remind you about the rules of professional conduct. Everything you learn about this case is doubly confidential, clear?"

All Scrutton could do was nod. As he watched Godber stalk off in the direction of the robing room, for a moment his brain slipped into semi-consciousness, permitting him to breathe but otherwise shutting down all systems. When he came to himself, it was to find one idea alone urgently demanding to be actioned.

The recent conversation had taken place not far from the pay phone he'd used earlier to call his father. Scrutton raced to it and shoved in a shilling, heedless of expense.

"Hello . . . Dad?"

"Yes. Alistair, what—?"

"Dad, listen. Have you done anything about those shares yet?"

"I spoke to Morrison ten minutes ago."

"For God's sake, call him back and cancel everything."

"Why?"

Scrutton looked to right and left. There was nobody about. "I had a tip," he hissed. "Now it turns out there's an injunction covering the info. *We could go to jail!*"

There was the briefest of pauses. Then he heard his father say, "Right, thanks."

As Scrutton replaced the receiver his whole body was trembling. Ten minutes . . . they might have dealt already, that was an eternity on the Stock Exchange floor. He leaned back against the wall with his eyes closed.

At that moment, he almost hated his father. Charles Scrutton had preached the work ethic to Alistair throughout his schooldays. Only when at Oxford had he realized that the old man always han-

kered after the easy money, and was stuffed with
cant. After that, he'd paid more heed to what Charles
actually did than to anything he said, and that's why
now he was on the brink of ruin: all because he'd followed his father's example, like a good son.

Never again, though. Never again as long as he
lived would he run such a risk. The sweat, the
strain, nothing could compensate for them. He
cursed the moment he'd seen Frank's notebook.

He opened his eyes. The notebook. *Where was it?*
"Oh no," he breathed. "No, no, no . . . "

As he ran back along the corridor his mind
replayed everything that had happened since he'd
left court, like a high-speed film. He'd sat down on
a bench, talked to the girl, what had they talked
about? Don't think about the girl, don't think about
anything except that bloody book, you put both
notebooks down on the seat beside you, the pink
and the blue, then Godber called you . . .

He saw the books lying on the bench while he
was still yards away and slowed to a walk. Thank
God, he said; irrationally, because he didn't believe
in an all-knowing deity, not really, although some
events came close to converting a man . . .

There was no sign of the girl he'd talked to earlier. He flopped down on the bench, thankfully taking off his wig. He undid his waistcoat and then, to
improve matters further, three buttons of his shirt.
Let the chest breathe a bit . . .

He looked down at the bench beside him, reaching out to pick up the notebooks. His incipient
smile froze, along with his hand. Then he was back
in the nightmare, only this time it was a hundred-
fold worse.

The panic fueling him earlier had made his memory sharper than usual. He could, with perfect clarity,
see himself coming out of court with the notebooks
under his arm. He'd put them down on the bench

beside him. When Godber called, he'd left them there, the pink book on top. Now the blue notebook covered the pink one. And . . . Scrutton grabbed up Frank's book to make sure, already knowing in his heart what the answer would be . . . the sheet of foolscap paper he had used to mark the place was gone.

Someone had looked inside the notebooks. Inevitably, that someone would have noticed the folded marker and turned up that page first. Someone pretty, with a devastating smile, who also happened to be a *reporter*.

The corridors were starting to throng with people again after the lunch break. Scrutton had to go back into court. He didn't know how he got through the afternoon. He took notes mechanically, obsessed by the knowledge that he ought to come clean. If he confessed to his own lack of care, the damage might be contained, as far as the clients were concerned. The plaintiff's solicitors would contact the press. The judge might even make an injunction stopping them from publishing anything that wretched girl had learned. But—what effect would it have on his career?

That was the question that tortured him. He could picture two outcomes.

In the first, the judge, counsel, everyone in fact, praised him for his honesty and straightforwardness. You made a mistake, they'd say; well, hah-hah, we were young once ourselves, my boy; shudder to think of some of the horrors we perpetrated; here, have a seat in chambers as a reward for being upright and true . . .

The script of the alternative daydream was very different.

There would be proceedings for contempt of court. He would be fined, at best. In addition, he'd be hauled in front of a professional conduct committee and disbarred, or, if he was exceptionally lucky, suspended from practice for five years. His picture would be in the papers. His parents . . .

The second daydream always ended abruptly at that point.

For some reason, the court rose early. Scrutton did not go to the robing room at once. Instead, he found his feet taking him along the transverse corridor at the north end of the law courts, to where the lord chief justice sat.

He bowed and entered junior counsel's row, as was his right, even though he had no connection with the case being heard, a criminal appeal. "The chief" sat bolt upright, having to stretch his hand far out to take notes. When he interposed to ask a question, his voice echoed slightly in the lofty courtroom. Counsel on the receiving end began to waffle. Scrutton knew that the question had been loaded; that it emanated from an acute brain, the kind that effortlessly cut through crap.

There were three judges in this court. "The chief" occupied the center seat, the seat of power. Looking up at him, Scrutton wondered whether, at the start of his career, he had ever made a mistake. Somehow he doubted it. Why? Because the man had been lucky, that's why.

Scrutton did not wait for the court to rise. He stood up, bowed again, and left. As he walked to the robing room he knew that he would never want anything as much as he wanted the peerage, the gold chain, the bows and the scrapes . . . and above all that seat in the middle, the throne of English law.

The first thing he did on returning to chambers was surreptitiously replace Frank's notebook in the exact spot where he'd found it. At tea he kept to one side. If people noticed the haggard expression on his face, they did not comment. Afterward he toyed with some papers, for the sake of appearances, while he thought about trying to trace the girl, but apart from knowing that her name was Roz Forbes his ignorance was total. Anyway, even if he did manage to find her, he could think of no reason why she might agree to help him. Roz Forbes looked to him like a lowly reporter, given the rotten jobs because she was female; that single paragraph in Frank's notebook represented the scoop, her one great chance of a lifetime, just as sitting behind Godber had this morning seemed like his.

Was she even now dithering over whether to publish data she'd obtained by stealing from a confidential source? No. *You* steal, *I* use my initiative . . . wasn't that how it went? In her place, Scrutton thought, I'd do the same. And she was protected by an armored shield: the convention that reporters never disclosed their sources.

He raised his head and stared at the bookcase opposite. Of course: Roz Forbes wasn't going to talk. And if he, too, kept his mouth shut, they might suspect, but they could never prove. That's right! . . . nobody was going to blow the whistle on him. All he had to do was stay dumb, no matter what pressures they brought to bear.

At six-thirty, Scrutton drove his orange MGB to the flat in Primrose Hill that his father had bought for him on his twenty-first birthday. Once home he opened a fresh bottle of Johnnie Walker and began to drink steadily. At first he mixed the spirit with water, half and half, but after a while he was taking it neat. While he drank he walked up and down, running every possible scenario through his brain. It was one o'clock when he finally fell down on the sofa, knocking over the whisky bottle as he did so. It hardly mattered; only a couple of fingers remained.

He awoke a little before six, feeling like death. After swallowing several glasses of water and putting the coffee percolator on, he dragged himself out to the newsstand on the corner, where he bought a copy of every newspaper they had. He scattered them over the living room floor and went down on his hands and knees with the eagerness of an evangelist repenting of some diversion from the straight and narrow.

He scanned all the business news. Then he turned to the home pages. Finally, in near desperation, he leafed through the foreign reports, the editorials, even the letters.

Nothing.

Scrutton got up off his knees. For a moment he stood still. Then he flung up his arms, cried, "Whoopeeeee!" and began to dance around the room like a boy who'd just survived his first French kiss.

Life had never seemed so sweet to him as it did that day. The sun shone; well of course it did! On his way to the Temple he stopped off at a florist's and sent his mother some flowers, not because it was her birthday or any other particular occasion, but because he felt full of gratitude that he needed to express in concrete fashion. All the girls he drove past were pretty; the river glittered silver as he swanned along the embankment; Reg Valance, opening the morning mail, looked positively handsome. To cap it all, Dennis Lighterman had finished his case in the Court of Appeal, so Scrutton's services were no longer required in Court Fifteen.

"How did yesterday go?" Frank asked.

"Wonderful." Scrutton beamed at him. "Fascinating."

His own pupil-master usually worked at home on Friday, if he wasn't in court, and the other barrister who shared his office was busy elsewhere, so Scrutton had the run of the place. He wrote an Advice on a complicated Landlord and Tenant point, did the crossword, and planned the coming weekend.

He briefly considered phoning Louise, only to dismiss it; she and Frank would almost certainly want to spend time together. But then, just before lunch, one of his Oxford cronies rang to say he was going down to Cowes at the weekend for a week's bumming around on the Solent; would Scrutton care to make up the numbers? He would. On the way out of chambers he bought early editions of the *News* and *Standard*, just as a precaution, but, as he'd assumed would be the case, neither contained any mention of the court case.

The feeling of euphoria that gripped him continued throughout a sun-soaked weekend on the Hampshire coast. On the Saturday afternoon he played tennis spectacularly well, even by his standards. His mother, a one-time county champion, had coached him since he was five years old, thrusting him and his elder sister Susan toward greatness. Susan, however, never cared for tennis. Or for anything else much, come to that.

As he sat on the sidelines, sipping Bucks Fizz, Scrutton found his thoughts turning to Susan, as they tended to do a few times each year. She'd always wanted to get away. Even as a young child, she'd pestered ma and pa to send her to summer camp. Then one day Alistair had come down from Oxford at the start of the Long Vac. to find mother on the tennis court, knocking up with Charles. After they'd been playing for half an hour, Belinda had said casually, as they changed ends, "Did you know Susan's going to live in the States? Something on Wall Street . . . "

In fact, she'd gone the week before, becoming a retail sector analyst for one of those huge brokerages with improbable names suggestive of Russian or Polish origins. And that was the last he'd seen of her.

Alistair drained his glass, wondering if Susan had ever traded on insider information. If so, presumably her luck had held every bit as firmly as his, for she was still doing the same job.

Yes, the Scruttons had always been lucky, he

reflected as he went in to change. Take the sleeping accommodation, for instance . . .

Scrutton had a room to himself on Friday, but to himself and one other on the Saturday. His companion that second night was a Somerville PPE graduate he'd been eyeing for some time, and Friday's run of luck, Scrutton luck, ran on . . .

It lasted, in fact, until Monday morning, when he went into chambers to find Reg Valance and Dennis Lighterman involved in quietly urgent conversation.

Lighterman saw Scrutton and dried up. "Come into my room," he said to Valance in a curt way that Scrutton had never heard him use before. As the two of them went out, Scrutton's eyes were drawn to a newspaper lying on Valance's desk. He approached it cautiously, some evil instinct already telling him the worst. The paper, a tabloid, was opened at a page toward the back. As he picked it up, a name rushed up to fill his vision.

Roz Forbes.

The item occupied the whole of one column, and was printed in darker ink than the rest of the page. They'd given her a byline; that was his first thought. Lucky kid.

He guessed at once what had happened. She'd been checking the story for accuracy. Somehow she'd found enough confirmation to go ahead. And for nearly three days now, he had kept his crime to himself.

He read the article several times before the sense of it sank in. Forbes had been clever; she said that a writ had been issued, which was anybody's right, but made no mention of the proceedings in court, thereby avoiding penalties for contempt. She reported the resignations of three directors, merely stating that they intended to start up a similar company of their own. The takeover bid, however, was written up in full. There were embellishments, but the gist of the article centered on that one vital paragraph in Frank's notebook.

Why had Lighterman not said, "Good morning," as he usually did to pupils? Did he suspect? Did he *know*?

Scrutton dropped the paper, battening down the desire to storm up to Lighterman and ask why he hadn't greeted him; this was no time for childishness. So instead he went to his pupil-master's room, quietly bade him Good Morning, and set to work.

The storm blew for a long time. What made it worse was the fact that it largely blew in Scrutton's absence.

Those concerned with the case, including Frank Thornton, had first to face the wrath of the judge. He charged the solicitors on both sides with responsibility for finding out who had talked to the press.

They began by requesting statements from all the lawyers, their clients and anyone who had been present in court for however short a period. Versions were cross-checked and, as far as possible, verified. Over a period of days the atmosphere in chambers grew progressively more unpleasant, while outside the rest of the press caught up with Roz Forbes' scoop. The plaintiff's share price rocketed. Lighterman betrayed his anger in occasional outbursts, often directed against Frank, who as his pupil provided the nearest target. Scrutton could see how unhappy his friend was, but whenever he tried to discuss things Frank would shut him up.

"Can't you see," he'd say wearily, "that's the trouble—talking too much? That's why we're in this mess."

Then came judgment in the plaintiff's application against its three defecting directors. The company lost. Since this had been in the way of a preliminary hearing, it had the right to insist on a full trial later, but in the meantime the defectors would be free to get on with establishing their new business and by now no one was interested. The share price dropped back to what it had been on the first day of the hearing and went on falling.

At least, Scrutton thought bitterly, father managed to stop the trustees from buying. It was his only consolation.

Several times he was tempted to make a clean breast of it. Let's get this over with, he imagined himself saying to Lighterman in a firm drawl; let's limit the damage, shall we? But he well knew that by this stage the only damage that could be contained was other people's. He was doomed.

Inevitably, someone remembered that he had stood in for Frank one day; and then Scrutton, too, had to make a statement.

The solicitor who interviewed him was in his forties, polite, a little overawed, perhaps, at finding himself in barristers' chambers on such an unusual mission. He began with an examination of Scrutton's pink notebook.

"It seems you didn't . . . er, you didn't have much opportunity for notetaking that day?"

"No," Scrutton agreed. "I'm a pretty grim hand at taking notes at the best of times, and that day I was so busy rooting through the papers trying to make sense of what was going on that I wrote even less than usual."

"Lucky for you, perhaps?" the solicitor observed, as he handed back the notebook.

"I'm sorry?"

"Nothing. Now I'd like to ask you a few questions . . . "

But Scrutton wasn't listening. What had he meant, *Lucky for you, perhaps?* In connection with his pink notebook . . . he'd not written much and that was lucky . . .

That could mean only one thing: *they knew the*

information had come from a notebook.

What else did they know?

He fought to concentrate on what the solicitor was saying.

"Can I focus your attention on lunchtime for a moment? Did you see anyone then? Either to talk to, or see in the sense of seeing somebody do something that struck you as odd?"

The solicitor's throwaway comment, "Lucky for you, perhaps?" had already convinced Scrutton that they knew about the Forbes girl. So he could not afford to lie about having seen her.

"I remember . . . " He turned his head slightly, as if concentrating on the carpet might assist his memory. "I remember we rose just before one o'clock. I came out of court . . . Mr. Godber was busy talking to the plaintiff's managing director, as I recall . . . " His voice slowed. "I sat . . . down. Yes, on a bench."

He waited, under cover of pretending to rack his memory, but the solicitor offered him no help. Scrutton opened his mouth to say: "There was a girl sitting next to me, she was from the press, her name was Roz Forbes." But, somewhere in the complicated path from brain to throat to tongue to utterance, fear wrenched the wheel from Scrutton, sending him down the road he'd chosen to turn his back on, the *wrong* road.

"I seem to remember there was a woman sitting there. Yes—she said something to me."

"What did she say?"

"It's very hot, isn't it—something like that."

"Nothing about the case?"

"No."

"Did she tell you her name?"

"No."

"What else was said?"

"Nothing. Mr. Godber called me away at that point."

"When you went away to speak to Mr. Godber, did you take your notebook with you?"

"I . . . I'm not sure." Scrutton stared at the solicitor, but the man's face alone would have won him a place in any world-ranking poker team. "I don't think so."

The solicitor wrote for a few moments. Then he said casually, "Did you carry just the one notebook down to court?"

"Just the one."

When the solicitor looked up, there was no longer anything over-awed about his expression. "Sure?" he rapped.

For a second, Scrutton floundered helplessly. *They knew!* But by now he was in too deep to do anything except say, "Quite sure."

The solicitor nodded and said, "Thanks very much, Mr. Scrutton. I'm sorry to have troubled you."

The interview was over.

He'd expected this to be the prelude to a resolution. Someone would announce the result of the inquiry, heads would roll. But nothing happened, and the atmosphere in chambers perceptibly lightened. Nobody wanted to discuss what was now past history.

Scrutton worked hard through the long, hot month of July, every night afraid to sleep on account of the dreams that had begun to plague him, every day fearing a summons to the head of chambers.

The summons, when it came, emanated from another quarter, although in a sense it was indeed the head of chambers that Scrutton had to deal with.

The last week of Trinity term arrived, and barristers everywhere were working long hours to clear their desks in time for the summer vacation. At seven o'clock one evening Reg Valance put his head around the door. "Still at it, Mr. Scrutton?" he asked.

"As you see."

"I'd like a word. Uncle Reg knows just the place."

To Scrutton's surprise, "just the place" turned out to be a basement drinking club down an alley off Theobalds Road, north of Gray's Inn. Valance led Scrutton to a back parlor with a darts board on one wall, where they could be alone. Scrutton was wondering what might be safe to drink, when the proprietor of this dingy establishment solved the problem by carrying in a tray on which stood two glasses and a half-full bottle of Chivas Regal.

"And some water, Ted," Valance said as he sprawled back in a faded leather armchair. "Assuming you 'aven't upped the price of it since last week."

The water came, along with ice in a pint beer glass. Valance mixed the drinks, then took off his tie and opened his shirt at the collar. "Cheers," he said comfortably.

"Down the hatch," Scrutton responded, wondering what on earth this all meant.

"Thought we'd have a little natter," Valance said. "About recent events."

"You're referring to that nasty business with the press?"

"Yes." Valance took a swig and held his glass up to the light. "Lovely drop'a scotch, that. A lot of to-ings and fro-ings, and not a rat's fart to show for any of it."

Scrutton said nothing.

"So they're closing the file and putting it away nice and tidy, at the bottom of the drawer. We don't want any scandals, now do we? Especially now that we're at the end of term, and there's people's futures to be decided."

Scrutton looked at him and understood that he was here not to enjoy himself, but to learn. "If you've got something to tell me," he said, with a rash attempt at hauteur, "spit it out, like a good fellow."

"Other 'alf first." Valance poured whisky into both their glasses before lolling back. "There was a little confabulation last Friday, Mr. Scrutton. Head of chambers held a council of war. What to do about that leak to the press?" Valance shook his head, tut-tutting in mock severity. "Dear me, you should have heard some of the language."

"And?"

"And . . . it turns out that the plaintiff's solicitors wrote a letter to the editor of the newspaper concerned. A frosty, you might say, letter, which got itself a dusty answer."

"They weren't prepared to reveal their sources?"

"They were not, Mr. Scrutton. But they'd reckoned without everyone concerned from top to bottom being a lawyer. So there was badgering and blackmail and pleading and I don't know what else. And in the end, the editor wrote to say that, as it was a special case, he didn't mind telling the solicitors this once—strictly a one-off, mind—that there *was* no source."

Scrutton stared at him, eyes and mouth all open. "What?"

"There never was no source," Valance cackled. "No one said a thing to that Forbes woman."

"But then how—"

"I'll tell you, Mr. Scrutton." Valance leaned forward to rest his elbows on his knees. No trace of humor hovered about him now. His face had turned ugly, the eyes screwed up and menacing. "There was no source, but there was a notebook. A blue one. With somebody's name written on the outside, in script, with a border around it, but the reporter can't, or won't, remember whose name it was."

Scrutton's mind flashed back to his interview with the solicitor. The man had asked, "Did you take just

the one notebook down to court?" And then—"Sure?"
He returned to the present with a jolt to find Valance
in the middle of asking him a question.

"What?"

"I said, Can you think of anyone who writes his
name on the outside of his notebooks in fancy
handwriting and then draws a line around it?"

Scrutton swallowed hard.

"Left on a bench, it was. They wouldn't say when,
or what time of day, or nuffink like that. Only that it
was left lying around on a bench somewhere."

There was a long silence. Scrutton spoke first.
"You were telling me about a chambers meeting.
Last Friday . . . "

"Ah, yes. Some people were rather hard on Mr.
Thornton."

"They're sure it was him, then?" Scrutton could
have bitten his tongue out, but too late to worry
about that now.

"Nobody's certain of anything, that's the point.
You really must take that cloth out of your ears,
young man; it spoils your good looks. But Mr.
Thornton's an honest sort of boy, know what I
mean? He couldn't swear he knew where his notebook was every minute of the day. His memory's
not as good as yours; *you* were positive you hadn't
taken that notebook out of chambers."

Scrutton poured another glass of Chivas, without
asking permission. His friend had been honest, all
the way down the line, and right now he didn't
want to think about that.

"So what was a boy to do?" Valance asked.
"Most people felt sorry for Mr. Thornton; one mistake and so on. But one mistake is all it takes.
Especially if you've got the wrong accent." For an
instant the clerk dropped his air of worldly wisdom.
"Can't have the wrong accent in chambers, now,
can we?" he said viciously. "Anyway . . . my opin-

ion was sought. And given. So." He raised his glass. "I think you'll find that before you break up for the hols, there's a certain offer going to be made to you, Mr. Scrutton. Congratulations are in order."

Scrutton felt too drained to feel anything. Valance wants me to thank him for getting me into chambers, he thought dully. He's demanding my gratitude. My feudal homage. But instead, he knew only anger.

"So you backed me, did you? Valance."

Members of chambers used the clerk's surname. He was a member of chambers now.

"I did. *Mr.* Scrutton."

"Now why ever would you do a thing like that?"

"I will tell you," Valance said, leaning even farther forward. "We're going to have a real conversation now, our first and our last, so you pay attention. I've made better men than you, Scrutton. Enough to know when to back a hunch. You're shit, but you're a clever piece of shit, and I like that. You'll go far, with my help."

"Oh yes? Since when have you thought *that*?"

Valance's smile reminded Scrutton of a battle-seasoned old tomcat faced with a greenhorn of a mouse.

"Hard to say," he said. "Maybe it was when I saw you come back into chambers from court that day, with Mr. Thornton's notebook tucked under your arm. His *blue* notebook." He shook his head, chewing his lower lip. "Nah. That weren't it. I can remember the moment, now. The actual minute. It was when I heard as how you'd sworn blind you took just the one, *pink* notebook down to court."

He knocked back his glass. "'Ope you 'aven't made any plans for going away this August," he said. "'Cause from now on, young man, you're going to be *busy*."

CHAPTER

8

LONDON. THE PRESENT

Condon pulled up outside one of a row of terraced houses in Ederline Avenue and for a
moment the three men sat there silently con-
templating the street.

"Quiet," Brennan said at last.

Pat O'Halloran was in front next to Condon, the
driver. He half-turned and said, "Mrs. Clark's used
to looking after the Salvation Army. Widow-
woman, in her sixties or thereabouts. Knows how to
keep a tight lip."

Brennan nodded. "Do me a favor, Pat. Take the
boy and go buy all the newspapers. Come back
again at four. Wake me if I'm sleeping."

"I will. Oh, Martin . . . "

Brennan, already half out of the car, stopped.
"Well?"

"I'm sorry to mention this, I was hoping—"

"What is it, Pat?"

O'Halloran chewed his lip. "There's been a bit of
pother up Cricklewood way," he said at last.
"Phone calls to Dublin: Why's Brennan here, who

authorized it?—you know the kind of nonsense."

Cricklewood was where the leader of the three-man cell that directed the Provos' English operations had his headquarters. A man called Mountjoy, as Brennan recalled . . .

"What did Dublin say?"

"They told Mountjoy to get stuffed; what you did was your business, Council business, and he wasn't to poke his nose where it could do no good. But, Martin . . . "

O'Halloran's tone had been growing steadily more apologetic. By now he was almost wheedling.

"Dublin didn't know you were coming. They weren't best pleased. I've had three calls on three successive nights, you know how dangerous that is. If you could see your way to having a word with them, now . . . "

The Army Council, rulers of the Provisional IRA, had not known that the Krait was coming to London, because Brennan hadn't told them. This would be enough to merit a court martial for anyone but him.

"I'll phone Brother Mark tonight," Brennan said. "Set his mind at rest. All right?"

"Thanks."

Brennan got out and watched the car disappear around a corner before turning his attention to his surroundings. A quiet road in south London, its solid Victorian houses showed all the signs of slightly rundown respectability. Lace curtains shielded clean windows from prying eyes; there were colored glass panels in frames above the front doors; each tiny but well-kept front garden had its tiled path and yellowing privet hedge.

When he pushed open the wrought-iron front gate, all twists and curls, its hinges squeaked, and flakes of white paint adhered to his hand. His knock was answered by an elderly lady wearing an apron over a thin floral print dress, her gray hair done up in a bun and protected by a net.

"You'll be Colonel Lloyd?"

"Yes, ma'am. But I'm more at ease if people call me John."

"And I'm Elsie Clark. Whatever am I thinking of, keeping you on the doorstep in February! Come and warm yourself. Would you like a cup of tea?"

"If it's all the same to you, I'd rather see the room."

She took him upstairs. His bedroom was sparsely furnished with a bed, table, easy chair, wardrobe, and bookcase, but everything looked clean and the sheets were dry under his hand. He wasn't sure he could live for long with the wallpaper, which came in an unattractive pattern of mauve and olive-green, but then if all went as it should he'd be out of here within the week.

"Now," Mrs. Clark said, "I'll leave you to rest, but before I go I'll just run through the rules." She laughed, a surprisingly strong sound to come from such a slight body. "Me telling the rules to an officer like yourself, fancy!"

She opened her left palm and began to tell of her points with her right forefinger.

"Cooked breakfast's included and you're more than welcome to share a bit of supper with me; I don't charge for that because I like the company and cooking for two's easier than cooking for one. Use all the hot water you like . . . "

Brennan watched her while she spoke. She had a large black mole on her chin from which three curly hairs sprouted. He longed to pluck them, it would have made a good face even better. He liked Mrs. Clark, despite her being English. If it became necessary to kill her, he would use a single blow from the side of his hand, as instantaneous as it would be painless.

"That's wonderful," he murmured when she'd finished. "We're going to be such friends, I can sense it."

She went out, closing the door behind her. There was no key in the lock. The first thing Brennan did was root around in his bag for a rubber wedge which he used to secure the door, kicking it home until it would go no further. Then he unpacked swiftly, wondering what Customs would even now be making of Mr. Challas's abandoned gray Revelation, until all that was left in the case was his Mo 951 Beretta.

He lay back on the bed, testing the gun's mechanism while he worked out what he could say to Dublin to allay their unease. He needed a clear run, without interference from the Cricklewood hierarchy or, worse, Dublin itself. Brother Mark, whom he had promised to telephone, was the code name of the Army Council's secretary, a longtime friend. He would listen to what the Krait had to say, he would understand; but his was one voice among several.

Somehow, he was going to have to pull the wool over their eyes. Because if the Army Council got so much as a sniff of his real business . . .

His own eyes were starting to droop. He hesitated a moment, then laid his gun on the bedside table where he could reach it instantly if danger threatened.

He did not need to bring this Beretta Mo 951 into England at all, and he'd certainly been crazy to do it the way he had; but that was what his life was all about. Taking on the British and trashing them. Again. And again.

Pat O'Halloran was a good man, he reflected. The Provos in Cricklewood could have fixed Brennan up with almost any weapon, but it wouldn't have been the same. Apart from the intermediary who'd sold the Beretta to the Krait, no one but he had ever touched it. This gun had saved his life on three occasions, and if he had gone in for carving notches on the butt there would have been sixteen.

The Krait erupted into a giggle and was still again. Part of the mystique surrounding him derived from his knack of blending into the landscape and then lying motionless for long periods, like the thin, black-and-white ringed snake which gave him his *nom de guerre*. And like that snake, he needed to strike only once, at beyond the speed of sound, before dissolving away to nothing.

He'd taken on the British and won. Again.

But it hadn't always been like that.

There once was a time, right at the start, when the British had beaten him. Twenty years and God knew how many deaths later, the score still wasn't even.

It would never be even.

Brennan suddenly wanted to stay awake. He knew that if he slept now, Sean would come to him. He always did when exhaustion threatened.

February. The cruelest month.

"My brother," he cried; the words echoed only in his mind, but he could hear the tears, even so.

COUNTY SLIGO. FEBRUARY 1969

Sean Brennan climbed into Martin's sleeping bag and held him close. "News," he whispered. "Guess you."

Martin, still half asleep, could only mumble.

"It's my turn," Sean breathed. "Come at last, it has. And it's *big*."

Martin was awake now. Outside, a storm wind hurled rushes of rain against the window, ice-cold from its ocean winter crossing, but here, tucked up with Sean, the harsh world could not enter. He returned his brother's hug and murmured, "Whass' time?"

"Gone two. I just got back. They're asleep."

In such a large household, "they" could have meant anyone; except that when spoken in the cold, scornful tone Sean had just used, it always meant mother and father.

"When?" Martin asked quietly.

"Two nights from now. Bank job, up north."

"Will they give you a gun?"

"Yeats says yes."

Martin knew Yeats by reputation only. Apart from being a wondrous flautist, he was a district commander in the Provisional IRA; and last autumn he had taken Sean, along with some other local boys, into the backlands beyond the Curlow Mountains, where he'd taught them to shoot. Sean could strip, clean, reassemble, and fire the old British Army issue .303s better than any man between Dublin and the border. Two nights from now, he would be putting theory into practice. Martin, who had been rejected by Yeats as too young, felt envious.

"Can't I come?" he implored.

"Yeats'll let you drive me to the rendezvous and pick me up again."

Martin's heart soared. His chance to serve The Cause at last! For Sean, notwithstanding his facility with a rifle or a rake, had never managed to master the art of driving. But then a terrible doubt wriggled into his mind and he involuntarily clutched Sean's arm. "Will dad let us take the car?"

"He will that," Sean replied; and his own whisper sounded grim.

He was right. Next morning, he and Martin came down to breakfast to find their mother frying eggs on the black, grease-coated range, while dad cast his eye down the columns of a week-old newspaper.

"Liam Yeats called by early," he said to the paper. Martin felt surprised, not on account of the news, but because of the way in which it was delivered. His father normally liked to look his children in the eye when he greeted them, ever ready with some cheery, stupid comment.

"He said I'd be doing him a favor if I let you two boys borrow the car this Friday night." Now dad removed his glasses and wiped his forehead, but still he did not look at them. "So that's the way of it," he said, turning over the page. "That's the way of it . . . "

Dad strongly disapproved of the Provos and their "shenanigans," his collective noun for murder, robbery, and arson lumped together. But he and his family lived in a part of Ireland where loyalty to The Cause was axiomatic, taken in at birth with mother's milk, and neutrality was like all other luxuries: beyond reach. When sons chose to answer the bugle's call, parents turned the page of the newspaper, keeping their eyes on yesterday's deaths rather than contemplate tomorrow's.

Friday came at last. Supper was a silent meal. "They" munched stolidly on their food, while the other children gazed in awe at Martin and Sean, going to be soldiers for The Cause. No one had told them. They all knew.

As Martin looked along the table he felt a sudden twinge of sadness. But then he turned his eyes on Sean, who caught the gaze and held it fast. Yes, Martin thought, I'm leaving now, and I don't care. It's right.

A little after eight o'clock, the boys drove away from the farmhouse, singing at the tops of their voices:

And I shall hear, though soft you tread above me,
And all my grave will warmer, sweeter, be,
For you will bend and tell me that you love me,
And I shall sleep in peace until you come to me.

A glance in the cracked mirror showed Martin neither lights nor any member of his family come out to wave farewell.

Their destination lay at the end of a long, winding track that led at first through fenced fields before entering a deep vale. About a mile after leaving the road, Martin pulled up in a farmyard where several other cars were already parked. Not a light showed anywhere, but Sean seemed to know what to do. He knocked on the farmhouse door, using a special tattoo. It opened a crack to reveal only darkness. Then a voice from within said: "You're late."

The door opened wide enough to admit them and immediately closed again with a bang. Someone struck a match, revealing Liam Yeats not six inches from him. Martin jumped back, knocking his head against a low beam.

"That's a nervous puppy you've brought with you, Sean." Yeats sounded unfriendly. "Make sure he doesn't yap, will you?"

They followed him into a large kitchen, lighted only by a storm lantern. The single window had been covered with black cloth. Several people sat around a table on which were mugs, and a deck of cards. Thick tobacco smoke did little to mask the smell of men's fear. Martin's eyes strayed to the fireplace. Leaning against the wall nearby, barely visible in the firelight, stood half a dozen rifles; beside them, a brown metal ammunition box with yellow letters on the top. For a while no one spoke.

"We'd best be getting away," Yeats said at last. Several men stood up, but there was no eagerness about them. Martin looked from face to face. The uniform tightness of their expressions frightened him. This wasn't how it was supposed to be: you went out to fight for the cause with a song on your lips, or a word of bright comfort for your comrades-in-arms. These men looked like bank robbers preparing for a raid.

He remembered, then, that they were indeed going up to Omagh to rob a bank, but the recollection only served to muddle him. He wanted them to look like what they were not; he wanted them not to be what they most resembled.

It doesn't matter, he told himself. Many a bad thing's had to be done in the name of The Cause.

Good men can't fight without arms. Arms cost money. Banks have money, and in Omagh it's British *punts* they have. God's sake, man; what does it matter what they *look* like . . . ?

But despite these fine words, he felt afraid for Sean. Suddenly he was overcome by an urge to embrace his brother; he held him close, and for a mad second came close to crying out, "Don't go!"

When a hand gripped his arm he released Sean and squirmed around to find Yeats' pitted face glaring down at him. "You . . . take care of our guest, there."

He pointed to the far side of the fireplace, where a single figure sat swathed in shadow, the lantern light not extending to his face. Martin nodded vigorously.

"See you do." Yeats continued to gaze at him through those grim eyes of his, as if Martin was the enemy, not the damned English. Then Yeats dropped his arm and seconds later he found himself alone with the silent figure by the fire.

Martin sat down at the table and nervously began to shuffle the pack of cards. Car engines died away, leaving only the rise and fall of the wind to disturb the silence. He wanted to speak, but something intangible about the other presence kept his lips sealed, so he dealt for a game of patience instead. Before he began to play, however, he moved the lantern, placing it more squarely between him and the fireplace. Now the seated figure no longer existed for him.

He didn't want to admit how scared he was.

No one had told him that he would have to spend time alone with a stranger. Was he one of the hard men? Martin asked himself; was he a butcher? A little mad, maybe? Had he been put here to guard him, Martin Brennan, while the others went about their business?

Outside, somewhere neither close nor distant, a door banged in the wind. The intermittent "clack-*clack*" was getting on his nerves. He wanted to go and fasten the door, but Yeats had warned him to stay put, and Yeats did not need to be in this room to rule it still.

A wild night was building itself in the darkness; gusts of wind, sudden bursts of rain against the windows, the ever-banging door, these things layered themselves one across the other with mounting intensity. Somewhere out over the Atlantic a storm bided its time.

The cards were blocked. Martin stared at them. Every column ended in a wrong color or a useless value. Pit-a-pat, pit-a-pat, pit-a-pat, went his heart; when he tried to swallow, it hurt.

A sudden, violent rain-squall hurtled against the glass like buckshot. Martin turned toward the window with a gasp. Seconds later, his eyes reverted to the table in time to see a hand, yellow as the lantern light was yellow, scuttle across from the opposite side of the table, while a shrill voice cried, "Red ten on black knave."

Martin leaped up, his chair flying backward. When he tried to speak his tongue betrayed him, he could utter only gibberish. And all the while, two slim, yellow hands with tapering fingers busily arranged the cards, until at last the patience came out. Then the two hands clapped together softly, dazzling Martin with a rainbow of gold, and ruby and emerald, for rings adorned many of those long fingers with their perfect, almond-shaped nails.

Mother Mary, he thought; they've left me alone with a woman. *Who can play patience upside-down!*

Then, only then, did the person on the other side of the table rise. A disembodied face rose to hover above the lantern, all light and shade and mystery. It was yellow, like the hands: a long, narrow oval marred by a squat nose with high-cut nostrils. Now the mouth slowly extended itself in a closed smile. The process seemed to go on forever, pushing the already prominent cheeks higher and higher, until Martin feared the face would cut itself in half.

"You're a . . . a Chinawoman," he managed to say at last.

The other person began to laugh in a high singsong that put him in mind of a bird. "You are so charming, we will be friends. I am not from China. I am not a woman. My name is Siri Chaloem. I come from Thailand." One of those remarkable hands floated around the lantern. "How do you do?"

Martin, ignoring the hand, continued to gawk at the half-visible person opposite, now established as a man. He'd received minimal education; this was something not just beyond his experience, but beyond his powers of imagination. He didn't believe in ghosts, not really. But tonight he had to *order* himself not to.

The hand flapped. "Shake hands," said the voice; and it no longer sounded like a bird's. This new voice was horrid. "If you don't shake my hand, you're not polite."

He took it quickly, and felt his own squeezed gently by moist skin unlike anything he'd touched before. It sent a shudder through him.

"Mother of God," he whispered. "Who *are* you?"

The weird face sank slowly out of sight. Martin heard the scrape of a chair leg and guessed that this frightening visitation had sat down, an impression confirmed when a moment later the voice, now neutral, said: "Sit!"

He obeyed clumsily, his limbs still shaking.

"We are going to be friends," Chaloem said. "It is written strongly in your face. I can read your history there and your future, too. The distance between your nose and your mouth is great. That means long life. But it makes you ugly."

A cackle of laughter jangled through the dark room.

"What . . . why . . . ?" Martin cursed himself for

weakness, but he was still recovering from the shock.

"Why am I here? Because I buy things. I sell things. Tonight I have come to sell. On a boat that leaked and nearly sank, all but killing me, so tonight the price will be that much higher." The Thai's voice vibrated with gleeful malice. "Your friends have gone to get the money. When they come back, then I shall sell."

"Sell . . . what? Guns?"

An unseen hand pushed the lantern sideways, to reveal once more that haunting visage opposite.

"Guns, and things *like* guns. Weapons. I buy weapons of another kind."

"Another . . . I don't understand. What do you buy?"

There was no response. For a while, this did not bother Martin. He continued to stare across the table at that perpetually variable, fascinating landscape of a human face, which seemed to grow larger and larger until it blocked out everything else, even sound.

By the time he began to struggle it was too late.

Being hypnotized was another utterly new experience. At first Chaloem's eyes merely glowed. Then they started to pulsate. Martin realized, as if through a thick, molten fog, that the silence had itself become a sound and he likened it, in his confused way, to a one-note hum. He wanted to look at the Thai's mouth, to see if he was making the noise that wasn't a noise. That was when he discovered that he couldn't close, or move, his eyes.

Chaloem said, "I buy this"; and the last word seemed to expand itself endlessly in a series of sibilants.

Martin heard a command to look, although the Thai's lips didn't move, and he obeyed. There, on the table in front of him, was a pyramid of the purest white powder he'd ever seen. Its brilliance dazzled him, like a pile of diamonds reduced to dust. Then he felt his hand stretch out. He took a pinch of the powder between finger and thumb. He raised it to his nose. And he did not want to do any of these things.

His mouth opened to scream. He could feel his throat muscles working, though nothing came out. His hand hovered beneath his nostrils. Because he'd resisted the lust to inhale with all his strength, his heart was thumping like a drum. He knew he must breathe now, or die; but the choice no longer rested with him.

"No," he cried; but still the sound wouldn't come. No, no, no, no . . .

The crack of a rifle came to him through the silence, making no more noise than a distant door being slammed. For a second he must have passed out. When he once more located himself in an ugly present, the chair opposite his was empty, he could breathe again, and none of the terrible, white, dusty diamonds had entered his body. Just as he noticed these things, hands grabbed him from behind and he was under the table with Chaloem holding him fast.

The kitchen door was flung open; he saw two pairs of legs enter the room. As he watched in terror, one pair collapsed and he heard Yeats curse. Then the lantern went spinning into oblivion and he could see nothing more.

Window glass shattered. Outside, the shots became a fusillade. He heard oaths and a gargling scream. A torch flashed on. By its beam he saw the black drapes suddenly bulge inward under the impact of some object hurled from outside. The torch beam went crazy; he was alone, now, and he had a lightning vision of Chaloem over by the window, bending to the floor. The Thai flung down the drapes and stood before the shattered window, one arm raised as if to throw something. The world outside lit up in a blinding billow of flame as the grenade exploded, a hot blast of air enwrapped Martin, and hard nuggets spattered the table top above his head.

After what might have been seconds, or hours, the shots outside dwindled away. Yeats was cursing steadily from near the fireplace, and overlapping the blasphemies he recognized his brother's voice. Sean's groans sent spasms through Martin's body, hot as lances. Instinct told him that these were the last noises you made, right at the end, when pain had taken you over completely.

He crawled out from under the table. Somebody re-lit the lantern. The room was filling up now, filling with exhausted men who brought their terror with them, and with oaths, and with the hot, abattoir-smell of fresh blood.

By the light of the torch, he found Sean. His face was unmarked; but his shirt was red from waist to neck, and when Martin undid the buttons with trembling fingers it was to reveal a hole. Not the neat bullet hole of a martyr's end, but a cavity containing twisted multicolored tubes and shards of bone, as if some mad anatomist had hacked him open to look while he was still alive.

"Sean!" he shrieked. "Sean, don't die, man!"

He fell forward to hold his brother, but the hole gaped and sagged and Martin rolled away, holding both hands to his eyes. When he managed to look again, Sean's head had drooped over to one side. There was no light reflected in his wide-open eyes.

Something terrible was happening to Martin. Raw pain stretched from his toes to the crown of his head. The worst of it was in his chest at first, but slowly it began to move down to his stomach, where it expanded like a football being inflated. Water gushed from his eyes. "Sean, Sean," he cried, over and over again. He could not cope with this. Could not, could not, *could not*. The horror of losing his beloved brother and only friend, the physical disasters happening inside him, agony, grief . . . no man could know these things and live. He didn't care. Dying meant only that he and Sean would be together again. But why did it have to take so long? And why did it have to *hurt* so much?

He lay there, hallucinating, in a state that was neither life nor death. He had gone so far that when Chaloem's hand descended onto the nape of his neck it acted like a trigger.

"Don't touch me!" he screamed. *"Don't . . . touch . . . me!"*

But the Thai's grip did not loosen; and Martin's body took an unpleasant revenge for so much terror, so much grief. His bowels opened, sending forth into the small, hot room an unspeakable odor of corruption and filth.

"Come," Chaloem whispered, his voice steely with authority. "They have caught the man who killed your brother."

Martin tried to shake him off, but the hand remained clamped to his neck. He rose without knowing how. Horrible warm liquid ran down his trousers. "Let go of me," he shrieked; but the Thai kept his grip and when Martin began to struggle he tightened it.

"Come," he hissed again. "You have work to do."

Martin found himself outside, in the farmyard. Two men stood over a third, who lay on the ground moaning. In the light cast by Chaloem's torch, Martin saw that he was wearing British army fatigues.

"What happened?" Chaloem murmured.

"SAS out on a frolic, I reckon," one of the Irish muttered. "Just the two of them. Oh sweet Jesus, what a night . . . "

"Hold this," Chaloem commanded, handing him the torch. It was clear from his voice that he had nothing but contempt for this band of fearful half-men. He released his grip on Martin, who sank down to his knees in a mire of his own excrement.

"Look at me," the Thai ordered. Martin dully raised his eyes, and saw that Chaloem was holding a thick cane, some nine inches long. Now he pulled on both ends and the cane parted, leaving two barbarous blades in either hand. "See," he murmured. "This man killed your brother. Gouge out his eyes."

The soldier lying on the ground was not so badly wounded that he didn't understand. "No," he cried. "God, you can't . . . "

Chaloem waited for Martin to obey. But shame had immobilized him.

The Thai knelt down and cut out the soldier's tongue.

"Now," he said, looking at Martin, "it will be easier." He held out the stilettos. "Avenge your brother! *Kill him!*"

"I . . . I . . . c-*can't.*"

Martin avoided the Thai's gaze, praying he wouldn't speak again, wouldn't add to the burden of dishonor that humiliated him. But Chaloem did speak. What he said was: "You're spittle, child." He rocked back on his heels, holding the knives high above him, and drove downward in a sudden, vicious movement. The soldier convulsed; all his limbs rose in a macabre dance of death; and Martin cried out in grief at the knowledge that the opportunity of paying his brother's blood-price had been taken away from him forever.

Through that scalding realization, as if from a great distance, he heard Chaloem say thoughtfully, "But will you always be spittle, I wonder . . . my darling child?"

CHAPTER
9

LONDON. THE PRESENT

From his seat in the dock, Frank Thornton had an unimpeded view of the judge, separated from him by a great void of space and circumstance. He was building up a psychological profile of the lord chief justice from those myriad tiny details that give away the inner man. This judge was impatient, "Shall we get *on*?" being his favorite question, as if this state trial was but one more administrative nuisance to be got through before the weekend.

The attorney-general, on the other hand, had all the patience in the world. His tactic was to build the case up piece by tiny piece, one detail heaped on top of another, until the dead weight of the whole buried the accused. Sometimes Frank knew that the jury couldn't see the joins between the real world and this web of deception being spun for their benefit.

Sir Patrick had done an excellent job expounding the law, he reflected. (Frank prided himself on giving any devil his due.) Treason, the jury was told, was a crime that could be committed only by someone who owed allegiance to the Crown; aliens didn't qualify. If only he'd had the sense to take out American citizenship when it was on offer! Too late now . . .

A voice interrupted both his reverie and the prosecutor's droning voice. "Shall we get on, Mr. Attorney?"

"The chief's" only doing his job, Frank reminded himself. Just as you always tried to do yours, no matter what. And the prosecutor *was* taking his time over the opening speech. He'd only just got to Louise's part in all this.

So many figures from the past, rising up to haunt him. Roz Forbes, sitting there in the press box, never once taking her eyes off him. Alistair Scrutton. And now Louise . . . The attorney-general, good orator though he was, came nowhere near raising her ghost for the jury's benefit.

Louise Shelley had never liked the law's "gray men," he remembered; a final taunt she'd flung at him, when their affair was over. Strange, then, that she had somehow ended up married to one of them . . . the wrong one, as it turned out.

LONDON. APRIL 1969

"Your mother phoned," Louise said. "Some woman's been trying to contact you."

Frank heaved the plastic carrier bags onto the table in the kitchen of the small apartment where Louise lived. Where he lived too, most of the time.

"Oh? Who?"

"How should I know?"

He sighed. "Look, I don't have any other girl-friends, if that's what—"

"All I said was how should I know?"

She made tea for herself, using a tea bag and without offering him a cup. It was Saturday, his turn to fix dinner, and although he wasn't overfond of cooking the prospect suddenly pleased him, because she'd go and watch television, leaving him to it, and that would give her a chance to calm down. Though why she needed to calm down he couldn't begin to guess. She hadn't always been like this. Louise was changing.

"I'd better phone ma and see what's up," he said.

But as he reached the door a sensation of inarticulate, almost painful longing overcame him and he ran back to where she sat at the table, putting his arms around her from behind in a strong hug.

"I love you," he murmured into her ear. "You're the only woman I've ever loved, the only one I ever will love, you're my heart, my soul, my whole life." He squeezed her hard, suddenly overwhelmed by her beauty, the apple-loft scent of her body, the texture of the hair against his cheek. She smelled so fresh, so sweet! Air expanded inside his stomach, making him heady with the remembrance that this exquisite being loved him as he loved her; that they would be together until the end of time.

His eyes lighted on her engagement ring: an emerald, set in platinum. The stone was tiny, all he could afford, but Louise didn't set any store by such things.

"I'm so lucky," he whispered. "I love you so much, so much . . . "

"You'd better phone," she said in a flat voice. "Your mother said it sounded urgent."

He released her, but slowly, reluctant to loosen his grip on the most precious person in the world for fear she might take flight as an angel before he could return.

"Hi, ma," he said as soon as the familiar voice at the other end of the line answered.

"Darling! Are you all right?"

"I'm okay. How's dad?"

"He's well. What's happening at work, Frank?"

"Oh, lots." He hesitated, wondering how best to sell the white lie, the one that would ease his mother's concern. "Fascinating."

"Everybody says the civil service is dull."

"Not the income tax department, ma. We get a lot of interesting cases."

A momentary vision of his small, overheated office in Somerset House, shared with three other lawyers, rose up to mock him, and he suppressed it with unaccustomed vigor. "Some of the tricks people get up to," he all but snarled, "would make you cringe. Ma, Louise said something about a woman trying to contact me."

"Oh, yes!" His mother sounded intrigued. "Now, that was strange, Frank. She rang late Monday night, well, your father had already gone to bed, actually, and I answered it, and she said, 'Can I speak to Frank?' And I said, 'Who's calling?' and she said, 'Oh, he won't know me, my name's Roz, but he won't know me.' So I said, 'He's not in and I'm not expecting him this week', well, it's not her business where you—"

"Er, did she say anything else?"

"She said she'd write you a letter. And she did. At least I think she did, because one came for you Thursday and I didn't recognize the handwriting, so I popped it round to you when I was out shopping. Was it important?"

He couldn't keep up with this. "What letter? I haven't had any letter."

"Well, I put it through the letter box."

Frank said nothing for a while. Louise hadn't mentioned a letter, and it certainly wasn't among his pile of mail propped up against the baseboard next to the front door.

"I expect it got lost when whoever it was cleaned the flat," he said at last. Which was a joke, he thought, because no one ever tidies this place up unless it's me, and I've done it so often that now I'm on strike. But he didn't like his mother to know that, because it reflected on Louise, so what he said was, "I know where it'll be, don't worry."

He sensed his mother wanted a longer chat, but he was suddenly anxious to find out what the missing letter contained. As he put down the phone he felt uneasy. The prospect of being written to by an unknown woman was mildly exciting, but it would become less attractive if Louise found out about it; and she already knew that this woman, whoever she was, had tried to telephone him . . .

Suppose she'd found the letter and guessed (known?) that it came from another female? What if she'd actually *opened* it?

Oh, come on! He knew a second's anger at his own suspicious nature. He loved this girl, dammit. She didn't open other people's mail. And anyway, he had nothing to hide; whatever the letter's contents might be, they were innocent. How could they be anything else?—he had a fiancée.

"Louise, ma said something about a letter . . . "

She glanced up from the *Daily Express*. "Behind the bread bin."

"Did you put it there?"

"No."

But you knew where it was, he thought to himself as he retrieved the letter. You knew exactly where it was, and presumably you recognized the name on the front, mm . . . ? The *addressee*, Mr. F. G. Thornton, not entirely unknown to you, I think, Miss Shelley . . .

His anger expanded, he was on the point of saying mentally, triumphantly, "*I put it to you . . . *" But then he stopped. He made himself count to ten. Cross-examination had ceased to be part of his professional life. Leave it out of the personal

life as well, or you'll poison yourself. Easy now.
Let it all go . . .

*Your best friend betrayed you. He swindled you
out of a place in chambers that was rightfully
yours. You're better than him. Cleverer, sharper,
more able. You're better, better, better. And he was
your friend. And he cheated you.*

Frank had been staring at the kitchen wall for a
long time. When Louise touched his arm he started,
came to himself to find the letter crumpled and
moist in his hands.

"Frank," she said gently. "I'm sorry. I didn't
mean to sound edgy. I'm tired, that's all. Nothing to
do with you."

Her words were sweet; but to Frank they sounded
artificially so, as if she'd injected them with saccharine, and like saccharine they left an aftertaste.
Sometimes that's what love boils down to, he
reminded himself. You feel dreadful, but because
the other person needs you, you do what has to be
done. You make the effort.

"Don't apologize," he said, turning around to
take her in his arms. "It was my fault. I came in all
worked up."

"I know. Thanks for doing the shopping."

"That's okay. Let's see what's in the letter—can't
have you fretting about my secret loves, now can
we?"

"I wasn't fretting."

Frank heard the renewed note of impatience
waiting in the wings and quickly said, "No, of
course not."

He sat down and opened the letter. It was hand-
written in white ink on green paper. Frank's eyes
widened; he wasn't used to such displays of character on the page. "Dear Mr. Thornton," he read . . .

"Who's it from?" Louise called.

Frank turned to the bottom of the second sheet

and for a moment stopped breathing.

"Frank? Frank, whatever's the matter?"

"It's from that reporter," he said in a dazed tone. "She . . . she's written me a letter." And then— "Jesus *Christ*!"

He stood up, pushing his chair over and went to stand with both fists clenched on top of the dresser. Louise picked up the letter and slowly began to read it aloud.

Dear Mr Thornton,

I found myself starting this with the words, "You won't remember me," only I know you will, so I tore that up and here goes.

I've moved on since *l'affaire terrible*. A new, better paper, and promotion. No, I'm not writing this to spit in your eye, there's a point. I'm pally with the ad. manager, who's pally with the proprietor's wife. (Yes, that kind of pally!) The prop.'s got an American friend who wants to set up an office here with its own legal department. Fabulous money, brilliant working conditions, nobody over thirty need apply. Only problem is, at some point you've got to be ready to relocate to Texas.

Interested? They're advertising on Monday, but if you want an inside track it's yours. Ring this number, ask to speak to Harrison L. Gephard and be ready to interview this *Sunday*. (Sorry 'bout your w/e.) He'll expect your call.

Can't explain; wish I could.

Ever best,
Roz Forbes

Frank unclenched his fists and turned around, but for a long time he did not speak. At last he said, "What was that about a number . . . a phone number?"

"Oh . . . it's in a PS. Oh-one—"

"Yes, all right." He came toward her, a hand held out for the letter and she gave it to him, not thinking anything of it; but then he tore the letter into shreds and hurled them around the kitchen with wild sweeps of his arms. "That's for your *charity* . . . and that's for your . . . fucking . . . *guilt* . . . "

"Frank! Frank, stop it!"

"Why?" He rounded on her, eyes ablaze. "Scrutton screwed up my chances of getting a seat in chambers *and* in the process blighted my entire career. That's the only one I've got we're talking about, incidentally. This bitch helped him! And you . . . you tell me to *stop it*?" He guffawed: an ugly, sarcastic sound.

Louise threw herself down in a chair and said, "You're paranoid."

"Oh yes, I forgot, sorry. You've got a PhD in psychiatry, haven't you, there I was mixing you up with some scrubber who does the bed pans at four every morning—"

She rose and made for the door, but he grabbed her long before she could reach it. "Where do you think you're going?"

"Out," she flared. "For a walk and a smoke, until you've calmed down. You think everyone's in a conspiracy against the mighty Frank Thornton. Don't you? Well, *don't you*?"

He released her arm and stared at the floor, as if recovering from a minor accident that had left him stunned but otherwise unmarked.

"You say I'm just a nurse, Frank, and that's true. I'm underpaid. I'm overworked. I haven't got a tenth of your brains, or a twentieth of your education. But I'm doing useful work that has to be done by somebody. I haven't just curled up and died, taken the first job that came along in some tax office, turned my back on it all. And I haven't turned *pathetic*."

"Is that how you really see me?" he said, after a long pause.

She did not answer at once. He raised his eyes to find her gazing at him and something about her look made him flush.

"Ask me again when I come back," she said. "Not now."

"Louise—"

The sound of the front door slamming echoed through the flat, a forlorn sound. Frank felt heavy; his brain, his feelings, his body, all were dull, leaden. A constricted sensation around his eyeballs presaged tears, but men didn't cry. So instead he knelt down and slowly gathered up the scraps of Roz Forbes' letter before shoveling them into the waste bin. Then he did the thing that men do instead of crying: he went to the fridge and took out a bottle of beer, meaning it to be the first of several. But the Newcastle Brown merely congealed in his stomach, making him feel bilious and even more malcontent.

He had to cook dinner. He chopped meat and ground spices for a curry. Frank, still rebelling against the blandness of his childhood diet, hankered after exotic, spicy foods for much the same reason that years of force-fed Tchaikovsky had sent him screaming in desperation to the Stones.

After he'd laid the table there was still no sign of Louise, so he looked around for something else to occupy his mind. Perhaps Louise had left something in the laundry basket. His face brightened. Yes, he'd do her washing for her. A peace offering.

He went into the bedroom they shared and upended the basket on the bed. Apart from his shirts, socks, and underpants there was a pair of jeans belonging to Louise. He went through each pocket to make sure it was empty. In the last one he found a theater ticket stub. He stared at it in surprise. The date was about ten days ago . . . oh, yes,

Louise had been on night duty. She must have gone to a matinee.

Then the time of the performance caught his eye. Seven forty-five.

Frank sat down on the bed. He was trembling all over.

She could not have gone to an evening performance *and* done night duty; it simply wasn't possible. He knew that there must be a perfectly simple explanation for this. Perfectly simple. The trouble was, he needed to have it *now*! *This instant!* Maybe she'd lent her jeans to one of her other flatmates . . . perhaps she'd found the ticket lying around and picked it up, meaning to throw it away, and someone had interrupted her before she . . . what if a friend had given her the ticket and she'd accepted it, not realizing at the time that she was on nights that week, and then . . . ?

And then *what*? This ticket had been *used*!

He gazed at the stub, holding it up to the light, interrogating the small print as if that held the secret to the mysteries of the universe. But only when he thought to turn it over did mystery deepen into the realm of nightmare, for on the back was handwriting he recognized: Alistair Scrutton's.

Frank allowed himself to fall backward onto the bed, and lay staring at the ceiling for a long time.

Alistair had written something on the back of the ticket while it was still whole. Now, only a fragment remained:

> rant
> lock
> able

Seeing jumbled letters start to disentangle themselves into words, he pushed them aside. He divined everything, yes, as a traveler sees all the details of a night landscape to the horizon in a flash of lightning; Frank, however, wanted nothing to do with any of it.

But despite himself, his thoughts were suddenly enriched by the most terrible of all fertilizers, jealousy. Ideas sprouted like tropical weeds running wild: "rant"—that could only be part of "restaurant," and then the rest became easy; "lock" was all that remained of "o'clock," and "able" had once been "table." Usual table . . . *usual table?*

He sat, holding his stomach. His breath came faster and faster, he wanted to be sick. Louise and Alistair had a "usual table." They went to the theater together.

They went to bed together.

A cold hand wiped itself the length of his spine, leaving clammy traces all down his back. Ten nights ago, the date on the ticket, he'd slept alone in this bed, thinking of her in the ward. Men's Medical, she'd told him, what a bore, and he'd felt sorry for her . . . well, she'd spent that night with a man, all right, but it hadn't been medical and it can't have been a bore . . .

He held his forehead, rocking to and fro, before suddenly rushing into the bathroom, where he threw up. But afterward he felt no better. Frank, normally so articulate, found his inner voice rendered dumb. He regarded himself in the mirror, seeing only a ridiculous cuckold.

She was his fiancée. Her body was his property. She had no right to consort with other men. Frank closed his eyes, and found Louise waiting for him there with Alistair, laughter on their lips, their bodies naked, writhing on the bed, working their way to an orgasm so much more intense, imaginative, *pleasurable* than any he and Louise had ever achieved . . .

Frank went back to the room he shared with

Louise and flung himself down on the bed, pounding the mattress with his fists. He was howling. He howled himself into exhaustion. He slept for a while. When he awoke the flat was nearly dark. He knew at once that something had woken him. The front door. Louise was back.

As he slid his legs off the bed he found himself in the grip of a strange calm. It was a mixture of things, he decided, as he made for the door. Part of him still refused to look facts in the face; there was an innocent explanation and within minutes he would be hearing it. Another part of him, his realistic side, wished to proceed in suitably judicial fashion. All he required was the truth. In certain legal jurisdictions, he knew, a confession was an absolute precondition to the passing of the death sentence.

That's a strange thought, he said to himself, entering the lounge: adultery as capital crime. Yes. Anyone who did that to him deserved death. He went to sit down opposite Louise. She seems frightened, he thought. Good.

"Frank, we have to talk," she said.

"You first."

It would have been easy to indict her then, but not as pleasurable as waiting for her to dig her own grave. Let her preach awhile. Wait until she's put herself up on a pedestal. Then sling the rope around her neck and kick the pedestal away.

"You've changed, Frank. You're gray."

He looked down his nose at her. "What?"

"Do you remember the night you were called to the bar? You told me about the other guys, the Cambridge lot. You said they were gray. That they didn't even understand that a . . . a moot, is that right? . . . should be funny. You said you'd never get like them. But I think you were always like them. From day one. Only I never noticed. I never wanted to."

He stared at her, speechless. Somewhere back in

the last century he had come into this room prepared to deliver judgment and administer punishment. But Louise had mounted the bench ahead of him.

Frank had always thought it was strength of character in her eyes that made her beautiful. Now, transfixed by her gaze, he found himself describing it as something else. Willfulness.

"I could live with that," she went on. "It's hard, but I'd have found a way of coping. Maybe I might even have succeeded in changing you a bit." She laughed nervously. "Not that you can ever change a man. Not really."

Still he could not speak. But he was starting to take a horrid interest in her use of tenses. "I *would have* done . . ."

"You've become bitter, Frank. You blame Alistair for everything. There's no proof—"

"I don't need proof."

"You blame Alistair because you know you didn't leave your notebook lying around. You say he took it down to court and left it there. But he didn't."

"How do you know?" He shot her a triumphant look. "Eh?"

"Because you told me he'd denied it and the inquiry believed him. Frank, you can't possibly be *sure* it wasn't you left the bloody book lying around."

"I'm sure." He couldn't face her, though.

"Then why didn't you tell the inquiry that?"

"I was trying too hard to be meticulous. I was thinking like a lawyer." He grunted sarcastically. "Next time I'll play it like Scrutton."

"Why does it always have to come back to him?" she cried. "Anyone could have stolen your book!"

"'Anyone' doesn't happen to be occupying my place in chambers. Only Scrutton."

"But—"

"He had motive. He had opportunity. But above all, my darling Louise, he had the *intention*. And why are you always defending him, eh? Where were you on the night of the 25th last?"

"This is no time for jokes, Frank. You're not a trial lawyer any more."

She rose as if to go, but he jumped up and restrained her, sending his nails deep into her forearm. "It's no joke," he grated. "March 25th. *Where were you?*"

She looked down at him with something approaching fear in her eyes and said, "Night duty. I was on night duty."

He held her fast, never once taking his eyes from her face. Her own eyes swiveled back and forth, not quite focusing on him, and her complexion was now blotchy-pale.

"I'm so glad you didn't have to do your duty alone," he said; and with a flourish he released her, holding the ticket stub up to within an inch of her face.

He didn't know what to expect. A protestation of innocence? Anger—*How dare you go through my things?* Contrition—*Let's start again, darling, we can learn to trust once more?* Shame? Tears?

What Louise actually did was sit down slowly and say, "I'm glad you know. It makes things so much easier."

Frank's mouth fell open. "Easier?" he stuttered.

"You think I'm a slut, don't you?"

"*Yes.*" He ground out the word from deep inside his chest with a feeling of the most profound satisfaction.

"I know. I feel the same way about myself. I've hated every minute of these last few weeks."

"I'll bet you have."

"Frank, be sensible. Let's talk like adults, okay?"

"*You* tell *me* to be sensible!"

She raised her hands and opened her mouth, then evidently thought better of it.

"What are you going to do?" he asked after a long pause.

"About Alistair, you mean?"

"Are you trying to tell me there were others?"

She said nothing, although her knuckles turned white.

"Sorry," Frank murmured.

"You're not helping."

"You think I feel like helping?"

"No! I know how you feel."

"How's that, then?"

"Sick. Betrayed. Angry—above all, angry. I know, because I feel the same, only with myself."

"No one betrayed you."

"I did. I let myself down. When Alistair first asked me out, you were away. Work was shitty, two of my best friends had just emigrated . . . all right, no excuse, I just fancied a few drinks and a night out."

"Without telling me. Then or later."

"It was wrong of me."

"Then why—"

"Because sometimes people fall short, Frank. Or hadn't you noticed? When I said I'd go out with Alistair, it didn't mean a thing to me. But by the end of that first evening, I felt . . . muddled."

"Couldn't you have talked to me about that?"

"You're the last person I'd have talked to."

"When did you first have sex? Do you call him 'Kid,' like you do me? Where was the first screw?" He shot out his arm. "In that bed? *Our* bed?"

"Oh, for God's—"

"No, you don't! Don't you go taking refuge in sanctimonious shit! It's a straight question, you bloody well answer it."

"*No!* Not on that bed."

"In his flat?"

"*Yes.*" She stared at the floor.

"*When?*"

"That's none of your business."

He hauled her upright. "It is my business." His mouth was millimeters away from her face. The words sprayed it with spittle. "You're my *fiancée!*" He flung her back onto the sofa and raised his hand. She screwed up her face in anticipation of the blow, but made no move to avert it. Frank's hand wavered. Then, very slowly, he allowed it to fall back.

For a long time, neither of them spoke.

Louise took off the emerald and platinum ring. She laid it on the coffee table. Frank stared at it.

"Are you going to marry him?" he asked in a low voice.

"He hasn't asked me. If he did, I wouldn't know what to say."

"Louise."

"Yes?"

He began to speak, but then he paused.

Some instinct told him that the single most important thing left in life was to get at the truth. He had to find out all he could, because soon he and Louise would say goodbye, and then the opportunity would be gone forever. It mattered more than health, or wealth, or even the next breath. He felt like an explorer in unknown territory, hacking through jungle, heat, and flies, hauling his way to the next horizon and the one after that *because he had to know.*

He wasn't even sure what he wanted to find out.

"Louise . . . " he tried again. "Can't you at least . . . find some way of explaining *why*? You're not a slut. You're lovely. Hard-working. Caring. Thoughtful."

She was swallowing back tears now, but when she held up a hand to her face, using the other one in an ineffectual attempt to silence him, he could not stop.

"All I've ever wanted in a woman. And I . . . I failed. Somewhere along the road, I didn't measure up. I don't understand what happened. And if I'm ever going to go on living, I need to know what I did, you see."

"Stop it. Please stop."

His face was etched with anguish: it showed in his raised eyebrows, his sunken mouth, the half-closed eyes. Louise turned her head, forcing herself to look at him. She swallowed a couple of times, gulped back more tears, and said, "I don't deserve you. I never did. I'm just ordinary. A nurse. You're so . . . so . . . "

"Please."

"I . . . I used to listen to you. You'd come back from chambers—most people go to offices, you went to chambers, Christ—and you'd talk, and I'd watch your face. It was all so important to you. So serious. Nothing funny ever happened to you. Not like in the wards. Some pretentious little intern slips on the lino and lands on his arse. One of the naughty old men tells you a filthy joke. You laugh. It's life. Life never seemed to come your way, Frank."

"Being a lawyer's serious." His voice was bitter. "That's why I like it. It *matters*, what we do, goddammit!"

"And my work doesn't?"

He frowned. "What?"

"You never wanted to hear about my work. Whenever I tried to bring up some problem, or tell you a funny thing, you switched off. I watched it happen. Often. Your face tightened." She raised her hands to her cheeks. "Here. A . . . a stiffening. I'd lost you."

He could spot the flaw in her argument now. He

felt a sudden upsurge of confidence. Logic was on his side; he could still defeat her.

"Alistair's a barrister, too."

"But he's not like you."

"He is. He's far more ambitious than I ever was."

"But he knows when work's over for the day."

"He won't always be like that. Not when the pressure starts to build."

"I know. That's why I couldn't answer if he asked me to marry him. And there's something else about you, something I didn't realize until today. You're not open to change."

"When have I ever rejected change?"

"Today. When you tore up that letter. Somebody was offering you a chance of getting out of the rut, going to America, even. And what did you do? You tore it up. We were still supposed to be getting married, then." She beat her breasts with her hands, suddenly letting out the anger she'd repressed for so long. "Don't you think *I* might have liked to be asked? Well, *don't* you?"

He could have continued the argument. There were a dozen things he could have said. But one important factor held him back: the knowledge that he had lost. He had lost because—a rare insight—he'd tried to defeat an emotional response with logic.

He sank down into a chair and buried his head in his hands. The prospect before him was desolate beyond anything he'd imagined before. A lifetime spent without love, because he couldn't cross the divide; forever separated from the world of the emotions where real people enjoyed their existence.

After the silence had gone on for what seemed like ages, he slowly started to become aware of it as a concrete thing in the room, a wall between them. Every second was one less spent with her, the woman on whom he'd pinned all his hopes. She was hoping he'd go. Would she telephone Alistair as soon as his feet crossed the threshold, he wondered? "I've got rid of the creep at last, why don't you come round and we can . . . "

There was nothing to be gained by staying. "I'll pack my things," he said. A wayward thought struck him. "There's a curry on the stove, you'd better . . . "

She stood up without a word and went to the kitchen, closing the door behind her. He fancied he heard her crying, couldn't be sure. A huge wave of grief towered up before him and he wanted to vent the hot tears, but he knew this wasn't the place or the time.

He picked up the ring. As he did so, something released itself inside him and he knew then that it was really over.

Somehow he got himself to the bedroom, where he packed his suitcase, taking his time over it because it would be too dire if he forgot anything and had to come back. Only when he was sure that the job was complete did he tap on the kitchen door, and say, "Louise . . . I'm off now."

He felt stupid, but then what did one say on these occasions?

She opened the door at once. "Don't go . . . yet."

"It's best."

She swayed in the doorway; and he could see that she had been crying.

"Oh, Frank . . . " She fell forward into his arms. "Frank," she whispered. "Can you ever forgive me?"

He wanted to answer, "Not until the end of time." But some inner sense of self-preservation told him that he'd already behaved badly enough this evening and he didn't want to go away with even worse memories to haunt him, so he said, "Nothing to forgive"; and felt a modest pleasure at that.

His eyes swept the kitchen, trying to ensure that

nothing had been, would ever be, forgotten. He caught sight of the rubbish bin, where he had thrown the remnants of Roz Forbes' letter.

America. The other side of the world . . . The New World. A new life.

He disengaged himself from Louise and went across to the bin, where he retrieved the vital scrap on which was written the phone number. He put it in his pocket and turned.

"I'm so sorry," he said, not really knowing why.

He left her standing by the kitchen table, one hand resting on it while she used the other to shield her eyes and mouth. When he murmured "Goodbye," she did not move.

His last, inconsequential thought as he closed the door was that she looked like someone who'd stumbled on the scene of a particularly gruesome murder.

CHAPTER

10

LONDON. THE PRESENT

The first soft tap on his bedroom door was enough to rouse the Krait, transporting him in a flash from the rain-sodden farmyard in County Sligo, where twenty years before his career could truly be said to have begun, to a quiet terraced house in the London suburb of Norbury.

"Are y'all right, Martin?" O'Halloran said as the door opened.

"I'm just fine. Come in, the pair of you."

O'Halloran led the way. As Condon followed, his toe caught in a loose tongue of carpet and he stumbled. He reached out to steady himself. By mischance, his right hand brushed against the Krait's arm and convulsed in a grip.

Vestiges of the dream still clung to Brennan, as sticky spiders' webs adhere to a man who has pushed his way through thickets. Without thinking he grabbed hold of Condon's hand with one of his own and sent the other to the nape of the boy's neck. He swung around through a semicircle, leaning backward. Condon's head crashed against the far

wall as he landed on the bed with a grunt of pain.
Brennan came to himself with his knees in the
small of Condon's back and one arm around his
throat.

For a long moment, the only sound in the room
was Condon's labored breathing. Then O'Halloran
said, in a soft voice, "That's okay, Bren. Okay, now.
Everything's fine now."

"I won't be touched."

Brennan recognized the voice. It seemed to come
from somewhere high up above his head, a dark bird
of prey haunting the jungle's treetops. His own
voice.

"I won't be touched," he grated again; and this
time the voice came from within him. "Not by a
man."

"I know, I know," O'Halloran soothed. His own
voice sounded half-afraid, half-gentle, like that of a
father trying to coax his infant son down from a
roof. "You can get up now, Tomas. An accident, it
was."

Brennan released his hold on the young man; but
when he stood up, Condon stayed on the bed, shaking.

"I won't be touched," Brennan repeated mechanically. "Not by a man."

The dream peeled away, but not cleanly, letting
him see Chaloem's hand descend onto his arm and
allowing him a final whiff of his own excrement.
Ever since that grisly night, he'd had a horror of the
male touch.

"You'd best take a look at the boy," he said to
O'Halloran.

The older man helped Condon to his feet and
dusted him down. Tomas Condon was about twenty-two, or so Brennan guessed. His face still bore
traces of a disfiguring acne. Looking at the deep
black hollows under his eyes, Brennan wondered

what kept him awake at nights. He disliked men who were too thin, as was Condon, because they were either weedy or vain. This man, however, was just plain scared.

Brennan wondered if Condon had any idea that he'd come as close to death as the bullet to its chamber. For a moment back there it had been a snug fit between Tommy Condon and his death, all right. Tight, you could call it.

"Pat, tell this youngster a few things, will you?" Brennan sat down on the bed, continuing to stare at Condon. "Tell him what they call me."

"They call him the Krait, Tommy."

It was clear from Condon's expression that this left him none the wiser.

"It's a snake," Brennan enlightened him. "A black-and-white snake. You find them in India, Burma, Thailand. Those kind of places. They kill quite quickly. Not so fast you don't know about it, though."

"There's a story," O'Halloran said, seemingly anxious to bridge the silence that followed. "A nice story they tell about him. How he was bitten by one of those snakes himself. And he survived."

Condon stared into Brennan's eyes for the first time since the assault. "Is it true?" he whispered.

Brennan smiled. "In a sense," he remarked genially, "everything is true. Then again, not. Skip the stories, Pat. Just tell him who I am."

O'Halloran cleared his throat. "Mr. . . . Mr. Lloyd here, he's been working alongside the Army Council these many years. Y'know about the Council, Tommy?"

Condon nodded.

"They only bring him in when the going's rough, see? Keep him in special reserve."

Brennan tilted his head up, very slowly, until he was looking at O'Halloran. Something in his eyes reduced the other man to silence. Brennan twisted back until he was once again staring at Condon.

"What Pat's trying to say, is that I'm . . . unpredictable. So that even my own side thinks twice before calling me in."

Brennan paused, wondering how far he should woo Condon with truth. He knew what the records said in Dublin's "Castle of Mysteries," where Intelligence kept their files. Psychopath, that's what they said, because it made them more comfortable if they could believe he was mad.

Sometimes, Brennan felt mad. Whenever Sean popped up unexpectedly, for example, bumping into him on the street or scurrying around a corner with that queer laugh of his. But if Siri was right about reincarnation, seeing your dead brother didn't necessarily mean you'd gone insane.

He decided not to tell Tomas Condon too much.

"Sometimes," he said, "I work for myself, see? Because over the years, I've made the contacts the IRA need to stay alive. Libya. Iran. Places the Army fucking Council couldn't spell to save their lives, that's where I make money, Tomas. Some for them, some for me."

The young man licked his lips a few times, began a sentence, tailed off. "Where's the money come from?" he gasped out at last; and Brennan nodded heavily, a guru pleased with some brighter-than-average disciple.

"Drugs," he replied. "Whatever saps the health and the minds of good English boys and girls. Whatever turns them into tarts, rent-boys. A drain on the national health. That's where you'll find me, Tommy my lad. The pharmaceuticals business."

Condon's eyes were bulging out of their sockets. "That's a d . . . " He'd been going to say "dirty," but at the last moment he wisely changed his mind, " . . . a dangerous game."

"Aye, but there's money in it. And now that our brothers across the Atlantic are baring streaks of meanness, we have to trawl where there are fish. We need the money, you see. The IRA is an expensive, wasteful, ill-managed organization. Not like Glaxo. So it needs more money, each year. But for me, it would receive less. Get me?"

Condon nodded hurriedly.

"Now tell me another thing." He still spoke like the guru, concerned to draw out answers that the student knows without knowing. "*Why* does the IRA need money? Why, in other words, have its friends been deserting it? Eh? Come now, you're a bright lad, you tell me."

Condon said nothing.

"No?" Brennan slowly leaned forward to rest his elbows on his knees. "Well, it's because the IRA is *weak*."

"Weak?" Condon was having trouble accepting that one.

"Weak," Brennan repeated. "Our biggest problem: image. It's a vicious spiral—you know what that is? Because people think it's weak, they desert. The more they desert, the weaker it gets. Crack the image problem, and we can crack anything. Get me?"

"Yes."

"That's why I'm here. So now you know, Tommy. If you're wise, you won't forget anything you've learned today."

Brennan held the young man's gaze a moment longer, as if recording his features for some dread inner file, then slowly looked up at O'Halloran.

"What are you staring at?"

The other man's eyes flickered away. "I had a visitor this afternoon," he mumbled. "Mountjoy."

"Did you now?" An ugly thought struck Brennan. "You weren't followed here?" he asked quickly.

"No. I'm sure we weren't."

"Good. Because I've got nothing to say to the Brigadier, now or later. What did he want?"

"To warn you."

"About what?"

"He doesn't want any footprints leading up to his door."

Brennan laughed out loud.

"Y'see, Bren, the word's gone round that you're in town."

Brennan stopped laughing. His face tensed. "Already?"

O'Halloran nodded. "Somebody's been talking to the police here."

"Cricklewood?"

"Lower down."

"Mountjoy's got a traitor in his camp?"

"He's not admitting it. But . . . "

"But he has." Brennan drew a long breath and exhaled in a low, throaty growl. "That's Mountjoy's problem," he said at last, looking up at O'Halloran. "But when you see him again, tell him I've not come here to make trouble for his men."

"I will do that, yes."

Brennan could sense that O'Halloran was still troubled. And why not?—for in normal times he was attached to Mountjoy's staff and subject to his discipline. But deep in his heart he was the Krait's man and had been for the past decade. Looking at his old comrade, Brennan recognized that it must have cost him something to stand up to Mountjoy, with Dublin breathing down his neck as well.

Brigadier Michael Mountjoy. Now there was a madman *if* you liked . . .

"The papers," he said suddenly, making O'Halloran jump. "Have you got them?"

O'Halloran handed him a stack of newsprint. The Krait skimmed the tabloids, then concentrated on the others, leaving the *Times* until last. He turned to its leader page and snorted a quick laugh.

"That's her!"

"If you say so," O'Halloran muttered.

"It's her." He read a few paragraphs. "'Not such a blind lady . . . ' Clever, that. Pens a beautiful sentence, does Miss Forbes. If she should write for the IRA now . . . " He grinned across at Condon, who hastily left off rubbing his neck. "We wouldn't be weak then, Tommy."

"But . . . she wouldn't do that." A pause. "Would she?"

"She might." Brennan giggled. "We could commission an article, maybe. What else have you got, Pat?"

O'Halloran opened his briefcase and took out a cardboard file that he now handed to Brennan. The first document in it was a photograph of Roz Forbes.

"Nice looker," Brennan observed thoughtfully. He skimmed through the other papers in the file. "What's your view of her, Pat? Will she do?"

O'Halloran said: "That's for you to decide, Bren."

"I asked you a question."

"Then . . . I can't understand why it has to be her. Quite a few journalists have been fighting in Thornton's corner. She's a woman, and—"

"And brilliant at what she does. High profile, controversial . . . unique."

"But . . . in what way? *How* is she unique?"

Brennan smiled. "She knows Alistair Scrutton. She knows Thornton. Soft on him, she is. And however many journalists are fighting in Thornton's corner, only one of them's a woman who's soft on the accused and knows the Crown's top witness. D'you get it now?"

O'Halloran shook his head.

"It doesn't matter. Just don't assume that I've got my eye on Roz Forbes alone. There's another . . . "

No, whispered the voice of caution. Pat's a

friend, but he doesn't need to know about the other one. Not yet; maybe never. Even the best of us blab sometimes . . .

That thought was chilling. "Just you have a care," he said quickly to O'Halloran. "If so much as one word of what I've got in mind for this lady were to find its way into Brigadier Mountjoy's ears, just one . . . "

He left the sentence unfinished because he'd seen the fear catch light in O'Halloran's eyes and did not believe in wasting breath.

Brennan closed the file and shoved it under his pillow. "Get the car, Tomas," he said. "I need to make a phone call."

"Brother Mark?" O'Halloran said hopefully.

"Later."

Condon took himself off. Shortly afterward, the other two men emerged onto the street, where they got into the back of the car that O'Halloran had hired. As Condon drove away, Brennan picked up the mobile phone and dialed a number.

"Put me through to Chief Superintendent Wright, would you be so kind . . . Superintendent Meath, of Dublin's Kevin Street station calling . . . Is that you, Billy, for Christ's sake?" He laughed. "Long time no see."

There was a heavy pause at the other end of the line. "Where are you?" a quick, quiet voice said at last.

Brennan's "Leetle Leprechaun" surfaced, just for a second. "Sure, and oi'm on the phone, not a word of a loie."

"Cut the blarney shit. Just tell me where you are."

"I'm closer than you think, Billy." There was no humor in the Krait's voice now. "Alistair Scrutton. I mean to see him. So just arrange it, will you?"

"You're mad! The Prime Minister couldn't get to him."

"But I'm not the Prime Minister, am I, Billy?"

"Listen, forget it." The voice at the other end was panicky now. "It's not possible—period!"

"Then make it possible. Or they'll take your nice blue uniform away and put you in a cage. You know the cage I mean, Billy. The one with wild animals in it. Animals *you* put there."

"For love of God, think what—"

"Scrutton. *Soon.*"

Brennan put down the receiver, yawned and stretched, pushing his palms hard against the roof of the car. "I could fancy a curry," he said. "Where's good around here, Pat?"

PART TWO
TRIAL

CHAPTER
11

LONDON. THE PRESENT

The Thornton trial was a week old.

Roz strode into the cramped, smelly room, composing an expression of kindly concern. "Frank . . ."

He jumped up and all but ran around the table, squeezing past Andrew Mottram. "Thanks for coming," he said, as he took her in his arms. "I can't tell you how much it means to me when I see your face there in court."

"And the others." She did not tell him that she had arranged a rota, so that at least one of the handful of friendly journalists was always in court.

Smilingly he shook his head. "Yours is the face I look for."

"I'm just sorry I can't be there always," she said, kissing him. "If you promise to sweep me off my feet like this every day, I'll make the effort, though."

"You're more use to me outside. Roz, I've said it before, but I have to say it again . . . Thanks for all you're doing. You've been . . . " He struggled for the right word. "Well, superb. I don't know what I'd have done without you."

She shook her head, holding him at arms' length. "You're looking fantastic. Well done."

In truth, his face reminded her of another friend, a former alcoholic who liked to play Russian Roulette with glasses of sweet sherry. But she remembered what Frank must be going through, and awarded him top marks anyway.

She shook hands first with Andrew, then with Hugo Lutter, Frank's solicitor, a tall, suntanned man whose monocle and seemingly infinite collection of Huntsman's double-breasted suits made him a natural point of focus for the TV cameras whenever he left court. "Anything you need?" she asked him.

Lutter shook his head. "Your people are being marvelous."

"The letters keep coming," she said.

Lutter nodded encouragingly. "If the government held a referendum, we'd win hands down."

She only forwarded the letters of support, which was dishonest, because the other kind took up more space.

"How far have we got?" she inquired.

"The forensic's finished now," Mottram replied. When he shifted his immense weight, the chair on which he was sitting creaked in protest. "Plus evidence of arrest, and so on. Tomorrow, we get Tumin."

"To link Frank in with the IRA?"

"Yes."

"Ridiculous."

Mottram sighed. "You know that. I know that. But ideological commitment on the part of the fan club doesn't sway juries. It's Tumin's word against Frank's."

"But this man's got convictions for violence, for . . ."

She tailed off. Everyone knew that Padraic

Tumin had a record. But unfortunately Frank couldn't produce an alibi for the dates his evidence was going to cover.

Couldn't . . . or wouldn't? As the by-now familiar thought entered her mind, Roz squared her shoulders. There must be a showdown over that, and today was the day.

"Um, am I interrupting?" she asked.

Mottram shook his head. "We were just winding down." He piled up his papers. "I've got a long night ahead of me."

One of many, she thought, looking at him. She recalled Norman Birkett's grim joke about capital trials: "These cases take years off my life . . . and add years to the accused's."

"Can I have a word with Frank, then? In private?"

The lawyers mustered smiles as they went out, but Roz knew that once in the corridor their faces would be wiped clean of any emotion, leaving only a grubby patina of fatigue. She pushed the door shut and rested her back against it, feeling as well as hearing the heavy bolt slide shut.

"How are you?" she asked, after a pause. "Really?"

Frank rubbed his eyes. "I'm fine."

She wanted to ask him what you thought about in the quiet hours, when you were on trial for your life, but it seemed indelicate.

"Do you need anything—books, food . . . ?"

"People keep asking me that. They want to give me things, when all I'm longing for is green trees. Fresh air. A hot bath, in private." He grunted. "A man's real needs are so simple, aren't they?"

She moved away from the door and sat down. "Frank . . . " She'd arrived in this cell to take something off him, when she ought only to be supportive, and now she didn't know how to go about it. "Frank," she tried again.

"What is it?" Suddenly he reached out to take her hand. She flinched. She didn't mean to, but she couldn't help herself. It was like being waylaid by a ghost. Some small part of the aura of martyrdom already adhered to Frank Thornton, like mildew on a corpse.

"Frank, there's something I want to talk through with you. Though it's not your problem, it's mine; I can't stress that enough, okay?"

He removed the hand, as if sensing her ambivalent reaction to his touch, and nodded.

"I've decided . . . I've been thinking that it could be a smart move for me to resign from the *Times*."

"Great God, why?" He stood up and took a few steps around the cell, a frown creasing his forehead. "Why?" he said again, this time to the door.

"Channel Four have offered a debate, live. Nine-thirty next Wednesday, prime time. It's chancy stuff: you know about the *sub judice* rule?"

"Of course. You can't discuss a trial in public while it's still going on."

"Because it might affect the outcome, that's right. But Four are prepared to run the risk, by keeping the discussion general. They know they won't get anyone from the government on the other side, but plenty of other people will be ready to support this trial." She hesitated. "They've asked me to lead for the opposition. God knows why, but they have. John Mortimer's agreed to follow; he's great, top weight. But they want a woman. And I want to do it. I want to throw in every damn thing we've got."

He turned away from the door. "But why resign?"

"Because Howard won't play ball. Howard Boissart, you know—my editor."

"What's he got to do with it?"

"Everything." Roz took a tissue from her bag and used it to wipe her forehead. It came away moist and grimy. She glared at it, wondering why every damn thing about this trial had to turn into an uphill struggle.

"I've been given a lot of leeway," she hurried on. "Howard's been generous. But he's in favor of using treason charges against the IRA and . . . well, look, I didn't want to say this, but—"

"But mostly his readership's behind him." Frank once more came to sit down opposite her. "You think I'm such a baby I have to be protected from the truth?"

"No, of course—"

"They keep the tabloids away from me, you know that?" He shook his head in disgust. "Do you want to hear something funny? *I'd* be in favor of charging IRA men with treason!"

She stared at him, speechless. After a while he began to giggle quietly. But for the circumstances, she'd have assumed he was drunk.

"Frank," she said sharply. "Stop it."

He stopped dead, as if he were a sophisticated doll and her words had severed a voice-sensitive connection inside him.

"Howard won't let me do that broadcast," she went on, after a pause. "That's why I've decided to resign."

He considered her through half-closed eyes. "So why are you telling me? If you've decided."

"I felt . . . you ought to know."

He laughed, but this time there was nothing hysterical about it. "Come off it."

"What?"

"You *dread* resigning. So you want my approval."

"I don't need anyone's approval, Frank. I'm free, white, and over twenty-one."

"Yeah, yeah . . . " Just when she'd forgotten that he'd spent most of his career States-side he would sometimes lapse into Americana. "Whatever. But I don't approve. I disapprove, get me?"

"Why?"

"Because I'm thinking straight, which is more than you are."

"Goddamm it, Frank, why are you so *angry*?"

He'd been rubbing his temple, but now he clenched his hand into a fist and brought it down hard on the table. "Because resigning doesn't help me. And I'm alarmed when a free, white, and over twenty-one friend can't see that."

"So tell me: why doesn't it help you?"

"One." He unclenched his fist and extended the hand, palm upward, toward her. "This broadcast stands an excellent chance of being trashed before it can go out. Suppose the government puts its lawyers to work, or Channel Four get cold feet, or whatever. So where does that leave you? Without a job, looking just . . . plain . . . *stupid.*"

"But—"

"*Two.* Say the program goes out. It's over in, what? Half an hour? Who's going to remember it next day? TV programs are like perfume; they can be quite simply wonderful when the cork comes out the bottle and for a few hours afterward, but then they fade away like they never were. And three . . . oh, come on, you know what three is."

"I don't." You do, an inner voice told her, but she felt unreasonably stubborn. She also wanted to cry; the back of her throat was swollen and sore.

"Three is that this trial is not going to last forever. Then, no matter what happens to me, you'll be out on a limb. I don't want that to happen."

She stared down at the table, because by doing that she could keep the tears unshed. "I owe you one," that's what he was saying; "I'm fond of you." And now, as if to underline the message without spelling it out, he said, "Do you still use that terrible green paper and white ink for your letters?"

"You shit." She stood up, sending her chair over,

and retreated to the wall where she could contain her anger without his seeing, or so her dignity would have her pretend.

"Roz, Roz . . . " She heard him come up behind her, felt his hand on her shoulder, and she wanted to run; but in a cell you couldn't run. So instead she reluctantly turned around and allowed him to take her in his arms, wondering how it came about that a man on trial for his life found the reserves to comfort her.

"You have to stay right where you are now," he murmured into her ear. "That way, you can go on helping me. Play office politics. Let your editor have his little victories, and at the same time, claim yours. Like water dripping on a stone, Roz. On TV, you'd be a flash flood in the desert. Useless."

She knew she ought to be attaching weight to his words, but all she really felt was the weight of his body against hers. So long since Johnny, since *any* man had held her like this . . . Guilt made her tense; she wanted him to go on holding her, when the whole point of the meeting was to . . . oh, God! What *was* the point, why had she come . . . ?

Resigning. They'd been talking about her resignation and Frank was against it. She let out the breath she'd been holding with a heavy sigh. "I'll . . . I'll think about it."

"Good."

"But you've got to think, too. Promise me."

He started to say something, but she held a finger to his lips. "Just promise me."

"All right."

"And . . . " She hesitated. *Go for it, girl!* "And if you could try to trust me more," she burst out.

He knew what she was referring to; it showed at once in the way his face went dead.

"Roz, don't . . . not tonight."

"I have to know, Frank."

He tried to cut across her but she raised her voice, drowning him out.

"Tumin and Scrutton are going to say you conspired with a member of the IRA to kill the Queen. Scrutton says it happened on a certain night, in a certain place: your house. You deny that. *But you won't tell me where you were!*"

"No, I won't."

He was sitting down again now, not looking at Roz.

"Why?"

Maybe she had asked him that question a thousand times, or perhaps only a hundred and it just felt like a thousand. He answered it as he always did, with silence.

"Why won't you tell me where you were that night?" she repeated. "Sometimes, I wonder—"

Now it was his turn to override. "Sometimes you wonder if I'm really guilty, yes, of course, I would too. You must have had a hell of a day, you look exhausted, why don't you—"

"Frank, I am *trying* to help you." A long pause. "You've told Andrew Mottram where you were that night."

"Yes. And he agrees with me; since I can't prove it, there's no point in making a big fuss about it."

"But why insist that Andrew keeps it to himself? Why tell your barrister in confidence, when there's scores of people waiting, dedicated, to following up any lead, no matter how thin, if it even *might* help you? Why?"

No response.

"All right, I can see reasons why you might not want to trust me. I'm a journalist and journalists sometimes make trouble, but—"

"It's not that." He smashed his palms down on the table, making her jump. "You know damn well it's not that."

"You don't trust me."

"I *do*! *Trust*! . . . Goddammit, Roz, I—"

Looking at him, she knew he had been on the point of transforming their relationship, that his next words would promote them to a table where they couldn't afford to play. So without waiting to hear them she hurried on, "Then why—"

He stared at her for a long moment before picking up the thread. "Because it does no good," he said lamely.

"You really won't tell me?"

"No."

"And the jury? Will you tell *them*, when you're asked?"

He said nothing. After a while, Roz wanted to go over and put her arms around him, murmur, "It's all right . . . " But it wasn't all right. So she sighed and said, "Let's think about Scrutton, then."

He smiled at her, hearing that, and she felt the familiar heart-flutter his smiles always generated. "Have you got any paper?" he asked, pulling his chair up to the table.

Roz sat down, producing a pad from her briefcase.

"The one lead my solicitors had, when they were drafting the defense to Scrutton's slander writ, was his Hong Kong connection; in particular, that swine Lee."

"The lawyer?"

"Right. Now it didn't take much rooting around in Hong Kong to discover that Lee was a crook." He had lost some of his pallor, was becoming animated. "Scrutton began to go downhill, back in the late Seventies, about the time he first met Lee. Everything, *everything* leads back to Hong Kong, and that first trip he took out East . . . "

CHAPTER

12

HONG KONG. JUNE 1977

"Play 'em for all you can get," Reg Valance enjoined Scrutton in a grim voice. "There's big money on the bamboo circuit, as long as you remember one thing: *win!*"

Scrutton grasped the need to win as early as the preliminary conference in London with Mr. Lee, the Chinese solicitor retained by his clients. Mr. Lee was a heavily built Hong Kong citizen who wore an ancient blue suit that, together with his clammy, yellowish moonface and plastic-framed spectacles, hardly suggested vast wealth. It was Scrutton's first experience of a certain type of Chinese facade.

"Let me see if I've understood it," he said. "Your corporate client, and two of its directors, are charged in Hong Kong with false accounting and conspiracy to defraud the tax authorities; you want a criminal leader to make the running in court, and me sitting behind him to help with the financial aspects?"

"Yes."

"I see." Scrutton coughed, aware of a certain difficulty facing them, namely, that the clients were plainly guilty as charged. "Certain payments were put through to individuals in exchange for awarding government building contracts. The payments were a . . . " He meant to say "bribe," but one look at Mr. Lee's face suggested a better alternative. "Commission."

Mr. Lee nodded.

"And so a third company was induced to send false documents to the client's bank, resulting in payment for bogus professional services, and that was the money used for the commission? In essence, that's what happened?"

"No. It's what the prosecution *say* happened."

"I'm so sorry. Of course."

On the paperwork laid before Scrutton, the prosecution would have been mad to say anything else.

"The trouble I'm experiencing, Mr. Lee . . . " Scrutton slowly sat back in his chair, addressing himself to a point just below the solicitor's tie knot. " . . . is that we're lacking the sort of invoices and receipts and other papers that would help us paint a different picture." He raised his eyes to Lee's face. "Aren't we?"

For the first time in a conference that had already lasted twenty minutes, the solicitor showed signs of preparing to write. "Such as?" he murmured encouragingly.

Scrutton said nothing for a long while.

From oblique discussions with Valance he guessed that he was being asked to outline evidence that would then be manufactured in a colony renowned for its skill in making things. If he went along with that, he too would enter the manufacturing business, generating a fortune from this case and from the others that would inevitably follow as a rather similar kind of "commission" to the one under discussion.

It wasn't as dangerous as the share deal that had almost wrecked his career at the outset. He could claim that he'd given Lee hypothetical advice in all innocence. And Scrutton needed money. Since his marriage to Louise Shelley, earnings had somehow never quite managed to keep pace with the overdraft that was a necessary adjunct to the practice of every barrister, however successful.

The only thing that gave him pause was the knowledge that if this seeped out, somebody somewhere would make a note on the file they kept on you in the section of the lord chancellor's office which oversaw judicial appointments.

Quite early in his career, however, Scrutton had lost his former ambition to be a judge. Two or three years spent sitting in a variety of courts had taught him that judges did a thoroughly boring job. More importantly, they were underpaid. *Seriously* underpaid. So that sitting in his chambers, with Lee's pen raised ready to write, he did not exactly feel his career to have reached a watershed. Say rather, he had, more by luck than judgment, blundered out of the forest of thorns onto a major highway.

Scrutton cleared his throat. "It's alleged the clients paid for valuations that were never made," he said. "If they could somehow be produced . . . "

He broke off. Mr. Lee was writing in Chinese characters that took a long time to form and Scrutton did not want anything to be overlooked . . .

A few months later he sat in Hong Kong's Supreme Court building off Statue Square, examining his nails while he waited for the jury's foreman to finish delivering the verdicts. It was a good result. His leader had advised the clients to plead guilty to six of the lesser charges, none of which would involve going to prison, leaving only four to fight. The jury acquitted on three out of the four, including conspiracy to defraud the Revenue, and the judge sentenced everyone to pay fines. The clients couldn't exactly claim to leave court without stains on their characters, although in certain Hong Kong circles those stains would doubtless be viewed as attractive coloration.

"I hope you can find room in the diary this September," Mr. Lee murmured as he led Scrutton toward the robing room. "We have rather a big specific performance action coming up."

Scrutton knew a moment of outright jubilation. "I'd be delighted," he said.

"Mr. Valance tells me you'll be free."

"Actually, Mr. Lee, I'll be rather expensive."

They were still laughing as they turned a corner and found two people blocking their path: a European and a tall, lean Oriental wearing baggy trousers beneath a cream shirt.

"Now," Mr. Lee said, smoothly stepping to one side, "I wish to introduce you to two particular clients and friends of mine who have noted your part in this trial with interest. Mr. Scrutton, Mr. Siri Chaloem . . . "

In a sudden, dramatic gesture, the Oriental held out his hand palm down, as if Scrutton was expected to kiss it.

" . . . Who is from Thailand," Mr. Lee went on, as the two men shook, "unlike Mr. Lloyd here, who hails from Ireland."

The Westerner removed a pair of sunglasses, folded them, and tucked one of their arms into the top pocket of his jacket, leaving the lenses suspended outside. "Call me John," he said in a voice devoid of all emotion.

While Scrutton labored over small talk, he acknowledged that he didn't much care for Chaloem. These thin, smiling Oriental men with their way of drifting along the pavement in a half-walk, half-dance, made his flesh creep with their lithe effeminacy. This one's face was strangely gray, as if he had a blackhead problem.

Lloyd was very different: a "man's man," clearly someone who knew how to keep himself in trim. Several of the flat fingernails were cracked and broken, and his hands were peeling in places. Scrutton wondered why he covered up manual labor with such expensive clothes, a confused, unattractive image. Whereas the Thai resembled an unblemished brown egg, Lloyd's skin was pitted and covered with hollows, a veritable relief map of a face.

Scrutton guessed that the Thai was the older of the two, in his mid-thirties, perhaps. He looked as though he'd sprung, adult and fully formed, from some unnatural mother's womb. But the Irishman had lived.

"Do you know the Far East?" Lloyd inquired. His baritone voice contained a lilt that Scrutton would not have readily identified as Irish unless he'd been told.

"No. This is my first visit."

"Would you have a few days at your disposal, now?"

Scrutton hesitated. Deeply etched lines around Lloyd's mouth suggested a capacity for laughter, although his wide-open blue eyes did not: they might have been two marbles set in off-white icing sugar. But . . . *This is how it happens,* Valance had told him. *I'll keep the diary empty, after the trial* . . .

"I really ought to be getting back," he temporized, anxious not to appear greedy. Perhaps they were organizing a trip to Bali . . .

But it turned out that Siri Chaloem had other ideas. "Chiang Rai," he said, "is so much cooler than Hong Kong. And I would like you to meet my father, Alistair." (They'd adjourned to the Peninsula's bar and everyone was on matey terms by then.) "He needs a first-class English lawyer to advise him on a European situ-wayshun. Do say yes."

So Scrutton said Yes and felt pleased with himself until they drove out to Kai Tak airport and he saw their plane parked on the apron.

"Converted DC-3," Chaloem beamed. "Dad's private plane. Jet set, huh?" He clapped Scrutton on the back. "Don't worry, you'll soon get used to the high life."

Scrutton doubted if he would survive long enough. The plane was a twin 1200hp-engined crate. As he climbed the rickety steps into the cabin, he saw patches on the wings and found himself looking for the bits of string. More feet clanged on the steps, and an elderly Chinese wearing brown shirt and trousers hauled himself into the cabin. He settled down opposite Alistair with a weary grunt, as if the effort of boarding had cost him today's entire stock of energy.

"Hi there, General." Chaloem waved cheerily at the Chinese, who nodded and returned an emphysematous grunt.

"General Yang Po," the Thai explained to Scrutton. "Very great man. Great fighting man. Friend of my dad."

The flight was terrible. Whenever the plane lurched, or fell a few hundred feet, which it did frequently, Scrutton found himself thrown against its metal sides until eventually his body ached with a mixture of cold, fatigue, and simple pain. After what seemed like hours he saw green mountains sweeping upward from a broad, flat plain. A few moments later the DC-3 crossed a yellowish tributary of the Mekong. The mountains here were swathed in cloud, their tightly knit, forested slopes clinging ever closer together in a maze of impenetrable jungle. Then they were going down through razorbacked scarpments, to land in what looked like a field but was in fact Mong Hsat airport. As they taxied toward a rusty iron hangar, it began to rain.

Everyone suddenly seemed to be in a great hurry. Their transport, a ten-ton truck that had recently been painted, but not well enough to disguise its erstwhile military markings, raced out of the compound along a road that was little better than a track, and almost at once began to climb into the foothills. Through a steamy curtain Scrutton caught glimpses of people squatting in a sad, bewildered way outside battered thatched houses while the rain torrented down upon their heads. He had no idea what a rich Thai entrepreneur could want with him in such a hellish place.

The track steadily worsened, as the folds of the mountains relentlessly closed in on it and evidence of attempts at clearing disappeared. Scrutton's landscape reduced itself to a dark green backdrop enlivened only by rain that fell as if fired at the earth by an angry god. At last the lorry trundled off the track, its tailboard crashed down, and Scrutton found himself standing up to his ankles in mud.

Siri Chaloem led the way through the green wall as if he expected it to collapse before his confident stride. The jungle encroached on them like a deadening blanket. Mosquitoes swarmed around Scrutton. He tried to swat them, but it was useless—the more he killed, the more they gathered.

"Are there any snakes?" he called out hoarsely to Siri.

"Some," the Thai replied. "Watch out for banded Kraits."

Lloyd's unexpectedly loud laugh made Scrutton cringe.

Suddenly the four of them emerged into a clearing overlooking a valley and a great many things happened. The rain stopped; the sun came out; a vast flood of golden light unreeled itself down the face of the mountain on the other side of the valley, as if it were a stage set and the performance was about to begin. For the first time since they'd landed, Scrutton got an impression of serious cultivation, extending as far as the eye could see. But that wasn't what held his attention; for halfway between where he stood and the valley floor was a timbered, mullion-windowed Tudor mansion complete with curlicued chimneys, a vision of the Cotswolds transported to the Mekong jungle.

Two figures exploded out of a door set in the side of the house nearest him and began to sprint up the hill. He had a confused impression of red headscarves, vermilion sarongs, brown skin, Khmer visages. Boys, carrying long black things; umbrellas, how thoughtful . . . then he saw that what they carried were rifles. The leading runner yelled something; a panicky voice answered from to Alistair's left in a tongue he'd never heard before; Lloyd tackled him to the ground and the world exploded around Scrutton's head with a heart-stopping crump.

He came to his senses lying face down in the mud, an acrid smell in his nostrils. He raised his head. The Tudor vision of a moment ago was no more. He watched with stupefied horror as the structure disintegrated in a fireball of red and yellow and orange, while smoke billowed upward through its skeleton. He struggled to sit up, rubbing ash from his eyes, convinced that this must be a dream. But there was no remission. The nightmare continued.

The two boys had already jumped to their feet and now were pointing their rifles at him, while they gabbled in high-pitched shrieks. The nearest one pushed his rifle into Scrutton's chest, his finger tightening on the trigger. Then the voice he'd heard earlier to his left spoke again. In a flash the boy grounded his rifle, showed a mouthful of white teeth in a dazzling smile and reached down to help Scrutton stagger to his feet.

For a moment, all he could do was stare in wonderment at these two boys. They looked to him like identical twins, an impression heightened by their dress. Each wore a red sarong emblazoned with black and gold markings, a thick gold necklace, a twist of pink cord around the right wrist, headbands and, circling each bare ankle, several more gold chains. On their feet they wore what looked like brand-new Nike trainers. They could not have been older than fourteen. Now one of them brought his right hand up to his temple in a cheeky salute. The other imitated him with a falsetto giggle.

Feet trampled the undergrowth behind Scrutton and he wheeled around. But it was only an emaciated old man, with a few straggly hairs still clinging to his scalp, wearing long, once-white shorts and a singlet several sizes too large for his puny frame.

"I'm so sorry," he piped. "They're Akha tribesmen, and we teach them to watch out for strangers, you see." He sighed, and wiped one eye with his left hand. "Omigod." Then, as if that was not quite enough to designate disaster, he shook his head and repeated, "Omigod."

"My father," Siri Chaloem said. "Dad, meet Mr. Scrutton."

The old man extended his scrawny hand, a network of fine bones shrink-wrapped in bark-colored skin. "Omigod," he repeated in his reedy voice. "Omigod."

The Chaloems embarked on a rapid-fire question and answer session in which General Yang Po occasionally joined. They took five full minutes to reach their first pause in the conversation. Scrutton grabbed his opportunity. "What . . . *happened*?"

Everyone turned to stare at him. The older

Chaloem rubbed his eye again, while Siri, to judge from the workings of his face, chewed his tongue.

"Accident," General Yang Po said loudly.

"*What?*"

They continued to scrutinize him through narrowed eyes. Scrutton pointed at the smoking ruins of what had once been a Tudor house. "That was an explosion," he said, marveling at his own calmness. "The place blew up."

General Yang Po's eyes had by now narrowed into horizontal slits; he evidently wasn't accustomed to having his explanations questioned. "Accident," he yapped.

"But . . . but was anyone hurt?"

Siri stopped munching on his tongue and exchanged a swift look with his father. The jungle seemed remarkably silent. Apart from the crackle of burning wood and the occasional crash of a burned-out beam falling apart, not a sound disturbed the stillness.

"Omigod," the elder Chaloem said again. "I so wanted you to see one of my houses. Air-con, you know. Refrigerator. Johnnie Walker."

"*One* . . . of your houses. How many do you have?"

"Six . . . five."

Scrutton gawped. "All like that?"

The old man nodded heavily. "I love England. Go there every year. Stratford. Hampton Court. I offered to buy it."

Scrutton wrestled with an overwhelming sense of unreality. "Buy it . . . ?"

"Hampton Court. There was this American one year, you see. Bought London Bridge. I wrote a letter. Got a charming reply back. Charming. I must show it to you. British government said they still wanted Hampton Court. I wrote back. Said, if ever you don't still want it, let me know."

Lloyd raised a hand to his mouth and moved away coughing, while Old Chaloem sighed.

"Other houses are too far away," he said. "Sorry. Tonight you'll have to go rough, Mr. Scrutton. Leave your luggage in the lorry?"

Scrutton, mesmerized, found himself nodding.

"Boys will fetch. Good boys. Rin and Tin."

"Ri . . ."

Lloyd made a strangulated sound, as if his throat was troubling him. "The answer's no," he said at last.

Scrutton gazed at him. "No . . . what?"

"There's no third brother, also called Tin."

Scrutton laughed, in spite of himself. Everyone looked pleased, especially General Yang Po, whose face had slowly been taking on the aspect of some particularly vicious storm devil drawn from his own Chinese pantheon.

The lorry took them first downhill then up again, by a different road somewhat better than the last. The weather held. At last they pulled into another clearing. Sunlight illuminated a large, square thatched house built up from the ground on short stilts. Wind chimes tinkled from its verandah, below which sat two teenage girls, preparing vegetables. One of them disappeared inside while the lorry was being unloaded, but the other stayed to welcome them, raising her hands in a *wai*, the traditional Thai greeting.

Scrutton did not know how one was expected to acknowledge a *wai*. He felt embarrassed, as he always did in any situation beyond his control. He wanted to pretend he hadn't seen the girl, but some inner compulsion made him cast a glance in her direction. Then he faltered, staring unashamedly at the most beautiful human being he'd ever clapped eyes on.

He guessed she was about eighteen: a magnifi-

cent peach, just attaining its prime. Her skin was
flawless, and her flesh filled it out perfectly, neither
loose nor fat but with a firmness that was just so.
She looked unused. But at the same time, she invited use. She was, he felt, *ready*, and she had attained
that state sometime within the past few hours.

He lowered his eyes a fraction. The tee shirt's
manufacturer had stitched a curious message across
the lefthand side of it: "Life. Go for Something." He
smiled, then noticed the two small nipples inside
her tight shirt, longing to know if the breasts were
as firm as they looked, or if they would turn to
sponge beneath his caressing fingers.

Slowly, very slowly, he raised his hands together
and inclined his head, attempting a *wai*. "I'm
sorry," he muttered. "I haven't done this before."

Her lips parted in a smile, but she did not speak.
Scrutton became aware of the others waiting for
him at the entrance to the house and forced himself
to climb the remaining steps to the verandah.

The house was constructed of aromatic teak. Siri
showed him to a clean, comfortable room containing a bed beneath a mosquito net, and some sparse
bamboo furniture.

"You'd like a bath," the Thai said. "Come . . . "

At the far end of the passage was another room
with a single window looking onto the jungle. In
the middle of the floor stood a wooden tub, already
full of piping hot water. Several copper jugs were
ranged nearby, along with thick white towels, soap
and mysterious bottles of colored crystal. The only
other item of furniture here was a mattress covered
with a plastic sheet.

When the Thai had gone, Scrutton gratefully
peeled off his clothes. The tub contained a broad
seat so arranged that when he sat on it the water
still came up over his shoulders. He rested his neck
on the folded towel someone had thoughtfully

spread over the rim of the tub, and closed his eyes, falling asleep at once.

He was woken by two hands closing around his neck.

He shuddered and fought his way up through the water, arms flailing. A cry for help formed in his throat, but the hands dropped away before he could utter it. He wrenched his head around to see the beautiful girl he'd noticed by the steps standing with both hands held up to her open mouth.

"Sorrysorrysorry," he heard a voice whisper. When his heart had finally stopped pounding he managed to say, "You startled me."

"Sorrysorrysorry."

"Come round where I can see you."

She obeyed. Her black hair, adorned with a single red rose behind one ear, fell in long streaks over her tee shirt to meet a plain blue sarong that began just below her navel. Her stomach swelled gently, enhancing his earlier impression of serene maturity. The face was small, a tiny upturned chin its most prominent feature, and her dark eyes sparkled with vitality. He found it hard to think of a word to describe her coloring: caramel was the nearest he could come, and as the word floated into his mind to conjoin with "ripeness" he acknowledged that he saw her in terms of something sweet and edible, a product of nature to be consumed before her bloom faded.

"Do you speak English?" Scrutton asked.

She shook her head violently, answering him and contradicting herself in one gesture and then, as if aware of the paradox, slipped her upper teeth over her lip.

The teeth were small, he noticed, and faintly silverish, like pearls.

"You *do* speak English," he teased her.

Again the teeth appeared. "Little." She laughed.

At first it had occurred to him that he ought to

cover himself up, but he felt quite relaxed. More than that—he knew a treacherous desire that she should look at him. He'd never felt such a thing with a woman before.

She folded her hands demurely in front of her. "I learn a little English," she said, with careful precision. "From school. Oh." She frowned. She had a most endearing frown. "At school. You want I . . ." She made a gesture of rubbing.

"That would be nice."

She retreated out of view once again. Her fingers were supple and immensely strong. When she picked up the soap and began to wash him all over, he neither protested nor found it strange, not even when she soaped his genitals. She risked a peek at him from under her eyelashes and smiled quickly, before passing on to lave his thighs.

When he was clean, and she had showered him with tepid water from the copper jugs, she motioned him to lie on the plastic-covered mattress, first covering it with a towel.

"What's your name?" he asked drowsily, relishing the feel of her skillful hands as they worked oil into his skin.

"P'ia."

He had expected to feel a renewal of the desire that she had merely sparked in the tub, but now she worked on him vigorously, driving out all trace of the earlier eroticism. Before she could ask him to turn over, he was asleep.

He awoke to find that she had covered him with a towel and left. Outside, the cicadas were busily tuning up for their dusk chorus. Delightful scents filtered in through the mesh frame, mingling with those of soap, and oil, reminding him of the girl. His body felt clean, light, wonderful. The memory of P'ia hung all about him in the airy room.

He changed into fresh clothes. The sound of voices

lured him to the south corridor, and a vast room that occupied one whole side of the house. His elderly host and the other guests were sitting in wicker chairs on the verandah, now screened from the outside by a rattan blind. Innumerable candles set in glass bowls provided soft light. Chaloem the elder, now clad in slacks, shirt, and straw sandals, came forward to greet him. "Omigod what a day," he said mournfully. "Let's eat."

The meal was a mixture of delicious Thai flavors, with several Chinese dishes thrown in, perhaps as a sop to the general. John Lloyd, who sat next to him, proved a helpful guide, not only to the food but also to the region.

"You know the area well, do you?" Scrutton asked him.

"No one knows it well."

Lloyd lowered his voice a little, and the two men drifted off into a conversation of their own.

"You've seen the landscape, Alistair. It's heavily forested, there's hardly anywhere to land a plane, the mountains have never been properly mapped. Half the villains in the Orient have holed up here one time or another. Take him, for instance."

Lloyd nodded discreetly at Yang Po, who was laughing at some joke of Siri's.

"He fought as a boy with Chiang Kai-Shek—a lot of the Generalissimo's people ended up in the Triangle, when the communists took over, with nothing to do except farm opium."

Scrutton stared at the Chinese. "He's in drugs?" he said uneasily.

"Oh yes. So's Chaloem."

Scrutton jerked his head around. "God . . . he seems such a nice old man."

Lloyd chuckled. "These fellows see it as a business, like any other. No wonder they call this the Golden Triangle."

"But can't the government do anything?"

"Which one? You've got three governments up here, trying to police Burmese rebels, communist factions, and American traffickers. The tribes have got no loyalty to anyone, except themselves. Many of the border patrol units are on the take. Except for the Thai Rangers. They're mercenaries, but attached to the Thai Third Army, and they're vicious."

Scrutton's gaze was drawn to the three Eastern faces opposite, their features melting and reforming according to the whim of the candles. He could not see their eyes.

The seed of a terrible thought sprouted. He was in the house of a rich opium farmer. He had witnessed an explosion which—for the first time he acknowledged it to himself—could only have been caused by dynamite, gelignite, call it what you would, the central fact remained the same; his host either kept an astonishing stash of explosives, or was the intended victim of someone who bore more than a petty grudge.

Alistair Scrutton, to sum up, knew too much.

"Where do I fit in?" he heard an unfamiliar voice say. For a split second his brain did not recognize that it was he who had spoken.

"Well, now . . . " Lloyd smiled. Like Scrutton, he kept his voice low. "I'd hate you to feel, and I know that Mr. Chaloem would hate you to feel, that you had to 'fit in,' as you call it, anywhere."

"You mean I can just walk out of here any time I please?"

"Yes. Although I wouldn't advise it; the jungle's hard on first-timers."

"But . . . supposing I went to the police?"

"You couldn't lead them here in a month of Sundays. Anyway, which police did you have in mind?"

"Thailand's, of course."

'You'd find that a little tricky. You see, we're in Burma, at the moment. And in the eyes of the Burmese border patrol, you're an illegal immigrant." He raised his voice. "Gentlemen . . . Alistair here was asking where he fitted in."

The other three fell silent. Apart from the cicadas, nothing disturbed the stillness. A single giant moth flitted among the candle flames, undecided where to cast in its lot with death.

First Siri, then his father, turned to look at General Yang Po, who sat between them. The Chinese chewed on a toothpick for a while, evidently in no hurry to speak, keeping one arm slung over the back of his chair, the other resting on the table. At last he removed the toothpick.

"Lee say you do fine job in Hong Kong," he said. "I watch you this day." He raised his forearm from behind the chair and pointed at Scrutton. "You one cool gennelman. Useful gennelman to have around."

Scrutton stared at him as if hypnotized. He still knew fear, yes, but he had lived with terminal boredom long enough to be intrigued. If nothing else, he could dine out on this for decades. He felt increasingly confident, however, that there would be something else . . .

The Chinese general had tired of his struggle with the English language. He swiveled his pointing finger until it was directed at Lloyd, and jerked his head downward.

"Do you seriously want to be rich?" the Irishman asked Scrutton.

Something warm and disturbing, but not altogether unpleasant, flooded gently into the barrister's lower stomach. "Enough to listen," he said.

"You can safely assume that after your recent performance in Hong Kong, there will be other briefs. Substantial ones, involving a number of visits to that colony every year, with protracted stays in suites at the Peninsula, or wherever else catches your fancy. No one will query your hotel bills. Should you feel lonely, that problem can easily be solved."

The ghosts of P'ia's artful hands crept insidiously over Scrutton's thighs. "Go on," he said, in a thick voice.

"Before long, you will become a familiar figure in the East. Hong Kong is a small place. Judges, other lawyers, will mention your name with respect. Soon, policemen on duty at the court will recognize you, exchange a few words, perhaps even treat you to a salute. At the airport, your passage will become increasingly smooth. Once your cases are over, you'll do what all the top silks do when they come out East: fly to Penang for a few days' rest. There again, no one will be auditing your hotel bill."

The giant moth cannoned against one of the candle globes, flapped its wings in an orgy of despair and tumbled onto the table. Scrutton watched its wings fold and unfold in a slow-motion dance of death.

"Your suitcase will be much admired."

Scrutton frowned. "My suitcase . . . "

"A large Louis Vuitton, somewhat battered by your frequent journeys. Extremely heavy. A suitable accessory for a wealthy barrister, don't you think?"

"But I don't own a Louis Vuitton suitcase."

"You will buy one, in Bangkok, tomorrow. And I'm afraid you must use your own money for that, Alistair. It's sometimes necessary to lay out a little in order to recoup a lot."

"Why?" Scrutton's voice turned urgent. "What's behind all this?"

"Twenty thousand pounds a run. To be paid anywhere in the world, in any currency you choose, in any name you please."

"Twenty . . . " But the wind went out of him, he could not finish the sentence.

"Perhaps once a year, unknown to you, your suit-case will be swapped for another, exactly like it. I stress—you will never know which case you are carrying through customs. But on those rare occasions when the substitution is made, as soon as you arrive home, a courier will come to swap the cases back again. Your fee will be paid next day."

"You want me to smuggle drugs, is that it?" Scrutton felt the dead weight of disappointment drag his stomach downward; for a moment he'd thought they might be about to tempt him with an acceptable proposition.

"We want you to carry a suitcase, Alistair." Lloyd's voice had never sounded so mild. "That's all."

Scrutton opened his mouth to say, "Well, fuck that for a laugh!" But then he caught sight of Yang Po's speculative eyes upon him and he kept quiet.

"And if customs open that suitcase," he said at last, wanting them to see at least one of the infinite number of flaws in their plan. "What then, eh?"

"Then you explain that there has been a mistake and that the suitcase is not yours. Which will be demonstrably true. Your own suitcase will materialize, the misunderstanding will be cleared up, and hey presto! No problem." Lloyd leaned forward to fold his arms on the table. "But the chances of that case ever being opened are minimal. You are a respectable lawyer with an international practice. You wear a three-piece suit, carry your robe bag, do you not? Signaling to customs that here is a man of probity."

"You think they'd let me through without question?"

"Of course."

"And why? I'll tell you—because they think no

respectable lawyer would be that *stupid*, to risk everything by smuggling drugs. And I'll tell you something else: Customs are *right*!"

General Yang Po took another toothpick from the jar and set to work again, excavating imaginary morsels from cavities long ago picked clean.

"We would like you to think about it carefully," Siri Chaloem said. "Overnight."

"What's there to think about? That you should think I'm capable of—"

Siri laughed. "But we know you're capable of it! That's why we brought you here."

"That remark's unforgivable. Outrageous."

"Lee didn't think so. There's something you should hear."

Siri reached down. He stood a cassette recorder on the table and pressed its "Play" button. Voices. Scrutton recognized one of them as Lee's. The other sounded unfamiliar; he'd never heard his own voice on tape before.

"The first conference," Siri said softly. "In London. When you told Lee what evidence was missing, and what you required."

The tape ran on.

"The trouble I'm experiencing, Mr. Lee, is that we're lacking the sort of invoices and receipts and other papers that would help us paint a different picture. Aren't we?"

Siri let the tape turn a few more revolutions, raveling Scrutton up in its insidious, all-destructive power, while the room quietly emptied. Scrutton sat staring down at the table. When Lloyd's hand descended onto his shoulder he jumped half out of his chair.

"I'll see you to your room," said the Irishman.

Scrutton allowed himself to be guided along the corridor, to be left standing on the threshold of his bedroom, like a sleepwalker faced with a brick wall.

He had no memory of taking off his clothes and getting into bed; it was only when a pair of gentle arms closed around him that he came to himself with a shudder. Then a warm, moist tongue tickled his ear, deftly exploring its ridges and hollows.

He half-turned, his hands involuntarily reaching out to the girl. "P'ia . . . You're . . . you're not wearing anything."

She giggled quietly. "Neither are you."

When she rolled over to lie on top of him her skin felt warm and dry to his touch. Long hair flowed down either side of his chest like a sensuous silken web that sparked off a thousand new sensations every time she moved. She was surprisingly light. She worked her legs between his until she was comfortable, then darted a quick kiss at each of his nipples, making his back arch. "You like that . . . ?"

He stroked her back, marveling at its smooth tension, before allowing his hands to wander more freely. When he bent to kiss her nipples she whimpered, and strained against him.

Scrutton knew, vaguely, that he was alone, friendless, in the hands of drug-traffickers who intended to blackmail him into a vile crime. None of that seemed to matter quite so much as it had a moment ago. But when, just for a second, the horror of the confrontation over dinner did douse through him, and he froze, P'ia sensed it. With an agile twist of her body, she leaped onto her knees. Before he could work out what she was doing, she had knelt over him, her head toward his feet, and those long strands of hair were massaging his stomach.

To and fro she worked, banishing fears of drug-smugglers and blackmail. It was enough to unseat his reason.

No one had ever made love to him like this girl. She *wanted* him! And to Scrutton, who had not felt wanted for many years, that bordered on magic. When he could stand it no longer he pushed her forward. She wriggled down his stomach and, still facing away from him, sank down. For a second she held herself perfectly still. Then she rose and sank again. Hot charges of electricity ran from the crown of Scrutton's head down to his toes; every muscle in his body strained to its farthest limit; and with a cry of pleasure that was almost pain he emptied himself into her. She moaned while she milked him dry, and fell forward onto the bed.

For a long time, neither of them moved. Then, as if from a long way away, he heard P'ia call his name. He mumbled something. Her voice reasserted itself close to his ear, a gentle hand touched his cheek. "Good?"

"Yes."

The word came out in a long sigh. This, then, was what it was all about. In London, after the port had slipped down too fast, colleagues were sometimes moved to say, "Those girls can make you believe they love you." He'd listened to the stories, feeling strong. It was easy to feel strong on a wet December night in England. You knew that you'd never fall for the pretense. Not *you* . . .

"A-liss-ter . . . will you come back?"

He rearranged himself, uncomfortably aware that the sheet was soaked with sweat. "Why, do you want me to?"

"*Yes!*"

Her quiet vehemence surprised him.

"I have a wife in England," he said. "That's my home."

"Do you love your wife?"

"Of course."

"Why do you say of course?"

He had no answer to give.

"Can she love like me?"

There was an answer to that, but he did not want to say it.

"You are my first *farang*, you know? My first foreigner."

Something in her voice, something against which even his studied cynicism was not proof, told him she was speaking the truth.

"A-liss-ter. I was always afraid of the foreigner, with his face so cold. But now . . . please let me love you."

His eyes had closed, he was drifting to the borderline with sleep. "Can't."

"You can. I will never trouble you. Never." She sounded suddenly fierce. "I will keep you—here." She pressed one of his hands over her breast, above the heart. "You cannot stop me. And I will wait for you. Always."

At home, all that awaited him was Louise. She had turned cold and unresponsive with the passing years. They would never have a child now. But he could come back here whenever he wanted. And once you'd tasted ecstasy at a certain level, you passed through a door that closed forever. He studied the idea for just long enough to discover that he couldn't look away.

"I cannot forget you, A-liss-ter."

The Chaloems must have sent her to him. But since the two of them had made love, since the door had closed behind him, things were different. Only certain things could be faked; the tears in her voice, the clutch on his arm, they were real.

"You've only known me for a few hours," he mumbled. "How can you love me?"

"How? There is something I must tell you." She was crying openly now. "They said I must do this."

"I know."

"Yes. You know. You are clever man. But . . . but they didn't tell me that you were kind. And . . . and you don't know what it means to have a nothing life. Now, I have something. Little, little. But something."

When she laid her head on his chest he felt tears. Somewhere at the back of his own eyes lurked a sensation that he vaguely recognized but could not put a name to. Then he remembered: he, too, was starting to cry. For a loveless, childless marriage. Lost hopes. A romance that he had believed he would never know.

He began to stroke her hair, trying to mine the words that would explain to her why it could never be. But long before the first one came, he fell asleep.

He was woken by P'ia giving him a rough shake. "Wake up," she hissed in his ear. "You must *wake up.*"

He opened his eyes. Vestiges of gray light filtered through the blind. P'ia ran from the room, he heard her bare feet thump on the wooden floor of the passage. Scrutton leaped off the bed, heart aflutter. All his senses screamed danger. He pulled on his clothes and stuffed things into his bag with the efficient speed engendered only by fright.

Lloyd appeared in the doorway. "We're leaving," he snapped. "Grab your gear and come. *Now!*"

Scrutton followed hard at his heels; across the courtyard they ran, out into the compound, where the rest of the party were already waiting. Scrutton saw Rin and Tin race to take up position on either side of the entrance to the clearing, rifles at the ready. Siri was arguing with the truckdriver.

"Leave the lorry," Lloyd shouted. "They'll be coming up the track; no chance. Northern path!"

He grabbed Scrutton's hand and hauled him to the back of the house. Seconds later, they were thrashing through the jungle, twigs and creepers grazing Scrutton's terrified face. After they had gone about a dozen yards, Lloyd stopped, turned and knelt, pulling Scrutton down with him.

"What's up?" Scrutton breathed.

"Thai Rangers patrol, coming our way."

"*What?* I thought we were in Burma . . . "

"They don't give shit."

"But how—"

"That little incident you saw yesterday. The house blowing up." Lloyd raised himself a little to peer through the dense curtain of greenery all around them. "Some of the Burmese commies had been making a nuisance of themselves. Old Chaloem invited them to a parley."

It took a moment for the implications of this to sink in. "And they were at the house when—"

"Damn right they were. So someone's decided to go in for a little revenge."

Scrutton sank down on his haunches, sweating with the unaccustomed early morning exercise and dread for himself, for what might be happening to P'ia . . . "Where's the girl?" he whispered hoarsely.

"She'll be all right. Now *shut up.*" Lloyd gnawed his lips. "It's too quiet."

To Scrutton, however, the jungle seemed deafening. Monkeys gibbered in the trees, invisibly high above his head. Birds sang. Close to where he cowered the grass parted as something slithered through it, and Siri's warning came back to him in a rush of dread: "Watch out for banded kraits . . . "

Lloyd plucked his sleeve. "Stick to me, don't take your eyes off my back, *don't stop.*"

He ran forward at the half-crouch. Before long Scrutton's face was bloody with scratches and the pin-prick wounds of insects. Daylight came on fast, but he sensed rather than saw it, for here in the dense undergrowth, half-jungle, half-forest, it remained ever dim.

Suddenly Lloyd broke through onto a sloping, muddy path and he swore, forcing Scrutton backward. "Down," he ordered. When Scrutton hesitated, Lloyd pushed him over, pressing an iron arm around his shoulders.

For a moment, nothing happened. Then Scrutton heard someone coming up the path.

Whoever it was moved slowly. Feet squelched in the mud, making pappy suction sounds. The footsteps approached to within a few inches of Scrutton's head. And stopped.

Lloyd spoke softly. A boy's voice answered him. Next second, Scrutton was lying in the mud alone.

He raised himself a little. Lloyd stood talking to one of the young Akha tribesmen. Scrutton's pent-up breath drained out of him in a moan of relief. Other footsteps squelched along the path toward them. Siri and his father emerged through the early morning mist, General Yang Po at their heels, with the second boy bringing up the rear.

"They've surrounded the house," Siri said agitatedly.

"Where's P'ia?" Alistair asked. And then, when no one replied, "*Where's P'ia?*"

"She went with the rest of the servants," Siri said. "She'll be all right."

A muttered conference ended with them all making off down the track, away from the house. Suddenly the silence behind them was rent with automatic fire and yells: the Rangers were going in. The leading Akha began to run, with old Chaloem right behind him.

Scrutton loped toward a hazy rectangle of yellow that steadily brightened to the brink of whiteness at the place where the path left the jungle and emerged into the open.

The enemy were there ahead of them. For an instant Scrutton was looking at something framed against the sun, a purplish, man-shaped figure, and then the firing began.

The initial burst dropped old Chaloem, who collapsed and rolled over without a sound. A bullet hit the first Akha boy, punching him backward against

Siri. It wasn't a clean kill. The boy went on wailing for a long time.

Scrutton burrowed back into the jungle. On the other side of the path, Lloyd jumped up holding both hands clenched together. As he wheeled around to face down the slope, sunlight glanced off something metal. The two shots sounded so close together that one might almost have been the ricochet of the other.

"Run!"

Scrutton didn't need to be told twice. He bounded up and sprinted along the path. He caught a glimpse of old Chaloem lying with his legs apart, one hand raised as if to bid farewell, and registered the Akha boy vainly trying to hold in the guts that flowed onto the path; then he was running past two black-clad bodies. He saw Lloyd stoop to pick up an automatic rifle. They came out of the jungle onto the side of a hill, planted thickly with opium. The path continued downward to a stream, perhaps a quarter of a mile away, in a deep gully. No one stopped to look back, but Scrutton knew that the Rangers, finding the house deserted, would be close on their heels. They splashed along the gully, where trees grew close to the water, affording some cover.

Now round thatched roofs could be seen in the distance, just visible above the rise of the land. Soon they were coming into a village, past scruffy plots of vegetables, a rusty, abandoned bicycle, squawking chickens, astonished peasants.

The hamlet was laid out haphazardly, but ahead of him Scrutton could see an open space. Parked to one side of it were three jeeps, with numbers painted on their hoods: the Rangers' transport. They had left one guard. While he was still struggling to draw his pistol, Lloyd shot him through the heart.

Siri flung himself behind the wheel of the second jeep and fired the ignition. Yang Po hauled himself

up beside him. Lloyd grabbed Scrutton, pushing him
into the back seat. The surviving Akha boy clung to
the awning frame. Lloyd sprayed the two other jeeps
with bursts from the automatic rifle, and they were
away.

After they'd careered about half a mile, Scrutton
caught a glimpse of several people running ahead of
them, waving frantically. Even with their backs to
him, something about one of those quarter-turned
faces looked familiar. Black tee shirt . . . he knew
that on its left breast would be stitched the words,
"Life. Go for Something."

"*Stop!*" he shrieked. "*It's P'ia!*"

Siri slowed slightly. The girl's dust- and tear-
stained face lifted itself in a plea to be rescued.
Scrutton grabbed her, somehow managing to heave
her onto his lap. Next second Siri had dropped a
gear and was accelerating hard.

Afterward, when memory of that headlong rush
back to Mong Hsat airstrip had faded, as even the
worst nightmares do, Scrutton would remember
only a brief, unreal snatch of conversation.

Siri had surrendered the wheel of the jeep to
Lloyd and now lay slumped next to Scrutton in the
back seat, with one hand supporting his head, eyes
closed.

"I'm sorry about your father," the barrister murmured. And, when Siri lifted his haggard head, he
went on: "You didn't have time to collect your tape
cassette. Did you?"

For a moment, Siri's expression did not change.
Then, with increasing anxiety, he groped in one
pocket after another before relapsing into immobili-
ty, his face expressionless.

Scrutton felt many things. Fear, and relief and
pain were among them, yes; but what he principally

experienced on that ghastly road was exhilaration at being alive. It affected him curiously. He recognized that over the last few highly paid, risk- and responsibility-free years he had become a dangerously bored man.

"I've always wanted to own a Louis Vuitton suitcase," he murmured, bending to kiss P'ia's uncomprehending face.

Lloyd took one hand from the steering wheel, unbuttoned the top left pocket of his shirt, and glanced at the incriminating tape cassette forgotten by Siri in his haste. But Scrutton, pleasantly distracted with P'ia, never noticed.

CHAPTER
13

LONDON. THE PRESENT

Roz wasn't responsible for editing the *Times* today—it wasn't "her" paper, in the jargon—so while keeping half an ear on the fag end of Radio Four's "PM" program she tried to catch up with some admin. Her heart wasn't in it.

Deputy editors were, by tradition and nature, either office managers or makers of opinion, and she definitely fell into the latter category. Howard Boissart, her chief, knew that. He also knew that she found it hard to mold opinion in the way he wanted. Roz likened her job to the vice presidency of the United States: one rung from the top, you had to carve out territory to call your own, with scope for your ambitions, while at the same time not getting hung with some initiative that could finish your career and prevent you from taking that final step up. A real bitch, in other words.

Howard had a gift for dangling tasty, provocative, ultra-dangerous morsels in front of her and standing back to watch what happened.

Roz decided she really couldn't take the NUJ's

pay claim any further this evening, so she drifted
down to the back bench. She sat in the chair normally reserved for Howard, who was still juggling
obituaries upstairs, and pulled the Atex keyboard
toward her. The green line across the top of the
screen read: "Times/Sunday Times." She logged on,
entered her password, thus causing the headline to
change to "Times" alone, and retrieved the list of
stories provisionally slated for next day's Page One,
called "pie-hold," for p. 1 hold.

But even here, at the heart of things, she couldn't
concentrate. Her attention wandered around the
long room, where assistant editors had begun to
hover in groups, discreetly checking that their stuff
was not being downgraded. Snippets of subbing conversations caught her ear:

"That Australian story needs a map." "We've got
one."

"It might make the basement on page four."

"Black magic, rape, incest . . . can't we lighten
page three?"

The wastepaper baskets were starting to fill up,
now, and the noise level, while never obtrusive, had
risen a decibel or two since she'd taken her seat.

"Put the funeral into pie-hold."

"Who's in the wire room? Bert, I said who's . . . "

From the TV set in the corner behind her left
shoulder the prime minister's voice suddenly res-
onated through the room, signaling the start of the
ITN early news. Roz pushed her keyboard away and
swiveled to focus on the screen. The senior night
editor was doing the same.

"Tony," she heard him say, "where did we put
the cabinet reshuffle? Only it looks as though . . . "

A few early leavers heralded the start of the
evening exodus: secretaries, assistant features editors. Roz was on the point of joining them when
Andrew Morris, the foreign editor, slipped into the

next chair and asked if she'd like to read a tasteless telex from their man in Bahrain reporting on a ritual circumcision that had gone sadly awry.

"WD U LIKE THIS PIECE," it concluded. "IF SO TX WHICH PIECE U WANT SOONEST."

"What did you reply?" she asked.

He handed her a sheet of flimsy. "While Little Ahmed's predic left no dry eye in house, eye regretfully chicken."

"Coward. Who's our guy out there?"

"Rob Benson."

"Well, say 'Hi' from me and tell him Roz Forbes has a thing about ritual circumcisions. Doncha lov'em?"

"Speaking for myself, no."

When Morris left, Roz decided that she'd definitely had enough. She was supposed to be going out to dinner tonight. On impulse she scribbled a telex giving her hosts' phone number and sent it to Johnny via her Telecom Gold mailbox, reluctant to have secretaries giggle over her private affairs. If affair was the right word, when your man never showed . . . perhaps Johnny would be none the worse for a botched ritual circumcision . . .

On further impulse, she plugged into the Profile database, searching for recent press articles that contained both the words "Thornton" and "trial." She called up the texts of the latest ones. Was it her imagination, or had sentiment at long last begun to change? Careful, she warned herself; no wishful thinking. But these write-ups seemed less assured, less *arrogant*, and as she logged off her face was thoughtful.

There wasn't much traffic; the journey to Hampstead took less than an hour. Because the Campions knew absolutely everyone, she was not surprised to have the door opened for her by a bespectacled monsignor in full rig, a glass of sherry held shoulder high in his left hand. "Oh, you disappoint me," he said, stepping aside for her to enter.

"And why, pray?"

"I was hoping you'd arrive with Ben Saunders. Then I could do the old one about 'the press are here, my Lord, together with the lady from the *Times*.'"

Roz laughed. "So Ben's coming, is he? How are you, Paul?"

"I'm just fine, ducks. Yourself?"

"So-so. Which bit can I kiss?"

The monsignor examined himself with quick, fussy movements of his head. "Well, you don't look like a ring kitten to me. Try a cheek . . . "

"Is it allowed?"

"No, but I can always repent."

She kissed his wrinkled cheek and he giggled. "So *that's* what all the fuss is about. Ah . . . I see 'the press' has arrived, after all."

Roz turned in time to see Ben Saunders pay off a taxi and start up the path toward the front door. Her lips set in a hard line. She wanted a session with him—alone.

"Why are you butlering?" she asked the monsignor, deliberately turning her back on Ben.

"Because we're hard up," Annie Campion said, as she came forward to take Roz's coat. "This is Paul's voluntary work for distressed gentlefolk. Hello, Ben; come inside, do."

Ben kissed her cheek and treated Paul to a cheery nod. "A word," he said to Roz, and then—"Annie, could Roz and I have five minutes alone?"

"Of course, my dear, how about the first floor den?"

Ben led the way upstairs. He climbed slowly, using the bannister for support like a man whose recent acquaintance with sleep had been brief and passing.

"Well?" Roz said eagerly, as he closed the door behind them. "Give!"

"Couple of things. I managed to track down the right Thai fellah for you. Copper in Bangkok, he knows all about the Chaloems and that." Ben produced an envelope from an inside pocket. "Tell Lutter the info's in there: who to speak to, Thai procedures for subpoenaing a witness, the lot."

"Thanks." She accepted the envelope with real gratitude. Lutter had got nowhere with the Thai authorities, and not for the first time she marveled at the way Ben succeeded where others failed.

"Can this Thai say anything about Scrutton?" she asked.

Ben lit a cigarette. "Not a dicky-bird."

"So we've still got nothing to use against him?"

"No. And yes."

Her eyes lit up. "What?"

For a long time he said nothing. Then he yawned, stretched, and asked: "Remember when we had lunch at the Indian restaurant . . . you wanted to know what I'd found out and I wouldn't tell you?"

"Of course."

"Well, just recently, a ray of light or two has begun to penetrate. Not much, just a trickle."

"Tell me!"

But he kept her dangling a moment longer, and she could see from his eyes that he'd been looking forward to this.

"The money that Scrutton splashes around the roulette table comes from Thai heroin. Heroin that's bought by the IRA for resale here in England."

He must have enjoyed the look on her face. Roz was conscious of the struggle being fought there: fascinated horror battling it out with an irrational desire to believe, and total, utter incredulity.

"Are you even remotely serious?" she breathed at last.

Instead of answering her directly, he said: "Scrutton's got something going with Brennan, Roz. I'm sure of that, now. Scrutton and the Krait are *connected.*"

"But that's imp—"

"Brennan's in London. Right now."

"What?"

Roz sank down into the nearest chair. "But why . . . how do you—"

"Never mind how I know, dearie, that's not part of our arrangement. What I'm saying to you is that before I wasn't prepared to let you in on what I'd found out because I couldn't get within sniffing distance of a witness. Now maybe, just maybe, I am. So that's the score."

"But Ben, don't you see? I need access, proper access to your sources. Two heads are going to be better than one."

"No. It's too dangerous, Roz."

"Dangerous?"

"I've been warned: one false move and my witness, if there *is* a witness, will dissolve into thin air. In particular, I've been warned not to have any truck with you. Got it?"

"A man's life is at stake. Thornton could die because of your attitude, you know that, don't you?"

"No. It's my scoop, Roz. My career, my life too."

"You'd let Frank die, just for a front page splash, is that it?"

He turned a haggard face toward her. "You know it isn't."

"I used to think I knew you pretty well, Ben. But . . . "

"When you were doling out money, you mean? Handouts?"

"Don't," she said wearily. "Please don't."

"I was divorced, on my uppers, and you saw me

through. Isn't that how it goes?"

"It'd got nothing to do with you. I did it for Kevin."

"Oh yeah? You'd have let *me* starve, is that it?" There was a long pause. "I think we'll back off," he said at last. "Don't you?"

She nodded and turned away, not wanting him to read her face. The divorce had been a bad trip for him, and for his son, Kevin. Roz was one of the few people to offer time and a sympathetic ear—plus money, which he had taken, and repaid, in silence. The money was nothing, but the emotional investment had been enormous and they both knew he could never reimburse her for that.

"Look," Ben said quietly, "just take it from me, Brennan's here and he's up to something and the London IRA are shitting themselves because they don't know what."

Roz said nothing for a while. Funny, she was thinking, funny how the best of friends often find it hardest to communicate . . .

"So," she said at last. "Brennan's arrived just as Scrutton—"

"Is getting ready to go into the box, yes. A pretty long coincidence. That occurred to me also, my darling-oh."

"But this isn't public knowledge?"

"Right."

"So—"

"So I need a very large scotch indeed."

He made for the door.

"Ben . . . Ben, I'm sorry for snapping. I'm grateful, you know that, really I am."

"It's not my fault," he said, turning in the doorway.

Roz stared at him. "What isn't?"

"That you've let yourself get emotionally involved with Thornton."

For a moment, yes, she did actually wish she had let him starve, after his divorce, him and his brat Kevin too, for that matter. She was on the point of telling him so at the top of her voice when the realization that he was absolutely right about Frank hit her below the breastbone; she staggered slightly, and closed her eyes.

By the time she'd opened them again, Ben had let himself out and was already at the bottom of the stairs. It was several minutes before Roz could bring herself to follow.

Annie Campion maintained what was perhaps the last genuine "salon" in London. Her drawing room was full of elegant men and women, nearly all of whom Roz knew at least by sight. She stood on the threshold, looking this way and that for Ben, but there was no sign of him. Then Tom Campion came forward to greet her, and before she knew it she found herself ensconced in one-half of a loveseat, with Tom pressing a frigid gin and tonic into her hand and Saunders temporarily expelled from her mind.

Roz adored Tom. He was big-boned, with a somewhat fruity voice, and his lawn-short white hair had long ago become a trademark, instantly recognizable, formidably potent. His smile was shaped like a Spanish tilde, making his expression wry, even skeptical.

"How many committees are you running now?" she asked him. "I ought to update your obit."

He laughed as he bent to kiss her. "I'm between engagements. The race relations people are dangling carrots and there was talk of something in Brussels. But I've really got nothing on at the moment."

In his mouth, the graceful disclaimer assumed a rather specialized meaning. He was master of the Oxford college where he'd studied as an undergraduate, deputy chairman of the National Tourist board, author of half a dozen books on economics and a regular contributor to *Forbes Magazine*. His weekly column in Saturday's *Financial Times* was said to be read by more people in socioeconomic classes A and B than any other piece of repeat journalism. So when he said he had nothing on at the moment, Roz sighed and said, "I suppose that means they've just appointed you head of the civil service."

"That's next week. Talking of which, we've invited a bugbear tonight, specially for you."

She picked the slice of lemon from her glass and squeezed it. "Oh? Who?"

"Brian Oakley."

Juice from the lemon slice sprayed her face and she swore inwardly at Tom's power to make people's fingers clench. "He's not a bugbear," she said. "He's sweet."

"What? A member of the Tory cabinet. Hunting, shooting . . . hanging." Tom's bright blue eyes narrowed slightly and the tilde shaped his lips. "Wait there," he murmured. "I'll fetch him."

While he was gone she surveyed the crush, looking for Ben but without success. There were too many places for him to hide in this spacious room, a haven of chintzy comfort that scarcely hinted at her hosts' vast wealth. For all her remarkable sources, Roz had no real idea what they were worth. In England, it wasn't "done" to know about people's finances. She remembered how as a child her burrowings in mother's rosewater-scented chest of drawers used to reveal buff envelopes full of bank statements, vaguely suggesting that her parents "had money"; but neither of them ever told her exactly how much and she could never bring herself to ask.

The Campions certainly knew how to mix a social cocktail. Roz fielded a wink from a trade union general secretary, propped up against the wall next to the mantelpiece, one hand resting on the wrist of a pretty, pretentious fashion editor whom Roz disliked. She recognized a Northern novelist and his latest wife (or was it his daughter, so hard to tell these days), and an investigative journalist who'd made her name at the unexpectedly late age of sixty, with a regular TV slot dealing with environmental issues. Her husband, something on the *Guardian*, didn't seem to have come tonight.

Roz was just brooding on why couples no longer went around together as they used to, when Brian Oakley slid into the other half of the loveseat and said, "Hello."

Even before she turned to look at him her instincts fired, telling from the timbre of his voice that much was amiss. She started to tingle in that special way reserved for journos. Story. She could smell story.

"Hi, Brian. Is Marinella here?"

"Over by the window, taking the consolations of religion."

Roz followed his eye, wishing her own man still looked at her like that, to see Oakley's young Italian wife deep in animated conversation with Monsignor Paul. The jealous phrase "gorgeous, pouting" put its head around a door of her mind, only to beat a hasty retreat when she flung something at it.

"So," Roz said. "What have you been up to? The Downing Street mob."

She wasn't sure if he smiled, or if his lips had merely given way to a nervous tic. Tonight he looked tired, as ministers invariably did, but there seemed more to it than simple fatigue. She suspected he wasn't well, which was strange, because he was only in his late thirties, very lean, very fit, a gym enthusiast, she remembered.

"I've got something I want to ask you," she blurted out, suddenly reckless. "Is it true that Brennan's in England?"

He had iron self-control, but not even that was proof against this question. His face turned pale, he jerked his head around . . . and that proved to be his undoing, for it enabled Roz to read confirmation of Ben's rumor in the minister's eyes.

"Interesting," he said at last. "I was hoping to dazzle you with that one. Never mind. Are you ready to listen?"

"Here?"

"As good as anywhere—it's impossible to hear yourself think in this room, let alone eavesdrop state secrets."

He was trying hard to regain the initiative, but Roz was neither deceived nor inclined to sympathy.

"Now you wait a minute," she said. "On what basis are we talking here?"

"Deep background. No names, non-attributable."

"I can't stop you talking. It's a free country, for the moment." Then she caught herself up. "Sorry, Brian. You're indisputably the best of a bad bunch. *Don't*"—she held up her hands, palms outward—"take that as a compliment. But I'm listening."

"The Krait . . . *is* in England."

"But how . . . when?"

"Maybe the beginning of last week. We had a tip-off from the usual Sinn Fein grudge merchant. But he'd been right enough in the past for us to give him the benefit of the doubt. He told us to watch for a Salvation Army officer."

"Nice twist. Ah! There's a big Salvationist conference on in London at the moment, isn't there?"

"That's right. Anyway, MI5 came up with an American colonel who was supposed to be staying at a house in Norbury. The landlady recognized Brennan's photo at once, though he'd gone by then, of course. He didn't take the flight shown on his return ticket, we checked that."

"Why no publicity so far? I mean, surely—"

His lips extended into a humorless smile.

"I see. Outvoted."

"Red faces all round. Notwithstanding a maximum state of alert at all ports of entry, someone let him in. After our informer had done his stuff, but before Five had stretched and yawned and scratched its arse."

"And we know how popular failure is at Number Ten."

"Don't we just."

This was the first time she'd ever heard him voice a criticism, however oblique, about a cabinet decision. But she'd got her teeth into it by now and the gibes could wait.

"Any leads?"

"A couple. Everyone's looking busy."

"I'll bet!" She was angry—with Ben for sniffing the story first, and with Oakley for restricting it to deep background. "Brian, you've got to let this one rip."

He could not manage to keep a flicker of triumph out of his eyes. She saw it.

"Oh, you bastard! *She* told you to do it this way, didn't she?"

"I just want to make sure that the story's given to somebody who knows her stuff. To you, in other words."

Roz snorted. "Wrong department, sunshine! Howard Boissart is the man for you. He'll tow any old party line you throw him. I won't."

"Do me a favor, Roz," he said quietly; and then, as if to underline the real message, he repeated, "Do *me* a favor."

"Why should I?"

"Because Brennan's murdered women and children, here, in Germany and in Northern Ireland. He blew up Deal barracks, he masterminded Eniskillen. Our specialists are convinced he's a psychopath. Suppose he strikes again and people weren't warned to be on the lookout?"

"I'll warn them, Brian, in my paper in my way. And on something this sensitive I will *not* be a party to deep background from a cabinet minister. Put out a press release."

"But how would you *feel*?" He became animated. "Children blown to smithereens, innocent housewives out for a morning's shopping . . . you want another Harrods, is that it?"

"Don't be crass. And don't expect the *Times* to bail you out."

"I hear what you say." His tone was harsh. "Perhaps it's time word got around that the *Times* is a little less wonderful on the Irish issue than it used to be."

"What's that meant to mean?"

"It means that you're sounding like an IRA apologist."

She was ready to explode, but he cut through her protests in a voice that caused heads to turn.

"Don't you people understand what this war is all about? It's about *image*, Roz. Our image, the IRA's image. And if you write up a story like this with the wrong slant, it's a bonanza for the IRA."

She nodded forcibly. "The truth often hurts. No, Brian. File a press release; hold a conference. Unleash Ingham or whistle up Boissart, if you must. But I will not do this."

"I see. So, at last we know where the *Times* really stands on a number of issues."

"A *number*—"

Oakley had been staring at the wall, but now he turned bitter eyes to her and said, "At least you're consistent. The Krait. The IRA. That damn Thornton trial."

She had known for ages that he resented her attempts to derail the *Times* from the party line on Thornton. But the realization that he could score this kind of point while still in a cabinet that was desperate to keep secret its failure to contain the Krait took her beyond mere irritation into the realms of white hot anger.

"Now listen to me," she began. But then Annie started to shepherd the guests in to dinner, and Tom Campion joined them.

"I love a good fight," he said cheerily. "If it's knives, could I trouble you both to move into the kitchen? This carpet's a shocker for stains."

"Brilliant timing," Roz said, making a wry face. "We were just starting on the trial."

"Oh, that!" Tom beamed proudly. "Did either of you know that I was at school with the prosecution's star witness?"

"What, Scrutton?" Though Roz could hardly feel surprised: Tom knew simply *everyone*.

"What was he like?" Brian sounded eager to know.

"Ooh, like all of us at that age, pretty deplorable. Mind you, I was quite a bit older than him, we didn't know each other that well."

"Was he a bully?" Roz said.

To her surprise, Tom answered, "No. He was overbearing, rather than a bully. 'Bull-*ish*,' if you like. He used to take bods under his wing, was rather good at it actually. I think it suited him to be seen in the role of uncle-protector."

"Was he as clever as he makes out?" Brian asked.

"Sound. People used to say that about him quite a lot, as I recall. 'Sound in the classroom, useful on the games field.' That was Alistair Scrutton."

"Middle of the road," Roz murmured. She was wondering how Brian knew that Scrutton made himself out to be clever.

Some of the guests were congregating by the double doors to the dining room. Roz noticed Ben among them and felt a momentary reprise of the resentment that had suffused her earlier. How *dare* he put a scoop above a man's life? But then ... what was he having to go through in order to pick up his information? Roz faced the question reluctantly, wanting results, not moral hassles.

Now that the crowd had thinned out, she felt exposed. She became aware of people looking at the trio of which she formed part, and made an attempt to stand up. But Tom forestalled her by saying, "Brian, it's common ground where I come from that the Tory divisions are exercising on Salisbury plain. Am I right?"

Oakley's eyes narrowed. "Sorry, never did make much headway with Greek."

"Oh, come off it." Tom sounded uncharacteristically testy. "No one's been hanged in this country for years. You're playing it to the limit to see who blinks. A hike in interest rates, inflation up a couple of points, and *that's* when the Goddess of Mercy will wave her magic wand."

"The government that cares," Roz interjected bitterly. "Yes, I've heard that too. But I don't believe it."

"And why?"

"Because a swing for Thornton is a swing to the Right. There are no votes in mercy, Tom."

"Roz. Think, just for a minute. This is England. The death penalty's ancient history. European Convention, Sixth Protocol ... look into your heart and tell me: do you really believe that Thornton will hang? *Really?*"

Roz said nothing. There had been a time when Frank seemed like the most important issue she'd ever encountered, or was ever likely to. She had spoken at Amnesty meetings, she had maneuvered her paper this way and that, she'd become secretary to the Labor party's "Halt the Trial" campaign, on Saturdays she carted petitions around London, checking off postal districts, until her feet wanted to melt into the pavement. She told herself that she was doing it for Frank and for justice.

But in her bleaker moments, with half a bed yawning empty beside her and hours to kill before dawn brought orders to face another day, she knew what she was really up to. This was sublimation in its purest form: losing yourself in a noble cause. And the beauty of it, the quality that outshone all the others, was an innate sense of certainty that she must inevitably win. Thornton would not walk to the gallows. You simply did not hang people in this country. This was England.

The room had almost emptied now. When Tom loped off to shepherd the tail-end Charleys to their dinner, Roz and Brian followed him. One of the double doors connecting the two rooms was already shut. Roz assumed that Brian would stand aside to let her through, but instead he pushed the other door until it was ajar, wheeled around, and rested his back against the wall. His face was white.

"Tom's wrong," he said hoarsely. "God, he couldn't be more wrong."

Roz stared at him, torn between the memory of their recent quarrel and concern for someone she liked. "Brian, are you all right?"

He whirled around to place a hand against the wall, resting his forehead on it. "They'll hang him."

Roz's life stopped, just for the space of a heartbeat. Then she came back, but as somebody different. "What did you say?" she whispered.

"The PM wants to see how people react to an execution. It's a perfect opportunity. The penalty for treason's always been death. Everyone loves a Royal, hates the IRA."

"But the Sixth Protocol forbids—"

"We've never adopted it. And we won't," he added caustically.

"Brian, say you're joking."

"Joking!" He stood upright and turned to face her. "This weekend's poll of polls will give us a clear lead over Labor of nine and a half points. Last week, nine. The week before that, eight point nine. That's when the Thornton trial began. Before that—two!"

"And you're part of it. Part of this . . . this *vicious*, hardline, cynical . . . *orgy*. You. Brian Oakley."

"That's right," he agreed. "Me. And it's making me sick."

"Resign."

"I can't."

"Why?"

"Because I believe I can do more good on the inside."

"Bullshit! You want to know what you believe? I'll tell you, my friend—that having a chauffeur-driven Rover and a red box is the be-all and end-all of existence."

"We've known each other for Christ knows how long and you can say *that*?"

She resisted the urge to hurl back at him, "It's because I've known you all those years that I say it," for that would not only have been cheap, it would have been untrue. Brian Oakley was, at bottom, an honorable man.

"Look," he said. "On the personal level, I'd support you."

"Oh, thank God! For one minute I—"

"But nothing in life is simple. I'm a career politician. I need a following. And if I want to get anything done, this is no time to be seen breaking ranks with the most popular Conservative leader since Churchill."

"Even if it means the odd sacrifice. Just as long as *you* aren't the one who has to make it."

"No. Even if it means leading from the front."

One of the doors swung open to reveal Annie, beckoning. "Come on, you two. Romance can wait 'til after the pud."

"Coming," Brian mumbled. "Sorry." But as he moved to follow their hostess, he found time to say to Roz, "Remember—deep background."

"What?" She grabbed his arm. "You tell me these things and expect to remain non-attributable? You can't be *serious*!"

"I'm deadly serious. This is a leak, Roz. I've put my career on the line for you, and by God!"—his face tightened—"if you let me down, you'll wish you'd never been born."

She started to protest, but he silenced her with a cut of his hand. "Just remember this. A time will come when Thornton needs a friend in cabinet. Because he is guilty."

"You can't say that until the jury—"

"I've read the prosecution statements. As in any other trial there are gray areas, of course there are, but basically it's an open and shut case. He'll be convicted. And do you know what? I'll be the only man in England able *and willing* to speak up for him."

"You'd really do that?"

"I might," he said coldly. "It depends. Let's see how the Krait story runs, shall we?"

And on that brutal note he left her, striding to take his place halfway down one side of the table without a backward glance. So Roz swallowed her bile and plumped herself down next to Monsignor Paul.

"Spooning with a cabinet minister," he ruminated. "Are you in need of spiritual guidance, my beautiful child, or can you cope by yourself? Or were you, by any chance, discussing our friend Mr. Thornton?"

Brian Oakley was preparing to spread his napkin over his lap, but on hearing the churchman's words he dropped it and clenched his fists, looking about the table as if for support. Unless a cynically amused smile from Ben Saunders counted, he was out of luck. The conversation had already slipped into that well-worn groove while the others were waiting for the two late arrivals.

"Is it true," someone said, "that you got him the American job, Roz?"

She managed a tight smile. "Who's been rumor-mongering?"

"The gutter press?" Ben Saunders suggested.

"You really shouldn't talk about the *Catholic Herald* in those terms," said Monsignor Paul. "It's scarcely polite."

Roz waited for the laughter to abate, staring down at the cloth. She was grateful when someone filled one of the wineglasses in front of her.

"It's true that I helped him get the job, I suppose," she admitted at last.

People were falling silent and turning to stare at her, but suddenly she didn't care. She felt an urgent need to get the story off her chest, make confession; and what better opportunity would she have than now, with a prince of the Roman Catholic church by her side?

The chablis proved excellent, for which she was grateful, because something told her that this was going to be a long night. She took another sip and plunged.

"It was me that introduced him to Gephard."

CHAPTER
14

LONDON. SPRING 1969

When Frank Thornton walked into Harrison Gephard's suite at the Grosvenor House, that spring day in 1969, one thing filled his horizon: losing Louise Shelley, the woman he loved. After a sleepless night he'd risen early to drink black coffee and try to hypnotize himself into believing that life would somehow go on. He entered the suite as an automaton, indifferent to his fate.

His consequently laid-back air made a wonderful first impression on Gephard.

"Hi, there," he said, shaking hands. "How y'all doing?"

"How do you do?"

"Fahn, jes' fahn."

Gephard appeared to be in his late thirties, a tall, lanky Texan with an air of relaxed confidence. There was a very English look to him. Only his accent gave the game away, and soon even that mellowed into a mild, mid-Atlantic drawl.

"Well now . . . " He sat well forward on a sofa, resting his elbows on his knees and clasping his hands in front of him. "I'm in London to set up the first phase of our new English operation. North Sea oil. I got a smell of it back in Houston and it seemed mighty pretty to me. My daddy—another Harrison, by the way—Daddy's really the man in charge, but he's getting old. A real Anglophile: lives in Lincolnshire, most of the time, tending his beef and his art collection both. He's not interested in expanding any more. I am."

"I see. Excuse me, but I'm afraid I don't know anything about your company, Mr. Gephard."

"Call me Harrison. Well, truth is, we're big in Texas, and kind of small pretty well everyplace else, so don't feel bad about it. We're the Gephard Foundation now, though the company's had quite a few names since Big Daddy Geph founded it back in the last century. He was my granddaddy. Took a slice of land in what's now Houston from the Allen brothers back in the 1850s—none of this means much to you, huh?"

"'Fraid not."

"Well, at first, Big Daddy Geph had cattle. Then he struck oil. Built himself a refinery. Typical Texan story, this. He bought hotels, built a few houses. My daddy was the same; after Geph died, he just went on getting bigger and bigger. More hotels. Bought an airline; well, hell, I say bought, he won it in a poker game in Pasadena."

Frank's eyes widened. "Goodness. I thought that kind of thing only happened in films."

Harrison slapped his knees and leaned back, laughing. "You never saw Texas yet, right?"

"Right."

"We Texans say that when we joined the Union, we annexed the rest of the States. Only way to know Texas is to go there. Which brings me around to the point of our meeting, heck, I'm sorry, you must have things to do, this being Sunday and all . . . "

Despite his pain, Frank could not but warm to this man. "Harrison," he said, "I can assure you of two things. First, every word you've said I find fascinating. Secondly, I have nothing to do today, because I've just been jilted."

His facial muscles ached with the strain of keeping back tears as he said that. Harrison must have sensed it, for instead of replying at once he stood up and went across to the phone, which he used to order coffee from room service. By the time he'd finished, Frank was composed again.

"You're kind of unusual for an Englishman," Harrison said as he sat down again. "That's the Texan way, to show your operation scars right off."

"Oh, look, I'm sorry, I didn't mean to—"

"No, no, you don't understand! Thanks to my daddy, I love England. I have all my clothes made in London, I adore the climate, the theater, my *God!* how I adore your theater . . . but English people, well, I have to say I find them strange."

"In what way?"

Harrison eyed him good-humoredly. "Would you be offended if I said that many of you are tight-assed?"

"I'd agree with you up to the hilt," Frank laughed, thinking of his stint in chambers.

"So when you just burst out, 'my girl's written me a Dear John,' that's refreshing."

The coffee arrived, putting a stop to further conversation. Frank watched in surprise as Harrison gave the waiter folding money and wished him a nice day.

"Before he went semi-retired in this country, Daddy got himself into a mess," Harrison said, sitting down again. 'He'd no time for accounts, that kind of stuff. Now Europe isn't Texas; over here, you don't just build a fence around a chunk of land and say it's yours down the barrel of a shotgun. So

I'm starting up here the right way. I'm opening an operational headquarters in Aberdeen, next month, but I need an office here in London, too. That's where you come in . . . maybe."

"I'm listening."

"I need an in-house legal department, headed by general counsel with commercial expertise and the ability to communicate. I'm prepared to invest a heap of time in training the right man for the job." He put down his coffee cup and pointed at Frank. "Clear your head of legal double-talk. I need someone I can *deal* with. Someone I can call up at two in the morning and say, Hey! You get your butt moving right now, 'cause I want some *answers*. A mover and a shaker. And to be honest with you—"

"There aren't many lawyers like that in England."

"Right. That's why I'm looking for somebody not yet tainted. When I find the right guy, I'll pay him thirty thousand pounds a year."

Frank's jaw dropped.

"Yes. It's money. Whoever gets the job will earn it."

Frank put his cup down on the table. He was trembling slightly; the effect of more coffee on what he'd drunk earlier, lack of sleep, emotional trauma, all these things played their part. But what really gave him the shakes was the sudden conviction that he had to jump on this wagon before it passed him by. He yearned to do something, go somewhere, be someone different.

Unfortunately, it looked impossible.

"Harrison," he said. "I don't know anything about anything. I've got a first-class law degree from Oxford, a year's pupilage in good commercial chambers, and a few months working for the Inland Revenue. That's it. What you need is superman."

"You're thinking English. Try thinking American."

"You've lost me."

"I come from a country that's run by lawyers. They can do it not because they're good lawyers, but because they're good men who happen to be lawyers."

"Even so, I just don't have the kind of experience you're looking for."

"No one's suggesting that you do. If you were offered the job, and took it, you'd be working alongside one of my legal team in the States for the first few years. He'd train you up and make sure you knew all the key people. Then you'd take over as general counsel, Europe."

There was a long silence. Frank realized that the only thing holding him back was fear of failure. To take this job, and make a mess of it . . . wouldn't that be worse than not accepting it in the first place? But then a saying, bittersweet and wholly apposite, came into his mind: better to have loved and lost than never to have loved at all.

"There's one other thing," Harrison said. "Whoever gets this job has to be prepared to relocate to Houston at some point. Maybe you read someplace that we abolished slavery?"

"It isn't true?"

"Not if you work for Harrison L. Gephard it ain't. So what do you say?"

Frank gawked at him. "You're offering me the job?"

"Sure am."

"Then I say . . . yes!"

Harrison beamed. "Fine. Let's go have ourselves a drink in the bar, celebrate some."

As they reached the door, a thought struck Frank. He'd bought two theater tickets, meaning to take Louise, but that was out now and the prospect of going alone appalled him.

"Are you free next Wednesday?" he asked. "I've

got seats for the Aldwych. *As You Like It*, the RSC."

Harrison's eyes widened. "You're asking the boss to go to the theater with you?"

"Yes. You said you adored English theater. I like you. And I suppose I'm thinking American."

Harrison guffawed. When he put an arm around Frank's shoulders the young man resisted his habitual urge to cringe; after all, he would be among touchers from now on.

"You and me," Harrison said as they went out of the suite, "are going to be friends."

Harrison's wife, Wendy May, was a plump, heavily made-up woman. She wore tailored jeans over her hand-stitched rodeo boots, a rattlesnake belt, and a blue silk shirt that clashed unrealistically with ruby and diamond bracelets, one for each wrist. Frank liked her from the word go. She was fresh, candid and, he sensed, an honest dealer, even though Gephard had introduced her as a "realtor," which he gathered was equivalent to an estate agent.

"Harrison says you need a place to stay," she said. "So first thing we do is go buy you an apartment."

It was Frank's second day in Houston. He eyed her uneasily, still nauseous with jet lag. "I'm not sure I can afford—"

"Yes, you can, 'cause Harrison's lending you the money. He's briefed me good. Don't worry, he'll take it back off your pay check every month, and it's *important* that you buy."

"Why?"

"'Cause this town's about to take off. Harrison don't want you missing out on that. He likes you, son. You're his hunch of the month. You're going to help him rebuild this city from the basement up."

That same afternoon, Wendy May took him on a tour of the city. She began by showing him the house she and Harrison lived in out at River Oaks, to the west: a colonial mansion with porticos and a verandah and a vast swimming pool. The whole of the back of the house had been extended with a conservatory, as high as the second floor, which was where Harrison did much of his work, a light, airy, glass room seventy feet long and half as wide again, filled with trees growing almost to the ceiling, date palms, asparagus ferns, gardenias, and hanging plants of every description. Frank saw it and gasped.

"That's what you're aiming at, honey." Wendy May stood feet astride with hands on hips, making no attempt to conceal her pride. "This here is all about motivation. Stare and eat your heart out."

"It's beautiful."

"You thought Texans were all shit-kickers— that's what we call cowboys, by the way. It isn't so."

She lent him a map and drove him around, explaining the suburbs.

"Houston's a car city. You can't walk anyplace. It's too hot and it's becoming dangerous. And you don't want to go northeast. That's black."

He'd taken to the Montrose district, and Wendy May offered cautious encouragement. "Used to be more fashionable than now, until folks started to move out to places like Braeswood and Houston Heights. But it'll come back."

He found what he wanted down a leafy avenue off Allen Parkway, not far from the Buffalo Bayou, a newly constructed, eight-story apartment complex complete with janitor and underground parking. A fifth-floor apartment was vacant.

"Can I afford it, though?" he asked uncertainly.

"Sure you can. I know the realtor who's handling this sale, he'll come down a ways."

So later that week he'd signed the papers and become the owner of his own apartment. He furnished it cheaply and simply, his only concession to extravagance being when he blew the remnants of his savings on floor-to-ceiling shelves for the second bedroom, thus converting it into his library. When his books arrived from England and he stacked them, they looked disappointingly few. He had a lot of old Penguin paperbacks, some in orange covers, some in green, others yet in blue. Depressed by the small amount of space they occupied, he rearranged them by color, rather than by author's name. Afterward they still seemed lost against those vast expanses of wooden shelving, but the configuration pleased him.

Frank was a compulsive book buyer. During the next seven years, he circumnavigated the globe more than fifteen times on Gephard business and for pleasure. By then, the shelves were so full that he had to buy tables on which to stack his latest acquisitions. But he still kept to his original layout, placing every book precisely by the color of its jacket, so that entering the library was to find yourself inside a rainbow, with the deepest red spines flowing seamlessly through oranges, yellows, greens, blues, purples, and mauves. The room became a talking point at Frank's parties, which were themselves a talking point.

Eventually, Frank was never sure quite when, it became obvious that he wasn't going back to England after all. His destiny lay in America, and it was a glorious one. Success didn't spoil him, although he achieved it on a scale that would have ruined a man with less character. It was property that made his name and his fortune. He arrived in Houston to find a city preparing to reconstruct itself.

Texans had never taken kindly to zoning laws. A man bought himself a few acres and expected to be able to build on it what he chose, be that farmhouse or factory, apartment block or abattoir. Prior to the late Sixties, this hadn't mattered too much in Houston: the "Big Thicket," a pine forest that visitors unexpectedly found covering huge swathes of the state, grew up to the back gardens of its then still relatively compact northern suburbs, and for the most part what is now Greater Houston was flat farmland. The Gephards and a dozen like him had already started to change that by the time of Frank's arrival.

He rapidly came to know as much about the Houston property scene as any man alive. As a rare Englishman in Texas, he commanded a certain awestruck respect counterbalanced by a feeling in the state's good ole' boys that here was a Limey who could be overreached. They were wrong. Deals that looked so sweet at the time turned to ashes as vendors saw him roll back the city boundaries to the horizon and beyond. He became a specialist in lapsed covenants, knowing precisely when to buy sites that would shortly fall free of contractual restrictions on their use. He bought into Chimney Rock early, for just that reason; when the Galleria came along, the Gephard Foundation unexpectedly found itself sitting on neighboring real estate worth twenty-five times its purchase price.

By the early Seventies, the national bird of Texas had become the building crane. Frank heard that joke in a bar, thought about it, and persuaded Harrison to buy a small steel works that was going begging down by Galveston. They concentrated on cheap, easily manufactured scaffolding and cranes until they'd made the works pay for itself; then they branched into building girders and made yet another fortune.

Nineteen seventy-six was a key year for both men. Frank's mother died, of a brain tumor. One minute she was doing the washing-up, she turned to her husband, said: "Oh, God, this head," and died.

He was broken up by grief. His mother had some funny ways, she'd never lost her knack for embarrassing him in public, but he had loved her deeply. For a while he could not sleep or eat or work. Because he was a thoughtful man, he realized that much of what he felt could be attributed to anger and guilt. Why wasn't I there? he reproached himself; when she needed me, why couldn't I be by her side . . . ?

He knew that she had wanted him to go to America, to better himself. But she hadn't bargained for the absence of grandchildren; that had not been a term of the deal they'd tacitly struck before he walked out of the house on his way to Heathrow. He stood with head bowed in the crematorium chapel, so cold and clean and devoid of atmosphere, recognizing himself as a breaker of emotional contracts and human hearts. You did not have to pay damages for either, though. You walked away from the debacle and carried it with you at the same time; that was the only price.

Oddly enough, he began his real climb to power within the Gephard Foundation through another death. Because Harrison's father lived most of the year in England, Frank somehow never got to meet him. Then, in the summer of 1976, the old man died while on one of his rare visits to the States.

Frank read the account of the funeral in the *Houston Chronicle* and was surprised to see how much space the event commanded. The speaker of the House of Representatives attended, along with a dozen other members of Congress, and the president of the United States sent a wreath. Three of the South's most prominent Baptist ministers officiated at the burial, including Dr. W. A. Criswell, even then on his way to being the best-known preacher in the country. There were lengthy articles on Gephard Senior's upbringing in the west of the state, his war service in Europe (he'd been a colonel in the U.S. Marines), which saw the beginning of his love affair with all things English, his ranching and drilling empires, his charitable donations. Tucked away in one corner of an inside page was a bare reference to his four wives, although the bars of Montrose, where Frank sometimes drank, were also a fruitful source of information about several ladies who never quite made it to the altar.

One televised sequence stayed in Frank's mind long afterward. The burial had already taken place, and the hundreds of mourners were dissipating along the cemetery's pathways. Only a few cars had been allowed as far as the grave. One of them, a stretched limousine, belonged to the speaker of the House. The camera caught a few seconds of him deep in conversation with Harrison. The speaker moved slightly, to reveal Harrison's taut face. He was frowning as he looked into the middle distance, his lips pulled tightly together. Frank knew he was considering an offer, and for some reason that notion troubled him. He longed to find out what flavor apple the serpent had extended to his boss in the mellow sunlight of a Texan autumn afternoon.

But when, more than a month later, Harrison finally got around to summoning Frank, the mystery only deepened.

The Texan pointed his visitor in the direction of one of the wicker chairs set around the desk. He had dark patches under his eyes.

"It knocked me back," Harrison acknowledged. "Seventy-eight, but he'd pass for sixty right easy. Rode right up until the last day of his life. But Jeezus, what a mess he left behind him."

"Is there anything I can do?"

"Maybe."

Harrison, fiddling with a paperknife, seemed to lose the thread again. Then, as if suddenly becoming aware of Frank's presence, he said, "Daddy came from Jefferson, originally . . . you ever been to Jefferson?"

Frank shook his head.

"No, course not. Must excuse me, Frank." He sat up straighter in his chair, tossing the knife to one side. "Jefferson's in east Texas. Used to be a great town, but the railway passed it by and so it died. Daddy moved west, up by Lubbock. Big spread; million acres. More. Hell of a place to live, though. Flat. You can drive a day, exchangin' one horizon for another jes' exactly the same. Mesquite everywhere. Cockleburs." Harrison shook his head. "No wonder he settled in England."

Frank sensed that this rigmarole was Harrison's way of avoiding a difficult issue.

"Inheritance Act," Harrison said suddenly. "Ever hear of it?"

"What?"

Harrison fiddled with some papers on his desk, selected a letter, and slowly began to read. "The Inheritance (Provision for Family and Dependents) Act . . . it's an English statute." He paused. "Seems if a guy dies domiciled in England leaving a girlfriend, she can claim against his estate, and, well . . . Daddy had a girl, in England. Hell, he had several. One of them is suing."

"I'm so sorry," Frank said, conscious of how inadequate it sounded.

"Yeah. Me too."

"But you said something about domicile . . . was your father really domiciled in England? It's awfully hard to lose domicile of birth, and surely that would be here in Texas?"

"Maybe, maybe not. This English law firm thinks it could go either way. Now, look. I need someone I can trust real bad right now. Daddy . . . " He hesitated. "Daddy and me, we fell out. He did a whole heap of things behind my back. But even when I had it out with him, he kept right on wheeling and dealing and now I don't know the half of this mess."

"I'll do anything I can. You know that. But if you've got English solicitors working on the case—"

"Remember what I told you at the start, son? I don't just need a lawyer, I need someone to *fix* things! These English solicitors, they'll be milking me dry come next century, the rate things are going now."

"So what do you want me to do?" Frank asked.

"Go over there. Find out what this woman's game is. Solve it, Frank. No publicity, no big payout either. I'm sending you because you still think English, sometimes."

"How high can I go to pay her off?"

"Twenty thousand US. Initially."

"Do you want me to work with your London lawyers?"

"As little as possible. It's your case, Frank."

Frank rose. "Thank you," he said.

The first thing Frank did on arriving in London was read a file sent around by the solicitors acting for the estate of Harrison Gephard, Senior.

The case was being brought by a woman called Sylvia Thomas, who had sworn a long affidavit setting out her claim. From the formal phraseology, Frank sensed that much of it had been put together by her lawyers, although here and there, when she was dealing with fun times she and old Gephard had enjoyed, genuine emotion showed through.

Frank found it hard to assess the strength of her case. He read the 1975 Act of Parliament on which it was based, making notes, and studied the Opinion written by Harrison's counsel with great care, but at the end of the day he could see it boiled down to good, old-fashioned horse-trading. No, poker was a better analogy. Someone had to blink first.

He let the papers fall onto the carpet and clasped his hands behind his neck. Sylvia had had to give her address, on the legal papers. Therefore, one possible tactic would be to contact her direct. But the English solicitors wouldn't like that, he knew. They'd say it was improper. So he wasn't going to tell them.

Sylvia Thomas made no difficulties over meeting him; seemed almost glad at the prospect, in fact. When he murmured that he didn't want lawyers involved her giggle made him laugh in sympathy, and she said, No, she didn't think lawyers were a very good idea either.

When Frank first saw her striding toward the table he'd reserved in a discreetly underlit basement restaurant she seemed much older than he'd imagined. She was wearing a tight white frilly dress belted so as to show off an hour-glass figure supported by long, tanned legs. Her blonde hair looked as if it had been bleached by too much sun, and her face had that brittle look that he associated with money-grubbers of a certain cast.

Then she came into the light, upsetting all his preconceptions, and he rose in some confusion to greet a sweet, shy girl of about his own age who did not know whether to laugh or cry.

She was extremely tense. He recognized that she'd had to nerve herself up to this encounter over a long period. For the first half hour she veered between the excessive gaiety of feeble jokes and a strained silence that stood between them like a glass partition.

Frank worked hard to put her at her ease. Mostly he kept the conversation on old Gephard. That wasn't difficult. Sylvia Thomas came across as a nice, well brought up girl who'd strayed into unfamiliar company and found it more congenial than life in her parents' Cardiff front parlor.

"Where did you two meet?" Frank asked.

"At the races. The Derby, it was." She plainly hailed from "Welsh Wales." "I'd gone with my . . . I had a friend, then. Sort of."

She laughed. Sylvia had a most infectious laugh; Frank found himself looking forward to hearing it.

"We met a lot of people that day, and do you know, I *won*! I won *a hundred pounds*!" She stared at Frank through enormous round eyes, as if daring him to disbelieve such a whopping great sum could ever have been won by the likes of her.

"Well done."

"And there I was collecting, you see, and this American was standing right by me, and he must have thought I'd had too much to drink, well, I had, and . . . "

She fell silent, picking at crumbs on the tablecloth. Frank knew from her affidavit that she was thirty-one, but looking at her now he felt her to be much nearer twenty.

"Look," she said suddenly. "Cards on the table, eh?"

He waited.

"I had a good three years with Leo. He liked me to call him that, it was our pet name. Leo the Lion . . . "

When she looked away he thought she was going to cry, but she clenched her lips together and laughed again.

"Anyway . . . we had some nice times. I kept working as a model. With an agency. Well, I expect you know that. And some secretarial, when the jobs didn't come in fast enough."

Frank had been waiting for an opportunity to slip a vital question into the conversation, and here it was. "Did he help you out?" he asked casually. "Make you an allowance?"

"Sort of. Bits and pieces, here and there." She sighed. "Look," she said again. "I'm not enjoying this. I know your job is to see me off. My solicitor would be mad as anything if he knew I was here, talking to you. But I'm going to trust you, Frank, 'cause I think it'll be best in the end."

He nodded encouragingly.

"I didn't really want to bring this case. I've got a friend, a journalist, and he put me up to it, see? He says there's big money in it. Mine's one of the first cases under this new Act of Parliament, so all the papers are interested. But first I've got to prove Leo was maintaining me, haven't I?"

"And also that he died domiciled in England." Frank shook his head. "Difficult. But you know that, don't you?"

She laughed again. "Don't I just!"

They were both laughing now.

"I don't want to go to court," she said. "But I do need some money." Her face turned serious. "Harrison Gephard was mean as pig-shit."

Frank concealed his surprise. Her affidavit had given a very different impression.

"If we could share it—holiday, champagne, day at the races—Leo'd buy it. But things like a flat, a brooch, or a car for me: no."

She held out her right hand, letting him see a plain gold ring with solitaire.

"Five hundred pounds that cost him. It's all I ever had off him to call my own."

"But in your affidavit you say—"

"About the apartment and the bank account and, yes, I know all about that. All true in a way, and all lies. Lots of things were put into my name. But it was done for tax, or to annoy his son; you knew Leo didn't like his son, did you?"

Frank smiled noncommittally.

"It was always understood between us that those things belonged to him, and I'd have to give them back if he asked. What I'm saying is that I need five thousand pounds, Frank. Somebody's come along with an offer of this job in the Middle East, see." She looked down at the tablecloth, her face uncharacteristically flushed. "I'm not sure what it involves, not really. Maybe I'll like it, maybe I won't. But I want to give it a whirl and at the same time put this stupid law case behind me, right?"

"Got it."

"Only I owe the bank. And . . . " She studied his face, not laughing now, not laughing at all. "And I deserve something," she said. "I put up with him and his little ways for three years, and yes"—she held up both hands—"I know what you're going to say, it was my choice, I was the one who made the bed. But five thousand would see me right and it wouldn't exactly hurt you, now would it?"

Frank sat in silence for a long time. She was very beautiful, full of life, and at that moment he actually envied Harrison Gephard, Senior. She would be great fun between the sheets, he knew, but she was off-limits to him. None of that altered his wish that this evening should not end.

Harrison had authorized him to pay up to $20,000; considerably more than the five thousand pounds Sylvia was asking for. His boss need never know the ins and outs of this deal.

"What you're saying," he murmured, "is that we'll pay you five thousand pounds and never hear from you again; you'll stop the action, pay your own lawyers?"

"Oh." Sylvia gnawed her lips. "I'd forgotten about the solicitors," she admitted ruefully. "Could you . . . ?"

"We might be prepared to pay your legal costs. *If*

you'd go one step further and agree that there should be no publicity. You mentioned a journalist friend."

"Oh, he wouldn't be a problem!" Her eyes had grown wide with reproach. "He's ever so nice, really! Only trying to help me, he is."

"It would have to be in writing, Sylvia. No publicity, or no deal. Do you understand what I'm saying?"

She nodded. Frank sat back. He was dying to give this girl the whole twenty thousand dollars. She'd made life easy for him, he liked her, Harrison would never know about her offer to settle for five thousand pounds. But it wasn't his money, and he had a responsibility to his employer.

"Five thousand pounds and costs," he murmured. "It's a deal."

She stared at him, not realizing that she had won. When it finally did sink in the color rushed into her face. She gripped the edge of the table. She was shaking.

"I feel sick," she gulped, and flew from the table.

She returned several moments later with water still dripping from her hair and shot him an appealing grin.

"I don't know who you were expecting to meet tonight," she said as she resumed her seat, "but I know it wasn't me."

He laughed. "It most certainly wasn't. I think we should celebrate, don't you? What's your favorite drink?"

"Oh, champagne. Pink. Leo's one real extravagance; used to live on the stuff, he did."

"I'll see what they've got," Frank said, calling for the wine list, but Sylvia forestalled him.

"Laurent Perrier," she said, surprising him with the quiet determination in her voice. "Leo always said Laurent Perrier pink was the best in the world, and Leo was right. And since he's paying for it . . . well, in a way . . . "

Frank and Sylvia parted an hour later, with mutual expressions of regret that time didn't permit a longer acquaintance. Afterward, undressing in his room, Frank felt a little foolish as he untied the tape recorder concealed beneath his shirt. He could have used the tape, he knew, to destroy Sylvia's case utterly, and since, as he'd reflected earlier, it was not his money but Gephard's at stake, perhaps that was what he ought to have done . . .

"You've got no excuse," he said sternly to his reflection in the mirror. "None whatsoever."

Then he winked.

As he'd anticipated, the solicitors acting for the old man's estate were not best pleased to learn of his initiative, although they grudgingly had to admit that he'd achieved a fine result. Sylvia's lawyers, for their part, were apoplectic. Frank might never have known about their anger, were it not for a visitor who unexpectedly came to his suite while he was packing.

The bell rang. He opened the door to find an attractive young woman standing on the threshold.

"Yes?"

She wore a gray suit: an under-manager with the hotel, presumably.

"Mr. Thornton?"

"Yes. How can I—"

"We've never met in the flesh, but you do know me. I know you, too."

He stared at her. "How did you get in here? Who are—"

"I persuaded them downstairs to let me surprise you."

Looking into her eyes, seeing the determination there, Frank could believe it.

"My name's Forbes. Roz Forbes."

There was a great stillness around them, as if the world had stopped, leaving only them to carry on the human race.

"You're . . . *who*?"

"Roz Forbes," she said in a low voice. "I'd like to talk to you."

"Well," Frank said, after a long pause, "I really don't think I've got anything to say to you, Miss Forbes."

"Not even thank you?"

"*Thank* you . . . for ruining my life, for—"

"I'd rather we didn't air it in the corridor."

He was tempted to slam the door in her face, but his upbringing held. Just.

"I'll give you five minutes."

She came in and took an armchair without waiting to be asked. Frank, fuming, sat down opposite her. She had a nerve, forcing her way in here . . .

Although his visitor was, he reluctantly acknowledged, attractive in a way to which Sylvia Thomas could never aspire. Roz had, in one word, poise. She held her chin up and she looked you in the eye when she spoke, not admitting the possibility that she might be anything other than your equal. He'd always admired women like that, while at the same time fearing them. Frank secretly did not believe he could ever win such a woman.

"Well?" he snapped.

"I gather you've sunk my pal Sylvie," she said.

"Sylvie . . . Sylvia Thomas?"

"Yes. She's not exactly my friend, to tell the truth. One of my reporters has been looking after her. *Had* been rather, until you came along. He's rather furious. So are her solicitors, by the way."

"What's the Thomas woman to you?" he shot out.

"She's bringing . . . was bringing the first case under the 1975 Act. A big one, too. We were monitoring it, of course."

"We?"

"I'm with the *Times* now."

"Funny, I'd have thought they'd have been a lit-tle fussy about whom they employed."

"*Whom*, oh my dear, such standards!"

"Yes, I do have some. Unlike—"

"What standards, Mr. Thornton? Tell me, are barristers supposed to talk directly to the other party?"

With an effort he controlled himself. She was, he realized, angry. Since her anger was directed against him, he must be responsible for whatever it was that upset her. Which made him feel absolutely wonderful.

"There are rules," he said casually. "Professional ethics. Covering such things as stealing notebooks, taking advantage of people and wrecking careers." He smiled at her. "Personally I've never bothered much about rules. Have you?"

"Very funny." Her voice was low, venomous.

"Yes, I screwed Sylvia. We did a deal. Don't encourage her to break it—"

"As if I would! How dare you imply—"

"—Because I tape-recorded our conversation, and if Sylvie reneges, her case goes down the pipe. She wasn't being maintained by Gephard and I can prove that, Miss Forbes. It was a dishonest case, whipped up by somebody now revealed as your lackey. So if that's what you came here to discuss . . . "

He tailed off with a shrug, interested to see what she would do next. For a moment she just sat there, staring at him through narrowed, hostile eyes. Then she smiled.

The effect was magical. A moment ago his suite had seemed dark, even a little poky; now it shone. Against his will he found his own smile matching hers.

"I'm so glad," she said; again, her voice was low,

but this time its timbre was warm, responsive. "You've come a long, long way and I'm so very glad."

"Do you always patronize men like that?"

"Only in the mornings."

"It's afternoon."

"How dare they end British Summer Time without telling me?"

"No doubt they realize you can't be trusted an inch."

By now they were grinning at each other.

"Could I possibly be forgiven, do you think?"

Frank thought about that. He didn't only want to forgive her, he also wanted to ask her out to dinner; and the more he looked at Roz the greater became his conviction that inviting her to stay over for breakfast would be a quite simply wonderful idea, too. But then Alistair Scrutton's laughing face suddenly swam before his eyes and—"Perhaps one day," he heard himself say.

He was remembering details now; things he'd hoped not to have to recall again. Louise . . .

"Not today?" Roz asked.

He could see that it mattered and he wanted to help her, because that way he could get to know her better and the mere sight of Roz Forbes was churning the blood through his veins in a way that he had almost forgotten.

Everything about her was delightful. Except her timing.

"I'm afraid that would only be dishonest of me," he said; and as the words came out he knew that he was doing the right thing. By letting her go now, and not otherwise, he held onto his hopes for the future.

"I see." She stood up and he did likewise. "Well, perhaps it was a bit presumptuous of me." She licked her lips. "I'm sorry I led off about Sylvie. My way of covering up."

"Covering . . . ?"

"Shyness. I wanted to see what you were like, I . . . " She twitched her shoulders in a little shrug.

"You're forgiven for that, at least. Sounding off."

She was going out when he said, "Do you have a card?"

"Yes."

"Please give it to me. Just in case one day . . . "

She gave him her business card. Frank watched her walk down the corridor with head bowed and shoulders a little hunched, as if the carpet held some particularly potent secret.

He began packing again, but after a while he stopped fiddling with his suitcase and threw himself down into an armchair. She had a nerve! And yet, she was lovely. How funny, somehow, to discover that you'd been ruined by a lovely woman . . .

He looked around the sumptuous suite, reckoning that if this was what it meant to be ruined he must try it more often. Had she, in truth, done him a favor? Perhaps he'd been slightly churlish . . .

The last thing he did before leaving London was visit Harrods, where he bought two cases of Laurent Perrier pink champagne. He had one of them sent to Sylvia Thomas. The other was delivered to the then offices of the *Times* in Printing House Square, with an unsigned card that said simply, "Perhaps one day . . . "

CHAPTER

15

LONDON. THE PRESENT

W e're almost there," Condon said, moving to switch off the car radio, but Brennan had other ideas. He inserted the last bullet into the Beretta's magazine, held the muzzle against Condon's ear and said, "Leave it."

The car swerved. O'Halloran, sitting in the front seat next to Condon, cleared his throat nervously and said, "Why do you always have to needle the boy, Martin?"

"Because I'm a good teacher. Thorough."

"It's hard enough without—"

"I'm listening to the radio, Pat."

He was in fact listening to Roz Forbes chair a late night discussion program. A left-wing solicitor, someone from Amnesty International, a backwoods Tory MP, and an Oxford law don had been brought together to air their prejudices.

"Clever," Brennan muttered. "She can't speak out against the trial herself without risking her job, but she can preside oh yes, she can preside. Now not many people would have thought of that." He leaned back in his seat. "Drive around the block, there's a good lad. Take your time."

Condon swung left.

The discussion on the radio fell along predictable lines. All the well-tried arguments for and against capital punishment were trotted out, mixed in with the usual appeals to sentiment, morality and the animal instincts that had once drawn thousands of spectators to Tyburn. Roz had a deft touch with animals, Brennan discovered. There were five claimants to the microphone, but he only listened to one. She was superb; never more so than at the end.

". . . Well, then: the crime of treason, without rhyme or reason. Recent events have brought to the fore what one of our contributors tonight calls 'a rotten corpse that everyone thought would never stink again.' And with no organ of justice currently immune from close scrutiny, there surely could not be a better time for determining—and then burying—what is truly dead."

As the closing music filtered through her last sentence Brennan said, "You can switch it off now, Tommy."

He liked the way she'd introduced the word "dead," right at the end, where people would remember it.

"She's good," he remarked. "She's a fine woman."

O'Halloran started to speak, then seemed to think better of it.

"Yes, Pat, you were saying?"

"Nothing important."

"No," Brennan persisted. "I am anxious to hear it."

"Well, then . . . do you have to harp on about this Forbes woman all the time?"

"Ah, she's not the only journalist that interests me. There are others." And then—"One other," he added quietly.

"Maybe, but you're fixated with the woman," O'Halloran went on. "What's the game?"

"Chess. She's my queen. We'll go to the house now."

They were driving down Wellington Road. Condon took the first exit at the rotary and almost immediately turned left into St. John's Wood High Street, before making a right into Allitsen Road. Here, the houses were spacious and well protected by walls from curious outsiders, with their expansive gardens, swimming pools, and other trappings of discreet wealth.

"Nice and easy," he murmured. Condon slowed. A pair of tall gates reflected light from a street lamp; behind them rose a black shape, a mansion-fortress, with no sign of occupation visible. But . . . "He's there," the Krait said.

Condon parked a few yards down the road, and the three men got out. They no longer had Salvation Army uniforms. They were clad alike in loose-fitting black cotton garments resembling pajamas, belted at the waist with a sash; on their feet they wore black plimsolls. A cold wind spotted their skins with rain and Condon shivered. The Krait had sent him to Chinatown to buy these strange garments at a martial arts shop. When he'd asked why they had to catch their deaths like this, Brennan explained, as if to a tiresomely stupid child, that they did not show up in the dark, and burned easily.

He seemed particularly anxious that they should burn easily.

They stood in silence for a moment while Brennan sniffed the air. This was a high-class area much favored as a base by wealthy denizens of Hong Kong and other Far Eastern entrepots, who kept themselves to themselves. Brennan intended to visit one of them, living in the house behind the tall gates down the road. He did not have an appointment.

"I don't want us to be disturbed tonight," he muttered to O'Halloran. "What's happening over Mountjoy?"

"Your call to Brother Mark did the trick."

But the Krait continued to look about him with a dissatisfied air, as if sensing a Provo in every shadow.

At last he made a sign with his hand and the other two blended into the night. Brennan himself moved swiftly to the gates of the next-door house, which were open. He padded across the lawn to the fence between him and his target and quietly vaulted over it, landing at the crouch in a flowerbed behind a rhododendron bush. Now he was in the front garden of the house he intended to visit. He held himself immobile while again sniffing the air, as Siri had taught him. He knew the way through danger's forcefield: you listened and you used your nose, but most of all you felt.

Nothing registered. Of course not. They'd be inside. Waiting.

He slipped around to the back of the house. A door was ajar; someone stood outside on the terrace, smoking a cigarette. Brennan tensed, then reached for the knife strapped to his left forearm, loosening it in the sheath. For a long moment he remained perfectly still, friend to the darkness and one with it. The lone smoker slowly began to pace the terrace. When Brennan moved, the curtain of night scarcely twitched.

The smoker turned into the Krait's blow. A hand pounded into his chest below the sternum, stopping his heart, and he started to fall. Brennan caught him, put his hands around his chest, picked him up and brought him down hard, feet first, onto the terrace, breaking his back. He rolled the corpse into the angle between the kitchen wall and the terrace. Seconds later, he was entering the house.

Down a corridor, soft red light glowed. He edged

toward it until he could see that it came from a small room, a breakfast parlor, occupied by an Oriental. Brennan watched from the shadows as the Chinese finished his dinner, holding the bowl close to his mouth so that he could scoop up the last grains of rice. Then he burped and stood up, turning to the source of the red light: a cavity, set at chest height in the far wall, containing three porcelain deities, joss sticks, bowls of fruit, a book. He raised his hands together before bowing thrice. As he came upright for the last time, a voice said, "Good evening, General" and something metal pricked the nape of his neck.

General Yang Po lifted his hands. "You . . . ?"

"Turn around, slowly now . . . that's right."

Yang Po's eyes suddenly looked away, over Brennan's shoulder. The Krait saw. He was already holding his knife. Now his left hand shot out to the general's neck, shoving him back against the altar so that his head banged against wood, stunning him. In the same easy moment he uncurled himself around to face the threat by the door, his knife already covering the intervening distance in a trajectory borne of a sideways flick. The shape in the doorway bent double. Brennan heard a "whump," telling him that the pistol his would-be assassin carried was silenced. Wide, *damn!* The man rolled over onto his back, bringing his gun to horizontal. Brennan released Yang Po and dived to the floor. Another "whump," chips of wood showering his head, a groan.

Brennan, snakelike, slithered a few feet and risked a glance to the door, where O'Halloran stood with one foot on the attacker's forearm. The Krait launched himself forward to snatch up his stiletto, then knelt to deliver a quick thrust between fifth and sixth ribs, well knowing the shortest route to the heart.

When footsteps sounded in the passage he glanced up, already planning his next tactic, but the steps retreated to the kitchen and he heard someone vomit up his dinner.

"Pat," he sighed, "Pat, you're to do something about that lad Tomas. Only it's starting to be a farce, you know?"

Yang Po had aged greatly since the Krait last saw him. His skin was a mass of wrinkles, his muscles had withered away, the paunch hung in rolls. He wore several layers of clothing to protect him from the English winter, although nothing quite fitted. He looked like a sad old man at the end of his time, but the Krait never relied on appearances.

"Sit down, General," he murmured. "With your hands on the table, wide apart, that's right, like you used to make the communists do before Hsiang Mei strangled them . . . now there was a nice boy, whatever happened to him?"

"Died," Yang Po said in a matter-of-fact voice. "Viet booby trap." He shook his head. "Very sad."

"Very. Any more gooks in the house? Never mind; Pat, take a look, will you? And bring Tomas in here."

He sat down opposite the Chinese, where he could keep an eye on both the door and the single window.

"I wasn't expecting to see you this trip." Yang Po spoke stiffly. "How did you know I was here?"

A smile was the Krait's only answer.

"I see. What do you want?"

"To chat about Alistair Scrutton."

That stopped the conversation as effectively as a grenade. While Yang Po was still groping for a response, O'Halloran helped Tomas into the room. "There's no more guards," he said, and Brennan smiled approval.

"Sit the boy down," he said. "Give him a good

view, now. Are y'all right, then?"

Condon, his face white, nodded. The Krait's eyes reverted to Yang Po and he smiled. "New recruit."

The Chinese leaned to one side and spat on the floor.

"I heard this little story," the Krait said, after a while. "About how you felt that our legal-eagle friend had outlived his usefulness."

"Crazy. Scrutton's great. Terrific. I love him. We all love him."

"Now is that really so?" the Krait asked, adjusting himself more comfortably in his chair. "*I* heard that you were worried about this trial, because you felt Scrutton might say more than was welcome to someone in your position."

The general rocked to and fro, as if cogitating. "Risky," he said at last. "Got to be sure he don't spill no beans."

"You think he's likely to? When one word out of place will send him to jail for the rest of his life? Ooh, I don't think so, General. Alistair's canny."

"Even good men crack under pressure."

Brennan studied the Chinese face opposite. Yang Po's eyes disclosed no fear; only contempt. He did not rate Brennan, never had.

"I've told you before, General, Scrutton's mine. He was the best drugs-runner I ever employed. So you've picked a bad time to interfere, see?"

"I have my business to protect."

"And a piss-poor business it is too, eh? With the Medellín cartel undercutting you left, right, and center? And the U.S. Narcotics Bureau rolling up your network from New York to San Francisco? And the Thai army, with its new long-range flame-throwers, oh yes, I know all about your business. It's *my* business too, remember? Drugs for guns, your end and my end; and it's all falling apart."

The Krait had been toying with his knife. Now

he drove it down hard into the center of the table, where it stood just off vertical, quivering. Yang Po gazed at it, unmoved.

"Why did you kill Siri?" the Krait murmured.

"Because he was selling our people to the Thai Rangers."

Brennan's lips rolled back to reveal long teeth narrow at the gums. For a moment he couldn't speak.

"You lying bastard," another voice hissed. Condon's voice. No, not Condon's voice but a voice coming from over where he'd been sitting. Brennan turned to look.

"He's a liar," Sean said. "Can't you see it, Martin?"

As if in a dream, Brennan nodded.

"It's been a long time," he said, after a pause.

"It has that."

His brother was dressed in black pajamas, like the ones Condon had been wearing. He occupied Condon's chair, too, keeping his eyes on Yang Po's face, not looking at Martin.

"What shall I do?" the Krait asked.

"Tell him we've had enough of his lies," Sean replied.

A movement caught Brennan's eye. O'Halloran was staring at him strangely, he couldn't think why, because this wasn't Pat's business at all.

"You're lying," he said, turning back to Yang Po.

The general shrugged again. "Siri Chaloem was selling our people to the Rangers," he said. "Ten thousand *baht* a time."

"He was not." Sean spoke clearly, but Martin Brennan was aware that no one else in the room could see or hear his brother. That was his secret. His strength. Sometimes he didn't know what he'd do without Sean.

Yang Po grunted a scornful puff of air through his

nostrils, as if trying to expel a bad odor. "You're a very stupid man," he said. "Know that?"

Brennan mastered his rage. He rested his elbows on the table and said, quite mildly and reasonably, "I'm not going to kill Alistair Scrutton and neither are you. I've built him and I've tended him lovingly, and he's going to become a judge one of these days, General, the IRA's judge, *my* judge, and in the meanwhile I'm using him in this trial to bring about results you couldn't even imagine. And you're not going to kill him either, for all sorts of reasons, first, because you'd never get near him, and second, and most important, because I can't forgive what you did to Siri and so you see I'm going to kill you, put your hands on the table, one on top of the other."

When Yang Po did not move to obey at once, Brennan reached across the table and arranged the old man's hands as he wanted them. Yang Po struggled but appearances didn't lie: he had no strength left in his aged, tired body. When Brennan was quite satisfied, he picked up the knife and drove it through the general's hands.

A deep groan erupted out of Yang Po, turning into a scream, then a series of gasps, then an undulating whimper without end. He tried to free himself, but the knife-point was embedded deep in the table and the more he fought the greater the pain became.

"That's the way, Martin." Sean's approval brought a grin to the Krait's face, and he shot his brother a glance of gratitude. Some duties were unpleasant. A man needed help . . .

He stood up, unknotting the sash from around his waist, before twisting it into a thin cord. He went behind Yang Po. He put the cord around his neck. He bent to the old man's ear and he whispered, "This is for Siri."

He crossed the ends of the sash and pulled. The

general's body heaved. He began to choke. The Krait, hearing that, released the pressure.

"Are you listening, Sean?" he said, eyeing his brother. "Shall I tell you something?"

Sean folded his arms and nodded.

"In Burma, our friend here used to command an army. Think of that . . . one, whole, army."

He pulled on the cord. Yang Po's face turned scarlet, the tendons on his neck strained out like bamboo canes, his mouth drooped open. Brennan kept up the pressure for about half a minute before letting go again.

"And in this army," he gasped, "there was a young officer, called Hsiang Mei. He was the executioner."

Yang Po's groans were pitiful enough to make Condon shiver. But there was to be no quick, merciful despatch.

"And this Hsiang Mei . . . " Brennan once more applied the pressure, " . . . was a good chap. He taught me this and that, you know . . . " His last word was lost in a grunt as he hauled on the cord. Blood from the crucified hands stained the table; every time the Chinese struggled he sawed a little more of his own flesh away.

" . . . and he told me, you can strangle a man . . . so that he takes half an hour to die. Can you believe it, Sean, eh?"

Brennan pushed his knee against the back of Yang Po's chair and redoubled his efforts. The general's body arched backward, his mouth opening in a dreadful rictus. Each long-separated breath came out in a high-pitched squeal.

"Sometimes . . . you garrote them . . . and they die quickly . . . but sometimes . . . you have to punish someone . . . because they *lie*. Because they kill your friends, Sean. For money."

Suddenly the Krait went berserk. He hauled on

the cord with all his might, as if he was trying to rend it apart. Yang Po's eyeballs rolled out of his skull, his tongue uncurled from his mouth; for an instant it seemed as if the cord would cut right through muscle and bone, bringing off his head . . . but then the last breath left him in a croaky, dying fall, and the Krait wrenched him backward off the table, so that the knife blade split the hands up as far as the knuckles to break through the skin, and then Brennan threw him aside as easily as you toss away a cardboard box when cleaning out the attic.

The Krait rested his weight against the table, panting with exertion. Sean stood up and began to move toward his younger brother, his favorite, but Martin backed away until he was cowering in one corner of the room, hands held out in the shape of a cross. He shook. His knees buckled. Sean had almost reached him when he uttered his first screech.

Condon and O'Halloran might have been wax-works. Their faces were cotton-white, they could neither move nor speak. Only slowly, between bouts of sobbing, did Brennan's terror distill itself into words they could understand.

"Don't . . . touch . . . me. Don't . . . touch . . . me. Don't . . . don't . . . don't . . . "

CHAPTER

16

LONDON. THE PRESENT

R oz was woken by her radio alarm at five to eight, theoretically just in time for the weather forecast, although today she didn't hear much of that. She felt grim, but the last vestiges of sleep stood in the way of finding out why. Then she remembered: Johnny had called late the night before and they had talked for a bleak ten minutes, using their own special shorthand so that if the international operator was listening in she wouldn't understand.

The Radio Four news rolled over her huddled form, leaving her indifferent. " . . . neighborhood of St. John's Wood. The police are treating the incident as murder."

She pulled the purple duvet up over her bare shoulders, shrinking into its protective warmth. There was something special Johnny had to talk about when he got back, he'd said. Then there'd been this long pause. Something we've been putting off, he went on. Lots of clicks and mutters and hisses as the satellite swung. Oh yes, she'd said, not wanting to sound over-keen, despite the pounding of her heart. A proposal. *At last!*

And then he'd said the words she thought she'd never hear. "It's not working," that was what he'd said; and for a blind second she'd fought to convince herself that he meant only the documentary he was filming. "We have to talk."

" . . . heroin dealers. Sources close to the Home Office have indicated that Martin Brennan, sometimes called 'The Krait,' may be connected with these triple murders."

Roz sat bold upright in bed, reaching for the volume control.

"It is now thought that the Krait entered England within the past few days and the public are urged to be on the alert. Extra security precautions are being taken, particularly in connection with prominent public figures."

The phone rang; Roz snatched it up. Ben Saunders' voice: "Heard the news?"

"Brennan's on the rampage."

"Right. I'm up there, now, so can't talk long. Listen, Roz, I'm dropping out of sight for a while, see?"

"Why?"

"'Cause I'm being trailed and I don't want to lead them to you." He paused. "They're interested in you."

"Who is?"

"So be careful who you let in the flat, and watch what you say over the phone, okay?"

"Ben, *who*—"

"I'm tired of being the shuttlecock, Roz. Time I went and bought myself a racket." There was a confused pause, while Ben mumbled something to a colleague outside the phone booth; then—"I'm going to get the truth for you, the real truth, and then I'm going to bring it to you on a silver plate."

"Ben, *please* give me your number, I'll call you back."

But the only response was the sound of more pips, followed by the buzz of an abandoned line.

Roz swore, then propped herself up in bed with the telephone tucked under her chin and Filofax at the ready. Brian Oakley's number was engaged, but she got through to her home news editor first time.

"Give Brennan space, George, lots of space."

"Will do. Couple of things might interest you . . ." She heard papers being shuffled. "Here we are . . . school in South Shields. Carpentry class built a gallows . . ."

"What?"

"A scaffold. In their spare time. Last night, some kid went and hanged himself on it. Mass hysteria, questions for the local authority, et cetera, et cet-er-a. Want a follow?"

"I want a bloody leader. What else?"

"We've got a press release on next month's National Union of Prison Officers conference. There's a motion to stop members having anything to do with an execution."

Roz was scribbling in her Filofax. "Go on."

"Background paper . . . ninety percent and over of membership recruited since abolition of capital punishment . . . joined up on a particular basis now shown to be false . . . de-da, de-da . . . I guess you want it covered, do you?"

"Yes, and I want interviews *before* the conference opens, plus notes on likely key speakers."

"I'll flag. That's it."

"All right. I'm coming in late. Get someone up to South Shields and go in hard. I want a big, cruel photo for page one and stuff the policy. Write naked emotion, George."

"Anything you say, boss. It's your paper today."

"And I want half a page on Brennan no later

than tomorrow. Full profile, plus pic."

"Who's going to write that?"

Roz thought. "I am."

She slammed down the phone and bounced out of bed, feeling more alive than for many days past. Johnny was right, she told herself as she fixed coffee. It hadn't been working for a long time past. But all that meant was failure of communication. They needed to talk things through. Then everything would be fine, she commanded her reflection in the mirror, as she tugged a comb through her hair. No question. And now, to work; never mind about personal things, skip the emotions, save them for the South Shields story.

"Are you all right?" she asked her reflection. And the woman in the mirror screamed at the top of her voice, *"God damn you to fucking hell, Johnny, you fucking bastard! I hate you, hate you, hate you."*

"Better now?" the original inquired brightly; and her reflection nodded.

"Let's go."

In the taxi from Battersea to the Old Bailey she sorted through her post. A check from the BBC, proofs of the "Halt the Trial" campaign's latest leaflet, invitation to speak to the Haldane Society of Labor Lawyers, no, she couldn't find time . . .

The memory of Ben's telephone call haunted her. Why were "they" interested in her? Who were "they"—Brennan? The IRA? Roz gazed out of the window, gnawing the tip of her thumb and cursing Ben for being so secretive. Today she felt cold, and very alone.

Barricades were still in place outside the Old Bailey, although this morning they served no useful function. A lone protester ambled up and down carrying a placard, but public interest in the trial was at a low ebb. Roz could change that. She had ammunition now.

Frank jumped up to greet her, giving her a quick kiss, but she held him close, today not above taking comfort from a man under threat of execution.

"I think there's a rule against it," he said with a smile, gently disengaging her. "Smooching with suspects."

"Cuddling cons?" Roz smiled, only half apologetically, at Hugo Lutter. "Sorry."

"I'm wildly jealous."

"Later, darling, later. Listen, guys. Brennan's in town."

Frank turned away with a tetchy sigh. "We've gone through all this bef—"

"I *know!*" Roz swallowed, got a grip on herself, and continued. "But Ben believes there's a connection."

"Can you prove it?"

"Oh, Frank, you know we can't. But it's too much of a coincidence, him turning up halfway through your trial. He's wanted everywhere, his profile's never been higher, there's a recent photograph of him in circulation, yet he's here."

"Where? Exactly?"

"Frank, *please* don't switch off. Scrutton's giving evidence today. We have to destroy him. I *know* you've tried to remember everything. But I have to ask you again. Can you think of anything, no matter how trivial, that ties Scrutton to the Krait, or that might link you with the IRA?"

Frank slumped back into his chair. "You're asking me to go back over years spent abroad . . . I must have met thousands of people, hundreds of Irishmen, God knows, perhaps some of them were IRA, *I don't know.*"

"Look," Roz said. "Brennan's IRA, he's here for a reason, you are the reason. You *must* think back. You left London after sorting out Sylvia. *What happened then!*"

Frank closed his eyes and tried to concentrate.

* * *

On his return to Houston he had rapidly grown in stature within the Foundation, warmed by the sunshine of Harrison's gratitude and friendship. The two men's liking had grown into something deeper, productive of great dreams. Many a weekend did Frank spend at the mansion in River Oaks, and when the Gephards produced another child, Jodie, her proud parents invited him to be one of the godfathers. He accepted joyfully.

It was while he was standing by the cradle, looking fondly down at the child, so helpless and endearing, that he first conceived the notion of taking out American citizenship. But next day he was due to fly to Perth on Foundation business and he shelved the idea until he had more time to consider it. Rarely a month went by without Frank flying off somewhere. On his frequent trips to the four corners of the globe he henceforth found new pleasure in shopping for his godchild, who early in life acquired enough presents to stock an international bric-a-brac store.

Then came the retirement homes, and the first of Frank's personal fortunes.

After his mother died, he'd been faced with the problem of what to do with his father, Sid. Frank offered to take him back to the States, but Sid couldn't face the transition, so instead Frank got him into the best home money could buy. That set him thinking. Not long after Jodie's birth he took Harrison out to lunch and expounded a theory.

"Old folks," he said. "Like my father. Maybe they lose a loved one, maybe they're just tired, a little afraid of a world they no longer know."

"What about them?"

"They want somewhere safe, with their own kind. People with shared values, Harrison; that's important. We should build for them. A village in the sun where they can form a genuine community, with people to check on their welfare, and resident doctors, and restaurants with dietitians."

"I don't know . . . it's not something I'd ever considered."

"Florida's done well out of this already. We should be chasing them. There's a good coastline, a warm climate, Texan values are rock-solid in a shifting world. Less crime than in Florida, which I see as a big selling-point."

Harrison shook his head. "I'll think about it," he prevaricated; but those words were sounding in Frank's ear with ever-increasing frequency. Harrison seemed to have put himself on hold without telling anyone why. When months passed and Frank had heard nothing further, he decided to go it alone. He approached some key operators who'd done business with him over the years and soon had his own consortium, with a plan to build fifty retirement homes near Rockport.

They sold all fifty at what was intended to be a pre-sales-campaign exhibition at San Antonio, on the basis of drawings and artists' impressions. Over the next few years, Frank and his partners bought and built and sold in a cyclical swing that seemed to have no end.

Meanwhile, Harrison had been spending more and more time in Washington, D.C. One day he invited Frank to the house and over lunch he asked him, "Would I make a good congressman?"

Frank laid down his fork. He was remembering the funeral of Harrison's father, the Speaker's discreet appeal by the graveside, all those subsequent visits to Washington; and he wondered how he could have been so stupid not to see it.

"I'd rather you became governor. Think of the contracts you could award yourself . . . "

"One thing at a time, son. What about Congress?"

"If it's what you and Wendy May want, go for it. But I'd like to know who'll mind the store here."

"That's just it," said Wendy May. "And don't look at me like that, Frank Thornton; just 'caus ah'm married to the brute don't mean I can tame it. Ah don't see mahself in Washington and that's a fact."

But when election time came, and Harrison performed as a Gephard should, she of course went with him, taking the children too. Harrison's last act before migrating to Washington was to appoint Frank the Gephard Foundation's general counsel (worldwide).

His new responsibilities were awesome. The foundation had offices in places as far apart as Alaska and Indonesia, twenty-nine in all, and Frank spent a good part of each year visiting them. As well as his property expertise, he had acquired a working knowledge of seven different judicial systems, some of which played by the book and some of which needed regular financial oiling. He likened himself to a fine old organ, capable of producing the most diverse sounds from one end of the scale to the other, and he was never bored.

Only Elaine, his wife, was bored.

He had met her during one vacation, in San Francisco. She came from New York, where she ran her own photo library. They were both unattached and when he told her how he planned to drive down the coast to LA, taking in Big Sur, San Simeon, and the Getty, it had seemed the most natural thing in the world for her to tag along.

Their courtship was a wonderful, easy-going relationship that, he told himself, suited them both. She had a career and loved it, but although she retained her New York base, they met, and vacationed together, frequently; not a month went by without their spending a couple of nights in the same bed.

Long before Harrison ran for congress, Frank had introduced Elaine to the Gephards, and she became his frequent partner at their parties. Harrison helped dig out an opportunity for Elaine to relocate to Texas. She kept many of her old clients, as well as finding new ones. Almost before they realized what was happening, they were married.

Once a year or so, usually while basking beside some pool in Maui, or Baton Rouge, they talked about having children. But for the moment there seemed to be no reason for changing a lifestyle that both found eminently enjoyable, and convenient. It worked, Frank honestly believed, because they didn't spend too long in each other's company. But he never thought to ask Elaine for her views on the matter.

In 1985, Frank's father had died after a short illness. He flew back to England and the knowledge that now there was no one waiting for him at home.

It didn't feel quite the same as when his mother died. Grief was there, yes; but time and distance seemed to have softened the edges of personal loss. Afterward he wandered around the house, touching furniture, pausing here to pick up a vase, there to examine a framed photograph. As he locked up the house where he had spent his lonely childhood, knowing it was for the last time, he acknowledged to himself that he no longer missed England, and again thought of taking out American citizenship. Now that both his parents were dead, he couldn't muster a single reason not to.

Sid Thornton's affairs were quickly wound up; Frank found himself fretting in his hotel suite with an unexpected extra day to kill. He considered looking up Alistair Scrutton, only to dismiss the idea.

They had nothing to say to each other.

Roz Forbes was a different proposition. They'd exchanged a number of letters by then and whatever might have held them apart when they were young was now history. But Frank couldn't make himself feel right about it. He was a married man and something told him to steer clear of too much personal involvement with Roz. In the end he phoned her but, when she suggested dinner, pleaded conflicting appointments.

On an impulse he changed his flight, going straight to Houston instead of via New York, as he'd originally planned. He was alone: no parents, no children. What he had now was all he would ever have. He and Elaine needed to start a family.

He arrived in mid-afternoon and took a cab to the Galleria, where he bought an eternity ring that he knew Elaine would like: a solitaire set in a plain band of gold. Nothing pretentious, nothing gaudy. He toyed with the idea of telephoning her at work, arranging to meet for a reunion dinner, but suddenly what mattered was holding her in his arms as a way of saying to God that he was not alone, after all; that his father's death had not robbed him of everything. He liked that idea. As he approached the door to their apartment, he harangued his Creator. "Made it," he said. "Made it to home base. You can take everything except her, God, but she's mine. She's all mine. To have and to hold. From this day forward." He inserted his key in the latch. "'Till death us do part," he said aloud, and his heart was singing.

Then a man came out of the bedroom into the hallway, wearing only a towel.

He left the apartment without a word, knowing that he'd been here before, with Louise, and conscious of how bootless explanations were. He'd checked into a hotel and proceeded to get drunk. He lost forty-eight hours out of his life, awakening to a dawn that held no promise.

He remembered that he'd made tentative plans to contact a friend in the mayor's office and explore what was involved in applying for citizenship. No need for that, now. Frank rolled over and went back to sleep.

When he'd sobered up a bit he phoned Harrison in Washington.

"I need a favor," he said. "Let me head up London."

There was a long silence at the other end.

"Harrison, are you there? I know that Charlie's due to retire next year, you'll need someone for London."

"Yes, but I also need you here, Frank."

"Who else knows the UK as well as I do?" He heard the whine in his voice and did not care. "Who else has got my kind of expertise?"

"This is kind of sudden, isn't it?"

"With my father dying, and everything . . ."

"Everything? What's everything?"

Frank hesitated. Then he broke down and told Harrison the whole story.

"I'm really sorry, son. Really I am." A long pause. "Frank, I'll level with you. London's taking on new importance. What with Europe, the free market they're all talking about come next decade . . . I need a married man there. Someone who can handle the entertaining. Now if you and Elaine could patch things up . . ."

But they couldn't. Elaine moved out very quickly. Their divorce was soon arranged, with Frank keeping the apartment. He started to drink, steadily and often. Within a year, his performance at work had begun to suffer and people were talking in mean whispers. By rights, it should have ended in only one way: collapse, followed by the long, slow process of drying out, a Golden Goodbye, endless decline.

One night he came back from the bar and instead of tumbling into bed as he usually did he picked up the TV's remote control. Commercials swiftly gave way to news. Frank stared, his fuddled state not allowing him to understand what the newscaster was saying. China, Russia, Panama, Texas.

Texas . . .

One word caught his attention, then another. Very slowly, like a malfunctioning robot, he adjusted the sound control. It *was* Harrison Gephard up there on the screen, beaming into camera, with no sign of the tortured doubts that had so disfigured his face at his father's funeral.

Frank reached out for the phone. When a young girl answered he recognized her voice and said, "Jodie . . . "

"Frrraaank!"

"Hi, honey. Listen. I would like to talk to the next United States ambassador to London."

"You betcha!" A pause; then, echoing down the line as if from far, far away: "DaaaAADDD . . . "

When Harrison came on the line Frank said, "In England, you're going to need a friend."

"Funny," he replied; "I was about to call you."

CHAPTER

17

LONDON. THE PRESENT

Scrutton took the book in his right hand and put his soul in play: "I swear by Almighty God that I will true answers make to all such questions as may be put to me."

Frank was convinced that his old rival did not want to be here. He had come to give evidence under duress. But what threat, or promise even, could be strong enough to force a man into conniving at judicial murder by giving perjured evidence?

Looking at Scrutton, Frank could almost hear his thought processes as he'd dressed that morning. He'd been right to eschew black jacket and pinstripes, which would have identified him too closely with The Establishment; his dark Prince of Wales check was just the thing. No breast pocket handkerchief, no jewelry, unless you counted the rimless spectacles with their gold bridge. Well-manicured clean hands folded on the edge of the box, but standing upright, like a soldier. *Very* good . . .

" . . . particular interest in legal education?"

"Yes. I've always believed that the profession

can't survive unless it nurtures its young."

"So you joined the Young Barristers' committee of the Bar Council?"

"I was invited to do so. Although at a time when I myself was not so young."

Timid laughter escaped into the court, like gas through a badly-fitting gasket.

"You played a leading role, I think, in improving the prospects of black and Asian students after they'd qualified?"

"Hardly a leading role. I sat on various committees."

"Is it right that you invariably had a pupil?"

"Until I took silk, there was never a time when I did not have one."

As he gave that answer he stole a glance at Andrew Mottram, who fielded it with ironically raised eyebrows, and Scrutton quickly looked away. Frank had spent hours, days, working out with Mottram what line of cross-examination he should take, but this led nowhere. Pupils were, by definition, young. That Scrutton's were nearly always female could be taken as more than a coincidence. But as far as the defense team knew, Scrutton had never laid a finger on any of the girls and could at least take genuine pride in what he had done to safeguard the profession's future.

Sir Patrick chose to dwell on his financial contributions to pupilage scholarships, the time he'd given up to seminars and conferences, the encouragement he'd been constantly ready to give. Perhaps the attorney-general guessed that Scrutton did all these things to compensate for his own inability to father children, for immediately afterward he asked, "Are you married, Mr. Scrutton?"

"I am a widower."

"When were you married?"

"In 1970. I married a girl called Louise Shelley."

"How did you meet her?"

Frank saw the peek that Scrutton darted toward him. His eyes were hard and fierce, and they glittered like antique jewels.

"I was introduced to her by Mr. Thornton."

"Where did you live, after you were married?"

"At first in Primrose Hill. Then in 1978 we moved to Nettlebed, where I still live."

"Were there any children of the marriage?"

"No."

No. Louise had told Frank that her husband used to bet that their first would be a boy, until one day the topic ceased to be amusing and they didn't mention it anymore. She had a wistful theory that everything would have been different for him if only they'd had children. His own flesh and blood, to love and cherish. An incentive—Frank smiled bitterly at the memory of her words—to goodness.

"You have described yourself as a widower. When . . . no, I should put it another way. Did you remain married to Louise until her death?"

"I did."

"When did she die?"

"In July 1988."

"At that time, the defendant had returned to live in England. Have you any reason to suppose that your wife met him between the date of his return and her death?"

"No, apart from something Mr. Thornton said afterward."

"Yes, we'll come to that 'something' later on. Mr. Scrutton . . . I'm sorry to have to ask you about these matters, but I must do it: how did your wife die?"

Scrutton's knuckles whitened on the lip of the witness box. "There was an accident," he said in a low voice. "She . . . she drowned."

"Where did that happen?"

A long pause. "At my . . . at our home. In the swimming pool."

Sir Patrick embarked on a muttered conference with the treasury solicitor's representative. During the pause, Scrutton with extreme reluctance found his attention dragged back to Frank, who had continued to stare at him throughout.

Frank knew that Scrutton was lying when he said he had no reason to suppose that Frank and Louise might have met. On the contrary, Scrutton knew everything about the two lovers. That was why he'd killed one of them.

CHAPTER

18

LONDON. AUTUMN 1987

When Harrison L. Gephard became United States ambassador to the Court of St. James's he realized that he was undertaking one of the loneliest jobs in the world. He was also the first to admit that his knowledge of England, while extensive, could not compare with a native's. He needed someone independent who could be relied on to sort out the truth from the lies fed into the system by the State Department. Needed, in other words, Frank Thornton.

"You'll be taking on two jobs," he warned Frank. "Running my company and holding my hand. Holding my hand's going to be the toughest assignment. Still want to come to London?"

"More than ever. But you told me that for London you needed someone with a wife for hostess. I'm divorced and I'm not likely to get married again."

"Smarter guys than you've said that." Harrison sighed. "Guess you get the job anyway."

Frank bought a pleasant, semi-detached house in

Abbotsbury Road, hard by Holland Park, commuting to the office on the Central Line. Because he had never cared much for his own cooking he took to having a proper lunch each day. England had become more health-conscious in his absence, and ethnic cuisine was now less of a curiosity than a requirement of the young and upwardly mobile. Years of Texan chili had done nothing to blunt the edge of his liking for exotic foods. Everything came together perfectly in a Japanese restaurant off Paternoster Square. At lunchtime the restaurant was usually packed, so that lone customers like himself would often be asked if they minded sharing a table. Frank was sitting by himself one day, with the *Wall Street Journal* propped up in front of him, when he became aware of a female hand pulling out the vacant chair opposite. He prepared an acquiescent smile in anticipation of the "Do you mind?" or, "Is anyone sitting here?" which custom dictated, but this woman said nothing.

She sat down. Frank raised his eyes. And froze.

"I'd have known you anywhere," Louise said. "Waiter, bring me a scotch, straight up, will you?"

He stared, food and newspaper forgotten, utterly swept away in a deluge of memories.

"Hello, Frank. You are Frank Thornton, aren't you?"

He nodded slowly, uncertain whether he shouldn't just stand up and walk away from this slightly mad-looking throwback, with her knife-sharp features, almost French in their perfect definition, and chic black-and-white dress, and her pricey make-up exquisitely applied, and hair with stray curls that were not gauche but teasingly sexy.

"My God," he managed to stutter at last. "It's been so many years . . . "

"You don't look pleased to see me."

The waiter brought her drink. She had been fingering a jade brooch worn at the neck of her expensively cut dress, but now she dropped the ornament and wrapped her long fingers around the glass. "Cheers," she said.

Frank watched her, wondering what had inspired her obvious taste for alcohol.

"Yuk!" She made a face and put down the glass. "I asked for scotch. That's Japanese."

But he noticed that her glass was half-empty.

"So how's you?" she said, sounding bored.

"I'm fine, thanks. You?"

She heaved a theatrical sigh. "So-so."

"What an incredible coincidence, us running into each other like this."

"Coincidence be damned. I've been following you." She drained her glass, need triumphing over discrimination. "Ever since I read about you in the *Times*. That article the girl did, your pal Forbes. When you landed the English top job."

"I see."

He knew the article she meant: a flattering piece.

"I read the papers every day, you know. The appointments page. And the indexes. And those lovely, lovely ads for distribution agents in Seoul. There's bugger all else to do in Nettlebed, except read. What's good to eat here?"

He tried to tempt her with sushi, but Louise disdained anything raw. "They must have that teppan-stuff . . ."

To his surprise, she didn't order another drink. Perhaps the first was just to soothe her nerves; after all, she had no means of knowing how he would greet her. *He* did not know how to greet her. Many times in the distant past he'd mentally lived this moment when they would see each other again, and he could say all those things he'd bottled up inside him since she walked out. Now there was nothing to say. Gall had a shorter shelf-life than he'd imagined.

"Tell me everything," he said, really wanting to know, because she was not the least what he would have expected. She'd hardened with age, like a conker that had been knocked about a bit and come through. It showed in her eyes, narrower than he remembered them; in her skin, tanned by too much sun, and possibly lamps, to a curious shade midway between orange and hide; in the way she moved her body with quick, controlled gestures. She had lost all trace of spontaneity. Here was a woman who forecast and arranged the events of her life much as he manipulated cash flows.

"Oh, everything . . . what a bore. Well, I married Alistair. I suppose you knew that."

"I'd heard."

"You thought I was after him, didn't you? Well I wasn't. For a long time I didn't even particularly *like* Alistair." She chewed her steak slowly, looking sideways; the effect was to convey extreme, if unintended distaste. "But there didn't seem to be anyone else . . . "

He guessed she must be in her mid-forties. Small clefts had materialized at the sides of her mouth; sign of an unhappy face. Her voice was affected, too: these clipped, bored tones weren't really her.

He caught himself in the middle of a rueful smile. People changed.

"What are you grinning at?"

"I was just . . . just wondering, do I look the same?"

"Or are you like me—raddled?" She pushed her half-finished plate aside and opened her handbag, from which she drew a long, thin cigarillo without asking if he minded. "No, you're not raddled." She blew a long stream of smoke at the ceiling through extended lips, before lowering her eyes to examine him more carefully. "A few more wrinkles. Careworn, but that's what power does for you. You

should see Alistair . . . no, you shouldn't." She tilted her head on one side. "Sad. You look sad."

"Ah." He hesitated. "Mum and dad have both
died. There's been a fair amount of turmoil lately."

"Sorry to hear that. I liked your people."

Her words jarred his memory. Call night; Alistair
talking about his "people" as if he were a king with
subjects. Louise used to laugh at that kind of thing.

"Let's go," she said, stubbing out her cigarillo; it
seemed she'd acquired a penchant for not finishing
what she'd started. Or perhaps it had been there all
the time?

Outside in the square she said, "Are you free?
Only I want to talk."

"Come back to the office."

"No, I spend all my life inside, I need to get out.
There's a seat over there . . . "

She led the way to the bench and sat down gracefully, crossing her legs and tucking them aside, so
that one of her Bally shoes drooped away at the
heel.

"I've got nobody to talk to." She turned slightly,
her eyes running up and down his face, from left to
right, quizzing, testing. "Except you."

"I can't think how I could—"

"It's Alistair. He hasn't changed. People like that
don't. They just uncover a little more of the shit
each passing year, that's all."

"I'm so sorry."

"Are you? Are you really?"

"Yes."

She grunted. "My marriage," she resumed, "is
what tragic heroines call an empty shell. Only I'm
no heroine. Not even tragic, really. Just pathetic."

"Do you have any children?"

"Christ, no." She laughed scornfully. "I've had
all the tests. There's nothing wrong with *me*."

"I see."

"Alistair needs a wife for the same reason he needs good suits: to impress and reassure. That's what holds us together. That, and . . . "

"And what?"

She eyed him, saying nothing for a while. "Let's walk," she said eventually. "It's not as warm as I thought out here."

They strolled along Newgate Street toward the Old Bailey, keeping to the sunny side.

"Are you married?" she asked.

"Divorced."

"Poor Frank."

"I've had some fun along the line."

"And you're rich, aren't you? Stinking rich."

"I'm not poor, let's put it that way."

"I'm poor."

"But Alistair's in silk now, isn't he?"

"Oh yes, he's a QC, rolling in it. But I don't get a penny."

"Surely he gives you an allowance, or something?"

"No. We have a joint account. 'You just buy whatever you want, my dear.'"

"Sounds pretty good to me."

"You've never been on the receiving end."

He felt mystified. "Of what?"

"Someone else's guilt."

They walked on in silence.

"Frank," she said at last. "I want to come and talk to you, sometimes. Can I do that?"

"If there's anything I—"

"I'm frightened, Frank."

They were standing by the traffic lights outside the Old Bailey. A cold wind came out of nowhere, whipping itself into a sudden frenzy, so that her skirt floated up and she didn't care, just stood there, looking at him through those fretful, half-closed eyes while somewhere close by a man wolf-whistled.

"Frightened . . . of what?"

"Alistair."

Before he could say anything she went on hurriedly, "Look, I'll be in touch, 'kay?"

He stared after her as she ran across the road toward Holborn and he knew then that he was going to have to find a way of coming to terms with this.

He got through the afternoon somehow. At six o'clock, his secretary came in with a list of calls for him to return and a typewritten sheet setting out his engagements for the next day. He was due in Aberdeen for lunch, after which he would have to visit an oil rig and be back in time for dinner with the Foundation's Scottish advocate. He knew he ought to study the field's production figures, but his mind wasn't on it. For the first time in months he went home with an empty briefcase.

He poured a generous tot of Jack Daniel's and began to move restlessly around the first-floor living room overlooking the garden. He found himself examining objects that had never caught his attention before: furniture, knick-knacks, lamps—things that had been imported wholesale by an interior designer whose name he couldn't even remember. This wasn't his room. It was merely a place where he camped.

No person, man or woman, had ever engraved the seal of another personality on his life.

He'd been unlucky twice now, first with Louise and then with Elaine. He had loved Elaine fervently, or so he believed. When she left, the lights died. Somewhere in the resulting darkness, rage, and loss, and self-pity and despair knotted themselves like clothes that had been tumbled together for too long in dirty suds. Unfinished business. Excess baggage.

Now Louise Scrutton, née Shelley, was back. And the question was: what did he want to do about her?

She had been making up to him this afternoon. He could have his revenge on Alistair, if he wanted it. He could make them both pay.

She was so beautiful.

She was Alistair's wife.

She was available.

Saturday morning came, along with four bouquets of flowers.

Frank was lying in bed reading the *Independent* when the front doorbell rang. He threw on a dressing gown and ran downstairs to find a delivery man on the step.

"There's been a mistake," he said. "I didn't order flowers."

The man consulted his clipboard. "Mr. Frank Thornton, Abbotsbury Road, sign here."

Something made him look over the man's shoulder. On the other side of the street, leaning against a lamppost with her hands in the pockets of a white raincoat, was Louise. She had a mocking smile on her face, as if she looked forward with interest to seeing how he would deal with this.

Frank accepted the flowers. "Won't you come in?" he called to Louise.

Her lips twisted in a smile of sorts and she sauntered over. She was carrying a large package, he noticed, but what principally caught his attention was her apparel. She wore a vermilion beret, a long white Burberry, black silk stockings and the same patent leather shoes she'd been wearing that day at the restaurant. She looked very French, very chic. The outfit took years off her, too.

"I knew you wouldn't have any flowers," she said as she crossed the threshold. "Men never bother." She thrust the parcel at him almost as though she meant to throw it away. "It gives me a real kick to spend Alistair's money on you, darling."

The parcel turned out to contain a pair of wonderful glazed vases ("Bencharong; don't ask me where that is, all I know is they cost a *fortune*!"). While he showered and dressed she filled his house with roses, and gladioli, and pinks, and mimosa, and daffodils, and tulips and colors enough for a dozen rainbows, and scents, such scents! She almost succeeded in transforming his house into a home. Was that the product of long summers spent in Nettlebed, he wondered; flower arranging Monday afternoons, bridge Tuesdays . . . ? (Lovers Wednesdays, from five until seven? He'd thought a lot about that, since their last meeting.)

For some reason she insisted on keeping her raincoat on, even after he had made coffee and escorted her back into the living room. She ambled across to the bow window. "Why do you live in a prison?" she asked.

"Mm? Oh, the shutters . . . I haven't had time to unlock them yet. All these houses have them."

"We don't have shutters in Oxfordshire. I don't know why. Alistair's paranoid about security. I must tell him, when I get home: Frank's got shutters, darling, terribly posh."

He kept his eyes on the coffee pot while he poured. "Does Alistair know you're here?" he asked lightly.

"Does he fuck! I told him I was going clothes shopping, which is true." She unbelted her raincoat. "Do you like it?"

He glanced up and the pot jerked in his hand, spilling hot coffee over his fingers. But he scarcely noticed, for underneath the Burberry she wore nothing except a lacy black suspender belt. She raised one knee, at the same time caressing the back of her neck, and moue'd him a kiss.

"Good . . . God."

As she advanced toward him he noticed her breasts still had enough resilience to bounce. The nipples were just as he remembered them: large, deep red and even now expanding with blood to stand proud from those tanned breasts. He made to stand up, but she was on him before he could get more than halfway, planting her lips on his and cementing them together with both hands clasped behind his neck.

"Hi, Kid," she made time to whisper. "Welcome home . . . "

She chewed his lips before exploring his mouth with her tongue. Her breath smelled almost imperceptibly of smoke, and of the spray she had used to mask the underlying taint. Another, musky scent was rising up to overpower the flowers that saturated the cool room. For a moment he dithered; then his fingers were closing around her breasts and thought gave way to emotion.

He had not had a woman for months. She wanted him. She had no opinion of her husband, herself, or him; she was a slut. Why not . . . ?

He began to apply techniques he'd learned from Elaine, a part of him reserved from the fray and pleased with his performance. Then the unexpected happened. He lost control.

Suddenly they were on the floor, fighting with their mouths. She was tearing at his shirt, his trousers, his underpants. They were naked, except for the suspender belt. She had her legs wrapped around his neck and was moaning into his mouth, but he wouldn't let her free, not even to breathe.

Technique went to the winds. He rammed his way inside like a soldier taking the spoils of victory. He came almost at once, but she thrust her pelvis upward and outward in a desperate attempt to hold him fast. For a few moments he squirmed with teeth clenched, mastering the exquisite pain;

then he was once more pumping away. Now he could afford to be cruel. He made her wait. He teased her to the brink of orgasm, only to retreat and regather his forces, while she panted and clung to him like a drowning woman going down for the third time.

Then she changed. She was pushing him away, both fists pounding at his chest with ever-increasing desperation. Her head arched backward, he bit her chin and she screamed, but he was not ready to let her go. Only after her face flooded with hot blood and her moans turned to gasps did he mount onto his knees and, hauling her buttocks up into his hands, inject her with all the grief and anger he'd kept pent up inside him over the years.

He came to himself kneeling, like a pious man at prayer.

Frank sat back on his haunches, dragging in huge breaths. Louise collapsed away from him. When he bent down to lick her warm fur, a sip of liqueur after the banquet, he saw that a patch of carpet was soaked right through, and he laughed.

Alistair, he thought, *you can't do that!*

His laughter woke her from a deep swoon. Her eyes opened a fraction. She drew several breaths as if the simple act required greater strength than she possessed. Her tongue flickered across her lips. She tried to sit up and failed; in the end she abandoned the effort and rolled over onto her side where she lay, heaving long, wet gasps.

Frank rested his back against the sofa and gazed at her without speaking. He perceived, as if through a white gauze, the beginnings of disaster.

"My God," Louise said. "My God, it's been so long . . . "

Suddenly he was curious. "Don't you make love with . . . ?"

She laughed hoarsely. "Joke."

But he couldn't leave it alone. "What about other men?"

She raised her head. For a long moment their eyes met; then she looked away with a shrug. "There've been . . . technicians. Men who twiddle a few knobs and say, 'There you are lady, that's fixed it for the moment.'"

Frank discovered that by reaching out he could pick up his coffee cup. The contents were cold, but he didn't care. He needed something, anything to refresh him, to flush away the sour taste already forming on the root of his tongue.

Louise slowly extended her entire body in a stretch that ended with a spasm, and sat up. "I need to take a shower," she said. "Then I want us to go to bed and talk. I can say things to a naked Frank that I can't say to a moron in a suit, okay?"

Following her upstairs, he knew an extraordinarily strong desire to get rid of her. In his briefcase he had a long telex from the Department of Trade and Industry to be annotated before Monday; they were negotiating the eleventh round of North Sea licenses, going for Central 22/13B, the "golden block" . . . he ought to telephone Ambassador Gephard, arrange their weekly meeting . . .

She spent a long time in the shower before appearing in the bedroom, toweling her back with brisk, diagonal strokes. When she threw the towel onto the floor and went across to her handbag, for an inhospitable moment he thought, "Oh God, she's going to smoke . . . "; but she turned back to the bed with only a breath-freshener spray in her hands.

"Open wide, be a good boy."

She gave them both a squirt. He wondered whence came this obsession with masking. "A good bar of soap and a tube of toothpaste are the only cosmetics a girl needs"—that's what Sister Shelley used to proclaim. Or was it a plain bar of soap and a good girl . . . ?

"Frank," she said, propping herself up with one hand. "Know any good divorce lawyers, do you?"

"Serious question?"

"Serious."

"I can make some inquiries."

She lay back and put an arm around his chest. When she moved her feet, his copy of the *Independent* fell to the floor with a rustle. For a long time she didn't say anything. Then she surprised him by asking, "What would you think if I said I was being followed?"

His head jerked around. "Are you?"

"I think so."

An unpleasant thought entered his mind. "Were you followed here today?"

"Don't know. Maybe. But the street was empty when I came in; I checked."

Frank knew that landscapes which looked deserted sometimes weren't. And there was such a thing as a telephone directory—if the followers already had a tentative surname, all they needed was to see this woman start walking along a certain street and then let the phone book complete the picture for them . . .

"Why would anyone want to follow you?"

"Alistair doesn't say anything, but he's madly jealous. Possessive—Christ! Sometimes I have to account for my life minute by minute. And then there's the others."

"What others?"

She darted forward to kiss his earlobe, but he pushed her back. "What others?"

He sensed with irritation that she was working out whether she dared trust him. Then she said, "Does the Bamboo Circuit mean anything to you?"

He thought. "Some English barristers go to the Far East, don't they?"

"Right. They go on the Bamboo Circuit. Alistair does it all the time. He's made contacts out there, along with a whole heap of money. It started in Hong Kong, years ago, I know it did. He went to Hong Kong and came back acting strange."

"In what way, strange?"

"He began to look at me as if he couldn't quite work out what I was doing in his house. As if I didn't fit. He had a woman out there, I'm sure of *that.*"

"He said so?"

She shook her head violently. "A wife always knows. Anyway, I didn't give a toss. We were two polite people sharing a house by then. He had his work, his committees . . . As if I cared!"

You cared, Frank thought.

"Then he started to get ratty about his work. No explanation, just foul tempers."

"Didn't you ask him about it?"

"I used to. Gave up, after a while. He'd just say he wasn't prepared to discuss cases with anyone. Pompous ass."

Frank felt meanly satisfied with this description of a marriage. "These others," he murmured. "You said something about there being others."

"Oh, yes. Chinks, mostly. Clients, he calls them. But clients don't come to their barrister's house at one o'clock in the morning, do they? And he's been cheating the tax man, Frank. That, and fixing evidence for those clients of his."

"How on earth do—"

"How do I know? Because when they're having a cozy drink in the study, sometimes I creep down and I hear things wives aren't supposed to hear. You men. You always like to talk, don't you? I read somewhere that women don't talk much at meetings, and that's why they never make the top jobs. Well, that's a load of bull. The reason they don't talk is that they know half the things men say are crap anyway."

Frank's lips twitched. He'd chaired enough mixed-sex meetings in his time to acknowledge there might be something in that.

"I study their faces, sometimes. These people who come and go. I look at them and I just . . . know that there's something rotten going on. And Alistair's in it up to his jelly-neck." She levered herself up again and studied his face. "You think I'm crazy," she concluded.

"I didn't say that."

"No need. Anyway, I'd rather I was going barmy than face up to the truth. Sometimes."

He began to speak before realizing that he didn't know what he meant to say. He stopped and tried again. "What it comes down to is that your husband sees strange people at odd hours, is that right?"

She hesitated. "Strange people . . . some of them have . . . "

"Yes?"

"Some of them have guns." With sudden, unexpected force she turned her body into his, and he could feel the wetness on her cheeks. "Oh, Frank!" she cried. "You've got to help me. I'm so . . . so s-*scared*."

CHAPTER
19

NETTLEBED, OXFORDSHIRE.
THE PRESENT

Outside, it was almost dark. As Scrutton watched, two shapes detached themselves from the shadow of the leafless oak and began to saunter along the boundary. One of them had something under his arm. Scrutton knew what it was, because his father used to carry a twelve-bore in just that way and one gun was much the same as another, he supposed . . .

His bodyguards.

Something soft rubbed against his leg. When he absentmindedly reached down to stroke Freddie's ear, the golden retriever looked up at him through soulful eyes, causing Scrutton to shake his head and say, "Not tonight, boy. Have to wait for the weekend, old chap; can't walk in the dark . . . "

As he turned away from the uninviting prospect outside his vision inevitably traversed a yew hedge to the left, with the wooden roof of a summerhouse just visible beyond that. The pool. The swimming pool where . . .

"God damn!" He drank deeply from the glass

before putting it down on a table and drawing the curtains.

Mrs. Foster, his housekeeper, summoned him to dinner. He ate only a little, wrestling with the queasiness that never left him now, but quickly, as if afraid someone might come in and whip his plate away before he could finish. His doctor had told him that as well as being bad for the digestion, this contributed to his weight problem. Scrutton grunted contemptuously at the recollection. Cigars were bad for him too, apparently, although he'd made it clear on countless occasions that he never inhaled; people (especially doctors) simply refused to *listen* to things they didn't want to hear. Drink never hurt anyone, not in moderation, though try telling the doctor that, with his "units" of this and "units" of that.

A movement hooked his eye and he jumped, staining the cloth with claret. Had the drapes really twitched? No; imagination. The curtains were made of pale mauve velvet. He stared at them, wondering what they reminded him of. Then he remembered: Louise, her lips, that day when . . .

He felt like getting up and going to make sure there was no one standing behind the drapes. Ridiculous! But he did it, all the same. Light flooded out of the room behind him, illuminating the roots and first few inches of the hedge.

Beyond that lay the pool.

He allowed the curtains to fall from his hand. He must plan his evidence for tomorrow. A Romeo y Julieta would help him concentrate, along with a small glass of armagnac.

By the time he'd dislodged Freddie from his armchair and sat down he was in better humor. There was nothing wrong with him that a good long holiday wouldn't cure. Perhaps a cruise, when this ridiculous trial was over . . .

The trial. Scrutton roasted the tip of his cigar in

the flame from a silver table lighter and squinted at the ceiling. The chief seemed to be writing it all down, which was something. Trouble was, he'd got one of those faces like the side of a house, you never could tell with the chief.

Scrutton remembered how once he'd longed to be Lord Chief Justice of England, and chuckled. The idea of taking a massive pay cut while at the same time adopting the social life of a Trappist monk had its ludicrous side. He'd almost told the Lord Chancellor that . . .

The last week of July 1988. A phone call in chambers. Could he see the Lord Chancellor at the House of Lords? I don't want to be a judge, he told himself. But now that the summons had actually come . . .

The Lord Chancellor sat at one end of an enormous table which for the most part was covered with piles of papers and heaps of Hansard; keeping his place with his finger he had looked up to gaze at Scrutton across the tops of his spectacles and said, "I presume you'd like it in the Queen's Bench, Scrutton?"

Scrutton had been expecting preliminaries. This approach floored him. When he kept mum, the Lord Chancellor continued, "Unfortunately, that isn't possible. You can take a Family Division appointment in October, or wait another twelve months and hope the Tories are still in power then; it's the High Court bench, either way. Think it over, let me know by the end of the week, goodbye."

Now, sitting in his armchair with a good cigar on the go, he could look back on that strange meeting at the House of Lords with detachment, even a degree of humor. He remembered the afternoon well. He didn't want to be a High Court judge, he'd told himself as he hailed a cab and had himself driven off to Paddington. He was through with all that nonsense. The knighthood. The red robes and ermine. The bowing and the scraping. The power.

NETTLEBED, OXFORDSHIRE. JULY 1988

He thought a lot about power, on his way back to Reading. It was a beautiful summer's day and he sat alone in the first class compartment, puffing on a cigar as he watched the countryside flow by. Not power over the people appearing before him—he genuinely no longer cared a fig about that—but power, at long last, to clean up and be free. For Alistair Scrutton no longer felt dangerously bored. Those haughty progresses through Customs, once so gut-twistingly marvelous, had begun to pall. Deep inside, he knew his luck could not last forever.

By the time he collected the Daimler from the station car park he'd all but decided to accept the offer of a judgeship, although he'd wait out the year in the hope of the Queen's Bench job, of course: the family division was part of the High Court, but being a judge there somehow lacked *cachet*. On the drive home he kept chortling aloud; so many years pretending he didn't want to be a judge and now here it was, on a plate.

As he closed the overhead door, throwing the hot garage back into near-darkness, from somewhere behind him a voice said, "Scrutton."

He wheeled around with his heart in his mouth, for he recognized that voice. He'd know it in a crowd, while half asleep, on the other side of a room he would know it.

'You!" he gasped. "What the hell do you want?"

The man walking around the Daimler wore slacks and a short-sleeved open-neck shirt; he might have been the Scruttons' gardener, were it not for the obvious horror his appearance had provoked in the householder. That, and the travel bag slung over his shoulder.

"I've told you, Brennan, I don't want you in this country, I don't want you in this *country*."

The Krait laughed. "You and plenty of other people. Unlock the door, we'll go inside."

"Mrs. Foster, my wife—"

"Aren't here. I know where *Louise* is, though. We'll discuss that." He nodded toward the door. "In, Scrutton."

As soon as they entered the kitchen, Brennan went across to pull down the roller blinds.

"I could fancy a beer," he said, smiling, not the least bit tense.

Scrutton went to the fridge and fished out a couple of cans of lager. "You're mad," he muttered. "Coming here in broad daylight."

The Krait unslung his shoulder bag and tossed it onto the table. "There's an envelope inside. Take a look."

Scrutton reluctantly unzipped the bag. It contained the kinds of odds and ends a man might take away for the weekend; also, a camera with several lenses and rolls of film, and a brown Jiffy-bag. He opened the latter. Photographs. He sat down, spreading the photos across the table. As he saw the first one his face changed and his hands began to move more slowly. Louise. Louise and a man.

He couldn't understand what he was looking at. Or rather, he knew perfectly well but his self-esteem wouldn't quite let him register the truth. Street scenes. Louise. Louise waving. A man by her side, taking her arm, looking into her eyes. A house. The two of them going up the steps to the front door. Going inside, the door closing.

He raised his eyes. "Who?"

The Krait finished his lager before replying.

"Name of Thornton," he said at last. "Frank Thornton."

"No."

A long time seemed to tick away before Scrutton could speak again. "No," he repeated. "Can't be. Can't . . . "

"You know him?"

Scrutton made himself study the photos again. Frank Thornton, yes; older, grayer, but unmistakably the same Frank he remembered from Oxford days. He felt hot and cold at the same time, his breathing became forced, he sensed the rage within him and feared it.

"Tell me," he said.

"Your wife," Brennan said, pulling out a chair, "is having an affair with Thornton. Has been for months."

"I'd no idea. No idea."

The Krait leaned across the table. "You know the rules," he said. "No scandals allowed."

Scrutton looked at the photos. He'd arranged them in some kind of chronological order. The meeting. The greeting. The going inside together. And what had happened after that . . . ? They'd been engaged, once. Louise didn't love her husband, had never loved him, he suspected. Frank came back into her life, and bingo!

"I'll talk to her," he grated.

"You'll stop her from seeing this man."

Scrutton had withdrawn into an unpleasant territory all of his own. When he raised his eyes to the Krait's face, they were cold. "I'll deal with it in my own way."

"Or others will. You're a good man, Alistair. Priceless, even. We wouldn't let anything disturb that."

Something of the barrister's innate cunning filtered up to the surface, undeterred even by terror.

Brennan didn't know that his creature had just received the offer of a High Court judgeship. He'd close the Swiss bank account. He could stop gambling, such a stupid way of covering up illicit income . . .

"You're thinking something nice," the Krait said, and he sounded interested. "You're smiling, Alistair. That's good."

"You described me as priceless, it made me smile."

"Well, and there I was imagining that you planned to ditch me; it shows how wrong a man can be. And I'm glad. I'll tell you why. You see, there's still important things for you to do."

"Such as?"

"Such as accept the judgeship they'll be offering, one of these fine days." The Krait prodded the nearest photo. "Assuming there are no scandals, no—"

He broke off. Seconds later, Scrutton heard the sounds that had fazed him: a car's engine, the crunch of gravel. "My God," he croaked, "that's Louise."

Brennan knew the house well. Without another word he snatched up his bag, sprinted through into the drawing room, and from there exited via the terrace. Looking out of the kitchen window, Scrutton saw him race across the lawn to lose himself behind the huge oak in one corner of their sprawling garden. Hearing the front door click, he whirled around, immediately catching sight of the lager cans. He thrust them into the waste bin and was about to send the photos after them when instinct made him pause.

He could always tell her that he'd been having her followed by a private detective. *And he wanted her to see those photographs.*

He braced himself for immediate confrontation, the start of his opening speech already clear in his mind. But Louise, not realizing he was home, denied him immediate satisfaction by passing out to the terrace through the same french doors the Krait had used earlier. He saw her go behind the hedge and knew she must be heading for the pool.

Scrutton followed her.

Earlier, the sun had been shining, but now it was after six o'clock and a thin but even layer of cloud had slowly drawn itself across the sky, sealing in a heat that had imperceptibly become humid. Scrutton walked through the gap in the hedge, shedding jacket and waistcoat. As expected, Louise had gone into the summerhouse on the far side of the pool, where they kept a small fridge. He knew what she would be doing. Suddenly he fancied a drink himself. Something strong.

He skirted the springboard, going by the deep end, and quietly approached the wooden shack. But instead of the expected clink of glass, he heard her talking. Then he remembered: there was a cordless telephone in the summerhouse. She must be calling somebody.

He paused. Whom could she want to ring, so soon after coming back from . . . where had she just been?

The answer came to him with the irresistible logic that was jealousy's forte. She'd spent the day with her lover, and now she was phoning to reassure him she'd arrived home safely.

He went forward again on tiptoe, straining to hear.

" . . . like I've been tingling for days. Where did you learn how to—" A pause. Delighted giggles. She'd never giggled for *him*.

"Oh, darling, no, I can't, I really can't. Alistair would suspect something if we . . . and the hotel people would . . . but what would I *say* to him?"

Rage lurked somewhere deep inside him, like a

tiger readying itself for the kill. But not yet, no, not yet. Let her finish with her lover first.

Then his mind played one of those treacherous tricks and he thought of the times he'd phoned P'ia from his room in the Oriental. He'd set her up with a gift shop in Bangkok, which did well, and often he would lie on the bed during the siesta hours, when trade was slack, talking down the phone to her about nothing and everything . . .

P'ia was history, now. He'd long ago paid the price of freedom and she had been part of it. He no longer had a mistress; he was damned if his wife was going to have a lover.

Scrutton walked forward. His shadow fell across Louise, causing her to look up with a start. " . . . Do phone before you deliver," she said smoothly, "only I'm often out in the mornings." She retracted the aerial with a snap. "Hello, you're early."

"Had a meeting. It finished at three, it was Friday, I thought I'd . . . " He tailed off, suddenly realizing that he was not the one on trial. "Can't I come back to my own home when I please?"

She stood up and went to the refrigerator. "Drink?"

"Whatever you're having."

Louise poured two slugs of vodka, added ice and tonic and handed him a glass. She was pink and alive and somewhat flustered, not meeting his eyes. She often seemed that way now; funny he hadn't twigged the reason before. He gulped his vodka and promptly went to fix a refill.

"Where've you been today?" he asked.

"With friends."

"Who?"

"Oh, for God's sake, you don't know them. I might just as well ask who your bloody meeting was with."

"The Lord Chancellor."

She had already launched into another sentence, but these words brought her up short. "Oh," she said uncertainly. "What did he want?"

"He's offered me a High Court judgeship."

"Seriously?"

"You don't find me a likely candidate?"

"It's not that. But . . . " She stood up and followed his earlier example, piling her glass high with ice cubes and this time omitting tonic water. "Yes," she said turning to face him. "If you want the truth, I think he must be off his head."

"Why?"

She folded her arms across her chest and thrust her way past him onto the concrete apron surrounding the pool. "Because you're rude to people," she said over her shoulder. "I thought there was a move to get away from the likes of you, on the bench."

"Thanks for being frank." *Frank.* Frank Thornton . . . He took a long swig to cover his seething temper. "What's got into you?"

She shrugged.

"You look like a whore who's made enough to knock off for the day."

She wheeled around, but she must have seen from his face that he knew, for she lowered her eyes and began to traipse around on the same spot, like a dancer practicing basic steps.

"Do you want to talk?" she asked, after a while.

"About?"

"About me and . . . and Frank." She looked up on the last word, flinging it at him with evident satisfaction.

"Proud of it, aren't you?"

"Does it show? Tell me darling, is it the same look you used to wear after Bangkok—smug and guilty? Ooh . . . and I didn't even remember to buy you a lovely new watch to compensate, did I? *So* sorry."

"How long has this been going on?"

"Months. Practically since he got back to England."

"You . . . slut."

"Nice, coming from you."

"I've never been unfaithful to you in my life."

She threw back her head and laughed at the sky. "You wouldn't convince a jury, sweetheart. Your face is enough to hang you ten times over. Are you really going to be a judge?"

"Don't change the subject."

"I'm not. We're going to have to think about this." Her face softened a fraction. "Look. I don't love you, you don't love me, all right? There's no kids to mess things up. Plenty of judges have been divorced before, you've often said it."

He stared at her. "What are you—"

"Doing it quietly. A quickie, isn't that what lawyers call it—no mud-slinging, just mutual incompatibility."

He still did not understand what she meant. "You . . . you want a divorce?"

"You bet. I'll move out. Tomorrow, if you like."

"Like hell you will!"

"So what do you suggest, then? You could buy a pad in town, I suppose, until we sell this place. Don't worry, I'm not going to take you to the cleaners. Frank's loaded."

"It's not the money."

"No? What then?"

"I'm not going to let you go, that's what. Jesus Christ, Louise, listen to yourself! Listen to what you're saying."

"You're *not* going to try to tell me how much you adore me, are you?" she scoffed.

"No. But if you think I'm going to abandon you to Frank Thornton without a fight, you're out of your mind."

"You can't stop me."

She tossed back the remains of her drink and turned as if to leave. He caught her arm. "Louise!" There was a note of pleading in his voice and he despised himself for that. "Be sensible, you can't just—"

"Let *go*." She shook off his hand, backing away from him. "Don't think I don't know all about your sordid little fucks out east. *And* the types you mix with out there."

She turned her back on him and went back into the summerhouse, where she picked up the phone and dialed a number.

"I think you'd better explain," he said quietly as he came after her. "You've got nothing at all on me, but if you think I'm going to be blackmailed by a cheating little slut of a wife, now, just at the point when—"

"Hello! Frank? Louise. Alistair knows about us. He's—"

Scrutton tried to wrench the phone from her hands.

"Frank!" she screamed. "For God's sake, help me. Call the pol—"

Alistair slapped her face so hard that she fell back against the table, knocking it over. He wrested the phone from her and flung it away from him. It landed in the shallow end of the pool.

For a moment neither of them could move or speak. Then Louise came upright and pointed at the pool. She was giggling.

"Bubbles," she said. "Look at all those tiny bubbles. That's Frank, darling, trying to speak to me. Like in the cartoons." She clapped her hands and bent double, still laughing. It was then that he hit her.

His fist would have landed smack in the middle of her jaw if she hadn't seen it coming and tried to duck. Her reaction diverted the punch awkwardly onto her chest. All the air went out of her in a throaty grunt. She staggered sideways, flailed, and toppled into the water.

Alistair ran a hand through his hair as he turned away with a shrug. Since the pool was unheated, it stayed cold until September. The shock of falling in should sober her up. Calculating bitch! How could anyone seriously think he'd allow her to drag him through the divorce courts . . . ?

He'd have to deal with her threats, though. That ugly reference to the Far East was unnerving.

He turned back to the pool to see Louise floating face down, her golden hair weaving and braiding itself around her head like a rare seaweed. For a few seconds, Alistair stared. Then he plunged in and struck out awkwardly across the pool.

Spluttering and choking, he somehow managed to drag her down to the shallow end until his feet touched bottom. He hauled himself out and reached down to cup his hands under her shoulders. With phenomenal effort he managed to lift her onto the apron. Clumsily he thrust a hand under her blouse. No heartbeat. He bent to her mouth, could feel no breath. Her face was deathly white, the lips the same pale mauve as the lounge curtains.

"Louise!" he screamed. *"Louise!"*

He pulled her jaw down, took a deep breath and breathed gently into her mouth. No effect. He tried again. Still nothing. Alistair sat back. His heart was beating like a machine gun, his head filled with noise, he pounded the concrete with his fists, he could not believe this was happening. It was not happening. *Not, not, not!*

A hand slapped his cheek, very hard; and Scrutton came to himself to hear the last of his own hysterical screams die away to silence.

Brennan was kneeling beside Louise's body, one

hand held to her neck. At last he looked up and said, "She's dead."

Scrutton stared at him. Dead. A word. Part of the English language. But nothing to do with him. Nothing whatever.

"What . . . what are we going to . . . " He wiped his face, knowing he should finish the question but stuck for the right words.

"Be a man. We have to work out what you're going to say."

Scrutton rocked drunkenly to and fro. Seeing his lack of comprehension, Brennan explained. "When a man kills his wife it's a damn serious thing, now isn't it? Isn't it? Only you're the lawyer, man; you should know."

"*Kill* her. But I didn't . . . I *couldn't* have . . . "

"The camera doesn't lie."

He rose. Only then did Scrutton notice that a camera with a telephoto lens was suspended from his neck on a thick black canvas strap, and his jaw dropped.

"But that's ridiculous. You saw what happened, you know . . . "

"I know."

"Then you can say . . . you can help . . . " A part of him, he belatedly discovered, still functioned. "You can't use those pictures. They're no good in court unless you call the person who took them." His courage was increasing as he thought it through. "You need to call a photographer. *And you haven't got one!*"

"Oh, we'll find a photographer, Alistair." The Krait's voice was gentle. He looked down at the corpse, then glanced sideways at Scrutton, a dreamy smile playing around his lips. "You're a lawyer, you know how it is. All it takes is money."

CHAPTER

20

LONDON. THE PRESENT

The first thing Roz did when she arrived at the Old Bailey was phone Ben Saunders, fingers crossed and eyes closed while she prayed. He wasn't in.

Damn, damn, *damn*. Mottram would be starting his cross-examination of Scrutton tomorrow at the latest, and he possessed precious little straw of brick-making quality. Ben had to come through with the goods, he simply had to. *Where was he?*

Roz rested against the side of the phone booth and counted options along with her change. One, she could write Ben off—no good, he was their only hope. Two, telephone everyone who'd ever met Ben Saunders on the off-chance that they might have some news of him—no good, she'd done that already, ten times over. Three, go looking for him.

That might work. She hadn't cruised the pubs yet . . .

Roz finally slipped into court at ten to eleven, still pondering her best chance of laying hands on Saunders. As she settled down beside Joe

Simmonds, Sir Patrick was saying, " . . . before that day at the funeral?"

"No."

Joe slid his notepad along the bench for her to read, but she pushed it away, keeping her eyes fixed on Scrutton. He had presence, she realized with a sinking heart. You could see that he lived too well, but there was no denying the man's authority. He might have been one of the Crown's expert witnesses; the pathologist, perhaps, or a gunsmith.

"But on that day, you *did* see Mr. Thornton, is that correct?"

"Yes."

"He went to the service?"

"Yes."

"And afterward, at the committal, was he there?"

Yes, Roz thought to herself. So was I. And God, what a performance that turned out to be . . .

SWYNCOMBE, OXFORDSHIRE. AUGUST 1988

Roz did not attend the funeral in a professional capacity; she went because she knew the chief mourner and was sufficiently nosey to expend a precious day off. But since the ceremony dissolved into one of the most scandalous episodes of a scandal-wracked year, she would have ended up with a scoop; except for the awkward accident of becoming prime witness in a potential court case that prevented her from using it.

The church was at the end of a lane and visitors were supposed to park down one side of a track which in its heyday might have accommodated the rector's Ford and the hearse without too much difficulty. This afternoon, fifty or more cars were vying for space beneath the row of beeches that lined the avenue leading to the old stone church. Because it was a swelteringly hot day, some tempers were shorter than the occasion required. A number of the mourners were lawyers, and Roz had remarked before that they did not excel at cooperative activities.

She took one look at the crush, slammed into reverse, and got herself a quarter of a mile down the lane without stopping. There she found a handy lay-by, where she parked, and was happy to walk the rest of the way. This was England at its summer best. Green trees and hedges lined lush pastures in which sheep grazed, and gentle hills broke up the horizon, like a backdrop taken from some storybook designed to convince children that there once had been a better time.

St. Botolph's church fitted perfectly into this picture, its spire half-hidden behind a lofty oak in full leaf. Because she was early, she took a stroll through the churchyard, examining the moss-covered graves, still damp to the touch after days of sun. Like most people, she sometimes fantasized about being buried in a spot like this. You forgot about the rain and the bleak midwinter days when death came to take possession of its allotted acre.

The church interior was blessedly cool, and sweet with scents of polished antiquity. She looked for Frank, feeling sure that he must have read the press accounts of the inquest, and confident that he would come. This deep inner conviction surprised her. They'd met once or twice since he'd taken up residence in England, first so that she could write a profile of him, and then socially, but she still did not think of them as being close.

She could see no sign of him, however, although by now the church was almost full. A little after three o'clock, Alistair Scrutton followed his dead wife's coffin up the aisle, hands clasped behind his back, head bowed. From her place beside a pillar, Roz could not see his face, merely the solemn bearing, silver-gray hair, and dark clothes of a distinguished lawyer, recently widowed.

She was not a religious woman, but the simple, dignified service moved her. When Alistair took spectacles from his breast pocket and began to read the lesson, his resonant voice filled the church from font to spire and Roz knew herself to be a participant at something that transcended spiritual divisions. Death *did* level.

The rector of Swyncombe delivered the address. Roz, listening between and behind his words, realized that he hadn't known the deceased well. His assessment of Louise was beyond possibility of challenge; phrases like "a well-known, friendly local figure" and "a source of constant support and comfort in his professional as well as his private life" were scarcely contentious.

After the service, people formed knots in the churchyard, waiting out the inevitable lull before the burial. Roz drifted away, hugging the wall of the church, not wanting to be drawn into Alistair's circle. He had already positioned himself near the grave, apart from the throng. She saw several mourners, mostly women, look at him with assessment in their eyes, obviously wondering if he was in need of consolation.

For the first time, she noticed something odd about his appearance. Although the day was hot, he wore a black coat and gloves, as if determined to carry convention to its furthest limits.

The rector appeared in the church doorway, accompanied by an undertaker, and made his way toward the grave. It was then that Roz caught sight of Frank Thornton. He stood alone by the lich-gate, leaning against the stone-and-flint wall with his arms folded across his chest. If he saw her looking at him he gave no sign of recognition. Only when the throng had formed a complete circle around the grave did he silently move to join them. Roz brought up the rear, positioning herself in such a way that she always kept Frank in view.

The interment was soon over. Scrutton scattered earth on the coffin; perhaps that's why he's wearing gloves, Roz vaguely thought to herself. People started to go, but something made her look back at the grave. Alistair stood in conversation with the rector, who at last touched his arm and walked off. By now the crowd had dissipated, leaving Frank high and dry. He approached the grave, keeping his eyes fixed on Scrutton, who did not appear to notice him.

Roz withdrew behind a tree, determined to see what would happen next.

"Alistair."

Scrutton raised his head. "I'm sorry," Roz heard him say. "I don't—"

"Frank Thornton."

For a moment the two men looked at each other in silence. Then Scrutton said in a weary voice, "Your usual idea of good taste, I see."

"Look, I don't want—"

"What *do* you want, Thornton? You could have paid your respects, if that's how you see it, some other time. This is hardly the occasion."

"I need to talk to you."

But Scrutton turned away and made as if to follow the departing mourners. Frank let him go a few steps. Then he said, "You can't walk away from this. I won't let you."

His voice had risen in pitch and Roz wasn't the only one to hear.

"It's nothing to do with you," Scrutton observed over his shoulder. "Leave it."

"Like hell I will!" A few strides brought him to Scrutton's side and the other man flinched.

"Don't make a scene, it's not worth it."

"Then let's go somewhere less public."

"I've told you, there's nothing—"

"And *I've* told *you*, Scrutton, there's things that need to be said."

Several people were waiting in a group by the lich-gate, staring at the two men. Scrutton bit his lip, then began to walk swiftly toward them. Roz sensed his fear, and her pulse quickened. She came out from behind the tree.

He was halfway to the gate when Frank said, "You killed her, Scrutton. Murdered her."

For a second there was total silence. Then the waiting group began to talk in outraged whispers. Scrutton stopped. He stared at the path for a moment, before wheeling around to face Frank.

"You're distressed," he said mildly. "It's understandable. Go home, we'll talk some other time."

"We'll talk now. I was on the phone to her when you cut her off. She was terrified."

"I wasn't there when it happened." Scrutton was losing control; his voice reverberated with anger. "The coroner—"

"You told that inquest a pack of lies."

Several yards separated the two men, who by now were making no effort to keep their voices down. Scrutton swung around and made as if to march off down the path, but the movement brought his eyes into direct contact with Roz's. She saw his face change. The transfiguration happened in a flash, but she could have taken an oath as to what she saw: rage, terror, and guilt.

"You heard!" he called; and she realized that Scrutton was talking to her. "You heard what he just said to me."

Roz shook her head violently, but Scrutton was having none of that. He strode up to her. "You're my witness," he snapped. "I want your name and address."

"My name's Roz Forbes," she said. "Remember?"

Scrutton stared at her uncomprehendingly; but behind him she heard Frank mutter, "Oh my God."

"I'm a journalist," she went on. "And we've met before."

Scrutton stepped back, wrestling with memory. "Met . . . before?" he whispered.

"When we were both very young. In a court corridor." He would have liked to retreat, but her stare held him rooted to the spot. "You want a witness, you've got one. I can be contacted at the *Times*. Ask for the deputy editor."

Then something happened which irked her for months afterward. Scrutton turned his back and spoke a single, low sentence to Frank, who continued to gaze at Roz for a few seconds longer before nodding assent. To her amazement, the two men walked swiftly away, thrusting through the outraged gaggle by the gate. She saw them get into a Daimler and drive off. It was all over within seconds, leaving her with a deflated sense of anticlimax.

As she made her way back up the lane to her own car she would have given anything to know where the rivals had gone and what they were saying. Later, when they were preparing Frank's defense, she came to learn his version. But it wasn't until the trial itself that she heard Scrutton's.

LONDON. THE PRESENT

"Where did you go?" Sir Patrick asked, "after that unfortunate graveside contretemps?"

"I drove the defendant back to my house."

"What happened when you got there?"

"I showed the defendant into the living room. I offered him a drink."

"Why?"

"Why?"

"You'd had a violent and public quarrel; hardly the sort of thing that merits hospitality, perhaps?"

"I wanted to give us both time to calm down. To reflect." Scrutton hesitated. "It had been a very trying afternoon. I thought it might help us both if we took a drink."

"How many drinks did you have?"

"I had one. He had three. He helped himself."

"Did you protest at that?"

"I did. He ignored me."

"Now please tell us the substance of what was said."

Scrutton looked up at the ceiling, then down at the floor, obviously gathering his thoughts.

"I began . . . I began by saying that his outburst had put us both in an impossible position. I was conscious of my position at the bar. Unless he agreed to make an equally public apology, I'd have to sue him for slander."

"What did he say to that?"

"In effect, that he stood by the allegation."

"That you'd murdered your wife?"

"Yes."

"Now we've heard the background from police witnesses, but to recapitulate: the coroner found that death was due to your wife falling into the pool where the sudden shock of cold water caused a spasm which killed her. In substance. Is that your understanding?"

"Yes. A doctor told the inquest that there are five or six cases every year. Something to do with the extreme contrast between the heat of the day and the coldness of the water. Our pool is unheated."

"Were you present when your wife died?"

"I was not." His voice lowered. "I . . . I found her. When I came home later that afternoon."

"The coroner detected a bruise on your wife's chest and held that it was recent?"

"Yes. It happened on the morning of her death. I was carrying a tray, thinking she was still in bed when in fact she'd got up, and we walked straight into each other. The corner of the tray landed smack against her."

"Please go on with your account of the meeting with Mr. Thornton."

"Well, he was very upset. Hysterical, I'd have said. It didn't help me. My own state of mind was . . . "

Sir Patrick cleared his throat. "Yes. Yes. Please go on."

"He . . . he began to stride about, repeating his allegations. He said that my wife had been on the phone to him when she was suddenly cut off, just before the time of death as found by the coroner. I was surprised. I didn't know the two of them had met. But he said . . . " Scrutton took a deep breath, resting his weight on the ledge in front of him. "*He* said that they'd been having an affair."

Roz gasped. Apart from that, the court was utterly silent. When the chief murmured, "Would you care to sit down, Mr. Scrutton?" she jumped.

"No, thank you, my Lord."

"What happened then?"

"I . . . I was astonished."

Roz, too. Frank had maintained throughout that he and Louise were friends, nothing more. Suddenly she guessed, no, *knew* why he'd refused to tell her where he was on the one night above all others when, if he was to defeat the Crown's case, he must have an alibi. He had been in bed with Alistair Scrutton's wife.

Roz looked across the court at Frank, reading confirmation in his eyes, and somehow she managed to smile.

She had not known jealousy for so long. How petty, how sordid, how thoroughly *nasty* an emotion it was, and, in the circumstances, how ridiculous! Frank's sex life was his own business, she'd been tied up with Johnny, Frank could be described as attractive, certainly, but . . .

The trial, she discovered, had been going on without her. She did her best to listen, but what felt like the start of 'flu was gathering in her chest and stomach, making concentration difficult.

"You had no knowledge of this affair?" Sir Patrick asked Scrutton.

"None. I still can't accept it."

"Did you tell Thornton that?"

"Yes. It was then that he drew a gun on me."

The silence in court grew oppressive. Roz could sense that neither prosecutor not witness wanted to be the first to break it.

"Did you have an opportunity to examine that gun?"

"Yes."

"How did that come about?"

Scrutton swallowed a couple of times. "At first, he was waving it about wildly. Then he . . . he seemed to break down. He began to sob. He threw the gun on the table between us."

"Did he say why?"

"He . . . he begged me to kill him. 'Put me out of my misery,' those were his exact words."

"Can you describe the gun to us?"

"Ah . . . a revolver. Wooden handle, with a plastic plate let into each side. And a . . . a circular badge, with lettering on it. I thought it was an *M.* and an *R.* Done artistically."

Sir Patrick called for an exhibit. The gun was handed up to Scrutton, who examined it.

"It looks identical to the one I saw after the funeral," he said.

"The *M* and the *R* you see engraved there indicate that this is a Manurhin MR-73. A French revolver."

"Yes."

"It was found in the accused's car on the day of his arrest."

"I see."

The exhibit was handed back.

"What else happened on that occasion?" A long pause. "Mr. Scrutton . . . ?"

"I tried to keep calm. Tried to soothe him. I was very frightened."

"Did you touch the gun at all?"

"No."

"Did he?"

"Mr. Thornton picked it up when he left the house."

"In the event, did you decide to sue him?"

"I felt he'd left me with no choice. He'd accused me of murder, publicly. I knew he'd repeat the charge, he was in that kind of state. So I issued a writ for slander."

"Did he defend that action?"

"Yes."

"On what grounds?"

"His pleadings claimed that the words were spoken in jest and would have been taken as such by all who heard them."

"In *jest*?"

The attorney-general allowed the words to hang in the stuffy air for a long time, while everyone present repeated them silently to him or herself.

"Was there any other defense pleaded?"

"I believe the specialists call it 'vulgar abuse,' not capable of amounting to defamation in law."

"Did he plead that the allegation of murder was true?"

"He did not."

No, thought Roz. Because he couldn't. He had no evidence. She had often wondered whether what Frank claimed about Louise's death was true. Now, looking at Scrutton in the box, she found herself suddenly believing it. There was something about this heavy, slack-jawed man that repelled. *If only the jury would see it!* "I want now to go back in time, to the period after Mr. Thornton returned to the UK, in 1987. Did you meet him then?"

"Not 'meet,' exactly. I went to his house, in March 1988, the year before last."

"How did that come about?"

"I read about his return to this country in the newspapers and decided to visit him. We'd been close friends, once."

"Did you make an appointment first?"

"I tried to, but Mr. Thornton was extraordinarily well protected by secretaries, and so forth. It did just cross my mind that he might not care to see me."

"Why?"

Scrutton coughed. "There had been a time, many years ago, when he and my wife were, I think, close. She chose to marry me, and perhaps . . . "

"Quite. Did you go to his house, in the event?"

"I did. I was anxious to renew our friendship and I felt that a face to face meeting was the best way of dispelling any lingering animosity that might have arisen from the circumstances of my marriage. So I called around, uninvited, one evening, during the last week of March. Rather late; I'd been in a conference that had overrun. It must have been almost nine o'clock when I rang his doorbell."

"Did he answer the door?"

"No. But I assumed he was in, because the lights were on. So I tried again, but still no answer, so I went round to the back."

"Explain that, please."

"Mr. Thornton has a house in Abbotsbury Road, by Holland Park. There's a garden at the rear; I'd seen the back gate as I approached. I walked along the passage to the kitchen door. There was no light on in the kitchen, but I could see a light in the hallway and when I pushed on the door I found it open."

Sir Patrick's junior was tugging his gown. The two men had a whispered conversation that ended with the attorney-general turning back to the witness and asking, "Yes, I'm reminded . . . can you put a precise date on this?"

"I have my diary with me. May I . . . ? Ah, yes: 30th March; the Wednesday before Good Friday. 'Frank.'"

"Did you make that entry before or after your visit?"

"After. That same night."

"Why?"

"Because of what happened at the house. It made such an impression on me, I knew it could be important."

"Tell the jury about that, will you?"

"I entered the kitchen. I think I may have called the defendant's name, I'm not sure. In any case, nobody answered. I walked through into the passage. A door was half-open. I could hear voices."

"How many?"

"Just two. The defendant's and one other man. Clearly I'd come at a bad time. I turned to go. I suddenly felt bad about the whole thing. Here I was, trespassing, I suppose; I wanted to get out."

"Did you leave then?"

"No."

"Why not?"

"Because of what I heard."

"Which was . . . ?"

"I'd almost reached the inner door leading to the kitchen when the other man raised his voice. He sounded . . . impatient, as if he wasn't getting through and it irked him."

"Did you hear what he said?"

"Yes. He said: 'Your revolver, the one we gave

you, of course.' He may not have said 'of course,' not those actual words. But that was the sense of it. Of his tone."

The attorney-general paused. Roz became aware of her heart beating disagreeably fast. Looking around her at the rapt faces, she wondered if others felt the same. This was it. The nub of the trial. The point on which all else hung; on which Frank might hang.

"Did you hear anything else?"

"Yes. I stopped and quietly walked back a few paces. I was intrigued. Mention of a revolver, and so on."

"What did you hear?"

"Thornton was saying something about risk. A big risk for small reward, something along those lines. He sounded frightened. Argumentative."

"And after this mention of risk . . . ?"

"The other man—he was very calm, controlled—said that there would be no risk; all the defendant had to do was have the gun in the right place at the right time and it would be taken off him by the man."

"The man?"

"He sort of gave the words capitals, you know? Capital T The, capital M Man. He used the expression several times."

"Did you at any time see this other man, the one at Abbotsbury Road?"

"No."

"Do you remember anything special about him?"

"I'm sorry . . . ?"

"His . . . how did he sound?"

"Oh . . . Irish, I think. I can't pretend to be an expert."

This last disclaimer in response to Mottram, already rising to his feet with a protest.

"Do you remember hearing anything else?"

"Yes. The Irishman . . . sorry, the *other* man, spoke of someone called Gephard. I gathered that this Gephard and Thornton were associated, but I don't know how."

"Did this Gephard have a first name?"

"Not in the conversation I heard, no."

"How was his name used?"

"The other man said that Gephard was the key, because he was close to the palace. He said—"

"Let me stop you there. Close . . . to the palace. Are those the exact words used?"

"Yes."

"Go on."

"He—the other man—said that Thornton needed a way in and Gephard was the key, because he was close to the palace."

"You say, 'because'? Are you certain that this is how the matter was put?"

"Yes, I am."

"Thank you. Was anything else said in your hearing?"

Scrutton thought. "Thornton was . . . " He shook his head, as if angry with himself. "He used the word counterproductive. He said that several times. 'It's going to be counterproductive, why won't you see that?'—I recall him using those precise words. Then again: 'a harebrained scheme.' And he said something about his fund-raisers in the States having better things to spend their money on."

"Are you sure he referred to 'his' fund-raisers? Possessive?"

"Absolutely."

"How long were you there for?"

"I would say . . . ten minutes."

"You left after that?"

"Yes. By that time, I was afraid."

"Afraid of what?"

Scrutton did not answer immediately. Then— "Of not getting out of that house alive."

CHAPTER

21

LONDON. THE PRESENT

Next day, Roz awoke an hour earlier than she'd meant to. The duvet had fallen off the bed, leaving her half-frozen. She hugged it around her and peered out at what was still semidark Battersea. Several early commuters fought their way up the street behind their umbrellas, contending with a mixture of sleet and rain. As she watched, it suddenly occurred to her to wonder if those people really were what they seemed to be. *They* are interested in you, Ben had said; and now who in her life could be guaranteed innocent?

But then the sight of those same umbrellas reminded her of something else—tiny fishing-boats, no more than coracles under canvas, struggling for the safety of Hong Kong harbor before typhoon struck—and she let the curtain fall from her fingers. Other times, other loves. That Far East tour with Johnny had been, oh *shut up!*

Roz bundled herself back into bed and closed her eyes, but once you let a thought into your head the day was *there*, another enemy to be thwarted and coped with and got through. She was more unhappy than she'd been for months, not just on account of Johnny, either.

Frank had complicated matters by holding back on her about his affair with Louise. This made Roz feel confused and unhappy, like an adolescent schoolgirl hung up on her favorite master when he got engaged. As if it was any business of hers whom Frank Thornton slept with. Pathetic!

She wondered what he was doing. Exercise? Slopping-out? (Vile phrase for a ghastly practice.) He was so . . . solid. He hadn't crumpled. Manly; that's the word she'd choose to describe Frank if she were doing a feature on him.

Roz wriggled her shoulders, frowning. She hadn't owned up to that before, but it was true. Frank Thornton was sexy. Come off it, she lectured herself; it's just his situation. But no, that didn't seem right.

Sexy.

She snuggled down in bed. Her finger strayed to her crotch and remained there. Johnny barged in first, but she ejected him without ceremony and beckoned Frank. It worked. It worked surprisingly fast and with unforeseen intensity.

Andrew Mottram was waiting for her outside court. "Anything?" he asked her.

Roz shook her head. "I can't even raise Ben Saunders on the phone. He's taken indefinite leave. I'm going to do the rounds of the places where he drinks tonight."

He sighed. "You're doing your best, no one could have done more, but . . . "

"But."

"At least there's Scrutton to look forward to." Mottram's face brightened a little. "I've never cross-examined one of my learned friends before."

"What's he going to be like under pressure?"

"Hard to say. He was always a formidable court operator. Very succinct. A bit oily and ingratiating toward the judge, and unless you were one of his cronies, downright arrogant to opponents."

Mottram thought. "If I can only get him to show off a bit, the jury might see through him."

"Good luck, Andrew."

She was under no illusions. Today, Alistair Scrutton faced cross-examination. If Mottram broke him, the jury would acquit Frank. If Scrutton survived the ordeal, Frank would hang. The case had been stripped clean down to the bone.

Roz had a feeling Mottram would open with their one fast ball and she was right.

"Mr. Scrutton, some years after you began to practice as a barrister, you went to Hong Kong to do a case, correct?"

Roz counted slowly up to five before Scrutton said, "Yes." The pause was his only sign of perturbation.

"Instructed by a Chinese solicitor called Lee?"

"Yes."

"Who introduced you to a man called Siri Chaloem?"

An even longer pause. "Yes. He was a Thai."

Roz found herself thinking of white noise. Silence became a substantial, tangible thing.

"Did you know that Mr. Chaloem subsequently died?"

"I'd heard . . . something to that effect."

"From whom did you hear it?"

"I can't remember."

"But you were enough in touch with that part of the world to hear?"

"Yes. If you put it like that."

"How would you put it?"

Scrutton said nothing.

"How did Chaloem die, do you know?"

"I understood . . . "

"Yes?"

"I understood that he was murdered."

"He was murdered. His father, too, was murdered; did you know that?"

"I . . . forget."

"Did you ever meet his father?"

"I may have done."

"Did you?"

"Once. I think."

"Did you know that the Chaloems, father and son, were in business together?"

"I knew nothing about them. They were friends of Mr. Lee who offered me hospitality. That's all."

"How many times did you meet them, over the years?"

"Perhaps . . . half a dozen."

"What, both of them?"

"I think so . . . "

"Mr. Chaloem the elder was killed in 1977, wasn't he?"

Scrutton hesitated. "It must have been his son I met those half-dozen times."

"You came to know him well, then?"

"As acquaintances. I don't see where—"

"Did you know that father and son were drug-peddlers?"

Scrutton lurched forward to grip the edge of the box. "I most certainly did not."

"Both murdered, at different times, by other dealers in that dreadful trade?"

"No."

"I have a *Bangkok Post* from last July here; do you wish me to read the report?"

"I'm happy to accept what you say." Scrutton's voice was hushed.

Mottram turned to the bench. "My Lord, we shall be calling an inspector of the Royal Thai Police to give evidence on these—and other—matters. Now. Mr. Scrutton. Will you also accept from me that Mr. Lee's in prison?" Mottram held up a piece of paper. "I have the certificate of conviction here, along with the Hong Kong Law Society's order that he be struck off the roll."

"I . . . I had absolutely no idea. Am I allowed to know why he was—"

"He was found in possession of a boat containing a quarter of a ton of processed heroin, which, according to the evidence led in Hong Kong and presumably accepted by the jury, he intended to market for one particular client. Can you guess the name of that client?"

Sir Patrick rose to lodge a protest, but Mottram cut him short.

"Chaloem," he said. "It was Siri Chaloem. Wasn't it?"

"If you say so."

"How many times over the years did Mr. Lee employ you professionally?"

"I really couldn't say."

"Our researches suggest twenty-three?"

"All right."

"How many times did you visit Hong Kong for professional purposes altogether, Mr. Scrutton? Think carefully, please; we have copy ticket stubs from the airline."

"I . . . I'm sorry, I don't carry the figure in my head."

"Twenty-three; does that sound right?"

"If you say so."

"Mr. Lee employed you twenty-three times and you visited the colony twenty-three times. No one else there ever employed you, did they?"

"No."

"Did you know that your only client out there had a profitable sideline in narcotics?"

"Most certainly not."

"Sure?"

"Of course I'm . . . I'm sure."

"Once the cases were over, you used to go on holiday, I think? To the Genting Highlands, for the gambling? To Macau, for the gambling? You are what's called a heavy roller, aren't you, Mr. Scrutton?"

The witness took temporary refuge in silence. "I sometimes indulge," he said sulkily.

The lord chief justice laid down his pen. He leaned forward to rest his elbows on the bench and clasp his hands in front of his mouth. These movements were utterly soundless. Not a single person in that court failed to observe them.

"Mr. Mottram." Something about the chief's voice activated echoes that ignored every other speaker. The two quiet words batted around the room like a squashball before coming to rest. "I don't want to ask the jury to withdraw, so I'll just remind you of a line of poetry: 'Willing to wound and yet afraid to strike.'"

He unclasped his hands and slowly sat back to grip the sides of his chair, not taking his eyes from Mottram's face.

Mottram bowed, and shuffled papers around on the lectern, telling Roz of his disappointment. That line of questioning was, she knew, their strongest point; and all it amounted to was innuendo.

"This gun," Mottram said thoughtfully. "The one Mr. Thornton . . . *brandished* in front of you after your wife's funeral." He paused. "Was it loaded?"

"I'm sure it was."

"Why are you sure?"

"If someone pointed a gun at you, you'd assume it was loaded, wouldn't you?"

Good, Roz thought. You look flustered, Scrutton. Jury won't like that.

"Just answer the question, will you. Why did you assume that gun was loaded?"

"I'm certain it was."

"That's because it wasn't Mr. Thornton's gun, was it? It was yours."

The courtroom became as silent as an empty church.

"You're saying . . . it was *my* gun?"

Mottram rested his arm on the lectern and rested his weight on it. "Yes. Is that true?"

"I've never owned a gun."

"Mr. Thornton will say that after the funeral he *did* go back to your house, and there *was* a gun produced. By you. He struggled with you and snatched it away, which is how his fingerprints came to be found on it."

"But mine weren't." Scrutton made no attempt to disguise his triumph.

"No. You wore gloves to that funeral, even though it was a hot day, and you never took them off. Why?"

"Is that right?" Scrutton was rocking back and fro in the box, plainly agitated. "Did I not remove—"

"Our witnesses will say you did not."

"I don't remember. I was wearing gloves, yes, it seemed . . . proper."

"When the temperature outside was in excess of seventy degrees?"

Scrutton made no reply.

"Did you scatter earth on your wife's coffin?"

"I can't remember."

"Minute traces of earth were found on exhibit one, the Manurhin MR-73 revolver. Our case will be that those traces match the earth in the churchyard where your wife was buried."

"It's possible."

"How?"

"I've told the court already, he flung the gun on the table and that's how I came to see it."

"You picked it up, in other words."

"I must have done."

"Without leaving fingerprints? And when you were giving evidence yesterday—" Mottram leaned back and snapped his fingers. His junior handed him the daily transcript. "—Yesterday, you told my Lord and the jury that you did not touch the gun. I have it here."

Scrutton was silent for a moment. Then he said: "That occasion was very fraught. Certain things stand out strongly in my mind. Other details have faded. I may have touched the gun while still wearing gloves. If there is churchyard earth on it, that is undoubtedly how it would have come there, unless . . ."

"Unless what?"

"Unless Mr. Thornton also had soil on his hands."

"Did he throw earth on the coffin?"

"I did not see him do so. He may have done when I was not looking. Just as I may have touched the gun."

Silence descended once more. It's like Wimbledon, Roz thought despondently. Back and forth lobs the ball; just when you're sure the Number One seed can't possibly recover, he makes that magic shot from the baseline . . . and after each game the whole audience subsides as the tension goes out of them, but there's still a set to go and all to play for . . .

The problem facing the defense was one of motive: why should Scrutton lie?

Earlier in the trial, the prosecution had called Padraic Tumin, an IRA gunman presently serving a life sentence in Dartmoor, who'd told the court that while in prison he'd become aware of a plot to kill the Queen—"something," as he laconically put it— "we've had on the list for half a century." An Englishman having strong connections with the American ambassador was to carry a revolver into

Windsor, where the real assassin would be waiting to take it from him.

At the time, Roz imagined that Mottram had exterminated Tumin. There was a string of previous convictions, including one for attempted murder, and the conception was so preposterous! Who was the "real" assassin? Mottram had scoffed. How did he plan to penetrate a polo match? *Why* would the IRA kill the Queen, when the *only* effect had to be to negate whatever residual sympathy the cause might enjoy on both sides of the Atlantic?

But now Roz was starting to have second thoughts about Mottram's heavy use of ridicule. Two could play at that game.

"I wish to be sure I understand the question you're putting," Scrutton said after one particularly barbed exchange. "You are, in effect, calling me a liar; have I understood correctly?"

"You have."

"But why would I concoct such an extraordinary lie? True, Mr. Thornton was being tiresome after the funeral. I'd dealt with that by suing him. True, he'd threatened me with a gun. I felt able to overlook it. We'd been friends, once. All I wanted was for him to go away. Yet you apparently suppose that I come here to perjure his life away, as an act of revenge?"

Scrutton shook his head sorrowfully, leaving spectators unsure whether he was regretting the slur on his character, or the rotten quality of Mottram's intellect.

"Doesn't that analysis rather leave your wife out of account?"

"My wife?"

"She'd been having an affair with Mr. Thornton?"

"That is a *lie*." Scrutton flushed a painful shade of scarlet. "Ours was a close marriage; we had no secrets.

If she was having an affair, I would have known."

"Why would the defendant lie about that?"

"I cannot begin to guess."

"I put it to you that you knew they were having an affair and you were jealous."

"Untrue."

"You were there when she died."

"Not so."

"You struck her. The pathologist's report revealed a bruise over the left breast."

"And the coroner concluded, after hearing evidence, that it was entirely consistent with her bumping into the tray I was carrying."

Roz's notebook was wet with sweat; she gripped it so hard her fingers hurt. *Say it,* she cried silently to Mottram. *Say: You killed your wife, didn't you?* But she knew it was hopeless; and when the QC sheered off the point she cursed their impotence.

Mottram had at last come to the evidence they could not avoid or explain, the Big Lie, as Roz called it: the meeting between Frank and an unknown Irishman at Abbotsbury Road.

"Let's assume that everything you've told the court about that meeting is true," Mottram said. "What happened afterward? Did you call the police?"

"No."

"Why not?"

Scrutton said nothing.

"Come on, Mr. Scrutton, think! Here was something fishy, yes?"

"I suppose so."

"You *suppose* so? With talk of guns, *Irish* talk? Don't you read the newspapers? The Hanover bombing, Enniskillen . . . was there *no* connection in your mind at that point?"

"There may have been. I preferred not to face it."

"You, a public figure, a lawyer? You ducked the

issue, is that what you're asking the jury to believe?"

"I had my reasons. I'm not proud of them."

"Tell us what they were."

"One. It seemed flimsy, insubstantial. Two, I could see that Mr. Thornton was at the end of his tether, doing and saying things that were not typical of him. Three . . . "

"Yes?"

"I was . . . " Scrutton wiped his forehead. "I was afraid."

Mottram had not been expecting such a patently honest answer. When he followed it up, too quickly, his voice rose in pitch. "Of what were you afraid?"

"The IRA. I had visions of . . . of an unbearable life. At the bar, you hear things. Police escorts for informers, armed bodyguards by your side day and night. Judges blown up, that happened in Northern Ireland . . . they don't forget."

"Is that right?" Mottram's voice had turned silken. "Then why are you here, giving evidence, if you're so afraid?"

"Once Mr. Thornton was arrested, and the story came out, I knew I had no choice. There was still a conflict inside me, but it could be resolved in only one way." Scrutton looked down and was silent for a moment. "My earlier fears were right. I have bodyguards now. There are no plans to relieve me of them. Ever."

Roz closed her eyes in near despair. She did not believe a word of this. But her brain told her how it must sound to the jury, who knew nothing of this actor before he strutted onto the stage and spoke his lines.

Next morning the Attorney General re-examined Scrutton. There were no surprises. At lunchtime, Mottram was waiting for her as she emerged from court.

"Have you heard from Saunders yet?"

"Not a dicky-bird." She sighed. "He sounded so confident, at the start. They say he's in and out of the office, but he never returns my calls. I've tried Kevin, that's his son; I've tried his ex; I've tried every lead I can think of."

"I'm sorry."

Something about his inflection upset her. "Andrew, tell me it's not going as badly as I think it is."

He smiled, but made no reply. Back in court, she watched him cross-examine the Crown's last witnesses. With his huge bulk and determined mouth, he reminded her of a strong, hard-working and endlessly patient ox.

At last Sir Patrick rose and said, "That, my Lord, is the case for the Crown."

There was an instant stir, some murmured conversation. The under-sheriff plucked the chief's robe and glanced at the clock, evidently querying the timetable, for the judge addressed himself to Mottram.

"Would you like a clean start?"

"I'm obliged to your Lordship, I would."

"Tomorrow, half past ten."

He rose, bowed, and swept from court.

Down below, in the cells, Frank was looking more cheerful than Roz had seen him for some time.

"How are you doing, sunshine?" she asked him.

"Not so bad. Yourself?"

"I'm all right."

"Is Johnny behaving himself?"

He doesn't know, she realized; I've been so intent on shielding him that I forgot to come clean.

"Oh, rain's stopped play. Too bad."

"Roz, I'm sorry. What an idiot that man must be."

Something about his tone made her look him full

in the face. If she hadn't known better, she would
have thought his expression almost gleeful.

"If it was me," he said, "I'd marry you like a
shot."

She smiled at the compliment, feeling moved
because he so obviously meant it.

"You need a holiday," he said, "when all this is
over."

"Let's go to Paris together. Everyone says how
filthy rich you've become, I feel like squandering
some of it on champagne and perfume and choles-
terol."

Frank laughed. "It's a date."

They fell silent. Mottram stared at a pad, sliding
his fingers up and down his green Bic. Roz had rid-
den the conversation into a marsh, she realized, and
now it was up to her to extricate them.

"Apologies time," she said. "Frank, I've been an
idiot."

"Why?"

"The way I nagged you over where you were on
the famous night when . . . you know."

"Oh. That. Yes, I . . . was with Louise, that
evening."

"It's none of my business, really, but I think I
know why you kept quiet. It was to protect her
memory."

"Partly. I told Andrew here, and he agreed with
me; no point in raking over what couldn't be
changed. Louise is dead; she can't help me by giving
evidence."

He would not meet her eyes. "Partly," he'd said;
that was *partly* the reason . . . but what else could
there be? He looked sheepish. Why on earth should
he care whether Roz knew he'd been to bed with
another woman? Unless he felt as attracted to her
as she did to him, oh *bullshit, bullshit, bullshit!*

"And now, if you'll excuse us," Mottram said to

Roz, "Frank and I have got things to discuss."

She rose to leave. On impulse, she went around the table and kissed him on the mouth. He smiled, nodded, raised his hand in farewell. She walked out close to tears, feeling like an old rag that had been wrung to the point of extinction.

She didn't fancy going back all alone to her flat and it was too early to have four drinks too many while in pursuit of Ben, so she hailed a cab and went to Wapping. Her desk was covered with messages. One stood out as if written in red ink: *Ben Saunders phoned; please C.B.* She was dialing before she'd got to the last word.

No reply. She held the message under the light, not recognizing the phone number and wondering if she'd punched in the right digits. London exchange . . .

Someone picked up the receiver at the other end. "Yes," whispered a voice.

"Ben? Is that you?"

"He's not here."

The line went dead.

Roz replaced the phone and tapped it in a thoughtful rhythm for a few seconds before sitting down at her desk.

She didn't like this.

Ben had gone underground, that she realized. But if the voice she'd just heard was anything to go by, he'd delved much deeper than he should. A memory from their lunch at the Indian restaurant came back to her with sudden force: he'd said he could get in a cab and find men with chains and iron bars . . . and then later, *they're interested in you* . . .

She dialed the number again. Busy signal. She sorted through her other messages, tipped the lot into her wastepaper basket and tried again. Busy.

"Ben," she said to the wall. "If you're not all right, my love, I'll kill you."

Her phone made a tiny click, as if it was about to

ring, and she snatched up the receiver, but it was only Howard Boissart.

"Heard you were in," he said. "I was just on the point of uncorking a rather superior bottle of Bourgogne Aligoté. Care to come over?"

She wanted a drink and a shoulder to cry on and she knew that Howard would provide high-quality both. After a moment's hesitation, however, she said No, very politely, and set off in search of Ben.

Frank started well without ever having spoken a word. He climbed into the witness box to take the oath in a steady voice. Well-groomed and straight-backed, he easily matched Alistair Scrutton for presence.

He outlined his career since quitting England in 1969, leaving Mottram to draw out the highlights but without any hint of self-denigration. What a marvelous life, Roz thought. Nothing to connect him with the IRA or crooked Hong Kong solicitors. Surely the jury must *see* that!

But she still couldn't find any trace of Ben Saunders, and Mottram had little to fall back on apart from his client's way with words.

Frank gave his version of the funeral in straight-forward fashion. Yes, he had gone back to Mr. Scrutton's house; he realized he was making a fool of himself in public and serving no useful purpose. He'd been short of sleep, he felt exhausted; not an excuse, but perhaps an explanation.

"What happened?" Mottram asked.

"We went into a downstairs living room."

"Did Mr. Scrutton offer you a drink?"

"No. Nor did he drink. We talked. He told me he was damned if he was going to have his career wrecked just because his wife had been . . . " Frank paused, glanced apologetically at the judge, and went on: "Had been fucking around with some jerk executive from an oil company."

"He used those words?"

"Those very words."

"Had you been having a sexual affair with his wife?"

Frank colored. He brushed his hair back a couple of times and rocked on his heels. No one who witnessed it could doubt how painful the moment must have been for him.

"Yes," he said in a low voice.

"Did Mr. Scrutton know about it?"

"He plainly did."

"He has given evidence to the effect that he did not; did you hear him give that evidence?"

"Yes. He's mistaken."

"How did you react to his rather unpleasant remark concerning his wife and the 'jerk executive'?"

"I'm afraid I completely lost my temper. I said some things that I now bitterly regret."

"Such as?"

"I again accused him of having murdered his wife. I'd read reports of the inquest and I knew about a bruise on her left breast."

"Standing here now, do you still believe Mr. Scrutton killed Louise?"

"Most certainly not."

"Describe how the meeting developed," Mottram said.

"We quarreled, violently. Mr. Scrutton produced a gun."

"Produced from where?"

"A sideboard."

"What did he do and say at that time?"

"He came up to me, very close, and held the gun pointing at my face."

"How close?"

Frank demonstrated by holding his hand a few inches from his nose.

"Do you know if the gun was loaded?"

"No."

"Did he say anything?"

"He said something like, 'I'm dangerous when I'm crossed. My friends won't like it if you cross me.'"

"Were you surprised to see that gun?"

"Astounded. In America, some of my friends own firearms, but I'm aware that in England handguns aren't easy to come by. And that a QC should have one struck me as quite amazing."

"Were you frightened?"

"I was. We were both mad as hell by that time. His face was red, he was shaking, he became incoherent."

"What did you do?"

"It was instinctive, a gut thing. I grappled with him."

"Did you touch the gun?"

"Yes. He didn't put up much of a fight. I'm stronger than Mr. Scrutton. In the end I got it off him and I pointed it at him and I said, 'Back off.' Something like that."

"Did he back off?"

"Yes."

"How did he look to you?"

"Amused."

"*Amused?*"

"Yes. He was laughing. By that time, I'd had enough. I was . . . afraid of what I might do if I stayed."

"What did you do with the gun?"

"I took it with me as far as the gate to the highway. There, I threw it onto Mr. Scrutton's lawn."

"And after that?"

"I walked to the village and phoned for a cab to take me back to where I'd left my car."

Mottram turned for a muttered conference with his junior, while the court relaxed in one of those welcome, midset breaks from tension. But no lemon-barley water, Roz thought glumly; her throat craved something cold.

The players were coming back onto court.

"I want to take you now to a particular day, last year, in March. The thirtieth. Mr. Scrutton gave evidence about entering your house that evening and overhearing a conversation between you and another man. Did you ever, at any time or place, have such a meeting as Mr. Scrutton described?"

"No."

"Do you have any contact with the IRA?"

"No."

"Have you ever had such contact?"

"No."

"Did you discuss killing the Queen with any person?"

"No. I have never discussed killing anyone."

"Did you ever provide assistance to anybody who, to your knowledge, intended to kill the Queen?"

"No."

"Or encouragement?"

"No."

The regular, monosyllabic denials followed one another like a barrage of shells, knocking the Crown's case to pieces, or so it seemed to Roz. God, he was magnificent!

"Do you remember what you were doing on the evening of thirtieth March, 1988?"

"Very well."

"What was it?"

Frank drew a deep breath. "I . . . "

"Yes?"

"I spent the evening in bed with Mr. Scrutton's wife."

Mottram waited for the murmuring to still before he resumed.

"Let's take it in stages. What time did you meet?"

"We had arranged to meet at the house, at seven." He permitted himself one quick smile. "She was late, as usual."

"What happened then?"

"She cooked supper for us. After that, we went to bed."

"Until what time?"

"About ten."

"Did anyone else enter the house between seven and ten?"

"No."

"Would you have known if they had?"

"Certainly. The burglar alarm was set and all the entry doors were locked."

"Mr. Thornton . . . how can you be sure that all this happened on the thirtieth?"

"My diary. I made the entry while we were speaking on the phone to make the appointment."

The exhibit was produced and verified.

"It says here: '7. L.'?"

"It does."

"Meaning?"

"Meet Louise at seven o'clock."

Mottram paused for a moment. "Did you love her?" he asked.

Frank had been looking at his barrister. Now he turned his head until he could stare straight into Roz's eyes.

"No," he said quietly.

Frank lowered his gaze, and Roz knew beyond all possibility of contradiction that, in some extraordinary fashion, for him the trial had ended.

"Two o'clock," said the judge, rising.

* * *

"It's going to be all right," Roz breathed as she left the court with Joe. She had difficulty speaking, because somewhere behind her eyes tears were starting to gather, she couldn't imagine why, the curse must be coming early this month. . . .

"Mm."

"You don't agree?"

"This is the easy part. Anyone can give evidence in chief and sound like a saint."

The wisdom of his assessment began to show through early in Sir Patrick's cross-examination, later that same day.

"Why should Mr. Scrutton concoct such a tissue of lies?"

"I don't know."

"Can you suggest *any* reason?"

"He was jealous, I've told you that."

Steady, Roz mentally warned him; hold steady, boy. . . .

"Jealous enough to put you on trial for high treason? Jealous enough to hang you?"

"Certainly."

"A Queen's Counsel with everything to lose? You do know, don't you, Mr. Thornton, that in this country we choose our judges almost exclusively from the upper branches of the barristers' side of the profession?"

"I'd heard that."

"Mr. Scrutton had a lot to hope for?"

Frank's shrug suggested mulish refusal to face facts. Roz wanted to give him a good shake.

"Very well. Let's turn to your alibi for the night of thirtieth March. Did you confide in anyone that you were having an affair with Mrs. Scrutton?"

"It's hardly the kind of thing you—"

"Did you?"

"Of course I didn't!"

"So the only person who could corroborate your

alibi for the night of the thirtieth is Mrs. Scrutton herself?"

"Yes."

"And she's dead."

"Is that meant to be a question?"

The judge tapped his notebook with his pen. "Mr. Thornton, just . . . just *think*, will you?"

"I'm sorry, my Lord."

The judge subjected him to a long stare before nodding. "Go on."

"Mr. Thornton . . . do you remember Mr. Mottram cross-examining Mr. Scrutton about the layout of your house?"

"Yes."

"Mr. Scrutton told us about the fixtures and fittings he saw, is that a fair summary?"

"I suppose so."

"But when Mr. Mottram came to ask you for your version of events, I didn't hear you allege that Mr. Scrutton was wrong about any of that. Did I?"

Frank said nothing.

"Mr. Thornton, let me be clear: Did Mr. Scrutton get the details of your house wrong, or did he get them right?"

A long pause. "He was right."

Roz felt a chill envelop her and she shivered.

"Still think it'll be okay?" Joe asked, as they came out of court at four-thirty.

"I have to get hold of Ben," she muttered.

But in Pennington Street there were no messages, not even an invitation to drink wine with the editor. Roz drew a notepad toward her and began to scribble.

"Dear Howard, I've been mulling over my position here for some months now and—"

She ripped off the sheet, scrunched it up, and flung it into her wastepaper basket.

"Dear Howard, When I first joined—"

The phone rang. She picked it up while continuing to write. "Forbes."

"Christ, at last you're *in!*"

"Ben!" The pencil dropped from her fingers. "Ben, where are you?"

"Never mind that. Where the hell have you been?"

"In court, I . . . what's up, you sound—"

"Scared, darling." His unusually high-pitched voice rippled up and down. "Spelled S-H-I-T, scared, got me?"

"What on earth's happened?"

"Valance."

"You've found him!"

"He's living in Peckham. Robbers' Row, they call it. Got no money, but drinking himself to death. Who's paying? Don't ask me. Someone doesn't want him talking, Roz."

"Mottram's going to be calling Frank any time now, we *have* to see Valance tonight."

"I am not happy. I am *not.*"

"But, Ben—"

"We need friends when we go in there. Lots of 'em. Meet me the day after tomorrow, six o'clock, London Bridge station caff. And *be careful!* You're being watched."

"Can't you do anything sooner?" she wailed.

"Darling, I will not kid you. This is going to be difficult like you would not *believe.*"

The line went dead. Roz replaced the receiver with a hand that shook. Ben had sounded really scared. The memory of his voice haunted her.

You're being watched.

Those words echoed in her ears when she woke up next morning, like a premonition of danger, and stayed with her throughout the day. Every time she turned her head, it seemed to her that someone looked away. She began to persuade herself that she recognized unknown passersby from a previous occasion, and found herself running when normally she would have walked, or thinking twice before approaching the block of flats where she lived, afraid to stay on the street but scared to go home . . .

Frank's cross-examination ended early, with none of the fireworks she'd been anticipating. Harrison Gephard came next, and did Frank proud. Yes, he had known the defendant for years. The man had never stepped out of line. He was moral, upright, and true; he was godfather to Gephard's child; as an employee and as a man he merited only the highest commendation. Listening to him, Roz felt a little of her confidence return.

"When I was appointed ambassador to London, my first thought was to bring Frank with me."

"Why?" Mottram asked.

"Because if I was going to grapple with one of the toughest diplomatic postings in the world, I felt I had to have one true friend by my side."

Mottram left it there; but the attorney-general had a question or two.

"Did he *want* to come back to England?"

"Yes. He'd been pressing me to send him for some months."

Roz brooded on that. She could see where it led: if there *was* a plot, Frank had to be present in England before he could play his part.

And so at last they came to the final day, and speeches.

Roz stayed in court for as long as she dared, but dogging her throughout the interminable afternoon was fear of missing the rendezvous with Ben. She stole away at the last possible moment, conscious that within minutes Frank's life would be placed in the jury's charge and that the long, drawn-out battle would be over.

She arrived at London Bridge a few minutes early,

just as the news vendor by the main entrance was putting up a fresh billboard: THORNTON: JURY OUT. She stopped dead and stared at it, as if it were a corpse lying in the station forecourt. No, that couldn't be right, some smartass home news ed must have jumped the gun . . . not yet, not yet . . .

She walked on. The cafeteria was designed in smart, new, high-tech style. She took her lemon tea to one of its upper terraces and settled down to wait.

Ben came fifteen minutes late, carrying a large whisky.

"Long time no see," she said as he slumped into the seat beside hers; but he wasn't in the mood for small talk.

"It's off," he said tersely.

"What do you mean, it's off?"

"I mean that Valance is being held locked up in a basement pigsty by the IRA, darling, and I can't find anyone stupid enough to want to go calling."

"What about the scoop of scoops?" she demanded angrily. "This is going to save your hide, remember?"

"One problem." He drank half his whisky. "I'd like to be alive to savor my triumph."

She looked at him. He'd lost a lot of weight. His face drooped with fatigue and worry. She remembered the piece about him in Private Eye's "Street of Shame," a fortnight ago: "Meanwhile, Sinful Saunders, hanging onto his desk by the dirt under his fingernails, has been behaving even more outrageously than usual, with not even his professional [*Shorely shome mishtake, Ed.*] colleagues at El Vino's knowing where to find him." Yes, she thought despondently; that's about it.

"Ben," she said. "Let's go to the police."

"No."

"Why?"

"Give me time, Roz. I can't share this story with anyone. Let me raise a few of the boys, people I can trust."

"But there's a man's *life* at stake!" She put a hand over his, where it lay on the banquette beside her. "The story will still be there, Ben," she said softly. "Your story."

He snatched his hand away and finished his whisky.

Roz sighed. "All right. Tell me where Valance is living."

"Why?"

"I'm going to see him."

He laughed offensively.

"Somebody has to. All I want is the address, Ben. You get what I get, the minute I've contacted Frank's lawyers."

"What you'll get is a knife in the ribs. Listen, Roz." He brought his head closer to her ear. "Remember me telling you about my swing through Asia? How everything just fell nicely into my lap?"

"Yes."

"Well, it's the same here, only more so. 'Come on in,' they're saying, 'the water's lovely.' And we're going to get sodding well drowned."

"Okay."

"Aaah . . . " He lurched up and went to the bar for more whisky.

"You've lost your objectivity," he declared, as he fell back into his seat. "You just assume he's innocent, when there's plenty of evidence apart from Scrutton's to show Frank did it. Fingerprints on the gun. Tumin. Thornton pressing Gephard to let him come back to England. Scrutton, oh Christ yes, Alistair even knew what color Frank's curtains were."

"Of course; break Scrutton and we break the

case. That's an objective judgment, Ben; it doesn't come from me, it comes from Mottram and Lutter. That's what they believe."

"I'm not bothered about what they believe. It's what *you* believe that's getting me going."

"I don't understand."

"Don't you? Don't you remember your little confession to Uncle Ben, back there in the restaurant? About how you screwed Thornton and've spent the rest of your life trying to make it up to him?"

She stared at him. "You think I'd do anything to get him off, don't you?"

"Yeah. Anything at all."

Roz thought about that. "Maybe you're right," she said at last. "Tell me the address, Ben."

"Too dangerous."

"Well, what about this . . . You're the only person on our side who knows where Valance is. Suppose something happens to you, before you share the info. Then *no one* will be able to get hold of Valance. Which means, Frank's dead."

He bit his lip. "I've been thinking about that, too."

For a long time he said nothing more. She could see he was wrestling with temptation and had the sense to stay quiet.

"I'll tell you the address," he said at last, "on one condition."

"What?"

"That you don't try and go there alone. You've gotta wait for the all clear from me."

"Oh, *Ben!*"

"I mean it, Roz," he said sharply.

"But you can't be—"

"Will you just *shut up!*"

People at adjacent tables stopped talking and looked in their direction.

"Tell me the address, Ben," she repeated quietly.

"And you'll promise not to go there?"

Clearly he wasn't prepared to escort her, so it had to be done.

"I promise I won't go there, or tell anyone else about it, until I hear from you. But you've got to be quick."

He stared at her for what seemed like ages, and her heart steadily sank. Journos didn't come any more experienced than Ben Saunders. Few judges or clergymen could have matched his experience of human iniquity. He must know she was lying. She didn't seriously expect him to tell her. But then—

"All right," he said. "I'll give you the address. But *only* because I've got to tell someone to make sure it doesn't die with me, got that?"

"Yes."

"Promise."

"I promise."

Did he want her to lie? she wondered as she wrote down the address he gave her. Was this his way of shedding responsibility, of handing on the baton to someone braver (more stupid?) than he?

"Where are you going now?" she said, as she put away her pen.

"Up King's Cross way. There's a few . . . no, never mind." He stood up. "See you, Roz."

On his way out, he stopped at the bar for long enough to swallow one last scotch. Roz followed him out and watched him weave his way through the crowd of commuters toward the tube. Only when she was sure that he had gone down the steps did she turn in the direction of the ticket office.

"Peckham Rye," she told the clerk. "Return."

CHAPTER

22=

LONDON. THE PRESENT

The cell door opened and a warder put his head around it. "Fancy a game of noughts and crosses?"

Frank stared at him. "What?"

"I'm the Bailey's resident expert, see?" The officer, a jovial middle-aged man, winked. "Got a pack of cards, if you'd rather. Beats looking at the wall and waiting."

"Oh." Frank smiled, relieved in one way because for a moment he'd thought the jury . . . " I don't think so, thanks. But could I have a cup of tea?"

"Coming up."

The warder went off. Frank noticed that they no longer slammed doors as they used to. Within a few hours he'd either be free or branded for the slaughter. Either way, people's attitudes were changing.

In the run-up to the trial, he had tried to anticipate and prepare for everything. But he hadn't faced up to how he would feel while he waited for the verdict.

They'd been out for thirty-eight minutes, now.

What *really* happened in the jury room? Did they discuss the evidence; or spin a coin and then chat for long enough to make it look as though they'd done a proper job?

He walked several laps around the perimeter of the cell, meaning to pace off one mile, but he could never get past the hundred without losing count and in the end he gave up.

There was nothing to do now, except think. Andrew Mottram had asked him if he wanted company, but he'd taken one look at the lawyer's haggard face and said, No, you go and rest.

Frank hooked his right hand under the back of a chair and bent his elbow to lift it off the floor. One . . . two . . . three. His forehead broke into a sweat. There was no strength in his arms any more.

Voices, footsteps, fast approaching. He dropped the chair, the door opened . . .

But it was only the officer, bringing tea. He darted a glance at the chair, lying on its side, then at Frank.

"Everything all right?"

"Yes. Thank you." Frank managed a smile. "I thought I'd try a bit of a workout."

The warder left. Frank set the chair upright and pulled the cup toward him. It was made of thick, off-white pottery. Four lumps of sugar sat in the saucer. Suddenly he hankered after something sweet, and he put two of them into the tea. He'd never taken sugar in tea. A new experience. He ought to look out for those more often.

When they called him, he would go into court and seek out Roz Forbes, and he would keep his eyes fixed on her until he left the dock again. If the verdict was an acquittal, he'd go straight up to her and kiss her. Then they would go out to dinner. Then they would go to bed.

If, on the other hand . . .

The tea tasted revolting. He pushed his cup away, spilling liquid into the saucer, where it stained the two remaining white sugar lumps a dirty shade of brown. Frank watched the lumps dissolve, very slowly, into dejected, sticky piles. The sight nauseated him. Then, without notice, a fit of shallow breathing struck him. He couldn't open his mouth to draw in air. He was gasping through his nose but the oxygen wouldn't enter, he was suffocating, *Jesus!*

He sprang up, hands to his throat. The chair went flying. *This was how it felt to hang!*

His teeth had clenched together. He struck his forehead against the wall, once, twice. On the second blow, something seemed to snap. His mouth flew open and he drew in huge breaths like a man who'd gone to the brink of drowning.

Frank leaned against the table, one hand to his heart, choking up phlegm. Slowly, very slowly, he recovered. He took out his handkerchief and mopped up the mess. He made himself sip the vile tea.

He felt like somebody who'd wandered by mistake onto a high wire across a chasm and reached halfway before looking down. He must not look down again. *He. Must. Not.*

Concentrate on Roz. No one, nothing else; just Roz. That way, he could stand anything.

Foolishly he allowed himself another peek across the abyss, but this time in the other direction: to acquittal and freedom. He yearned to spend a lot of time with that wonderfully vivacious woman. She was a giver of life. He needed Roz. Now that Johnny had abandoned her, he felt sure that she would come to need him, too.

Twice in his life he'd been cursed by love. Third time lucky . . . ?

Crazy!

No one in his position should think about a

future that might never be. Frank stared at the wall opposite, trying to empty his mind.

The jury had been out for sixty-seven minutes.

Roz turned left at the bottom of Rye Lane and promptly lost herself in a maze of narrow streets that seemed to have been laid out with no sense of civic pride, or even convenience. She passed a school, its high brick boundary wall topped with broken glass, and a grime-encrusted church. The houses were shrinking, becoming ever less cared for, more squalid. Several times she saw rusty corrugated iron sheets nailed to what had once been front windows. This part of London was a place to get out of, fast, before night fell.

Three men were ambling toward her. As they passed beneath one of the lamps she caught sight of close-cropped hair, jeans, and leather jackets. Their voices sounded shrill, and when one of them laughed, Roz automatically slowed. The laugh was feckless, uncontrolled.

Suddenly their voices dropped an octave, becoming secretive. One of them giggled. They'd seen her.

Don't run. Don't turn your back. Roz marched on, feeling in her handbag for keys, a comb, anything sharp or pointed that might serve as a weapon.

"'Allo, darlin'."

"How ya doin', then?"

The third man merely whistled; an artificially drawn-out, suggestive sound.

"Can you tell me the way to—"

"Can tell you all sorts of things, love."

"Wha-*hey!*"

They had surrounded her now.

"Can we *help* you, modom? Assist you in some way?"

"I'm looking for this address." She read from the paper.

"Whoo . . . you don't wanna go there. Them's wolves what lives there."

"We was going to the pub, come on, buy you a drink." One of the men had her by the arm.

"Oh, really?" she said, not struggling, somehow managing a smile. "I thought big lads like you didn't drink."

More whistles, "Wha-heys."

"Like big lads, do you?" one of the men leered. His face showed up mottled in the unforgiving sodium glare. "'Cause in that case, darlin', I got summing you'll want to see."

A hand cupped itself around her buttocks, gave them a squeeze, and began to slither about. With an effort that cost far too much, Roz managed not to turn and strike. She glanced over the shoulder of the man directly in front of her. The street yawned empty. She had to get out of this. She had to get out *now*.

"Do us a favor," she said. "I've got to meet my husband there, he's a solicitor, one of his clients is up at Newington Causeway tomorrow."

The hand paused, then removed itself. There was a hardly noticeable silence, but when the leader spoke again something had changed.

"Whass 'e up for, then? This geezer, tomorrow?"

"Grievous bodily harm."

"Strewth, that must be Tony Dicker." The leader whistled and turned to his mate standing next to him. "You remember, him what done that copper up at Clapham."

"Yeah, I remember. You a pal of Tone, then?" The speaker rubbed his nose. "Hard man, our Tone."

"Sorry, don't know his name. My husband keeps quiet about things like that."

"Lawyer that keeps quiet, eh?"

"Shit!"

More offensive laughter.

"Here, give us that paper." The leader snatched the address from Roz and held it toward the nearest street light. "Yeah, I know it. Down there, to the end, turn right, first on your left."

He handed back the paper. "Better watch yourself, darling. Them there's not all posh, like you and me. Know what I mean?"

"Thanks."

Cackles followed her down the hill to the corner, where she turned right and broke into a sprint. After a while she halted and leaned against someone's front gate, panting. The encounter had rattled her badly.

What was she doing here?

Roz straightened her shoulders and walked on. She was barging into danger, unaccompanied and with no back-up if things went wrong, for a cause that stretched her to the limits. And at this very moment she couldn't say why.

Being honest with herself, she knew she wanted to be a heroine. But so far from behaving heroically, she kept thinking of Frank in bed with Louise, hating it, hating him, above all, hating herself for being so petty, especially in a crisis like this. She'd wanted to discover her hidden strengths, but all she'd found so far were hitherto unsuspected weaknesses. And it was so irrational, because Frank had meant nothing to her at the time, she was with Johnny, then, and . . . and, *oh shit!* but she wanted out, knowing she couldn't get out, not now . . .

Ben had warned her not to come. *Why had he given her the address, when he must have known she'd go there: a place he was too afraid to visit by himself?*

The house was at the far end of a narrow cul-de-sac. Roz's shoes echoed on the pavement, sounding the alarm to anybody with an interest in hearing it. Halfway down the street burned a single lamp, casting just enough light to let her see that Valance's front door was a steel plate edged with studs, and that all the downstairs windows were boarded up.

Roz crossed the road and stared at the house. It was the end of a terrace, two-up and two-down, with one square foot of concrete at the front behind a low wall and no visible path around to the back. She swallowed. What now?

She swung around, thinking she'd heard a noise behind her, but the street was empty. It seemed so quiet. Roz had lived much of her life in London and knew how it should sound at different times of day. Here was different. Here did not conform to rules.

She began to walk back up the cul-de-sac. *Where were the people? Why so few cars?* Then, suddenly, she cracked. She ran, and only when she reached the intersection with the main road did she stop. All she wanted to do was flee from this Gehenna, back to the lights, warmth, and safety of the London she knew.

Back to the newspaper billboards: JURY OUT.

"It's so unfair!" she croaked through clenched teeth. *"Why me?"*

Somewhere in the darkness behind her, a door opened and closed again. She heard the distant jingle of keys. Then footsteps. Coming her way. Roz slipped across the main road and lost herself in the shadow of a parked car.

The entrance to the cul-de-sac opposite was bathed in orange light from a nearby street standard; but a few yards farther back it became a wall of darkness. The footsteps were advancing to that wall in a slow shuffle. Roz gripped the car's door handle, trying to instill some courage.

Then she saw him. *Valance.*

It never occurred to her to doubt that this was indeed Reg Valance, Scrutton's old clerk. He ambled through the black wall facing her like a phantom materializing into somebody's nightmare, paused, looked this way and that, then moved on. He walked with a stoop, both arms swinging loosely at his sides, making him seem neanderthal.

When he was about twenty yards down the main road, Roz eased away from the protection of the car and began to trail him. He crossed a couple of streets, then ducked down an alley. She followed in time to see him turn into the side entrance of a pub just before the alley opened onto another main road.

She let a minute pass, and followed him inside.

The second she crossed the threshold she was blinded by a gray-white wall of smoke; everyone seemed to have a fag on the go. Gradually her smarting eyes allowed her to make out the old-fashioned four-ale bar, the fruit machines, the tatty tables with their sodden beer mats, the cigarette burns in a paper-thin carpet . . . but not Valance.

She became aware of people staring at her through the smoke screen. Of all the people in this pub, with its stink of spilled beer and spent nicotine, only a handful were women, and none of them dressed, talked, or looked remotely like her. She began to make her way through the crowd. To one side of the bar was a door; on the other side of that lay the snug. As she moved toward it, she caught sight of Valance turning away from the counter with a glass in his hand.

Roz shouldered her way into the snug, conscious of hostile eyes on her back. The inner room contained only three tables, two of which were empty. Valance was sitting at the other with his hands clasped in his lap.

Roz dropped into a chair opposite his. "Mr. Valance?"

For a moment she thought he wasn't going to bother to reply. He sat staring straight ahead of him with a placid smile on his face, as if he had no complaints. He was wearing an old gray woolen overcoat, tied at the waist with an incongruous plastic belt, and his head was thinly planted with short hairs resembling, for color and texture, needles shed from a glass-fiber insulating blanket.

He slowly turned his head, until he was looking at her through two pinched, milky-blue eyes, and he said, "Why don't you get yourself a drink?"

There was something so unpleasant about this creature that Roz felt tempted to run for it. Instead, she stood up and went across to the bar, ordering a gin and tonic for herself and another scotch for Valance.

He didn't seem to have moved while she was away. Now, however, he picked up his glass and raised it. He was about to drink, when he lowered his hand and said, "Did you count your change?" His voice was reedy and completely flat, as if all the character had long ago been thrashed out of him. "You should always count your change," he said, "here."

He took several sips from his glass, as if the effort of mounting one genuine swallow was too much for him.

"Mr. Valance, I'm a journalist, my name's Roz Forbes. I need to talk to you urgently about the trial that's on now. The Thornton trial."

He said nothing, but continued to sip his drink as serenely as if he were alone in the snug.

"You used to be Alistair Scrutton's clerk. Scrutton lied at the trial. I need your help to prove it." She hesitated. "Money wouldn't be a problem."

"Money's not a problem for me," he said. "Anyway."

"Well . . . look, Mr. Valance, I'll level with you.

The jury's out but it's not too late to do something. I believe you can prove Scrutton's lying."

Silence. She became aware of a television over the bar, a chat show, brainless applause.

"Mr. Valance . . . if you're being threatened, if you're afraid—"

A man tramped in from the public bar on his way to the toilet; Roz turned her head and saw two doors in the far wall, one marked Men, the other, Women. She'd have to go in a minute, her bladder was hurting.

"I'm not afraid," Valance said. "Uncle Reg never 'ad no enemies. Not like Scrutton."

Roz's head swiveled. "Yes?"

"Our Alistair would fuck you up good and proper, he would. You could *rely* on him." Valance sounded almost proud, as if he was talking about a star pupil.

"Tell me about it. Everything you can remember."

Valance's lips thinned out into a smile. "Life's not long enough," he said. "For that."

Roz badly wanted to go to the loo. She forced herself to concentrate, but it was hard.

"Roses all the way," Valance was saying. "They kept him off the petty crime, you see. The rubbish never got a sniff of our Alistair. Did their porridge and kept their mouths shut, they did."

They kept him off the petty crime . . . *they* know about you, Ben had said . . .

"Who's 'they'?" She wriggled uncomfortably. One gin and tonic shouldn't be having this effect. "*Who* kept him off the petty crime?"

"The Chinese. And that other fellow. Thai, was he?"

"Chaloem!"

"Yeah. That's him. Poppy, I used to call him. Because he talked like a woman and he made a million out of drugs."

"Scrutton knew that?"

"Oh, yeah." Valance laughed, a glum sound. "He knew."

"But was he *in* it?"

"One lovely big party, it was. The drugs barons. The IRA. Golden Triangle. You scratch my back, I'll scratch yours."

Roz breathed "Thank you, God," and fumbled in her bag for paper and pen, only to realize with a fit of anger that she couldn't put off going to the toilet any longer. She clenched her fists. What if Valance did a runner while she was gone?

"Mr. Valance, I'll be right back, *please* stay there . . . "

As she pushed through the door she heard the TV over the bar suddenly fall silent in the middle of a burst of applause. "We interrupt this program to join Joshua Rozenburg outside the Old Bailey . . . "

Damn! Roz paused, but now her bladder was giving off stabbing pains and she ran quickly down a flight of steps to the toilets. There were two cubicles, one was occupied. She entered the other, only to find the lock had broken. Never mind, chance it . . .

The second she relaxed her sphincter a stab of hot pain flooded through the lower part of her body, an agony so acute that she squealed. She collapsed to one side, and if the partition hadn't propped her up she would have fallen.

Something in her drink. But she'd watched the barman pour it herself . . .

As if through layers of cotton-wool, she heard footsteps coming down into the toilet. At the same time, the lock on the adjacent cubicle was released and someone emerged from it. The door facing her swung open, revealing two men. One of them she recognized as the barman; the other, much younger, was a stranger to her.

The barman moved forward, but a voice commanded "No, Pat," and he stepped to one side, disclosing yet a third man. Roz's last coherent thought was that she knew him. Who? Where could she have . . . ?

Then she knew. She opened her mouth to scream, but her tongue filled her mouth and all that came out was a long hiss of dread.

"Good evening, Miss Forbes," said the Krait.

Frank came up the steps to find the last of the jury taking their seats. He scanned them eagerly, but the twelve people who held his life in their hands wore the uniformly tranquil expressions of those whose work was over and who could look forward to a well-earned rest.

The seat Roz usually occupied had been taken by someone else. Frank's heart gave a jolt. He looked everywhere, but there was no sign of her. He gripped the ledge of the dock in convulsive movements, his lips soundlessly calling her name over and over again.

The clerk was on his feet, reading the first count of the indictment.

"How say you, members of the jury; is the prisoner guilty or not guilty?"

A pause, during which no one in that courtroom breathed. Frank braced himself against the edge of the dock.

"Guilty."

An unearthly sound echoed through the court: no mere gasp, not a sigh, but a great outpouring of emotion, of grief and horror commingled.

"Silence!"

"By the second count, he is charged in that . . . "

Frank heard nothing more of what the clerk said, only the word guilty reverberating over and over in his brain, like a drum beating him to execution.

Guilty on both counts.

The clerk of the court was speaking again. "Prisoner at the bar, you stand convicted of High Treason. Have you anything to say why the Court should not give you judgment according to law?"

Frank knew that these words were addressed to him. He ought to respond. After days of sitting hunched and impotent, it was important to stand upright, show dignity.

He licked his lips, vainly trying to moisten them with a tongue grown dry as leather.

"I am not guilty," he said. "Of any crime."

A movement caught his eye. The chaplain, plainly clad in black suit and white dog-collar had come through the door behind the bench. Someone was lifting a square of black cloth onto the lord chief justice's wig. And for the first time, looking at that composed face, Frank saw a crack appear there: a livid whiteness, a tension which had not manifested itself throughout the trial.

"Francis Graham Thornton. You have been found guilty of two counts of High Treason. For such a crime there is only one punishment fixed by law."

The judge paused. Suddenly his face flushed the color of his robes and for a moment his lips moved silently, the play's star drying up at its climax. When he recovered, he spoke almost too quickly for the hearers to follow.

"The sentence of the court upon you is, that you be taken from this place to a lawful prison, and thence to a place of execution, and that you there suffer death by hanging; and that your body be afterward buried within the precincts of the prison in which you shall have been confined before your execution. And may the Lord have mercy on your soul."

"Amen," the chaplain murmured.

A dreadful pit of blackness opened in front of

Frank. He staggered. *Let me go down*, he pleaded silently. *Take me away* . . . but there was still one more ancient ritual to be endured. The clerk raised his voice above the hubbub.

"All those having anything to do before my Lords the Queen's justices may now depart. God save my Lords the Queen's justices!"

News of the verdict had reached the crowd outside. A sudden roar pervaded the court: an ugly sound, redolent of fury, and revenge, and blood, so that the clerk almost had to shout the final words.

"God save . . . the Queen!"

PART THREE
SENTENCE

CHAPTER

23

LONDON. THE PRESENT

Something soft and red flattened itself against the windscreen as Oakley's chauffeur accelerated, through a wave of invective and shaking fists, into the courtyard of Wandsworth prison.

"Good God," he cried. "What . . . ?"

"A tomato, Minister." His driver was an attractive blonde in her early forties whom nothing seemed to faze. "None too fresh, by the looks of it."

As she came around to help Oakley out, the governor hurried across. "Sorry about that, Minister, the police—"

"Mr. Howells?"

"Edward Howells, Governor. My chief officer . . . "

Introductions over, Howells led the way inside, where only a cold twilight filtered through the grimy windows.

"How long's that mob been out there?" Oakley said nervously.

"Since the trial ended. Executions mean trouble for everyone, Minister. Always."

The chief officer rapped on yet another metal

grille and it swung open to reveal more rows of cells converging to a high, arched window at a far distant point of perspective.

"Quiet," Oakley muttered. "Is it always like this?"

"In the afternoons, yes. They're out at work."

"Where is Thornton?"

"Hospital. Full check-up. Number One wanted a clear couple of hours without him being next door."

The three men tramped on.

"Morale?" Oakley asked.

"We're inside a powder keg, Minister." Howells glanced at the chief officer and lowered his voice. "There's only so much control I have over this. The inmates are restless, but that's not what's worrying me."

"Your men?"

"Precisely. No one can accept that what Thornton did could amount to high treason. Hang him for *that*?"

"It's not their job to understand the law."

"We live," Howells said quietly, "in an England I no longer recognize, Mr. Oakley. Your government is treating us like cattle. All right. But tell me— have you ever had to face a stampede?"

"All I'm concerned with is whether your officers will cooperate in England's first execution for more than a quarter of a century."

"There are enough hard-line royalists on my roster for you to be sure of that, Minister. Thornton *will* hang. Who sleeps afterward is another question."

"I shall, for one," Oakley snapped. He shook a finger at Howells. "You accepted the governorship of Wandsworth knowing that the last gallows in England is maintained here."

"I shall do my duty, Minister. Let's just hope the Home Secretary doesn't shirk his."

Oakley grunted. "What sort of state is Thornton in?"

"Still shell-shocked."

Howells halted before a cell door and the chief officer came forward with his keys. The governor stood aside for Oakley to enter. Then—"Are you all right?" he inquired.

"Yes." But Oakley's voice sounded unnaturally loud.

The room was twice the height of an ordinary cell. Where the ceiling should have been were two large parallel beams extending from wall to wall; between these beams hung three steel chains. Above them was another thick beam, to which those chains were attached. Straight ahead, beside the far wall, was a staircase going down into darkness. But perhaps the strangest feature of this odd room was the large rectangular hole that took up much of the floor.

"That's the only working drop still left in England, Minister."

"Thank you, Mr. Howells." Oakley's tone showed that he knew perfectly well what the hole was. "I have to report back that all is well, so let me see it function, please."

But before either of his companions could reply they heard steps on the staircase, and a man rose out of the pit. He came up slowly, whistling under his breath, with both hands thrust into the trouser pockets of his old, black, three-piece suit. When he reached the top of the stairs he turned, saw the party waiting by the door, and smiled. But he did not come to join them, not immediately. He stood on the far side of the drop, continuing to whistle the same tune: "While Irish Eyes Are Smiling."

"You know Florentine," the governor said uneasily. "Do you?"

Oakley shook his head.

Florentine skirted the hole in the floor with the confidence of one who had done this many times before. He was in his early sixties, though his hair, a mixture of sand and ash, was still profuse and well-brushed. He sported a white mustache in need of trimming where it overshadowed his upper lip, and that accorded perfectly with his voice when he spoke: an upper-class, military kind of voice.

"Minister . . . " He took his right hand from its pocket and extended it to Oakley. "How do you do?"

Oakley took it with a trace of visible reluctance. "Mr. . . . is it *Mr.* Flor—?"

"Used to be Major; now no longer. Also known as Number One, or The Chief." He laughed quietly. "I answer to all of 'em."

Nobody said anything for a while. Deep gloom pervaded this place, illuminated only by one window let high in the wall close to the master beam supporting the arrangement of chains. This had once been an ordinary cell. Now, however, it was designed not to keep prisoners fast but to send a select few on their way. It smelled of dust, and of something else that lived here and was part of it; something that had been kept locked up, moldering, for a very long time.

"I have to satisfy myself that everything's in working order," Oakley said at last.

Florentine nodded understandingly. "Very proper. Do you want to see the full show?"

Oakley shuddered. "No."

"Just the trap in action?"

"Yes."

Florentine squatted by the hole. "Arthur," he called. "Pass me a rope, will you? . . . No, not that, the new one."

Another figure rose out of the darkness. The governor introduced him as Wandsworth's foreman of

works and this time Oakley looked ready to shake
hands with slightly less manifest reluctance, until
he saw that the newcomer was carrying a rope.

Florentine took it and held it up. "Comes from a
tentmakers' in the Old Kent Road," he said engag-
ingly. "The old firm. Nothing changes in this job.
Six foot long. When the box comes in from the
Prison Commissioners, it must contain, by law, one
old rope and one new. Normally I'd use the old, but
in view of the lapse of time I propose to hang
Thornton with a new rope that's been stretched for
longer than the customary twelve hours."

When he stopped speaking, his voice remained in
the shape of a minute echo that floated above all
their heads.

"You'll notice there's no hangman's knot,
Minister. There never was. Very cruel." He shook
his head in condemnation. "Strangulation is something we prefer to leave to the Americans. Instead, a
metal collar, covered with chamois leather. We
attach it . . . thus." He reached up and connected
the rope's end to a link in one of the chains via a
shackle. "Get the trap up for me, Arthur, there's a
good fellow."

Arthur descended into the pit and shoved the two
halves of the trapdoor together. Florentine adjusted
a lever in the floor that Oakley hadn't noticed
before: it looked like something rescued from an
old-fashioned signal box.

"Now, Minister, what happens is this. The man
comes through there." He pointed to a leather-and-
stud covered door. "That's the C.C., on the other
side. I go in, pinion him, bring him onto the trap
where you see the chalk marks; my assistant ties
his ankles; then it's cap noose pin lever drop."

On the last word he knelt with the agility of a
young monkey, snatched out a cotter-pin, rose to
the half-crouch, and pushed the lever away from

him. The two halves of the trap fell apart with a crash that outsized this small room: Oakley's hands went up to his ears, he uttered an "Ooof!" of shock.

"The prisoner," Florentine said as the last echoes died, "doesn't hear that."

"How long does it take?" Oakley asked weakly.

"From start to finish, between eight and twenty seconds. I'm used to hearing the last strokes of nine o'clock strike as the doctor goes down into the pit."

Florentine spoke those words with a touch of professional pride.

"There's rather a big gap between eight and twenty seconds, isn't there? What determines the precise timing?"

Florentine observed him through eyes that had lost their earlier good humor. "Depends," he said bleakly.

"On what?"

But the executioner merely repeated, "Depends. Minister, there's one thing I'm not happy about." He pointed. "That phone, there, on the wall. It doesn't work. I don't know why it's been put there, but I don't like things that don't work and if it's staying it ought to be fixed. All right?"

Oakley eyed the governor, who nodded, and silence descended once more.

"Well," Oakley said at last, "that's it, then. Thank you, gentlemen." On the threshold, however, he turned back. "Mr. Florentine . . . "

"Minister?"

"How many men have you . . . topped, I think is the expression?" He smiled, putting on his best constituency-massaging expression.

"Enough to know what I'm doing, Minister."

Florentine gazed into Oakley's eyes for a long moment, without friendliness, unconsciously giving the minister a preview of what would be Thornton's last sight on this earth. Oakley wheeled quickly and marched off down the corridor, leaving Howells and his chief officer to follow.

"Seems all right," he muttered as they came out into the courtyard. "Something less to worry about, I suppose."

"I'm glad one of us has other things to worry about."

Oakley ignored the sarcasm. "Oh, there's always something," he said. As he slid onto the back seat of the car his hand lighted on that day's *Times* and his expression became somber. "This, for instance . . . "

Howells bent down to see him holding up the newspaper.

"Miss Forbes? The missing journalist?"

"Deputy editor, actually. Friend of mine."

"Sorry to hear that, Minister."

"The police are doing a first-class job. Busting a gut, as the saying goes."

"I'm sure they'll find her soon."

For a brief instant Oakley's brain insisted on reviewing the strings he'd illicitly pulled, the liberties he'd taken, the corners he'd insisted Scotland Yard cut, and, yes, he hoped they would find her soon, preferably before the prime minister found out how he'd been abusing his powers in the cause of finding a friend.

He looked up to find Howells staring at him. "Yes, well," he said hastily. "Goodbye, then."

By the time the car emerged through the main gate, the police had managed to get the crowd under control. No more tomatoes were thrown. Oakley caught a glimpse of posters: BAN HANGING; THOU SHALT NOT KILL. The mournful sound of a hymn briefly penetrated the car's comfortable interior, along with angry abuse, before fading away.

Seventeen days to go. It would get worse.

CHAPTER
24

LONDON. THE PRESENT

In the dream, all was darkness. Some men were cutting off her hands while others worked at her ankles. The pain went on and on. Roz wrenched her head this way and that, but her tormentors remained invisible, protected by the darkness that surrounded her. Then the darkness changed, and Roz realized that for the past few minutes her eyelids had been open. But the dream hadn't faded, it lived side by side with returning consciousness. And she did not know which was worse: the nightmare or the reality that beckoned.

She was lying on something hard. Cold. Damp.

She swallowed. Her throat ached. With agonizing slowness, her saliva glands started to come back to life.

Someone was moaning. Must be she.

Roz raised her head. She was lying on a metal-framed bed equipped with a thin mattress. Wire bound her ankles and wrists to the frame. The flesh had rubbed raw. Nausea flooded up her body: it was like being hung over and still drunk at the same time . . .

She felt so cold.

She was naked.

She turned her head a hair's breadth. On the wet floor, some feet away from her bed, stood a Camping-Gaz lamp. Its mantel shed a sickly trace of light over a few square feet of what, her brain hazily informed her, must be a cellar. Piers of crumbling brickwork rose to be lost in the gloom above. The walls were invisible. She felt herself to be floating on cosmic Chaos, buoyed up from destruction by this tiny island of impoverished light.

Sitting by the lamp was a *bikkhu*, a Buddhist monk.

Still in the dream, of course. Hallucinating.

He sat facing her with his legs folded in a classic meditation pose, both hands extended, palm upward, the tip of each forefinger touching its respective thumb. She could see his face quite clearly, in the light shed from the lamp. He'd shaved his head and his eyebrows, too.

Much time passed while Roz stared at him. She had never seen such an expression of utter tranquility on a human face before. It dawned on her that he was a Westerner. A European Buddhist, clad in yellow robes. Most strange.

She tried to speak. At first, all that came out was a dry clicking. The monk showed no sign of having heard.

"Please," Roz whispered. Torpor once more had her in its grip, she could feel herself slipping down into oblivion, this was her last hope. "Please . . . help me."

An unseen door crashed open; heavy footsteps invaded her consciousness; instinctively she wrenched away from them until the restraining wires gouged deep. Her head convulsed to and fro. In one of its swings to the right, she saw that the monk had opened his eyes. They were a very pale shade of blue. And then she knew where she had seen this holy man before.

Brennan.

"Wake up!" A hand roughly slapped her leg, making it spring against the wire that held it, and she squealed.

A hooded man entered her line of sight. He flung cold water over her; the wires dug deep into her flesh as she heaved; scream after scream filled the dank cellar.

"She is awake, Pat," said this quiet, reproving voice; and through a haze of agony Roz recognized it as Brennan's. "Leave us now. Please."

She was aware of feet tramping out, of a door slamming shut, bolts being drawn. Then silence.

The monk slowly unfolded himself and stood up. He disappeared into the darkness for a moment, before coming back with a blanket, which he threw across her naked body. He passed out of sight again. When he returned a few seconds later he was carrying a tape recorder. He pressed a switch, then looked up at her with a dreamy smile on his face.

"We are going to talk," he said. "And because what we say to each other, here, in this room, is important, we shall want to remember it."

When he sat down again, he did not adopt his former meditational pose. Instead, he stretched one leg out in front of him, bent the other and rested his forearm on its knee.

"Valance was the wrong man for you," he resumed. "He was good enough for Ben, but for you he was wrong."

Roz stared at him uncomprehendingly. Ben? Where did he fit into this nightmare?

"I want you to remember," Brennan said gravely, "that Ben Saunders is a good man. But I needed his input, you see. Had to have it, in fact. That's why I sold him Valance."

"You . . . sold . . . ?"

"Valance was the price I had to pay for you."

She saw, then. Ben had known she would come after Valance, yes, of course he had. But he'd been programmed. Bought and then tailored.

She wanted to scream, "You're lying!" But when she looked inside herself she did not know whether Brennan was lying or not. If she saw Ben again, and accused him of betrayal, he would deny it. She had no means of finding out the truth. That was the nightmare. Part of it, anyway. There was more.

"Forget about Valance," Brennan advised her. "What you nccd to know is why Scrutton perjured himself. And if you want to learn about Alistair Scrutton, you must come, not to Valance, but to me."

She gazed at him, hearing what he said but understanding none of it.

"At the trial," he went on, after a pause, "there was talk of someone called Chaloem. Siri Chaloem and I were good friends. . . . Can you understand what it was like for me, being rescued by Siri? Me, a good, Catholic boy?"

He made a strange sound, part chuckle, part cry of pain.

"Yes," he murmured. "Siri. There was a night in Sligo, years ago . . . Siri picked me up and made me a man."

Now he raised his voice and said cheerfully, "Tell me, Roz Forbes, have you ever been to Thailand?"

She could not speak one word.

"Ah, well. That's where Siri showed me temples and palaces, he taught me how to hold Mekong whisky, and he bought me my first woman." Brennan chuckled, this time without the pain. "Then he sent me back to Ireland to think things over, and left me alone for a long, long time . . . "

His eyes had never left her face. Now he leaned forward until they were almost touching, and he smiled at her.

"You see, Roz, to understand Alistair, you first have to know Siri Chaloem. And if you want to meet Siri, the person you must ask . . . " He gently tapped his chest. " . . . Is *me*."

Roz swallowed. Brennan's eyes were growing bigger and bigger.

"Do you know anything about Buddhism, Roz? No? Well, Theravada Buddhism is the kindest religion in the world, and the best. But it omits one story from the *Dhamma* which I've always loved: the story of the Master and the simsapa leaves. One day, the Buddha was teaching in a forest temple. And a disciple asked: 'Master, have you taught us everything?' Buddha picked up some leaves. He replied: 'Tell me: which is greatest, the number of leaves here in my hand, or the number of all the leaves in the forest?' And of course the disciple answered: the leaves in the forest. Then Buddha said: 'As the leaves in my hand are to the leaves of the forest, so is my teaching to you when set against all the truths in the world that I know. But I have taught you what you need, to find enlightenment.'"

He fell silent, eyeing Roz with a quizzical gaze, while she fought to put some meaning in his words.

"You mean . . . you'll tell me what I need to know, but there's more?"

Instead of replying with words he clapped his hands together in gentle token of approval.

"I first heard that story," he went on, "in May 1976, at a place called Muang Ngai, in northern Thailand. My pal Siri had got himself into a fight, I can't remember the details now, I'd arrived the day before, and there I was—on the run before I'd so much as unpacked. Monks, he said; we're going to become monks, Martin, you and I. You're crazy, I told him. Now whoever's going to take us in as monks?"

To Roz, staring at his graceful robes, the idea seemed less fanciful. Brennan looked the part; no, he *was* the part.

"You see, Roz, in Thailand, it's common for a young man to do a spell in a monastery for one *phansa.* That's what they call a Lenten season. And Siri knew where to go, of course." His face softened further. "Siri always knew where to go . . . "

He began to describe the monastery for her benefit, and while he spoke Roz found herself seeing the picture in his mind, as if some electronic wizardry now allowed direct transmissions from one brain to another, so vividly did he make the scene come alive: those foothills overlooking the town of Muang Ngai, where light breezes wreathed down from distant peaks to soften the worst of the midday heat; the dusty main compound, with its quiet *kuti,* where the monks slept; and above all, the forest temple . . .

"*Wat pa,*" Brennan said. "The temple glade. We monks would wander along to it in the afternoon, to study or talk or simply to drink water and smoke."

His gaze had been fixed on the middle distance, apart from her, apart from this freezing cellar; but now he turned and, with a beatific smile, murmured: "It was in that glade that I got my nickname, Roz. And died."

She blinked. He had pronounced the words with his usual clarity. She knew what he'd just said. But—"Tell me," was the only reply she could think of.

Again he made that gentle clapping motion in sign of approval, and the shiver that ran through Roz had nothing to do with the cold.

"I was sitting there with Siri, one lazy afternoon,

and I'd asked him what he wanted of me. He'd done so much for me, you must understand. And he replied, he wanted me to *learn*. Just that. By then I already knew that he was a magician, of course. He'd trained in Tibet, so it followed naturally, and I understood about the things he wanted to teach me."

Roz found herself nodding, as if under hypnosis.

"And do you know what he did then?"

Roz shook her head, in the same automatic way.

"He pointed to someone on the other side of the glade. This man wasn't a *bikkhu*, he was what they called the *waiyawachakon*. A layman who looks after the temple's money. And ours was a rich temple; it had several thousand pounds to its name, in those days."

Roz shuddered. "You . . . stole it, didn't you?"

He smiled, and held up his hands palm outward, shaking them gently to show that she must not jump ahead. But she sensed that he was pleased with her, nevertheless, and another shiver rippled through her flesh.

"Now that man kept the temple's money right there, in the *wat pa*, hidden underneath one of the big stone seats that were scattered about. *But Siri wouldn't tell me which one!*"

"Why?"

"Because he wanted me to promise him something. The money was going to be my reward, you see."

"Promise what?"

"That I'd learn whatever he could teach me. However hard the road, no matter how long it took. 'Learn' he commanded me, that hot day in the forest; and I said No."

Now it was the turn of Brennan's face to undergo a remarkable transformation. There could be no mistaking the fear that flashed across his face.

"He had those terrible eyes, Roz, terrible. They could roast a man. And he had this . . . this gray veil that descended over his face at certain times . . . "

Brennan slowly shook his head, then allowed it to fall forward until he was staring at the floor. After a long silence he seemed to come to himself again, stretching out his legs at the same time as he drew a deep breath.

"So we went on as before," he resumed. "I washed my robes, kept my possessions tidy: the alms-bowl, razor, needle and thread, mosquito net, umbrella, cup and saucer, cutlery, quilt, and pillow that every monk must have. I shaved my head and eyebrows once a month, abstained from drink, stayed celibate. I attempted meditation, with some success, and every day went out on *pai binthabat*, the dawn alms round, begging my rice. I fought the good fight with hunger, heat, and mosquitos, did what I could to acquire merit, bided my time. And"—he raised an admonitory finger toward Roz—"I dwelt much on Siri's information concerning the temple's cache of money. But only when Siri said we could leave did I decide to do something about it."

"What did you do?"

"I waited for the night before we were due to leave. Once I was sure everyone else was asleep, I set off for the forest temple. And there I had a problem. Which stone seat was the money under? I tried many, before I found the one. A cavity, containing a box. I dropped the match I'd been using to light my way and felt around in the hole. I had it, Roz! It was *there*, beneath my fingers!"

His large, round eyes were so close to hers that she could see the skein of blood vessels overlying their whites, and they did not so much as flicker.

"And then . . . something . . . *bit me*."

Slowly, oh so slowly, his eyes closed, and he swallowed.

"Well, now . . . " He swallowed again, but it was a painful thing for him, she could see that. "I dropped the box. For a moment, I thought, it's nothing, an insect. Then . . . "

After a long, long pause Roz whispered, "Yes?"

"Then . . . it was as if someone had taken a syringe of molten metal and injected it into my veins. I could feel it traveling along my arm, into my chest, all over my body. My heart was jolting, I screamed. I was falling. Everything . . . closing down. I was conscious but I couldn't breathe. Paralyzed . . .

"Suddenly I knew I must be hallucinating, for there was Siri, walking toward me slowly, oh so slowly. He flung his fan away, like a dagger. I heard a hiss; and he fell on top of me. Just before I went under I felt him stretching his limbs out to cover my own. And then . . . nothing."

He was silent for a long time after that. To Roz it began to seem as though he would not speak again in this lifetime, so it came as a shock when he blurted out, "I woke up in hell."

"Hell?"

"Whiteness. All white, everywhere. Only my right arm burned. Hellfire, I thought. I was lying in a bed. A bed in a white room, with a drip in my arm. Hospital. And, in another bed next to mine lay Siri."

"*Siri?* But—"

"Then the doctor showed up. Nice Thai fellow, Nopporn, that was his name. Nopporn. He couldn't understand what the hell was going on. 'Why aren't you dead?' he used to say. 'You should be dead.'" Brennan laughed tolerantly. "It seemed a taxidriver had found us by the roadside. I was paralyzed, Siri was in a coma, holding a dead banded krait in his hand. I mean, my *God*, a krait! No known antidote. None. And do you know the funny thing, Roz? He wasn't dead—just not breathing. Or, not breathing very often, let's say. A zombie."

The Krait heaved a long sigh.

"I got well," he said. "Except for my right arm; that kept me awake at night. The scars were terrible, I knew they'd never fade. The next thing was, they wanted me to leave. I was a burden on them, you see, and if I wanted them to go on caring for Siri I had to find the means to pay for it."

"There was always the money you'd stolen."

"No. I found out later that the money had stayed in the ground, untouched. Anyway . . . I went back to the monastery, collected our possessions, and paid the hospital. I found myself a room in the town and settled down to wait. Well, I didn't have to wait long. That Thai doctor had had enough. He wanted to turn off Siri's I.V., forget the whole thing. He gave it another seventy-two hours."

Roz looked into his eyes and saw something she had never dreamed might live there. She saw love. "How did you save him?" she asked, not understanding why, or how she knew.

Brennan smiled down at her. "I had a dream."

Her eyes narrowed. "What?"

"I was lying on this beach. It must have been Asia, there were palm trees, and thunderclouds over the ocean. And the sun!—I felt nauseous with heat. So I raised my head, in this dream, and saw somebody walking toward me, a monk. In his right hand he held open a paper fan. Siri. He knelt beside me and waved the fan to and fro, until I was cool. Then he said something. His lips didn't move, but I understood. 'The fan is the life'; those were his words, repeated over and over again, like one of his prayer chants. The fan is the life.

"As soon as I woke up, I went to the hospital, as usual. It grew very hot in the ward; maybe it was because I knew that, perhaps it was to do with the dream, but anyway, I did something I'd never done before, I took Siri's *bikkhu* fan with me. I sat down by the bed. After a while I picked up the fan and began to cool myself with it. Suddenly I looked at Siri's face. And his eyes were open. His mouth opened. And he took a breath. He sounded, you know . . . rusty, as if everything hadn't been used for ages. Then his hand jerked. It jerked again, only this time it bounced off the fan, like a message . . . So I started to wave it again. And before long, he was breathing properly. And I wanted to fetch the doctor, you see. I was just getting up, but then Siri spoke to me, as he'd done in the dream, wordlessly, without moving his lips. 'The fan is the life,' that's what he said. So I knew I must stay beside the bed. And that's how they found me half an hour later, fanning the face of someone they'd given up for dead."

The Krait smiled at Roz. "Do you understand?" he asked softly. She shook her head, causing his eyebrows to lift in mild reproof.

"Well. Next day, soon after daybreak, Siri spoke—spoke properly, I mean—for the first time. He said: 'You owe me.' I thought I'd misheard, but he said it again: 'You owe me.' And I said, 'Yes, I owe you one life.' And then, just like that time in the glade, Siri said . . . *'Learn!'* And when I said, 'Yes' . . . that's when he gave me the fan."

The Krait's voice died away to silence.

"He was saying . . . " Roz swallowed. "He was pretending that his life had been saved by his magic."

"Not pretending." The Krait shook his head gravely. "It was true."

"You don't believe that." When he made no reply, Roz croaked: "You don't, you don't, *you don't*!"

He answered her. He drew up the sleeve of his robe, revealing two blood-red circles rimmed with white, above the wrist.

"You don't believe that!" she screamed. *"Tell me you don't believe it. Tell me!"*

He put his head on one side and smiled. She knew with sickening clarity that in another time, other circumstances, she might not have been able to resist the secret promises of a face like his.

"Why am I here?" she asked weakly. "Please tell me. Not just so that you can tell me the story of your life?"

He smiled his dreamy smile again. After a while she felt sure he didn't intend to answer, but then he said, "Ah . . . You're here through no choice of mine, Roz Forbes. I can't control these people."

"These . . . the IRA?"

"The Provos, yes. For some reason, they think a charming lady like you has become too dangerous."

"Me? *Dangerous?*"

"You were helping Frank. Even before he was charged with high treason, you were providing him with information from your database, at the *Times.*"

"And you think that'll just grind to a halt, because I'm stuck here?"

"I don't. But I have to do what I'm told." He surveyed her with the kind of expression a father might show to his dying child. "It'll be all right," he murmured. "I hope. They've no reason to go on holding you, once Thornton's dead."

"Why?" she wailed. "Why do you want Thornton dead so badly? He's never hurt any of you."

"*I* don't care whether he lives or dies. It's not important to me."

Something about the way he said it made her realize that this was the literal truth. Whatever Brennan's plan might be, he did not require Frank's death, and she experienced a moment of ridiculous hope.

It did not survive his next words.

"But you see, my bosses, they're convinced the government will go through with this execution. Then Thornton will become an IRA martyr. And next time they kill an Englishman, or a corporal's wife in a German suburb, or a coach-load of schoolchildren, they can claim it's in revenge for the murder of one of their own."

"Oh my God." She squeezed her eyes tight shut, as if by doing that she could exclude reality.

"It's a question of image. You, a journalist, can understand that. They're going to make the world look at those of us who fight for Ireland in a brand new light. But as for you . . . I'll do what I can."

Someone flung open the door. A hooded man entered the pool of light, carrying a tray. Brennan inspected it.

"Rice," he murmured. "And water. I'm afraid they're putting you on a diet, Roz Forbes. A Buddhist diet."

The man put down the tray and disappeared into the darkness.

"We'll talk again," Brennan said, picking up the lamp. He switched off the tape recorder, removed the tape, and went to join his companion. "You were making inquiries about Alistair Scrutton," he said from somewhere on the other side of the black wall. "Yes. You should know about him. Al. My pal."

The door clanged shut, leaving her to silence and terror.

CHAPTER

25

LONDON. THE PRESENT

For everyone else in the world, just another Thursday morning. For Frank Thornton, perhaps the last Thursday he would ever see.

"Of course, the trouble is, the union." George stretched his legs out and examined his shoes. "Now, you'll be surprised to hear me say that, Frank, but it's so."

"Ain't that the truth," Nobby agreed lugubriously, turning to the *Mirror*'s sports page. "Ain't it just the bloody truth."

This Thursday, possibly the last Thursday of his life, Frank was trying to finish Paul Scott's *Staying On*, which the librarian had recommended as well-written and funny, although it didn't actually matter what he read, because his span of concentration had shrunk to a few minutes. So now he was glad to let the paperback flop onto his chest and say,

"What union?"

"Prison officers' union."

"Waste of bloody time," said Nobby, thumbing back to page three.

"And money."

"Right. That and all. Mind if we smoke?"

It had both surprised Frank and endeared them to him when they'd first asked permission to light up. No smoker himself, he'd eagerly granted permission; later, however, when his cell was thoroughly infused with the stink of stale tobacco, he had come to regret having done so. The smoke polluted *his* last few hours, not theirs. But . . .

"I don't mind," he said.

George Steeper and Nobby Gibson were usually on the day shift. George looked old enough to be past retiring age. Something told Frank that they'd wheeled him away from his home and his garden because he'd minded the C.C. before and they needed his expertise, but he'd never plucked up courage to ask. George was tanned the color of a pickled walnut, and the skin stretched tightly over his angular skull and sunken cheeks looked almost worn through by harsh weathers. The one thing that didn't quite match the rest of him was his nose: misshapen and bulbous, it sprouted like an unnatural growth.

Nobby, although much younger, had a gloomy outlook on the world. He invariably entered the cell saying, "It's going to rain later." "It's bleeding raining now," George had said, on one occasion. "Shows they're right then, doesn't it?" Nobby had replied in a voice of triumph. "Them weather forecasters."

George and Nobby passed the time when time was passing all too quickly by itself. And they stopped Frank dwelling on what lay nearby. Somewhere close to his cell was a scaffold. He had a terrible, unreasoning desire to know what it looked like.

Many things like that prowled on the boundaries of his conscious mind. England had abolished the death penalty, yet here he sat, in the condemned cell, awaiting execution. His fate was unjust, and terrible. Worst of all, the one person he really wanted to see had not come to visit him. He needed Roz more than ever, now. Yet she hadn't even sent word. *Why?*

He needed to make things right with her before the end. He yearned to explain about the big muddle that had only arisen because her Johnny always seemed to be there, occupying the central position in her life. He wanted to tell her how Louise would never have happened if he hadn't been weak, and thoughtless; how much he regretted not finding the courage to admit that he'd had an affair . . .

It was important, vital, that he have the chance to say to Roz: "I always chose the wrong women, because I never had the sense to choose you. In a way I'm glad it's over now, because I won't have the chance to foul up your life, but I want you to know that I respect you and care about you more than any woman I've ever met."

And then, when she said, "But I ruined your youth!" he would be able to say, "No. You made me a man." And then, "I don't want you to forget me, but you must live your life without pain." And then she would . . .

Sometimes, as now, thoughts of her threatened to bring on tears of self-pity, and he had to hold his book close to his face, so that the officers wouldn't see. Not that they'd mind. George Steeper was kindness itself. And Nobby always looked on the verge of tears anyway.

These were his last friends.

Frank tried hard to behave with dignity. He scrutinized himself every moment, watching for signs of weakness. He wanted these men to go away afterward saying, "Thornton was the bravest man we ever knew." It was pride, and people looked down on pride, condemning it as a sin. But it was all Frank had left. So now he swung his legs off the bed and sat up.

"What's wrong with your union?" he asked.

"Sorry?"

"A moment ago, you said something about the prison officers' union."

"Ah, well," said George, a man preparing for a long session; and—"Yeah, well," chipped in Nobby, folding up his paper. But before they could develop their theme, keys clanked in the corridor and someone threw open the cell door to admit the governor.

Everyone stood up. Howells approached Frank with his usual diffidence, almost as if he thought of himself as an intruder in his own prison, and shook hands. Frank often wondered what had led Edward Howells to this job. The governor struck him as a cultured man, ill at case in what was presumably his chosen environment.

"Everything all right?" he asked. The tightness in his voice told Frank that he both recognized this for a platitude and desperately needed its comfort.

"Yes, thank you, Edward."

Howells had insisted on Christian names from the start.

"Anything you need?"

"Well, if you had a cake with a file in it . . . "

Everyone laughed. Even the feeblest of a condemned man's jokes were deemed funny.

"There's one thing," he said quickly. "A visitor. Miss Forbes. I've been asking ever since I got here, but . . . "

A look of consternation flitted across the governor's tired face. "Sit down," he said.

Frank lowered himself back onto his bunk. Howells pulled a chair away from the folding card table in the middle of the cell and perched on the edge of it, like a nervous vicar invited to take tea with the lord of the manor.

"You haven't been getting the newspapers," he said. "Normally we'd let you have them, but . . . but we didn't want to upset you."

Frank stared at him. The idea of someone in his position being upset by anything in the papers struck him as ludicrous.

"The fact is . . . Miss Forbes has . . . well, she's disappeared."

Frank stood up and took a few steps around the cell, his agitation plain for all to see. The three men regarded him sympathetically, but in silence.

"Disappeared?" he said at last.

"There's a nationwide hunt going on for her. The police are stretched to their absolute limit—they say this is the biggest search for a missing person they've ever mounted. They've got a lead, Frank: she was seen in Peckham, the night you . . . the last night of your trial. She was talking to a man called Valance."

"They've found him!"

"No. He's disappeared, too. I've talked it through with my chief officer—we both know how much you wanted to see Miss Forbes—and we've agreed that from now on you've got to be kept in the picture. *Got* to be."

Frank slumped down on the bed again and covered his face with his hands. When George uneasily shifted his weight from one foot to the other, the squeak of his shiny, new, regulation boots made everyone jump.

"Now, Frank, there's another reason why we want you to see the newspapers." Howells put on a broad, unconvincing smile. "There's an enormous amount of support for you outside. Before, you didn't get much of that, but since your conviction there's been a definite change in the press coverage. You're an intelligent man, I know you won't go overboard—but I wouldn't like you to feel that nobody's fighting in your corner."

Frank removed his hands from his face. "Thank you." He could think of nothing else to say. Howells made several false starts at further conversation but eventually left, his hunched shoulders betraying a sense of defeat.

Nobby caught his colleague's eye. George yawned extravagantly and said: "There's them what runs the union, Frank, and them what does the work. Now, take a young man like Nobby here, with, let's say, what, Nobby? Twenty years left?"

The two warders embarked on a desultory discussion, but Frank no longer heard. He was back in his time capsule. So many days. Twenty-something. Three clear Sundays; enough to take communion three times, make peace with God. And it went so fast. When he was on remand, time dragged. Each day became a week. But now . . .

A line of Shakespeare's hovered on the fringe of his memory; something about Time: *"Who doth he gallop withal? With a thief to the gallows."*

Each hour, each minute, each second brought him galloping closer to a heinous, unmerited death; and the one person left in this world to love, the only woman who gave a damn for him, had vanished.

CHAPTER

26

LONDON. THE PRESENT

The second Ben entered, his editor was off his chair and closing the door behind him.

"Know what this is, Saunders?" Ron Macheval shouted, thumping the rolled-up report with his fist. "*This* is what's known, in the inky trade, as a P. 45."

Ben pulled a chair around until he could squat with his arms resting on its back, and said, "You shouldn't keep things pent up like this, Ron. Get it off your chest, why don't you?"

"Very funny, ha-ha." Macheval hitched his bottom onto the desk and stared at his home news editor. "Possibilities. One. You're totally mad. Two, we're all looking at five-to-ten inside for contempt of court plus conspiracy to pervert."

"Lovely headline, Ron. Mind if I write that down?"

"Three. The Provos'll be here tomorrow measuring up for the bombs and what fucking *color* would we like!"

He thumped the papers down on his desk with a

snarl. "That's just the possibilities. Now let's examine the certainties, shall we? One. You are F-I-R-E-D, out, kaput."

Ben surveyed him stonily. "Are you through?" he inquired.

"Not by so much as one-bleeding-tenth." Macheval wriggled his shoulders in the gesture of a man preparing to wing a golf ball over the horizon. "What *possessed* you?"

In the silence that followed, Ben drew out a pack of cigarettes and lazily offered one to his boss, who took it as if they were having a drink in the Wig and Pen.

"I was wrong," Ben admitted at last. "But I'm coming clean now."

Macheval scowled at him. He was a tall, heavily-built bruiser of a man with a tendency to sweat profusely. To combat that, he spent a fortune on male cosmetics. No matter what the weather, his face was always coated with tiny droplets of moisture, but it was *clean* moisture. His memos on the subject of personal hygiene were a source of constant merriment to his staff and to readers of Private Eye. He was known as "The Prince," partly on account of his Machiavellian-sounding name and partly because, like royalty on tour, he showered at least three times a day. So when Ben said, "I'm coming clean," he at once suspected a hidden slur. But before he could challenge him, Ben had taken up the reins once more.

"You've seen what I've managed to find out," he said, pointing at the papers lying on Macheval's desk. "It fits."

"Convince me."

"The whole concept of a plot to kill the Queen is a non-bloody-starter. Totally counterproductive. Guaranteed to lose the IRA whatever sympathy it's managed to scrape together."

"Ben, answer me one question. Just the one. Why do we make jokes about Irishmen?"

Ben started to speak, but Macheval held up his hands. "No. Let me tell you. It's because Micks are stupid, Ben. They keep their brains where the rest of us park the dinner we've just digested. Don't they? Eh?"

"That's one answer. What I'm saying is, there might, just might, be another."

"Such as?"

"This plot is, on the surface, ridiculous. So ridiculous that no one can see past it to the Krait's real intentions. So way-out, so daft, that no one's even bothered to try."

"His real intentions."

"Yeah."

"Which are what?"

"To get rid of Thornton, because he was getting close to Scrutton. That libel action. They were digging up dirt left, right, and center; what Scrutton did in the Far East, gambling—"

"Everybody gambles out there."

"Yes, but if Scrutton wanted to explain away his lifestyle, he had to gamble and *win*. He lost. And I know what you're going to say." Now it was Ben's turn to hold up his hands. "If they were so worried about Thornton, why not send a coupla fellahs around with shooters to knock him off?"

"As a mind reader, my son, you're perfect, it's as a reporter that you—"

"*Because* . . . no, listen, it's because that would still leave people dredging up the dirt on Scrutton. They had to turn Scrutton round. Build him up. Vindicate him."

"They could have done that in the libel action."

"But that would leave Thornton intact, wouldn't it? And if somebody blew him away afterward, some highly nasty questions might get asked, yes?"

"You're pissing in the wind, Ben."

"So why were all these geezers out East so keen to spill the beans to me?"

"But not to give evidence." Macheval collapsed into his chair and began to skim through Ben's report with a frown.

"Suppose there was something in it," he said after a while. "What's the IRA going to get out of all this?"

"Scrutton. A Provo judge on the English high court bench; Ron, *think* of it! What wouldn't they give for that?"

"And I suppose . . . " Macheval raised his eyes to the clutter on his desk, puckering up his mouth. "Nah . . . "

"Say it."

"I suppose they'd have their martyr in Thornton, wouldn't they? Their glory-boy. Haven't been too many of them. Blowing up squaddies' families more their line. Killing baby girls."

"Right! But if you get the government flaunting the human rights people, it's tyranny-rears-its-ugly-head time."

Macheval flung Ben's report back onto the desk. "But why *Thornton*?" he shouted. "If they want a treason trial, why don't they send over some dyslexic dick-head, stuff him full of amphetamines and shunt him up to Smith's Lawn, or wherever it was? Thornton's a lovely fellah; whiter than white."

"That's true whether my story's right or wrong. A less likely terrorist never got his collar felt. So somebody wins either way—the IRA have got their martyr, and the wishy-washy liberals can go around bleating what a terrible miscarriage of justice it all was."

"I'm not buying it. You've been stalling me for months—'This is the big one, Ron. It's coming through, Ron. Just a few more weeks, Ron.' And

look at the *money* you've spent! I mean, I've heard
of creative accountancy, but this could give, what's
that Russian sci-fi bloke, this could give Asimov his
next fucking *book*!'

Macheval swung out of his chair and came
around the desk once more. "Seriously," he said, in
a quiet, almost friendly tone, "give me one good
reason why I shouldn't fire you."

Ben's face was running with sweat. "Because," he
said, quietly, "if I'm right, this is going to be the
biggest . . . fattest . . . most glorious front, middle,
and back page all rolled into one *scoop* of your
entire career."

"*If* you're right." Macheval sniffed loudly. "And
not *your* career, I notice."

"Well, something might rub off. But I'm not
exactly bargaining from strength, am I? You might
as well say it; even before Thornton, I'd been on the
slide for months."

Another loud sniff. "What is it you want?"

"Cash. And authority to sign up Valance's story
for whatever it takes. That's the only reason I'm
here." He pointed at the report he'd written. "If I'd
had the readies, I wouldn't have let you come within a mile of that."

Macheval raised two fists above his head and
appealed mutely to an indifferent God.

"I know I can find Valance again," Ben went on
gamely.

"That's where it falls apart for me. *How?*"

Ben's face had assumed an extraordinary pallor,
as if he were about to go down with something tropical and rare. "Just take it from me," he said. "I
can."

"Come on, you've got to do better than that!"

"I've got sources, haven't I?" Ben stood up and
took a few restless turns about the room. "Special
sources. Yeah."

"So we're talking exclusive?"

"Yup. And exclusive means top dollar, *you* know that."

The one thing he *must* have was moolah. Brennan's intermediary had made that very clear: "As far as Valance is concerned, money talks; no money— no talk." The memory brought two scarlet spots into Ben's livid cheeks. "Look," he said hurriedly, "I can bribe or booze or beat the truth out of Valance, promise. But that means a safe house, where the IRA can't find us, and cash for two heavies."

"And if the IRA *do*, by some unhappy coincidence, find . . . *us*, as you put it? You could get killed."

"Yes."

"And where would that leave your Kev?" Macheval asked.

Ben stared at the carpet, chewing his lips.

"Nice boy, your Kevin. You just think about that."

"I have." Ben raised his eyes to Macheval's face. "But I'm not going to let this one go."

"But *why*, man? What's Thornton to you, at the end of the day? Eh?"

"I believe they're going to top an innocent man, some time next week. Tuesday, probably. I've got five days to come up with the goods and make it stick in time to save his life."

Sometimes Ben really believed all that. Sometimes . . .

"Yeah, well don't let the *Sun* know."

"What?"

"Word is that they've come up with a way of getting a man into the execution shed. Dead hush-hush."

"Oh, you're joking!" Ben stared at Macheval. "No, you're not, are you?"

"No joke. And just a minute . . . where's all this

high-minded guff coming from suddenly . . . saving
Thornton's life? It's not just the story any more?"

Ben's face set hard. "No," he said softly, after a
long pause. "It's not just the story."

Macheval gazed at him for a moment. Then he
said, "I think you should take a rest. Have a look at
something completely different, why don't you?"

"Different?"

"Yeah. Lots of other papers have come round in
support of Thornton now. He's got plenty of pals, he
doesn't need you."

"He does! I tell you, he does . . . "

"And it's not as if his is the only story in the
world. Roz Forbes, now she's a friend of yours—why
not get on the back of that one? You could write
that up really well."

There was a long silence.

"The Forbes thing's got a lot more going for it,
honest."

"Can't do that, Ron."

"But *why*, for Christ's sake?"

"Can't."

"Has to be Frank Thornton, does it?" Macheval
clicked his tongue. "Sentimental, Ben. Big mistake.
Big mistake."

"I don't think so." Ben ran a finger around the
inside of his collar. He had to win this one, *had to!*
"Just give me those five days. Give me five grand *and*
a contract to wave at Valance. At the end of that
time, I'll hand over to you the biggest story in the history of newspapers." He stood so he could rest his
weight on the back of his chair. "That's a promise."

Neither man spoke for about a minute. Macheval
slowly returned to his seat behind the desk, where
he sat toying with a pencil, his face screwed into an
intense frown. "Ben," he said at last. "Do you really, *really* . . . have to have more loot if we're to get
any hope of this story?"

"Yes. That, and a sky's-the-limit contract in my pocket to buy Valance, and one of the safe houses, where we keep the tarts and rent-boys once we've signed up their life stories."

Macheval slid open a drawer of his desk and Ben's heart leaped. But his editor merely took out a plastic tub, opened it, and tipped a yellow tablet into his palm. He knocked it back without benefit of water, making a face. Then he said, "You can have the petty cash for your thugs. *And* a contract for Valance. But when you walk out of this office, you'll have become like MI6, Saunders. As far as this newspaper's concerned, you won't even fucking exist."

CHAPTER

27

LONDON. THE PRESENT

After a while the guards ceased to wear hoods, allowing Roz to see their faces, and she knew that meant they would kill her, for now she could identify them.

Sometimes they brought her a few inches of icy water to wash in, and she made the effort. She ate the rice they provided, even though it was usually cold. Once, however, it was scalding hot, and having to wait for it to cool reduced her to tears. She was perpetually hungry, perpetually dirty.

Worst of all was the fear that she had been forgotten. Her parents, family, and friends knew her as an independent woman with a will of her own; perhaps they thought that if she chose to wander off without telling anyone, that was her affair. She cursed them for their stupidity and callousness.

Then the Krait brought her a newspaper. She read of the ceaseless efforts being made to find her. She wept with relief and gratitude, and an excess of guilt for those spasms of loathing those she loved, holding onto the hem of his yellow robe and wiping her face with it over and over again, while he gently stroked her hair.

He encouraged Roz to take a little exercise. She walked up and down, dragging the chain that shackled her to the bed, trying not to think of the degradation. She stank, even to herself. Tears constantly hovered at the backs of her eyes. She viewed herself with a contempt that she could neither dispel nor express in words.

Initially, she tried to keep alert. At school she'd always scored highest marks for composition, and never needed props in order to construct a fantasy world. So now she would go for endless, mental walks through the streets of London, pausing to stare into favorite shop windows, or treating herself to afternoon tea at the Ritz. But then that became too depressing and she tried mathematical calculations, until the frustration of not being able to hold the figures in her head drove her into a rage.

There were times, a few times, when she awoke into the real world, cast onto an eroding island of sanity that had survived the maelstrom. Then she was, she dimly realized, on her way back to infancy: to an era when she had been dependent on others for everything from a smile to a bowl of food.

Childhood memories came back to haunt her, one in particular: whenever her parents used to rent a cottage in the Cotswolds for summer holidays, she and her brother would climb the old brick wall to spy on their neighbors, who liked to garden naked. Sam, her brother, had been very shocked at first. Not Roz. Roz had skipped the horsy bit, graduating early to men.

Always, it seemed, looking back, the wrong men.

Martin Brennan—she soon came to call and think of him as Martin—did what he could to alleviate her distress. At first, she rejected him. But gradually, as what psychologists versed in kidnapping call "the slow death" crept up upon her, and the periods of recall became less frequent, she began to think of him in another light.

She felt especially vulnerable when he recounted his life story. He spoke so movingly about the deprivations his family had endured; of his brother's tragic death; of the sub-world into which he'd reluctantly allowed himself to be drawn, for lack of discipline and example.

"You want my sympathy," she'd snapped; at that time unsubservient.

"No, no." He laughed quietly, but then his smile faded. "Roz, a word of advice. Don't think of feeling sorry for me."

She stared at him, trying to divert the insidious suspicion that he might be offering her sincerity.

"There's people out there whose job it is to do away with the likes of me; you're on their side. The Black Berets, for instance; now there's a body of men I can respect . . . "

He told her about Germany's GSG9, with its access to the awesome Federal computer at Wiesbaden, and Holland's special assistance unit of the Mariniers, and special patrol groups and diplomatic patrol groups, and what the difference was, and how the latter always drove around in maroon cars. He taught her the trick of stealing a furniture van and turning up at your victim's house to carry him out rolled up in a carpet. He dwelt with melancholy pleasure on the logistics of collecting a ransom, when eleven million pounds was represented by one ton of paper, or three and a half tons of gold; oh how he longed, he said, for the cashless society!

She hung upon his every word. In a curious, twisted re-run of the *Thousand and One Nights*, she implored him to stay and tell another of his marvelous stories. Just one more, she would beg. And he, knowing what life became like for her when he exited through the wall of surrounding darkness, would smile, and say, "Next time . . . "

Because they'd removed her watch, she had no sense of time at all.

There were certain things she refused to discuss with Brennan. For instance, she would not plead with him to withdraw what he'd said about Ben Saunders, even though she longed to, because what was the point? But she did remind him, often, of his promise to tell her about Scrutton, not understanding why he always sheered off. Until one day, by chance, she found another route . . .

"Tell me about Siri," she said. "About what happened after he gave you his fan. What made him so *special*?"

For a long time Brennan said nothing, but sat on the floor with one leg folded up and his right forearm resting on its knee, a favorite position of his. Now, looking down on him from the bed, it occurred to Roz that her question had moved him and she could not understand why.

"Special," the Krait said at last; and the word came out in a long exhalation.

"There I was," he eventually went on, "just as Siri had said: spittle. No education. No hope, and of course, no more elder brother to adore. Just a mess of religious hatreds and bigotry. And he changed all that, you see."

"But something happened to him . . . after the business with the snake, I mean?"

"Scrutton happened to all of us. Even you."

"*Me?*"

"Oh yes. I first heard your name from Alistair Scrutton's lips. He knew a lot about you. He admired you. And the more he told me about you, the more I admired you, too." His voice tapered off. "You've a lot to thank him for."

"Scrutton? But . . . " Roz ground her teeth together. Martin *wanted* her to ask about that, so she wouldn't. Instead, in an inspired move, she fought her way back to the conversation's starting point and asked: "What's he got to do with Siri?"

"Scrutton was involved in the drugs business. Well, you'd worked that out for yourself. There came a time when he wanted to give it all up. But there were people in the way."

"You?"

"Me. And . . . "

Normally he talked easily and well, with the facility of a raconteur occupying his usual seat in the bar and surrounded by friends. But she had flummoxed him, it seemed. That pleased her. It made her so happy that she burst into tears, and he had to comfort her before he could embark on the story. His best story, he called it . . .

"This happened," he began, "in December 1976; and all because Siri was late picking me up at Bangkok airport. That wasn't like him. At first I blamed the traffic, you know how you do, but in the end I hailed a taxi. Well, half an hour later, there I was, still stuck in a jam on Rama IV Road. And then I caught sight of one of the Oriental Hotel's white cars on the opposite carriageway. Also stuck. Some poor johnny going to the airport, thought I. Then I took a closer look, and I realized that I knew this poor johnny. Alistair Scrutton."

By now Roz had recovered from her earlier fit of the blues and was listening intently. "He was carrying something? A shipment?"

"No. Not that time, I think, although . . . well, you shall hear. Until then, I'd been on my way to Siri's house, but there was something about the sight of Scrutton to set off alarm bells in my head, and I changed my mind. He had no business being there, you see. So I found a flophouse and waited for nightfall. Then I risked one quick phone call to Siri's place. No reply. Now that was strange, Roz. Siri was a rich man; he had plenty of servants to answer his phones.

"What to do? Calling by in person wasn't an option, not yet. Instead, I took myself off to the river, and a certain multi-story shopping complex. The shop I wanted lay down an ugly cul-de-sac; one of those double-fronted emporia, with an American Express notice pasted onto the glass and an ivory tusk on each side of the entrance. You know the kind of place I mean: always overpriced, always empty."

He paused for breath. Roz raised herself on one elbow, the better to study his face. Something grim lurking behind his ever-present smile warned her not to interrupt.

"I'd come to see a woman called P'ia. She was Alistair's mistress; had been for years. He'd set her up in this very shop, and the moment I clapped eyes on her I could see she was terrified.

"'Come into the back,' she hissed. '*Quick.*' So I followed her into the office, and the moment I shut the door she burst into tears and collapsed. 'Siri,' she wailed. 'What about him?' I said; 'Where is he?' And she replied, as by then I knew she would: 'Dead.'"

He rested his weight on his hands behind him, head sunk into his chest. Roz knew better than to speak. But when some treacherous, nameless emotion urged her to reach out and comfort him, it was only with difficulty that she resisted.

"Well . . . " The Krait sighed. "It was a long story she had to tell, but what it boiled down to was this. Siri had come to the shop the day before. Angry, as if—P'ia said—as if someone had betrayed him. He'd wanted to know where Alistair was. P'ia told him she didn't know, hadn't seen him for months. Which I did not believe, for had I not seen the man himself just a few hours before, on his way to the airport? But—why should P'ia lie to me, Roz Forbes? Why?"

Roz shook her head violently.

"There was more. Siri had seemed not only angry, he was afraid, too. And the minute he'd left, a couple of Yang Po's men had come in—"

"Yang Po? The same man that was murdered here in London?"

"The same. He'd been the Chaloems' partner for more years than any of us could count. In a way, he was Alistair's partner, as well. So two of his men had visited P'ia's shop, asking questions: Where was Siri going, had he brought anything, had he mentioned Brennan? Now that interested me, Roz, it really did, for I couldn't think of any reason why Yang Po should be bothering himself about me. Anyway. P'ia swore she'd told them nothing about Siri or me, and then they'd left. Next thing was, Lek—that's Siri's number one—phoned her in the middle of the night. She could hear shouting in the background, as if everyone was panicking." Brennan hesitated, drew a deep breath. "Siri's headless body had been thrown over the wall."

He sat forward to rest his arms on his knees. Suddenly he startled her by asking, "Roz, when you were a journalist, before you became an editor, I mean, did you ever interview someone and know that he was lying, even though you couldn't put your finger on how you knew?"

"Oh yes. There's a famous saying we have: 'Always ask yourself why these lying bastards are lying to you.'"

He rewarded her with a full, rich laugh that went on for a long time. "It's experience, isn't it?" he asked at last.

"Yes. That, and having done your homework before you go in."

He nodded appreciatively, one professional sharing with another. "Yes. Well, that's how it was with

P'ia and me that night. I knew she was lying. But I couldn't work out why. She was holding something back. Perhaps she didn't regard it as important, perhaps she was afraid. *But there was something.* I knew she wasn't going to tell me, and in any case by then I was . . . I was beside myself, Roz. But behind and beneath all the grief, questions were stirring. Who, apart from Siri, knew that I was coming to Bangkok? Had he told anyone? Worrying, that—very. So I bought myself a motorbike in the Thieves Market. I knew where to go: Chiang Mai, and the Triangle."

Roz noticed the change in him once he left Siri's death behind. He became animated, less introspective. Again, she felt his peculiar brand of magic brush her when he described the cool, scented air battering his skin as he raced up Highway One; she hugged his shadow as he slipped across the Burmese border in the far northwest, just down the Ruak River from a small town called Mae Sai; she helped him beach his bamboo raft and cover it with brushwood before skirting Tachilek and heading north on foot along one of the hidden trails used by traffickers. Dawn found Brennan—and Roz, too—holed up in trees overlooking an Akha village of some twenty bamboo and thatch huts.

The man kept them waiting for almost a week.

Brennan had brought fruit in his rucksack, along with some sweet, sticky rice wrapped in banana leaves for variety. Roz could taste it. Nor was she thirsty, for Brennan knew from way back where the village water supply flowed out of the hills through wooden conduits, and as long as they had water the two of them could live for a long time.

They exercised in the cool light of daybreak, before the village came to life. The first shaft of smoke from a cooking fire, rising into an utterly silent, green landscape, found them lying on their

stomachs, watching the path where it wound along
the side of the hillside below: the tiny hamlet's sole
means of contact with the outside world. They
watched while the heat built up and the sky turned
from blue to a pale yellow screen of heat and dust;
through the furnace of midday, when the village lay
cocooned in torpor; to the brass tints of afternoon,
and finally the subtle mauves and pinks of early
dusk. Then they would move down to the path, so
that even if the man came during the night, they
would hear his approach.

So far Roz followed him, moment by moment;
until suddenly, without warning, he pitched her off
the magic carpet.

"Sean came long after sundown, he always knew
the best time to find me."

For a moment Roz did not realize that she had
been discarded, that the journey was going on without her. "Sean . . . you mean—"

"'Hello, Martin.' That's what he said. Just that."

Looking at his face, it dawned on Roz that he was
still in reality, only a different reality from hers.

"I wasn't sure, at first. But then Sean said: 'Well,
and who else could it be, out here, at this time of
night?' and I thought, yes, by God! He's right—who
else could it be?"

Roz lay perfectly still, studying him. For the first
time in a long while, she felt frightened. Her body
was turning cold, the cold that followed an influen-
za night sweat.

"He'd come to talk about Yang Po, you see. Fill
me in, as it were. He was as near as your right hand,
Roz."

She snatched her hand behind her back.

"'We'll sit down, Martin. Have a talk.' That's
what he said. And we did."

Roz had no means of knowing which would be
worse: to speak or remain silent. Speak. Let him

think she was still with him, on their journey . . .

"What . . . did he say, Martin?"

"He confirmed my thinking: Yang Po's men must have expected me to go straight to Siri's house when no one was at the airport to meet me. That was why they hadn't answered the phone when I rang—they'd been there, of course—for when I hear an unfamiliar voice, Roz, I vanish.

"That left the mystery of P'ia. But Sean was very good on P'ia, oh yes, very good. Yang Po always knew where to find Siri Chaloem, he had no need to send his men to P'ia's shop. That was a blind. They figured I'd go there. They meant me to discover, quickly, who'd killed Siri."

He said nothing for a while. Roz was coming to dread these silences, the times when the ground rules shifted and changed, without warning or reason.

"Why hadn't they taken you on the spot?" she breathed. "In P'ia's shop . . . "

"Ah! Because they wanted me on their own ground, where they could slaughter unseen and unheard. Wanted me, in fact, either to go to Siri's house, like a butterfly to the killing-jar, or do what I actually did: go up to the Triangle. And Sean showed me the thing P'ia had been holding back. She knew what her role was, you see, Roz: to send me to my death."

"But why would she do that?"

Brennan grinned, shook his head. "Not all the questions had answers," he replied. "Not even Sean knew everything, then. Only later . . . Well, enough; I'll come to that."

He seemed to shiver slightly, as if feeling another persona slide beneath his skin, and when he spoke again his voice was different, less filled with foreboding.

"At last . . . Rin came."

"Rin?"

"Someone from Alistair's past. A man whose brother had been killed in front of him, during his first meeting with Siri's father. It was Rin's village I'd been watching, him I'd been waiting for. He came at daybreak, not expecting trouble; I took him very cleanly. By the time he came to, I'd got him suspended by the thumbs from a tree branch, with just the tips of his toes touching the ground."

The Krait painted a picture with his hands for Roz's benefit, although she could see it right enough without any help from him.

"He talked. In the end. He'd been working for Yang Po. At first, he spun me Yang Po's line, the one he'd put about among his men: that Siri had been betraying them to the army, for money. But it wasn't true, and Rin knew it. He confirmed all that Sean had told me. And he told me something else besides."

Roz sensed from his tone that this, what came now, was the answer to everything, the key that unlocked every door.

"Yang Po, P'ia, and Alistair had cooked up a deal between them. The details don't matter. What matters is that because of the deal, Siri had to die. And do you know what I said to Rin? I said: 'Oh, my friend, how can that general be so . . . damn . . . *stupid*?'"

"What happened then?"

Roz despised herself for asking that question, playing into his hands. But because the Krait was a master storyteller, she had to know.

"Then . . . ?" He heaved a sigh, staring into the middle distance as if she hadn't spoken. "Then . . . I cut him down. I watched him totter as far as the outskirts of the village before I hit the track; and, weak though I was, I didn't stop until I reached Thailand. Where I went back to our monastery, the one Siri and I had spent time in. And I cried from sundown unto sundown, as the Thais say . . . for my brother."

His face had turned melancholy. She caught herself longing to console him again and screamed to herself, *You stupid, bloody bitch! That's what he wants!*

"Your brother," she said. "Which one—Thai or Irish?"

When he did not reply, she went on, "You know it wasn't really Sean, there in the jungle, don't you? Just your brain, playing tricks."

He pursed his lips as if her words had made a deep impression on him and he needed to think. "You believe I'm mad," he said sharply. "Is that it?"

At first caution held her back, but then an awful, reckless courage drove up through her body, and in a kind of stupor she heard herself say, "You kill people, you talk to your dead brother, yes, you're mad, you're a psychopath."

He stood up and she knew he was going to beat her. But instead he merely surveyed her for a long moment before bursting into peals of delighted laughter.

"Roz Forbes," he said at last, wiping his eyes, "you're a mighty journalist. The *human* angle to every story." Another little bubble of laughter burst out of him. "I never told you how much I enjoyed that article you wrote about me. Am I really 'handsome in a wistful kind of way'?"

He picked up the lamp.

"So," he said. "Now you know about Scrutton. Everything Rin told me that day in the jungle was true."

"The deal Scrutton made with the others—"

"Caused Siri's death, yes. After that, I had to make fresh plans for Alistair."

"And Frank Thornton has to die."

"I'm sorry he got involved. I've nothing against him."

"I always knew he was innocent. Always."

"No." His voice turned matter-of-fact. "You weren't sure. Until I introduced you to Siri, until I told you what Rin told me, you could never be sure."

She hated him then, for knowing her better than she knew herself. She watched through a red haze as he switched off the tape recorder, removed the tape, and glided as far as the frontier where her range of sight gave way to darkness.

"You were wrong about one thing," he said, keeping his back to Roz. "Sean *was* there, in the jungle. Siri said so."

"Siri!"

"Yes."

"But he was dead!"

She flung herself back on the bed, making no effort to hide her contempt.

"Was he?" asked a quiet voice, one that she had never heard before.

Roz shot upright again. Still on the threshold of shadow, Brennan turned. She knew it was Brennan turning there, knew that in a second more she would see his quiet smile, the same as ever. But when he faced her it seemed, just for a second, as though another countenance had superimposed itself upon his own, and in the shock of semi-recognition she uttered a terrible, drawn-out wail, a scream made up of terror and grief and pain.

For an unearthly visage swam before her on the line where light gave way to void: upslanted, almond-shaped eyes, high cheekbones, a round face swathed in gray, all in gray . . .

Just for a second. Then the darkness mended itself to become complete.

CHAPTER

28

WANDSWORTH JAIL.
THE PRESENT

Visitors arrived in the afternoon, after exercise. Harrison Gephard came frequently, bearing delicacies from Fortnum's and encouraging news of Washington's latest diplomatic moves to have Frank reprieved. Some days he had word of new initiatives to find Roz: the primetime broadcast of a lookalike following her daily route to work, perhaps, or a fresh advertising campaign. And then one Sunday afternoon he brought his daughter, Jodie.

Frank stared at her through the mesh, struggling for words. She was young, still only fourteen and with all her life to look forward to, but already she had turned beautiful. Today, however, her face was blotchy-pale beneath the long, blonde hair and she gnawed a lip that trembled.

Frank glanced up at Harrison. "You shouldn't have—"

"No choice. She insisted." Harrison stuck out his jaw. "Though you needn't think I tried to dissuade her."

"What are you doing now?" Frank asked Jodie, once he could speak again.

"Oh . . . studying here at the American School . . . " She squeezed out a cheerful grin; but the effort cost her dear and when the collapse came immediately afterward it only caused them more grief. They sat there, wrestling with their emotions, while Harrison looked on helplessly.

"When do you take exams?" Frank stammered.

"June. Sometime. I don't know." She hesitated. "Frank, I just . . . just *know* you didn't do . . . what they said."

"Jodie, I—"

"And this is the most barbarous, *vicious* thing . . . " She was making no attempt to stem the tears by now. "If anyone's got to hang, it should be the British government!"

She wiped her face, keeping it averted.

"Jodie," he said at last. "Listen to me. You, your father, everyone . . . you've got to get over this. I want you to put it behind you."

"I can't *ever* do that!" she wailed.

"You must. You absolutely must. For my sake. Because I love you, and I want you to be happy. Please, promise me you won't let this thing turn to bitterness inside you."

He strove to inject his gaze with all the force of his emotion, as if by a mere glance he could stamp, indelibly, the right memories, the best ideals, into her brain; until at last she held her palms to the mesh and whispered, "I love you too, Frank. I'll be thinking of you, praying for you."

As Harrison led her away, tears streaming down both their faces, Frank buried his head in his hands. Then George touched him on the shoulder, one soldier-comrade to another, and he rose blindly to stumble from the room.

The evening of her visit, he did something he'd

meant to do long ago but lost sight of in the welter of preparations for his trial: he made out his will, using George and Nobby for witnesses. He left everything to be divided between Roz Forbes and Jodie Gephard, and as he signed it he recalled his mother's words spoken on Call Night all those years ago: "I'm very proud of you, Frank. You're the only one in our family to have done anything."

That day as on most other days, he played chess with Nobby after dinner. Jodie's visit had taken it out of him, however, so he lay down earlier than usual and tried to sleep. But sleep always came hard, and tonight for some reason the rage he felt against Alistair Scrutton boiled up inside like molten steel. He lay there, stiffly, with his hands clenched by his sides and his eyes clamped shut, given up to hatred.

He despised and loathed himself almost more than Scrutton; for these emotions brought him down to his enemy's level. But he could not quell them.

Rage is better than despair, he told himself. Sometimes, if it's strong enough, rage can even blot out fear. Fear of death. Of the coarse hempen rope around his neck. Of falling sickly through space, shrieking, into a void that was the more terrible for being unknown . . . and often the violence of his fear would bring him bolt upright, whimpering, ashamed of his weakness in front of the warders whose duty it was to save him for the slaughter.

That Sunday night, Frank had almost drifted off to sleep when he heard the familiar rattle of keys in the lock and opened his eyes in time to see Edward Howells enter the condemned cell.

One look told Frank the truth, making his heart catch and shudder. He stood up and said: "There's no reprieve."

"Frank, I am so . . . so desperately sorry."

Howells' face was drawn and white. He shifted his weight from one foot to the other, unable to keep still, but made no move to leave; and Frank realized that this wasn't quite all. "When?" he stuttered.

Howells breathed in deeply. "The day after tomorrow," he said in a rush. "At nine o'clock."

CHAPTER
29

LONDON. THE PRESENT

The safe house was an unassuming postwar pebble-dash and brick semi, backing onto a recreation ground in Tottenham. The tabloid's business tended to be transacted in an upstairs room, half office and half "my lady's chamber," as Ben called it: a soft sofa, mirrored drinks' cabinet, desk lamp in the tasteful guise of a pink, fake-marble Virgin Mary with a bulb screwed into her uplifted hands.

At one o'clock that Monday morning, the last Monday of Frank's life, Reg Valance lay on a sofa, snoring, while Ben Saunders chain-smoked and tried to cope with recent memories.

They'd promised him Valance if he delivered Roz. Well, he'd done that; but Valance had disappeared, all the same. A con trick, that's what he thought. Then, just as he'd abandoned hope, the phone had rung. The promised tip-off. An address, a couple of names, a time.

The snatch went exactly as arranged. He and two unarmed bandits had trounced a pair of IRA hard men while they walked Valance home through the back streets of King's Cross. Like something out of one of his better stories . . . God, the back-bench boys weren't going to believe this when they heard.

Nor should they, for it wasn't true. Brennan's men had deliberately ducked a fight. That was part of the deal. That, and delivering Roz Forbes into the Krait's arms.

She'll be all right, Brennan's intermediary had promised. But when Ben said: "You won't hurt her?" he'd just smiled.

Ben crushed *that* memory. The important thing was that he had Valance. But something he didn't have was time. Because a little over twenty-four hours from now, they were going to hang Frank Thornton.

He walked up and down, lighting one cigarette from the stub of another, trying not to think about what he'd been ready to sacrifice in pursuit of his so-called "career."

"Kevin," he said aloud to the pink Virgin. "I did it for my boy. If it wasn't for him . . . "

As soon as Ben heard Valance groan and stir he switched on the hidden tape recorder, careful to make no noise. One glance through the curtains showed him a sullen dawn, carrying the threat of snow. He quickly shut it out. Then he straightened his shoulders, said a quick prayer, settled himself forward in an armchair opposite Valance's sofa . . . and launched himself down the ski-jump.

"Mr. Valance, what a relief to find you safe and sound."

Valance peered at him through bleary eyes, squeezed almost shut against the trickle of light filtering through the curtains. "What the . . . who *are* you?"

"Press, Mr. Valance." Ben flashed his NUJ card.

"Where the hell am I?" Valance rolled upright, rubbing his eyes. "What time is it?" His narrow eyes shifted uneasily around the room, not settling anywhere. "Actually, I'm leaving. Way out is where?"

Ben laughed politely. "Oh, my goodness, Mr. Valance, be careful, sir, do. You're in a very bad state, what with the way those villains handled you last night, before we managed to rescue you. The hospital is where you're going, then the police to make a statement of course, that's obligatory—"

"Poli—"

"And you need to rest a bit. After a nightmare experience like the one you've been through . . . " Ben shook his head, hissing through his teeth. "Christ, I'm only glad it wasn't me. Those IRA geezers arc rcal shits."

Valance had managed to achieve the vertical. Now, hearing Ben say "IRA," he stopped moving. After an indecisive moment, he slumped back on the sofa where he'd spent the night. "'Aven't got a snort, have you?"

"Sure. Think I'll join you." Ben moved across to the drinks cabinet and poured two large shots of scotch.

"What's the game, then?" Valance said; and Ben uttered up a lightning prayer of gratitude.

"Well, you see, sir, it's this Thornton trial and the chief Crown witness, Scrutton. You knew him, I believe?"

"Just a minute. *Just* a minute. You was going on about the IRA. Now suddenly we're with Thornton."

"Right! The connection! I want to do a deal with you. Your story, our money."

Valance took a sip of his drink and smacked his lips. "How much are we talking about?"

"Fifty thousand pounds."

Valance's hand quaked, spilling whisky over his shirt front, and he swore. "Fifty—"

"Plus maybe a book deal—you can have it ghosted, natch—and TV tie-in. You've got quite a story to tell."

Valance sat up a little straighter, visibly preening himself. "You could say that," he muttered.

Ben let silence complete the work he'd begun, while Valance swilled scotch around in his glass, staring into it.

"Does anyone know you've got me?" he said.

"No."

"What did you do with them two pigs last night?"

"They should be waking up around this time tomorrow.'

Valance nodded gravely, as if this answer afforded him indescribable satisfaction. He fished a cigarette from one of his pockets and held it clenched between his teeth for a moment, before bending to the absurdly heavy silver table lighter.

"Are you with that Forbes cow?" he inquired, after he'd taken a drag. "The one they put me up to?"

"No, sir." Ben's voice had gone very quiet. "Not our department."

"Look, cut all this "sir" shit, will you? I'm Reg." Valance turned his head sideways on and sucked in his cheeks along with a lungful of smoke. He held his cigarette between the tips of his thumb and all four fingers, like a darts player. "Know Forbes, do you?"

"Acquaintances. She's *Times.*"

"And you?"

Ben told him. Valance's eyes widened in appreciation. "Getaway," he murmured. "Get . . . a . . . way."

"What do you know about Roz Forbes, then?" Ben asked.

"Ooh, this and that, you know? She sort of did our Alistair a favor, one time. Long way back I'm going now."

"Favor?"

Valance eyed him through a toxic cloud of gray-brown smoke. He looked sharper all round, now; hangover-scotch evidently agreed with him. "Fifty grand, you said?"

"Yup."

"What about my security, then?"

"Security . . . oh, you mean the IRA?"

"And the police. There's going to be questions asked, see? Why didn't I come forward before. Here, what day is it?"

"Monday."

"It said on the news they're topping Frankie tomorrow."

"That's right."

"Jesus." Valance looked away. Eventually his eyes fastened on the drinks cabinet. Ben rose and offered a refill.

"I daresay we could manage a one-way ticket somewhere warm, as well," he said, sweating. He had absolutely no idea whether Macheval would go to any extras. But apart from money he hadn't got a card in his hand.

"New name? Passport?"

"That's up to you, Reg. We can't go fiddling passports."

Valance sucked his lips. "Got a contract?"

Ben produced a three-page document typed on A4 paper. Valance studied it closely; and Ben remembered that he had once been a barristers' clerk. *Oh God, if Thou art there,* he prayed, *please let those wankers in Legal have got it right, just this once!*

"Got a pen?"

Ben opened his eyes, not quite believing what he'd just heard. Once he'd recovered, he lent

Valance his Biro, watched him sign at the bottom, and witnessed the signature.

"Now," he said. "Start with how Scrutton got to know Forbes."

At first, Ben made a pretense of taking notes, but after a while he sat back and just let Valance talk. It was all going down on tape, anyway. Even if it hadn't been, Ben couldn't have done anything about that. The enormity of Valance's story crept relentlessly over him like the onset of disease. By the time his informant had finished, his cheeks were burning, his eyes hurt, his mouth was dry as dust.

"What it comes down to," he said, after a long silence, "is that Scrutton built his career on a monumental lie."

"Right. But when you do the story, keep me clean, okay? All I did was let it happen. Stood by helplessly, yeah?"

Ben thought about the signed contract in his pocket. It was his story now, his and nobody else's. *He* would decide how it got written. And who got hurt.

"Tell me about the Far East," he said quietly.

"Ah, that's where Alistair got tangled up with Brennan."

Ben sat very still.

"Scrutton," Valance went on in a tone of affectionate reminiscence, "was brave. There's not many as would have risked it. But he risked *everything*. Know why?"

Ben shook his head.

"He thought life was dull. Back in the last century he'd have been a pirate, or whatever. He thought life was dull, and he enjoyed looking generous." Valance peered sideways at Ben. "You knew I'd had a spot of trouble, did you? Done time?"

Ben nodded.

"He got me a fine brief—didn't do me no good,

but Alistair paid. And afterward, his friends sent a nice car, put me up, looked after me . . . "

"His friends being the IRA?"

"I guess so. Irish, anyway." Valance's face hardened. "Bastards . . . I couldn't piss without one of 'em looking over me shoulder. I like a pint in the pub, now and then. I do *not* like minders coming with me."

His easy-going, almost superior tone had modified itself into something more sullen. Ben could see that his memories of the past few months were grim.

"And then there was 'Krait' Brennan," Valance went on suddenly.

"He came to see you, after you got out of stir?"

"Several times."

"Did he use his own name?"

"Didn't have to. We all knew Martin, didn't we? Even if we only open *your* bloody rag, we know him."

"What did he say?"

"Oh, he buttered me up. So grateful for my co-operation, they was."

"Co-operation?"

"Over Forbes. They were after her. I was bait."

Me too, Ben thought savagely. *Bait, worms. . . .* "And you agreed?"

"Yeah. Don't know why. They never talked money, not like you. Couldn't see what was in it for Reg. Know what I mean?"

Ben nodded. He knew exactly.

"Getting uneasy, I was. I could identify faces, see. Always a bad sign. My old mother used to tell me, 'Reg,' she'd say, 'Reg, darlin', never let a girl see your face until she's seen everything else.' Too fucking right!"

"Bangkok," Ben said brusquely. "Chaloem."

"Who? Oh, Poppy—the Thai, I know who you mean."

"What was the connection?"

"Drugs," Valance said equably, stubbing out his cigarette. "Where's the bog?"

Ben showed him. While he waited for Valance to come back, he checked that the tape was still turning in its concealed cabinet, and tried to quell the volcano of excitement bubbling up inside him. The enormity of what this grotty little man had to tell was beyond even his powers of hype.

"Drugs," Valance said again, as he returned to the room, wiping his hands on the shiny sides of his trousers. "Your actual Golden Triangle. And it *was* golden for Alistair."

Something had begun to trouble Ben. "Did he tell you what he was up to?"

"Not exactly, and not at first. But I knew."

"How?"

"Well . . . " Valance helped himself to more scotch and flopped down on the sofa. "Came a time when he was so busy that I needed to know where he was every hour of the day. If he took his wife on holiday, I had the phone number, that kind of thing. And he started to take these little one-day trips to Switzerland. And once, just once, he left a paying-in slip lying around on his desk, where I could see it."

Ben had a mental picture of Valance seeping through chambers at night, like a smell from the drains, turning over papers, rifling through drawers . . . "Go on," he said.

"I made a copy of that slip."

"Have you still got it?"

"You bet I have! Swiss bank, it was. And you know how those Swiss bank accounts are supposed to be so secret?" Valance tapped the side of his nose. "Well, they're not. Not if you've got a few good City solicitors that owe Uncle Reg a favor. So I began to collect names here, a detail there. And sometimes, when Alistair got uppity, didn't want to do some case I'd landed him, I'd drop a hint. And you know what happened then?"

"Amaze me."

"He'd talk. Not much. But enough to keep me quiet, as he thought. And the more he let drop, the more generous he became." Valance lit another cigarette. "I liked Alistair," he said. "Best of my lads by a long way."

By lunchtime, Ben had as full a picture of Alistair's activities as any man alive. It staggered him. In all his years as a journalist he'd never dreamed the like.

"It's unbelievable," he muttered when Valance finally wound down. "Incredible."

"Yeah," Valance agreed. "Like his evidence at that trial: incredible. You were right about that. I bet Brennan put him up to it. Alistair was suing Thornton for slander, and I reckon Thornton got too near the knuckle."

As a reason for giving perjured evidence when a man's life was at stake, that still didn't make complete sense to Ben. But he knew one thing: if the treason jury had believed a tenth of what Valance had told him, they'd have acquitted Thornton without waiting for the summing-up.

"Do you know where Brennan is now?" he asked.

"Possibly. They were talking one night. Must have thought I couldn't hear them. In the next room, they were. Started to argue. Raised voices. 'Clapham' that and 'Clapham' this. The next stage, Brennan said, over and over. Where we go next."

"Did you hear them mention an address in Clapham?"

"Might have done."

"So, tell!"

"Look, mate, I have done enough for you and your horror comic. I'm getting out as soon as the check clears. And *that* is *final.*"

Ben thought hard. He needed Brennan to make the story stick. He reckoned he'd already gone more than halfway toward saving Thornton's neck, but without Brennan, and a confession, there had to be doubt. Would an appeal court believe Valance? Apart from a copy of one lousy Swiss bank deposit slip, there was no paperwork to back his fantastic-sounding story. And why hadn't he come forward earlier?

Ben knew he couldn't afford to take the risk of going in to bat with Valance alone. *He had to have Brennan as well!*

"I suppose you don't know what happened to Roz Forbes?" he said slowly. "Only there's a reward out for anyone who helps find her. Deputy editor of the *Times*: important lady."

"She's with Brennan."

"What?" Ben's heart was suddenly beating very fast. He'd known that, of course he had, deep down, but when he heard Valance say it, *actually say it* . . .

"That's what the row was about," Valance said; "the one I overheard. He wanted to take the woman with them, to Clapham. The others wanted to . . . you know."

He drew a finger across his throat. Ben stared at him in dread. "Did they . . . ?" he croaked.

"Uh-uh. Brennan wins arguments."

"Okay. Listen." Ben drew several deep breaths, seeking words that wouldn't come. "She's a mate of mine, right?"

"You said you was acquaintances," Valance sneered.

"So I fucking *lied*!" Ben fought for control. "I've got to get her out."

"Then you'll do it without me."

"You're scared? We'll protect you."

"You could only protect me against the IRA."

"Well, Brennan *is* the IRA!"

"No, he's not. He's a magician."

"Oh, ha-bloody—"

"I've seen it. He can disappear."

Ben stared at him. "What's with you?" he asked slowly, not trusting himself to formulate a longer sentence.

"I've seen him disappear. Straight up."

The funny thing was, Valance so obviously believed what he'd just said.

"How did he do that, then?"

The only answer was a shrug.

"Oh, this is ridiculous," Ben said, after a prolonged pause. "Just . . . just tell me what you want, and I'll see you get it, only tell me the address."

"No."

"Look. Brennan will come after you anyway, once this story breaks."

A hunted look came into Valance's eyes. "But if he knows I didn't lead the fuzz to him, he might . . . "

"Might."

Valance said nothing.

"Whereas, if the cops manage to finger Brennan . . . you'll be in the clear. Because they will put him away for longer than you and I can ever hope to live."

Valance still said nothing.

"And then there's the reward for finding Roz Forbes."

Valance belched, scratched his head, and started to ransack his pockets in search of a cigarette. Ben handed him one. The hand that took it wasn't quite steady.

"I want time to think," Valance said at last. "And I want to see some evidence that you can deliver. You've got a boss, haven't you? An editor, or what?"

Ben nodded unwillingly.

"Tell 'im to start buying tickets, renting flats in Buenos Aires, or whatever. Yes?"

"I dunno. I'll have to—"

"Okay." Valance sat back, his face betraying its usual cunning. "Depends how much you want the address, doesn't it?"

Ben gazed at him for a long time. Everything had been going so well: Valance singing like a bird, photocopied deposit slips, and now this. Even after all his years in the tabloid press, Ben hadn't believed that a human being could stoop so low.

In a voice that might have ground glass, he said: "An innocent man's going to hang, all on account of you, you do know that?"

But Valance just laughed. "Me," he said, tapping his chest with mock gravity. "I could get kneecapped."

CHAPTER
30

WANDSWORTH JAIL.
THE PRESENT

Florentine left his overnight bag in the room they'd allocated him, and strolled over to the shed—an unemotive name for the strange cell Oakley had inspected some days before. The first thing he did had no obvious connection with next morning's assignment. He lifted the telephone that had caused him anxiety on his last visit, and dialed the speaking clock. Rather to his surprise, he got through first time.

His assistant joined him shortly afterward and together they performed all the checks prescribed by the Prison Commissioners' rules. When they had finished, Florentine drifted away, anxious to be alone.

He passed through the main courtyard, in search of a certain secluded garden that he remembered as being not far from the administration block. It was not quite where he remembered it. Here they buried executed prisoners, with only a square stone in the wall to mark their final resting place. Each headstone bore sets of initials and dates. Florentine had been responsible for putting most of them there, in a way, although that wasn't how he would have expressed it. He regarded his duty as beginning and ending with the implementation of decisions taken elsewhere. His job was to execute not men, but judgments.

Florentine's career as a hangman had begun in Malaya, during the fifties Emergency, when he was a second lieutenant. He'd killed a lot of insurgents in the field: more, in fact, than all the people he was later to execute put together. Emotionally and psychologically he dealt with that by explaining to himself that it was "them or you."

He knew from his own experiences that a person who'd killed once could easily kill again. All soldiering was based on that. Therefore, it was better to execute a murderer before he had the chance to strike again. *Them or you.* So when the Provost Marshal detailed him to assist at the execution of a British soldier who had murdered a prostitute, he simply brought a refined version of his philosophy of killing over to Pudu prison and watched, dispassionately, as one fine dawn the condemned man hurtled down into the pit, to be brought up with a jerk and a crack . . .

George Steeper came up behind him, his boots making no sound on the lawn, and tapped his shoulder.

"Long time no see, Charley," he murmured.

Florentine waved away the proffered Silk Cut and said, "I've given up, thanks. How are you, George?"

"Not so bad. Yourself?"

Florentine grunted. "Older."

"You don't seem surprised to see me," George said plaintively.

"I asked for you."

"Ah, so it's you I've got to thank."

Florentine nodded. "Going to snow," he said, eyeing the grubby black clouds that floated low above them. "Lucky they dug the grave early . . . "

"Not many of us left now," George said, as they started along the corridor, glad to be in the warm. "Small club."

"Mm. Now that Our Albert's gone."

"'Our Albert' was the name by which Albert Pierrepoint, England's chief executioner for many years, had been known to his colleagues.

"Tell me, George, what's your mate—Nobby, isn't it—?"

George nodded.

"What's Nobby going to be like tomorrow at nine o'clock in the morning? I know what *you're* going to be like."

"He'll be solid as a rock."

"Chaplain?"

"A bit nervy."

"They all are. In the pulpit of a Sunday, death can be made to sound attractive. At one minute past nine in a freezing shed, it's funny how many vicars see the light."

A tea tray was waiting for them in the hangman's room. "I'll be mother," George said.

Watching him pour, Florentine remembered how they'd started down this odd road.

On the day of his first execution in Pudu prison, George Steeper had been sergeant in charge of prisoner's escort. He'd done a good job. When Lieutenant Florentine was appointed Malaya's chief executioner, brought in for many civilian as well as all military cases, George usually acted as his assistant.

The two men had returned to England at the same time. Florentine soon became restless with army life, so he got out, and bought a hotel near Folkestone. It was inevitable that he should be invited onto the Home Office list of qualified hangmen. When "Our Albert" retired in February 1956, "Charley" Florentine took his place.

By that time, George had left the army and gone
into the prison service. The two of them met face to
face for the first time in ten years on the scaffold at
Manchester Strangeways, when George was again in
charge of prisoner's escort.

By the time of Frank Thornton's trial, Florentine
was one of only two men left in England who had
seen, let alone officiated at, an execution. George
was the other.

"What made you give up smoking, Charley?"

Florentine rubbed his mustache, picking gingerly
at the hair ends, as if wondering whether a trip to
the barber's should be on the slate. "Same reason I
cut down on the drink, a few years back," he said at
last. "Saw too many suicides."

"Don't get you."

"The fellows I topped all stood on that trap
because they'd walked there of their own free will.
They'd gone out and killed someone, knowing what
the law was. I started thinking about it. One day I
found I couldn't *stop* thinking about it. So I gave up
the fags and I keep to my twenty-one units a week,
thank you very much; and that way I won't end up
like them."

"Dead before your time?"

"From choice. Exactly."

"Have you sussed out Thornton yet?"

"Through the judas-hole," Florentine said,
extracting a sheet of paper from his inside pocket.
"And I've read the doctor's report. Height . . .
weight . . . " He held the paper at a distance, as if to
compensate for short sight. "Nothing extraordinary.
What's he going to be like on the night?"

George stirred his tea without answering for a
moment. Then he said, "Fine. Frank'll be fine."

"You had to think about that."

"Not really. He's got himself together, as they
say nowadays."

"Then all I have to worry about is the Number Two."

"Who've they given you?"

Florentine mentioned a name and George shrugged.

"Youngster. First time—naturally. George, I want you to watch him like a hawk tomorrow. First sign of fright, you put him on the floor and take over, okay?"

George nodded. For a moment they stared at each other, expressionlessly. Then they smiled.

"Hell of a long way from the jungle," George said.

"Is it?"

George began another smile but never quite made it. Florentine's eyes lacked humor, and George suddenly divined that Charley was no longer quite the same. He let his glance fall away, not wanting to hear about that.

"Think I'll go and check things over," Florentine said at last. "One more time."

They stood up.

"There will be trouble in the prison tomorrow," he muttered; and it sounded more like a promise than a prediction.

CHAPTER
31

NETTLEBED, OXFORDSHIRE.
THE PRESENT

Alistair Scrutton stood hunched by the french windows, looking across the darkened garden. Occasionally he would move away from the window for just long enough to pour himself another drink before returning to gaze out into the darkness. When the phone rang he didn't even turn his head, knowing that Mrs. Foster, the housekeeper, would answer it.

"Mr. Scrutton . . . " Mrs. Foster had entered the room, looking flushed. "Mr. Scrutton, I'm sorry to disturb you, but there's been an accident. My sister. She was knocked down by a car in Reading, that was the police, they say I'd better go."

"I see." He paused, dredging down for some appropriate response. "How awkward for you. Terrible. I'm sorry."

"Could I take the little car?"

"Of course."

A moment later he heard her drive away. But by then he was already standing in his accustomed place before the french windows, gazing at the night. A half-

413

formed, pallid image of Alistair Scrutton taunted him through the pane. He stared into his reflection. For an eerie moment, he seemed to be dissolving and reduplicating: a pair of Scruttons stood out there. Then horrid intuition told him that two men had come up to the windows, and he leaped back with a cry.

Two faces. Two white faces, one dour, one smiling. He did not recognize the dour man. But the other . . .

A pane of glass shattered. Scrutton watched helplessly as a hand inserted itself and opened the french doors. Freddie raced forward, barking his head off, but seconds later the dog's anger had turned to fawning acceptance. He knew one of the visitors, knew him well.

"Good day to you, Alistair," Brennan said as he breezed in. "Freddie, old chap, good boy, *good* boy, down now . . . "

"You . . . *you!*"

"And who else would be calling on yourself on a damned cold night like this one, eh? There, Freddie, get down. Alistair, I want you to meet my friend, Billy Wright. Chief Superintendent Wright, but he answers to Billy, don't you?"

He turned to the other man, just stepping across the threshold, and clapped him on the arm a couple of times.

Scrutton could only stare at them. "How the devil did you get past the guard?" he stammered.

"Well, now, you see, Alistair . . . " Brennan's voice was loud, jovial. He dropped a Gladstone bag on the carpet and kept up a running explanation while he went across to the drinks cabinet, where he poured a mineral water for himself, with something stronger for his companion. "There's ways, and there are ways. Billy here and I have been working in harness for many years, and when I said I had a hankering to see you for old times' sake he offered to oblige me. Right, Billy?"

The other man accepted his glass without comment. To judge from his expression, he had recently drunk gall and was holding the last sip inside his mouth.

"Billy knew we wouldn't want to be disturbed," Brennan went on. "So he tipped your bodyguard half a crown and told him to piss off. Well, no, I must be honest with you. He arranged to have him pulled after you decided you didn't want protection any more."

"I never said that!"

"A mistake, eh? Well, these things happen. Thank you, Billy, I needn't be troubling you further. I daresay Alistair and I'll make a night of it, as usual. Have a care, now."

Wright put down his glass on an occasional table and went out, closing the french windows behind him. The silence that followed his exit, punctuated only by the whistle of the wind through the broken pane, seemed to last for a very long time.

"I was asking myself what your plans might be," Brennan said. He sat down in Scrutton's leather armchair. "Now that the trial's over."

Scrutton lowered himself into one of the spindly dining room chairs with which Louise had filled the blank spaces in their lounge. Freddie looked at him almost apologetically, before going to put his head on Brennan's knee. The sense of loss inspired in Scrutton by this simple act of betrayal outweighed even terror, allowing the Irishman's next words to wash over him unheard.

"You've been a good lad, Alistair." Brennan seemed totally relaxed. "The funeral. The trial. I told you to wear gloves when you buried your dear, late wife; you wore gloves. I told you how to play the gun scene with Thornton, afterward; Johnny Gielgud couldn't have done it better. I broke into Frank's house, briefed you on the layout; you described it to the jury as if you lived there yourself.

And as for your *delivery*, well . . . perfect."

Scrutton said nothing, but tore his gaze away from Freddie to stare at the Krait, as if a real serpent had slithered through the defenses into his house.

"Perhaps you fancy a trip?" Brennan inquired. "I've been on my travels, too, you know. Thailand."

Two red spots kindled in Scrutton's cheeks, but still he did not speak. In the pause that followed he became aware of how silent the house was. His nearest neighbors lived a quarter of a mile away.

"I went up north," Brennan resumed. "To talk to some old friends." His voice lowered to a silken whisper. "You'll remember the north? And P'ia?"

Scrutton's eyes suddenly refocused from that point in the middle distance where he had been reliving his life. "P'ia?" he said stupidly.

"Oh, *you* remember, Alistair. The woman who loved you. And do you recall the boys you met on your first visit to the Triangle? Rin and Tin? Tin died. But I met Rin, not so long ago. In the jungle. One quiet dawn."

Scrutton was eyeing him with dread malevolence, but Brennan paid no heed.

"Rin and I had a talk about Siri. Who's dead, you may have heard. At first, Rin tried to tell me that Siri had been selling us out to the Rangers. But that was just a little tale, to make me laugh. We got down to the nitty, after that. And what Rin told me was . . . God, the crack makes a man thirsty . . . "

He stood up and went across to replenish his glass, at the same time pouring a large cognac for Alistair.

"What he told me," Brennan said as he resumed his seat, "was that Yang Po met 'the English ghost'—sorry, my dear chap—in Phuket. 1985, or thereabouts. Phuket, now there's a lovely place!"

Scrutton took a long swallow and waited.

"Well, it seemed Yang Po wanted to cut out my

pal Siri. But he couldn't, not completely. So he told the English ghost—that's you again—how to carry extra shipments, that Siri didn't know about. And you agreed." Brennan kept his eyes on Scrutton's face. "Didn't you?"

"You're talking nonsense." Scrutton shifted position, jutting up his chin.

"Is that so?" Brennan nodded his head, as if the news didn't surprise him. "Is that right, indeed? But Rin, you see, he used to bring Yang Po's extra loads as far as Chiang Rai; that's how he found out about it. And—this is the good part, Alistair—that's how Siri came to find out about it, too, because Rin sold him the information. Which made Siri angry enough to want to talk to 'foreign ghost' Scrutton. But you refused to go to his house, where he was surrounded by his men and could be safe. Instead, you proposed a meeting somewhere else. And— God, he must have been mad!—Siri agreed. He went to a rendezvous where his people couldn't guard him properly. And since you'd already tipped Yang Po off, he was able to take Siri unawares. Yes?"

Scrutton said nothing.

"Now, Alistair—a first-class brain like yours will have seen the flaw in this penetrating analysis. I mean, if it was all true, why didn't Yang Po kill you too? By that time, you knew a hell of a lot, it would have been much simpler for him to waste you."

Scrutton's face had taken on something of its habitual, confident coldness. But still he made no reply.

"And then it dawned on me. 'Alistair's had enough,' I told myself. He's getting out. That's why he helped sacrifice Siri. And *that's* where P'ia comes in."

Brennan gazed at Scrutton expectantly, but he could see from the man's expression that he wasn't following, didn't want to follow.

"Can't you see it, my dear chap? P'ia was the key to *everything*! She longed to bail you out of the drugs traffic, didn't she? Longed to make you clean, destroy the evidence against you . . . and so the pair of you made a deal with Yang Po. Something along these lines: Alistair will give you Siri; P'ia will give you Brennan as well, in exchange for Alistair's life and safety. And Yang Po bought it. After Siri had been killed, I was to be next, once P'ia had sent me up to the Triangle. Now I'll tell you a funny thing—did you know I saw you, on your way out of Bangkok that last time?"

"You . . . *saw* me?" Scrutton stared at Brennan, thunderstruck.

"Our taxis were going in opposite directions. You'd sold Siri, you'd sold me, you were on your way home, believing that stupid, unsophisticated Yang Po, the only threat left, could do you no harm as long as you remained safely in England. Although"—he chuckled—"You were wrong about that. Yang Po came in search of your head, and if it hadn't been for me he'd have got it, too."

Brennan fell silent. Neither man spoke for a long time after that.

What had Scrutton been thinking about in that taxi? Brennan wondered. What lies had he told P'ia: that he'd be coming back as soon as things cooled off? That he'd arrange to get her a British passport and fly her to England? Now, looking at Scrutton's drawn face, he guessed it must have been something like that.

"I could have forgiven you almost anything, Alistair," he murmured sadly. "You were going to be a judge, *my* judge . . . but Siri . . . no. I had to punish you."

"Why didn't you, then?" Scrutton stirred restlessly, displaying his first signs of curiosity. "You had the tape of my meeting with Lee, you had the photographs of my murdering Louise. What stopped you turning me in? I never understood."

"Because I saw an opportunity to kill two birds with one stone, and it appealed to my economical mind. I saw how I could use you. Picture this . . . a trial. A trial for high treason. Principal witness for the Crown: a QC. Eminent. Respected. *Credible.* The defendant is found guilty and hanged, or not hanged, it really didn't matter a damn, in my little dream; what mattered was setting the English legal system at odds with itself. Because you see, as I planned it, this eminent QC was lying, and shown to be lying, corrupt, evil beyond conception, Alistair, a demon in human guise; and English justice cocked it up as usual; while the English government lost whatever pretensions it might once have had to be civilized, and was rubbished throughout the world, by *me*"—he banged his breast with a triumphant, devil-may-care laugh— "Now isn't that a dream to be proud of, eh? An *Irish* dream, fit for a poem?"

When Scrutton made no reply, the Krait answered himself in a whisper: "It's a dream for a king; a story so grand, it can only be told . . . by a queen."

Brennan smiled, as if at some meaning hidden deep inside those last words. Then he gently pushed Freddie's head from his knee and leaned forward. "So there it all is, Alistair, my friend. Because you wanted out, you did a deal with Yang Po. Siri had to die, along with me, and you knew that, and still you signed. True?"

Scrutton swallowed the last of his cognac and set the glass down on the floor beside him.

"Yes," he said.

Brennan, watching him closely, saw how his face underwent a change as he spoke that word. It seemed to smooth itself out, become younger. When their eyes met, the Krait felt as though he was looking straight into the soul of a man who at last had cleansed himself and felt glad about it.

He stood up and went across to the Gladstone bag he'd dropped earlier. From it he extracted a notepad and a pen.

"We'll go to the dining room, you'll need a table."

Scrutton knew that he had no choice but to comply. Yet in a curious kind of way, he did not feel himself to be under duress from the other man. Everything came from within. He went to sit at the table, pen in hand, and waited.

"We'll start," the Krait said, "by making a note of your foreign bank accounts. For the record."

The confession took an hour. Brennan paced up and down the room, hands clasped behind his back, never once faltering. He kept a sharp eye on Scrutton until right at the end, when he made a longer turn than usual, going through the archway into the lounge, where he once again delved into his Gladstone bag. Even when he was doing this, however, the same regularly paced sentences continued to roll out.

" . . . The murder of my wife, Louise, was filmed . . . and the photographs . . . can be found . . . in my safe." Brennan returned to the dining room. "Knowing, as I did . . . about these photographs . . . and the negatives, which were retained by the IRA . . . I had no choice but to give evidence at Thornton's trial."

The Krait came to a halt behind Scrutton and read the last page over the barrister's shoulder before adding, "Nothing . . . could have been otherwise."

He had spoken those last words almost as if to himself. Scrutton turned, meaning to ask whether he was to write them down, but then he caught sight of Freddie lying on the floor in the archway, his head at an impossibly unnatural angle, and the question died in his throat.

Brennan was holding a length of good quality hemp rope. One end of it had been turned back upon itself in a five-ring hangman's knot. Florentine, with his horror of American gimmicks, would have predicted a cruel death.

CHAPTER

32

LONDON. THE PRESENT

While Roz was asleep, someone brought in the tape recorder and left it running on play-back. At first she merely heard a flutter of indistinct sounds. But she was roused, instantly, by the sound of the Krait's voice saying, " . . . as for you, I'll do what I can."

She struggled upright, forgetting the chain that bound her to the bed, and squealed when its cuff bit into her ankle. It was freezing cold in the vault. She sat there, shivering uncontrollably, while the tape unreeled and tears dripped down her face in fits and starts, like desultory rain on a window.

She hadn't realized that they possessed the means of monitoring her even when the machine wasn't in the cell. This, the master tape, chronicled everything.

She shuddered when she heard the guards' harsh rants. At the sound of herself using the bucket to empty her body of waste, she broke down and wept without ceasing. Then came the blows, the screams . . .

The tape rolled on dispassionately.

The door opened, admitting enough light to disclose a broken woman on a thin mattress, keening her heart out.

"Now, now, now . . . " As Brennan sat on the bed he placed a gentle arm around her shoulders. "You mustn't take on so. Oh, dear God, what have they . . . "

He got up to switch off the record of her degradation.

"Now see here," he said soothingly. "It's nearly over. Look. I've brought you some hot food. Chicken. Potatoes. Even a glass of wine. They've gone, the others."

He wasn't wearing his monk's yellow robe today, but instead a dark blue track suit and trainers. This change disorientated her. Without the robe to soften them, his bald head and shaved eyebrows merely made him look like a vicious punk.

Roz became aware of an unusual smell. When she drew a breath, the aroma went right down her gullet into her stomach, where it translated itself into a huge, nauseating void of hunger.

She looked at the tray on the floor, waiting for him to kick it over. But instead, he lifted it onto the bed frame and removed the saucepan lid that was keeping her food warm. "There, now," he said. "I'm no cook, but I could eat that."

Seeing the mistrust in her eyes, he gravely took a nibble of drumstick, washing it down with a sip of wine from the tumbler. Once he saw he had her full attention, he held up his arms, allowed a look of horror onto his face and made as if to keel over, before coming upright again with a smile.

Roz felt her lips mirror his. She made a grab for the tray, but he stopped her.

"No." His voice had turned firm. "You'll kill yourself. Let me cut it up for you. Small bites. And for God's sake, woman, *chew*!"

Brennan fed her with the tender concern of a zoo

keeper weaning some rare animal from its mother. She moaned while she ate, venting hoarse little cries of greed and raw pleasure and self-detestation for having sunk to this.

After he'd helped her clean the plate he gave her wine, a sip at a time, with long intervals between. Her stomach twisted itself into knots, her head turned light, she could not stand the sudden rush of well-being that deluged her. She fell back on the bed, wailing, pounding the metal frame in frustration. Then she must have slept awhile, for when she came to herself he was rocking her to and fro, singing softly, in a language she didn't understand.

Roz, gazing up through blurred eyes into his face, knew it must be an Irish song. He sang the words softly and slowly, milking each one for its burden of nostalgic balm. Listening to his voice, she felt her whole body loosen, and again she despised herself for what she had let herself become.

"There, now," he said, gently laying her back onto the mattress. "You'll soon be yourself."

"Thank you." Roz hiccuped, and burst into tears again. He let her cry herself out before reminding her, "Don't ever say thank you to me, Roz Forbes."

"Can't . . . help it."

"Yes, you can."

"Will you really let me go?"

"Indeed I will."

"When?" The real question concealed by those words suddenly detonated inside her skull. "They've . . . they've hanged Frank, haven't they?"

"Not yet. There's hours yet."

She stared at him, trying to work out if he was telling the truth. He was so handsome, so . . . *noble*, even in his severity. What a wasted life, she thought.

"You could save Frank," she sniffled. "Couldn't you?"

"It's out of all our hands now, my dear."

"But if you told them—"

"Who would believe me?"

The vault felt warmer. Her body was coming back to life.

"I'll say this," he went on, unexpectedly. "I've given him a chance. Just one."

"What chance?"

But he shook his head with a smile, and would not answer.

"Why?" she cried. "You made Scrutton lie. You fixed everything. Why give Frank a chance now?"

"Maybe . . . it's on account of you."

"Me?" She laughed, a horrid cackle. "Me," she said again, with loathing in her voice. "There is no me. Not now."

"Ah, but there will be again, soon."

"I'm never going to get over this."

But even as she said it, a voice inside her head shouted: *You must!*

"You will," he said, affirming that inner voice.

She was silent for a while. He hugged her again and she let him do it. She did not know why she let him do it, or what she wanted from him or why she didn't just try to claw out his eyes.

"Is it true, what you said about Frank?" she asked. "Is there really a chance?"

"One."

"Not . . . you're not going to talk about that magic rubbish, are you?"

"No."

"Only that's crap." She stared at her hands. They were filthy. Dirt had engrained itself in the tiny folds of her skin. However hard she scrubbed, she was always going to see that dirt, when she looked at her skin.

He was lying. He could never, never let her go.

He would kill her.

Roz did a strange thing. She leaned into him, as if for protection against herself, and said, "Don't go."

He gave her a quick hug.

"I mean it," she said, pushing him away enough to be able to look into his eyes. "Stay with me."

For a moment his face remained expressionless. Then he smiled tenderly at her and she flung herself into his arms and held him as if a slit might appear the length of her body and she could pull him inside and zip him into her for ever and ever . . .

His warmth was rising in step with her own. Suddenly strong arms were returning her pressure, mastering it. She pulled him down on top of her, letting go all her breath as his hot, hard body weighed her down.

She found herself hallucinating. She wasn't on the bed with Brennan at all, she was standing beside it, looking on with cool detachment. She saw how his hands went to the breasts of the woman lying on the bed, how they unbuttoned the filthy dress. His track suit was easy to divest. She was so thin! So *dirty*! How could he bring himself to . . .

He was amazingly skillful, for a monk.

There seemed to be no particular hurry. Roz, the real Roz, wandered around the vault, examining the tableau in the center of it from every angle; once even levitated above the two-backed beast to see how that looked. She felt dreamy, contented.

Then he despoiled her, and the vision shattered.

She fought, hard. "No!" she screamed. "*No, no no no nonono!*" She bit him. He smiled when she bit him. Smiled.

Roz was pinned down by a force greater than she could vanquish. This was rape. *No!* She loved it. This vile, degrading . . . *monstrous* crime, this sin . . . oh, how she adored him, it, everything.

She was mad.

When she began to climax, she knew she was mad.

Evil cannot overcome good.

How dare he?

How could she?

She never once thought of Johnny, or Frank. Only Brennan was real.

Her back arched off the bed. It was unbearable, unbelievable, what he was doing to her. She heard him start to grunt; the grunts became cries. She was aware of her nails tearing into his shoulders while her body described a bow above the bed, only her toes and the back of her head in contact with the real world.

His cries turned into a roar of heaven-sent thunder, the voice of God.

Roz fainted.

She floated up into awareness of lying on the bed. By turning her head slightly she perceived a shaft of light where the door was open. When she moved her right leg there was no longer a chain attached to it.

She sat up. Her head spun. As she recovered from the nausea fit, she saw, in the light flooding through the doorway, a chair. On it were clean jeans and a blouse, some underwear, a pair of shoes.

Everything fitted her. As she scrambled into these unworn clothes, something tinkled to the ground. She stooped to pick it up.

A tenpenny coin. One phone call's worth.

She was on the brink of remembering. *Don't do that!* snarled her guardian angel; and she obeyed. "I must not think," she said aloud. "About anything."

Between her and the door lay one final obstacle, a dark, rectangular shape. She stared at it. The tape recorder.

The tape wasn't moving. She found the play switch and pressed it.

"I mean it." Her own voice. *"Stay with me."*

For a moment she stood there, her face blank, listening to what followed. Then her first, recorded mewl of pleasure whipped out the pin and she exploded.

She picked up the recorder, staggering under its weight even though it wasn't a big machine, and flung it against the nearest wall. Blue sparks flashed as the lead snapped, but she didn't care. She strode across to the wreckage, picked it up again, and hurled it to the ground. She jumped on it.

The spool rolled away, like a child's hoop, spinning to a stop on the threshold. She threw herself upon it, scrabbling for the end of the tape, so that she could pull it to shreds, destroy the evidence of her . . .

The evidence.

She froze. From another era, another incarnation, a memory came back to her.

The tape covered everything. She hadn't realized that they were recording her even when the tape recorder itself wasn't in the cell.

She held it up to the shaft of light from the doorway with fingers that trembled. He'd talked about himself, about Scrutton, about everything.

She could save Frank. All she had to do was . . .

All she had to do was tell the world what had happened, here in this cellar.

For a moment she actually hesitated. She could see the headlines: a journo's dream. Then, without her brain having given any orders, she was stumbling up the stairs. She knew herself to be on the verge of breakdown. *Don't think,* whispered the guardian angel. *Do not think.*

She staggered up into a narrow passage. On her left, a wall, to the right, far off, what looked like natural daylight. A glass-paneled front door.

Nemesis waited for her by the gate, laughing. Brennan was wearing his track suit again. He stood with legs apart and his arms folded across his chest.

In his right hand he held a gun, in his left a fan.

She walked toward him. She was in an ordinary street, she dimly realized, not the one where Valance lived; orange lamps still burned, but dawn was already oozing over the flat, gray, suburban landscape, showing her terraced houses, parked cars . . . Nemesis.

When she was still a dozen paces short of the gate, she stopped. He continued to smile at her.

Her head was going round and round. A nasty mixture of hunger and vomit ground in her lower gut. She swallowed hard. She felt dizzy. He seemed to float up and down, and his lips didn't move, but she heard him say, "One chance."

Then she was looking at his stomach. She had, oh God! she'd fallen to her knees, too weak to walk.

A horn tooted. Headlights. Tires squealing, burning rubber. Men's voices. Shouting, everywhere.

She glimpsed the Krait look swiftly to his left and break into a run. Then she was staring at the stone slabs of the path. Her cheek hurt, where she'd grazed it when she collapsed. She'd bitten her tongue.

Ben careered around the corner to see Brennan standing in the roadway. He gunned the engine and drove straight at him, seconds seeming to pass in slow motion. He knew he must hit the man, who by now was running in the van's headlights as if for the Gold.

An instant before contact, Brennan flung himself flat. The van roared over him. Ben braked and was outside in a flash, with a couple of his helpers hurling open the back doors to join him.

Brennan was nowhere to be seen.

They ran this way and that. They searched nearby vehicles; Ben even rolled underneath one of them, chasing what turned out to be a cat. They peered over garden walls. They skimmed to the intersection, their heads flashing left and right.

The Krait had vanished from that dingy street like a puff of smoke.

"Ben," a weak voice called.

He swung around. "Roz. Oh, *Christ,* Roz, are you all right?" He ran over and helped her to lean against the wall.

"What . . . time is it?"

"Rozzie, darling, did he—"

"*Time?*"

"Half seven."

"Got . . . tape." She managed to hold it out to him. "Confession. Brennan. Confession."

For a moment Ben stood immobile. Then he extended both hands, like a celebrant accepting the alms-plate at divine service, and raised the spool slowly to his lips.

Only when he had kissed the tape did he think to look into her eyes. Just for a second, he imagined he caught a glimpse of gratitude and relief, tiny shards from a greater ruin. Then they too faded away, and with nausea in the pit of his stomach he knew he wouldn't be seeing them again.

"Roz . . . "

But in a stony voice she cut across him, saying, "I've got the tape."

"And I—"

"You've got Valance . . . Yes. *We can save him!*"

While they raced through the streets of south London, dodging the early rush hour traffic, she ransacked her memory for Brian Oakley's home number. She couldn't remember the penultimate digit.

Ben tried five different combinations on his mobile phone before finding the right one. Oakley's wife, Marinella, answered to say he'd left for the Home Office an hour before. Ben passed her over to Roz, who not without difficulty extracted his private number from her. But when she tried it, Oakley's secretary icily informed her that he wasn't to be disturbed by incoming calls unless they came from the prime minister personally.

"But there's a man's *life* at stake!"

"I'm sorry. It's more than my job's worth."

"*Fuck* your fucking job and *fuck* you, you—"

The line went dead.

"I'm not going to cry," she told Ben; and immediately gave herself the lie.

The driver, a hulking black Ben knew simply as Robbo, raced through a set of traffic lights.

"Where the hell are we?" Ben demanded.

"Balham High Road."

Ben ground his teeth. "Look, there's a cab over there . . . he's getting away, *block him*!"

Robbo planted the van diagonally across the cab's front fender. Next second, Ben was dragging him out, along with Roz.

"We split," he said to her. "I'm going to the Home Office, with your tape. I'll see Oakley if I have to murder every flunkey in the Civil Service. You're off, along with handsome here."

Ben produced a twenty pound note and thrust it into the outraged cab driver's top pocket. "These two," he grated, "want to go to Wandsworth Jail, yesterday, now *move*!"

He watched the taxi until it turned a corner, knowing that this would be his last sight of Roz Forbes and wanting to fix the moment in his mind.

The morning of any execution is dignified by a remarkable silence.

The chief officer awoke Florentine and his assistant at seven-thirty. Florentine accepted a breakfast tray, but the assistant declined. While he ate his egg, the executioner made a discreet study of the young man.

His face was white, he smoked incessantly.

In the half-hour this occupied, nobody spoke a word.

Florentine led the way to the execution shed. He hauled up the sandbag that had been stretching the rope overnight, so that there would be no "whip" when Thornton dropped. Meanwhile, his assistant went down into the pit, where he stood on a stepladder to push the two leaves of the trap together.

Florentine quietly slid the bolt shut, locking the lever with a cotter-pin. He retrieved two planks standing against the far wall and laid them over the trap, about three feet apart. These were for the condemned man's escort, in case they had to bear him up in the final seconds.

At a signal from Florentine, his assistant placed a ladder against the central beam, enabling the two men to make final adjustments to the length of the drop. When he was satisfied, Florentine noted down the figure and handed it to the chief officer, who looked at it, raising his eyebrows. But still he did not speak.

Florentine coiled up the rope and secured it with a piece of red twine, so that the noose dangled where Thornton's neck would be. He bent down, reaching inside a waistcoat pocket for a piece of chalk. With that he marked a T on the spot where he wanted the escort to align the condemned man's feet. That done, he stood up and took a last look around the green-painted room, taking his time.

At last the executioner turned to his assistant and gave him a quick thumbs-up. When the assistant responded in the same way, Florentine swiveled, nodded at the chief officer, and walked from the shed as silently as he had entered it.

The chief officer closed the door behind the three of them. He looked at his watch. It was eight-thirty-two.

* * *

Roz and Robbo had to finish their journey on foot. Outside Wandsworth Prison, a huge crowd spilled over from the pavements of Heathfield Road, pressing back against the fence of the nursery opposite. As they began to force a way through, Roz heard the occasional muttered, angry exchange, and she could feel tension around her like a tangible force. What struck her most, however, was the silence which hung low over the assembly in a pall of doom to match the rain drizzling down on their heads.

Several couples had brought children along. They stared straight ahead, while the kids twisted to look up, not understanding. Some people were crying; many prayed. Nearing the front, she saw that a small open space had been cleared in front of the prison's main gate. Stony-faced policemen stood there, gazing outward, but they were not attempting to control the crowd. There was no need. Violence and protest had failed. Today the throng merely waited, silent and powerless.

Off to one side a Salvation Army band had assembled. As Roz reached the police cordon, it struck up "Abide With Me." Close by, someone had parked a pick-up truck bearing the banners of Amnesty International and the "Halt the Trial" campaign. Three men and a woman stood in the back. They had brought loudspeakers and a microphone, but made no attempt to address the crowd while the hymn was being played.

Roz accosted the policeman nearest to her. "Who's in charge here?"

"Inspector. Over there."

"I need to talk to him."

"What's it about?"

"I'll tell the inspector."

"Look, madam, he's got more important things to do than *chat*, all right?"

"I have evidence that Frank Thornton's innocent. I urgently need to speak to someone in authority."

The policeman, though young, did not lack self-confidence. "Why don't you write a letter to the Home Secretary, tell him all about it?" he said kindly. "You shouldn't distress yourself any more today, madam. Not worth it."

"They're about to hang an innocent man!"

"We're none of us completely innocent, madam, are we? Now move along."

Throughout this exchange Roz had been aware of Robbo tensing up beside her. She knew that in another minute there was going to be trouble of an unproductive kind. She looked at her watch. A quarter to nine. Somehow she got a grip on the panic rising within her and tried to think.

The hymn was winding down. She glanced up at the truck and, after a second of uncertainty, recognized the chair of "Halt the Trial." Her heart leaped. "Jean," she cried. "Jean, it's me, Roz Forbes!"

Heads in the vicinity turned to look. Jean scanned the upturned faces around her, seeking the source of the voice.

"Roz," she shouted. "Up here . . . "

With Robbo's help, Roz shouldered her way to the truck and clambered up, snatching the microphone. Seconds later she heard her own voice echoing off the prison walls.

"My name," she said, "is Roz Forbes. I'm deputy editor of the *Times*." She faltered, closing her eyes while she prayed for physical strength. Her head was going round and round, she felt so *weak* . . .

Keep it short, keep it simple.

"For the past few days," she went on, "I've been held prisoner by Martin Brennan. The Krait. He framed Thornton. Thornton is innocent. I have the evidence to prove it."

For a moment there was silence. People looked up at her as if she'd gone mad. Then muttering broke out.

"I know this woman!" Jean had grabbed the mike away from Roz and was shouting into it. "The police have been looking for her, it's been in all the papers. *Listen!*"

The truck suddenly rocked as another man hauled himself on board. "I'm a reporter," he yelled. "*Times.* This *is* my deputy editor. Listen to her!"

He nudged Roz. "You okay?"

She nodded, but she wasn't. Any minute now, she'd fall over. Had to do something. Must. They were giving her their full attention. What to do with it? Looking helplessly from face to face, she knew incipient despair.

Ten to nine.

Then it came to her. Somehow this crowd had to be translated into a mob.

Before she could speak again, however, another policeman hurried to the side of the truck. He wore inspector's tabs. "We've been looking for you," he cried.

"Help me!" she gasped. "We've got to stop it!"

"How?" He seemed dazed.

"Let me talk to the Governor."

As he ran off, Roz lifted the microphone again. Somehow she managed to fight off dizziness, and took a deep breath.

"Inside there," she shouted, pointing at the prison, "they're going to murder an innocent man! A man condemned to death on perjured evidence. Lies! His oldest friend told a tissue of lies to frame him, *and I can prove it!*"

Someone fiddled with the amplifier, enabling Roz's next words to be heard inside the gaol.

"I was captured by the Krait. He held me prisoner. And he talked. He recorded himself, and me. He gave everything away. But when I managed to escape, I took the tape with me."

She cast a desperate glance over her shoulder. The inspector was deep in animated conversation with an officer, who had emerged from a side gate around the corner. The ring of police had shrunk in upon itself, leaving only a small, clear space in front of the prison. She could see, *sense*, their morale begin to sweat away.

"That tape's on its way to the Home Office." She paused. "Do *you* trust the Home Office?"

The roar that went up caused the inspector to break off his conversation with the officer, one hand instinctively going to his radio.

"Would you trust this government with *your* lives?"

A huge "NO!" rolled over her, half-drowning her last words.

"Then *stop them!*"

Even before she'd finished, seven hundred people were charging forward as one, smashing their way through the flimsy cordon. The inspector, terrified, darted through the side gate and the officer made to slam it. But Robbo, who'd been edging his way forward ever since Roz mounted the truck, was too quick for him. He turned sideways, thrusting his body at the inch-wide gap. A split second later, the entire weight of the human wave punched into his back. For an instant he hovered there, caught in a vise. But because Governor Howells hadn't anticipated this crisis, only a few warders were mustered on the other side of the gates to meet the onslaught. Robbo, drenched in sweat and breathless, was suddenly propelled through the wicket like a cork flying out of a bottle of agitated champagne.

He ran down a broad, dark passage until an inner

steel grating brought him up short. By now, twenty or more people from the crowd had joined him. They could go no farther without finding a way to divert through the guardhouse, off to one side. Several demonstrators were already bursting into it, but Robbo, who'd done enough time to know his gaols, stayed by the inner gate for long enough to cup his hands to his mouth and shriek:

"Thornton . . . is . . . *innocent!*"

And the prison answered him.

Frank swung around in his chair. "What's that?"

His heart was pounding fit to burst. His mouth was dry. He knew it was nearly time and he was terrified, but at least the ominous quiet had enabled him to make his last preparations. Now this . . .

"Sounds like a . . . " George had risen and was standing with head on one side. His eyes met Nobby's.

"Riot," Nobby muttered in confirmation. "Shit."

Outside, far away, they could hear the sound of a woman's voice, amplified through loudspeakers. Then the cons started. The banging was the worst thing. Clang, clang, clang, it went on and on, despite warders' voices raised in anger. Someone started screaming; the sound went on for half a minute, rising above the general hubbub, and was as suddenly silenced.

Frank sank down, gripping the table. Until now he'd been calm. But this . . .

He'd got it all worked out. If he went quietly, a lamb to the slaughter, wasn't that a kind of suicide? But if he struggled and screamed, they would remember that. And it would be so hard on *them*, the reluctant witnesses. Who cared about *them*? Frank did. So he was going to be calm. But now this. A riot.

Try not to think. *Try not to hear it.*

He had planned out each of his last moments on earth. A few words for everyone, mostly Edward Howells. Just a farewell, and thanks, with dignity and courage. Then, twenty seconds, that's all it took. George hadn't wanted to tell him, but Frank insisted. Short walk, hood over the face, rope around the neck and before he could draw another breath the trap would spring . . . instantaneous, George assured him quietly. Never a mistake. Never.

Darkness and rest would follow. Peace.

But in that last hideous second, when he was falling . . .

Frank shut off the train of thought with an effort. His fists clenched and unclenched on the tabletop. His breath came in a series of steady pants. He tried to blot out the noise, but it was hopeless.

What time was it?

George stood with his back to the door, now, trying to look unconcerned. Nobby took the chair beside Frank's. Nobody spoke.

The night before, he'd tried to think about all the good things. Harrison. Jodie. The fine work he'd done. But Alistair blotted out everything. Frank wasn't going to die in a state of grace. He was going down the drop with hatred poisoning the last beat of his heart. Sleep came just before dawn, but so did Alistair. Mocking him. Laughing.

The prison had become a bedlam of noise. He couldn't hear himself think. But when suddenly a fist pounded on the door of his cell, he heard *that*.

The door opened. Frank half turned. Before he could complete the movement a mustached man wearing a dark, three-piece suit with a white handkerchief in its breast pocket had tapped him on the shoulder. He was smiling. There was a trace of peppermint on his breath; Frank's last smell. "Good morning, Mr. Thornton," he said, swiftly pinioning his charge.

The prison clock struck the first beat of nine.

He swung Frank around, letting him gaze into his eyes: unexpectedly curious, perhaps even a touch compassionate. Frank's lips twitched. "Morning," he stuttered.

Another resonant clang from the distant clock. Two.

The cell was full of people: the chaplain, Edward Howells, others he'd never seen before. George slipped across to the wardrobe and slid it to one side, revealing a door that opened in the same instant. Hands were guiding Frank forward.

"I want to thank you, Edward," he managed to blurt out. Now his life could be measured in heartbeats, he was already through the door, slopping awkwardly in his laceless shoes, and there it was, *Christ!*—the object he'd shied away from in so many dreams, a rope coiled at shoulder height, the noose; then he was coming to a halt, seven paces, that's all it was, and George laid a hand on his arm.

The third strike of the clock.

"You all right, Frank?"

He nodded once. To his amazement, he found that death had come ahead to claim him—it was already over and he'd behaved well. Around the corner lay thought, like a robber ready to strike, but nothing forced him to turn that corner.

George squeezed his left arm. "Goodbye, lad," he whispered. "Good luck."

Four.

Florentine came into view while invisible hands bound Frank's legs together and whipped the handkerchief out of his pocket, it wasn't a handkerchief at all, it was a white hood, he drew it down over Frank's chalk-white face, so that he had to heave his last remaining breaths through cotton, it made a terrible noise, they were putting the noose around his neck now, why so tight, why so *quick*, never mind, you've only got to bear it seconds more, a last jerk on the rope, footsteps bounding away from him . . .

A crash. Frank choked out his last breath.

Nothing.

He was just aware of sudden chaos around him. A man being sick. Odd sounds, as if someone was being dragged away. George had dropped his left arm and was swearing somewhere close by the floor. Frank heard a voice say, as if from the other side of eternity, "For Christ's sake, get him *up!*"

A voice screamed in his brain: "*No, no, NO!*"

He felt his legs going. The fifth chime echoed through the shed.

A phone rang.

A phone rang.

Florentine had removed the cotter-pin from its hole and was rising from the crouch, one hand on the lever.

Everyone froze.

As the clock finished striking for the sixth time, the only sound in the cell was Frank Thornton's suffocating, tortured breaths, filtered through cotton.

After that lifeless second, the chief officer raced forward, nearly tripping over the inert form of the assistant executioner, who'd vomited then fainted as Florentine was about to spring the trap. In his haste to answer, the chief officer knocked the phone off its bracket. He retrieved it and for a moment just stood there looking shocked, almost moronic. Then he held out the instrument to the Governor.

"Home Office," he said. "For you. Oakley."

The clock struck seven, and Frank collapsed.

CHAPTER

33

WAPPING. THE PRESENT

Roz deliberately sought an early morning appointment, at a time when she knew the newsroom would be quiet. Like Frank in the condemned cell six weeks earlier, planning his last moments, she proposed to make a dignified and orderly exit.

She came out of the lift and turned left, going straight to her office on the mezzanine floor. Looking across the well of the newsroom she could just see the top of Howard Boissart's head bent over his desk in the inner office, and wondered if he were even now reading her article. No, re-reading: it had come out yesterday, twenty-four hours after her resignation took effect . . .

Howard hadn't noticed her. For the first time she removed her sunglasses. She was reluctant to do so, but she wanted to make a thorough job of clearing her office and you had to see properly for that.

She turned toward the desk and stood quite still. For on it sat a huge bouquet of red roses, pearled with fresh water. She had never seen so many flowers together in one place.

She approached them slowly, not knowing whose idea of a welcome this might be. There was a card, sealed. She opened it and read the one-word message. A smile crept across her face. She laid the card on the desk, next to the Beaujolais-tinted blooms.

By nine-fifty, she was done. As she walked around the mezzanine she looked down on the home news desks, where a few subeditors were sitting at their screens, logging on, or just removing their jackets, savoring gossip and that first weed of the day. It was a view she'd been familiar with for nigh on ten years, without, she realized, ever really taking it in. Tomorrow, no more.

She reached the doorway to Howard's room and stood for a moment, surveying the neat plaque:

THE EDITOR OF THE TIMES

Then she went in.

"Darling," he murmured. "How are you?"

"Vertical."

She shot him a thin-lipped smile and accepted his offer of a chair.

"It's lovely to see you," he said, and she knew he meant it.

"Thanks. Howard, I . . . what I mean is, can we do it quickly?"

His own smile faded. He looked down for a moment. Following his eyes, she saw yesterday's *Guardian* folded in half and lying squarely in the center of an otherwise empty blotter. It looked momentous, like a treaty. For a long while there was silence in the room.

"Even if you hadn't resigned, I couldn't have published that," he said at last. "I'm most desperately sorry."

"I know. I mean, I know you couldn't and I know you're sorry."

"I just can't believe it's going to do anybody the slightest good."

She let silence voice her disagreement. One of the things she'd discovered over the past few weeks was how many futile words spilled into the atmosphere, polluting it, every minute of every day.

"Some of this stuff is, well . . . " He fingered the *Guardian*, that hated opponent, in which the lengthy account of her recent experiences had appeared.

Again, she said nothing.

"As journalism, I hope I don't have to tell you, it's magnificent. But . . . "

"Yes?"

"But I wish you could at least have told me what was going to happen, and when. Reading your piece was a shock, for me and for many others in this building."

"I know. But because you're so powerful, in more ways than one, you might even have talked me out of it. Or talked others out of accepting it for publication."

He did not disdain the compliment.

"Will you be all right?" he inquired, after an interval. "I mean, severance pay isn't a problem, obviously, but . . . in the long term?"

"The psychologist's excellent."

"I'm so glad."

"If it's of any interest to you, she was in favor of my resigning. She says there are always problems when a hostage goes back to work. Hostages make trouble. They have a new list of priorities. Certain things no longer seem important to them. It can become infectious, apparently."

He remained silent, but she could see he was hearing nothing new.

"Howard, tell me something. What was it about my piece, length apart, that repelled you?"

He made a feeble attempt at a deprecating smile. "I never said—"

"That it repelled you, I know. But I heard it. Something you have in common with the Krait and that awful Thai familiar of his: you can speak without moving your lips."

There! The gauntlet was down.

Howard took a deep breath and let it go in a sigh, tossing his head at the same time. "The magic business . . . " he temporized.

"You can't believe the Krait really disappeared from that street."

"Ben Saunders can't either, I notice, his write-up was very different from yours."

Roz flushed at hearing that name, and looked away. "He hadn't endured my . . . experiences," she said at last.

"Ben thinks that Brennan hauled himself up off the road, underneath their transit van, out of sight, and somehow managed to stay there until—"

"I've read it," she said. "Thank you. What else is wrong with my piece?"

Howard couldn't quite meet her eyes. "The . . . *physical* aspects . . . " he managed to say at last.

"The sex."

"If you in—"

"You must be straight with me, because we're not going to see each other again."

He started to protest, genuinely upset, but she silenced Howard by talking right through him. "It's what I have to say about Brennan, isn't it? His triumph."

"You really do see it as a triumph, don't you?" His tone had become somber, with a hint of challenge. "It rings through every paragraph of this . . . " He fingered the *Guardian* with distaste. "This paean of praise."

"It was a triumph for him, yes. Brennan infiltrated

the highest branches of the legal profession. He nearly installed a judge on the High Court bench to do his bidding. Because he read the political scene so well, he instigated a treason trial and stood back while England fell apart on the issues of capital punishment and the unwritten limitations on a government's power to override the will of Parliament."

"I can't accept that."

"Even though it is true?" She looked down at her hands. "Even though he hanged Scrutton that last night, before he fucked me?"

He allowed a few seconds of silence to obliterate what she knew he regarded as an unpardonable breach of good manners.

"Scrutton left a letter," he said at last. "Along with those extraordinary photographs of his wife's drowning. The coroner found he committed suicide. In the light of the documents, he could hardly have done anything else."

"Despite that broken pane of glass, the dead dog? Someone arranged for his bodyguard to be withdrawn and broke into his house that night. Someone murdered Scrutton."

"Scrutton *himself* asked for the bodyguard to be withdrawn, according to the police. And—"

"The usual cover-up."

"—And we all know that people who intend to commit suicide quite often kill a favorite pet first. So Roz, I—"

"From the point of view of naked propaganda," she said, as if he had not spoken, "this has been the IRA's most successful exercise since the Easter Rising. That whole, wicked trial was part of a conspiracy directed not against one man, but against England. I'm quoting, incidentally. Brian Oakley sent a letter round last night. He's authorized me to give you a last scoop, Howard. He's resigning from the government. He wrote the words I've just quoted and apparently they represent the collective view of the entire cabinet. The sole difference between them and Oakley is that they blame me, because I wrote that article, and he doesn't. That's all."

Boissart made a note on his pad before continuing. His tone, when he resumed, was placatory. "I know that the facts, some of them, are, to put it no higher, consistent with this theory, but—"

Again, she spoke across him. "The IRA never meant to kill me. I wasn't important; the only reason why Brennan chose me, and not some other journalist, was because I knew both Scrutton and Thornton. My escape, with the tape, was staged from start to finish, as was Valance's. Everything the Krait has done, since Siri's death, he did mainly out of a desire to be revenged on Scrutton. That's what saved me, and Frank. He had no other interest at all in either of us. He didn't care a damn whether Frank lived or died."

When Howard spoke, he used the gentle, soothing tones reserved for a person who's been very ill. "It's an enormous edifice to construct on somewhat flimsy foundations."

"So the *Times* keeps saying. I have been reading our newspaper daily. It makes such a change from what all the others are printing."

"It's almost as if . . . no, forgive me."

"Say it."

"Sometimes I get the impression that the Krait is some kind of *hero* to you."

"He is the most effective terrorist alive in the world today. And he is at large. And unless they can face up to what he did, unless they heed my warning, they will not take him; that much I know."

"So your article says. Roz, can't you see that the cabinet are quite right for once; by publishing this account, you've played straight into his hands?"

"I published this account because I had no choice other than to report the exact truth, which is my job. He knew that." Suddenly Roz laughed, and Howard looked at her strangely. "I will show you something, before I leave," she said as she stood up.

She returned a moment later, almost obscured by the bouquet she carried in front of her.

"How very charming," Howard said; "I was sure that people here would want to . . . "

She held out the card to him. He opened it, a smile on his lips, and she knew he was placing some mental bet as to the identity of her well-wisher. Then the smile cut out as if it had never been, confirming that he had lost the bet.

The card read: "Thanks." Next to it, someone had drawn, in what her expert eye detected immediately as printers' ink, a long, black-and-white-ringed snake.

When she took the card back from him, his fingers did not even twitch.

It was raining hard as she came through the gatehouse and of course there wasn't a cab in sight, there never was around here. No point in wrestling with an umbrella as well as these roses. Throw the flowers away? She loved red roses. Everyone in her family did. That's why she always sent a bunch on the anniversary of gran's death. She clutched them more closely to her breast and began to walk up the hill, but then a familiar voice called: "Roz."

Her step faltered only for an instant. When the car drew up alongside her she did not turn her head.

"Roz! It's me . . . Frank!"

She would have liked to speak to him, then, but the tears were running thick and fast. He drove a few yards ahead of her, parked, and jumped out. Because the Krait's flowers blocked her view, what with that and the tears, she walked straight into his arms.

"Oh dear," she heard him say sadly. "You've already got some. At least mine . . . ouch! . . . don't hurt like yours."

She stole a glance toward his car. On the back seat

she could see another huge bunch of roses—white, this time. Frank looked fit, she thought. Handsome, as ever.

He gently pushed the bouquet of thorns aside and grinned into her eyes. "I've got to see my lawyers," he announced. "They're getting Scrutton's defamation action struck out, with costs. Hope to God Alistair had the grace to die solvent."

"Hope so."

"But your secretary told me they were expecting you at the office today, and I simply had to come here first."

"I've resigned," she said.

"I know, good."

Roz had already pushed past him, but hearing him say that brought her up short. "What?" she asked uncertainly.

"I had a lot of time to think, in Wandsworth. About the people who mattered to me. I knew that one of them in particular wasn't happy. Like me, she was in a prison."

She stared at him as if he were a total stranger, accosting her on the street.

"Roz. Get in the car."

She shook her head.

"Only it's teeming, and I'm drenched."

For a second she was almost tempted. It passed quickly.

"Sorry, Frank, but there's things you don't know about me. Things you can't ever know."

"If that's your wish. I trust your judgment that I don't need to know them. I shall never ask."

She stared at this somewhat ridiculous person, trying to work out why he continued to smile into her eyes.

"I used to think I'd failed twice," Frank said. "Once with Louise and once, in the States, with Elaine. I didn't really fail. I had bad luck, that's all. And my luck's changed now." He drew himself up a fraction. "I love you, Roz."

It would be impolite to laugh, she thought; hardly tactful. But the courteous disclaimer she'd planned came out all wrong.

"Don't . . . don't *say* that!" she snapped. "Listen, Frank, I don't want to make things worse by . . . oh, what the hell!" She sighed. "I'll say it. You've read my article in the *Guardian*?"

"Of course I've read it. I couldn't put it down. No one could. No one's talking about anything else."

She thought of the TV crews camping on her doorstep, the flood of invitations to appear on this, that, and the other, the queue of publishers flourishing their check-books, and it seemed to her that Frank Thornton was quite, quite mad.

"Let me spell it out," she said. "You can't love a person once they've owned up to something like that."

"Like what? Oh . . . " His lips produced a dazzling smile. "'Sex with the Devil,' yes . . . "

"You're a *Sun* reader now? How interesting. You don't really love me, Frank, so let's neither of us pretend, okay?"

He stepped back and opened the passenger door of the car. "Shall we find out?" he asked quietly.

"You're insane."

"Please. Get in."

She made him wait a long time before she answered.

"Frank, understand one thing, if I get in that car it's because I'm wet, and tired, and I'm fed up with doing my crying in public. There's no other reason."

"I know. Come on."

For a last, long minute she stared at the wine-colored roses still clutched to her breast. She let them fall from her hands. She got into the car.

After Frank had driven away, the red flowers continued to lie in the gutter, suffering the rain to wilt their delicate petals until they resembled nothing more than a deep, rich pool of blood: the product of some terrible disaster about which nobody much cared.

If you would like to receive a HarperPaperbacks
catalog, fill out the coupon below and send $1.00
postage/handling to:

HarperPaperbacks Catalog Request
10 East 53rd St.
New York, NY 10022

Name _____

Address _____

State _____ Zip _____

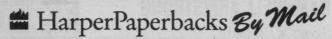

CAMPBELL ARMSTRONG

Agents of Darkness

Suspended from the LAPD, Charlie Galloway decides his life has no meaning. But when his Filipino housekeeper is murdered, Charlie finds a new purpose in tracking the killer. He never expects, though, to be drawn into a conspiracy that reaches from the Filipino jungles to the White House.

Mazurka

For Frank Pagan of Scotland Yard, it begins with the murder of a Russian at crowded Waverly Station, Edinburgh. From that moment on, Pagan's life becomes an ever-darkening nightmare as he finds himself trapped in a complex web of intrigue, treachery, and murder.

Mambo

Super-terrorist Gunther Ruhr has been captured. Scotland Yard's Frank Pagan must escort him to a maximum security prison, but with blinding swiftness and brutality, Ruhr escapes. Once again, Pagan must stalk Ruhr, this time into an earth-shattering secret conspiracy.

Brainfire

American John Rayner is a man on fire with grief and anger over the death of his powerful brother. Some say it was suicide, but Rayner suspects something more sinister. His suspicions prove correct as he becomes trapped in a Soviet-made maze of betrayal and terror.

Asterisk Destiny

Asterisk is America's most fragile and chilling secret. It waits somewhere in the Arizona desert to pave the way to world domination...or damnation. Two men, White House aide John Thorne and CIA agent Ted Hollander, race to crack the wall of silence surrounding Asterisk and tell the world of their terrifying discovery.